A SCROOGE AND CRATCHIT: DETECTIVES MYSTERY

TREASURE AND MURDER IN IRELAND

CURT LOCKLEAR

ISBN: 978-1-960146-77-9 (hard cover)
    978-1-960146-78-6 (soft cover)

Edited by: Melissa Long

Published by WARREN Publishing
Charlotte, NC
www.warrenpublishing.net
Printed in the United States

I dedicate this book to all Christians who have been and are still suffering under horrible conditions in totalitarian states. As always, this book is dedicated to the greater glory of God.

Praise for Curt Locklear's Books

Scrooge and Cratchit: Detectives

"Curt Locklear's mystery adventure novel, Scrooge and Cratchit: Detectives, A Dickensian Christmas Mystery reads like a good Dickens novel ... The plot evolves with vigor and excitement, and readers familiar with Dickens's original will be thrilled to welcome back some of Ebenezer's ghostly personages, including Marley (there are others too). Overall, a lively and fun read."

—5-STAR REVIEW BY READERS' FAVORITE REVIEWER,
EMILY-JANE HILLS ORFORD

Splintered

"Splintered by Curt Locklear is one of those novels that demands your attention because of its well-crafted and well-developed plot line. Everything was connected so well, every character was so perfectly drawn and described that I felt at one with them. The story itself was very engrossing. You can feel the emotion right from the get go and you will find it till the very last word of the novel."

—5-STAR REVIEW, TABIA REVNEER,
READERS' FAVORITE REVIEWER

Asunder

"Like Mr Locklear himself, the book is full of passion ...
for a good story, for history, and for the Civil War."
—ROBERT HICKS, *NEW YORK TIMES* BEST-SELLING
AUTHOR OF *THE WIDOW OF THE SOUTH* AND *THE ORPHAN MOTHER*

Reconciled

A Masterpiece of Storytelling
I have read a lot of those books and watched a lot of those movies. Most of them are
good. Some of them are great. But few authors tell the story as well as Curt Locklear
does. Reconciled is a masterpiece of storytelling and it tells the story of a lot of
different Americans and even some others whose lives were affected by this war.
—RAY SIMMONS, *READERS' FAVORITE* REVIEWER

Scrooge and Cratchit, Detectives

Curt Locklear reinvigorates Dickens for a new generation, bringing the beloved,
classic characters of Ebenezer Scrooge and Bob Cratchit further along their journey.
Now, they are on the case of a terrific Victorian murder mystery full of twists
and turns with loving echoes of Arthur Conan Doyle and Agatha Christie.
He'll keep you guessing all the way to the end with lots of nods and winks
to those paying close attention. And since it's Scrooge,
there's no shortage of ghosts, life lessons and the spirit of Christmas.
—CHRISTOPHER LASTRAPES, FORMER WARNER BROS.
MARKETING AND DEVELOPMENT DIRECTOR

STAVE ONE

DEATH ON THE MOOR: THE MYSTERY BEGINS

On a marsh in a small valley of the Wicklow Mountains of Ireland, a man in his late thirties, dressed in hiking attire, as if he had been out for a jaunt, lay dying on a mound of peat. His legs were dangled at odd angles into the soggy, black mire of the surrounding murky bog. His body showed no signs of injury, save for a few dirty hand-prints about his throat. A whiskey bottle lay in one hand. While his glazed eyes stared into a burnished sun setting in a crimson-and-gold September sky, his breaths grew shorter. All around him for miles were peat and bog, and the noxious gases of the marsh floated up like a phantom, twirling in a chill wind. In another moment, he stopped breathing. Lying atop his chest was a small wooden jewellry box.

A month later, across the Irish Sea, in a London alley near St Paul Church, a man wearing a black shirt and black trousers, and with a scarlet cape slung around his shoulders, moved stealthily, circling his opponent, Abigail Jiggins. In a swift move, he swung a stout, wooden staff, and struck a hard blow to the young woman's knee. The exquisitely beautiful woman crumpled to the cobblestone pavement. Struggling to her feet, she held horizontally above her head her own four-foot long, lacquered, hickory staff which had a wooden knob on one end—a shillelagh she had come upon and made her own. With excellent swings of her own staff, she was successful in batting off the continuous swings from the assailant.

Any passerby seeing the fight might be more alarmed by Abigail's attire. She was dressed in an unbecoming and scandalous manner for a woman—trousers, a tight-fitted blouse that was open at the neck, and heavy work gloves. Her long black hair was tied in a ponytail.

Finally stumbling to her feet, she began shifting her stance repeatedly, almost equivalent to a ballerina's swift turns, alert for any attack from her opponent. Her cheeks flushed, her dark eyes shining fiercely, she intended to fight the man hard and defeat him. "My shillelagh will bring you down!"

The man sniggered, his narrowed eyes mocking her.

While the man swayed back and forth and made rapid stabbing motions towards her with his staff, she slowly backed away. She glanced around the darkened alley and evaluated the stacks of crates and barrels stacked along the walls, wondering whether she could use them to her advantage. She also ascertained that it was a dead-end alley with no doors into the buildings. There was only a narrow exit to the street. That one escape route was blocked by her attacker who now stood still, grinning callously.

The man had jumped out at her only a few moments after she entered the alley and almost driven her to the ground. She barely warded off his blows.

Now, he was standing five yards from her and twirling his staff like a band leader's baton.

In the corner of her eye, Abigail could just see Ebenezer Scrooge, who had accompanied her into the alley. He was crouching in the shadows behind a barrel, his eyes fixed on her and her assailant and filled with dread. She perceived her friend and employer was trembling, one hand clutched over his mouth, the other hand on his sturdy walking stick. She feared he might try to come to her aid and quickly regret such a move.

The dark-clothed adversary suddenly swung his staff mightily then swung again and again at Abigail's head, but she blocked each blow with her own hickory staff. When he backed away a step and swept his staff high in the air to render a crushing blow, she leapt, spinning in the air, landed, and then swiftly advanced two steps. With amazing accuracy, she delivered a strike to the man's groin with one end of her staff and then struck the man's shoulder with the other end.

He plopped unceremoniously to his knees. Then he looked at her with dark, fathomless eyes and sneered. Springing to his feet, he swung wallop after wallop at Abigail, and though she batted them well, the last of his swings to her ribs sent her tumbling into a pile of barley sacks.

She lay there, holding her side, breathing great pants.

The man smiled and then offered a hand to her to help her stand. "Did good, learner," he said matter-of-factly. "Ribs heal soon." He placed his staff on the ground. "You be near ready."

"Thank you, Mr Wang," she said, rising, still holding her ribs tenderly, her inhalations forced. "For a moment, partner, I thought I had triumphed over you."

"Not this day." The Chinese man's English was broken, but his smile now was genuine.

Scrooge floundered his way out from behind the barrel. "I was under the impression, Miss Jiggins, that this was to be an exhibition of your new skill, not an outright combat. I was fully prepared to come to your assistance and—"

"Come now, Mr Scrooge," Abigail said. "This sort of fighting is not in your arena of expertise. You fight with the cognition of your brain to know everything about loans and monetary interests both backwards and forwards and, as the mood suits you, to do some detective work."

Scrooge hung his head for a moment then looked up. "I suppose you're right, Miss Jiggins. And I presume this partner, as you call him, is your trainer in this mode of combat?"

"Yes, Mr Scrooge, I give you Mr Mengzu Wang. I was introduced to him by our dear friend, Corporal Eugene Hart ... beg pardon, now promoted to *Sergeant* Hart. Eugene met Mr Wang years back when he served in the Queen's Guard while in Hong Kong and convinced him to emigrate to London. To my advantage, he did. And Mr Wang has trained me well. He barely gave me time to remove the maid's dress and bonnet I wore over my fighting attire. I appreciate the courtesy of two moments to disrobe, Mr Wang. It's most difficult to fight in a dress."

Mr Wang gave a slight bow to Abigail and then Scrooge, who tried to emulate the bow. They exchanged a few pleasant, awkward words. The man from China bowed to Abigail and once more to Scrooge, who again made a poor attempt at a bow. Wang swung his scarlet cape about him and slipped away out the alley as quietly as a rabbit.

From atop a barrel, Abigail gathered her bundle of more feminine clothes—a bonnet and a blousy maid's dress (not her usual elegant attire) and a long cape—and darted behind a tall stack of crates to change into more suitable street attire. Suddenly, she yelled, "Mr Scrooge, come quick!" Scrooge hurried to her side.

Lying prostrate on his stomach was a gaunt man in tatters of clothing. His britches extended barely past his knees, and his arms stretched forth from a ragged jacket. He seemed more bones than muscles; his breaths came in gasps.

STAVE TWO

A DYING IRISHMAN AND A BANSHEE

S crooge stared incredulously at the dismal vestiges of a barely living man. "L-let him b-be," he stuttered. "He must be diseased or a drunkard. Best to leave him alone."

Enraged, Abigail turned to Scrooge. "How dare you say such a thing! The man is dying."

The man opened one eye. "Faith," he coughed out. "Would ya be so kind as to gi' a poor fella a scrap to eat ...?" His sentence trailed off, and his eyes closed.

"Did you hear his accent, Mr Scrooge?" Abigail asked. "He's an Irishman."

"Yes, yes, an Irishman," Scrooge said. "And his country's potato famine is only growing worse; and the likes of him, and even whole families, are coming here, scouring for work and, I might add, taking the jobs from good Englishman. They'll do any work for a mere pittance and thus steal from an Englishman his means of supporting his family."

"'Tis a great pity." Abigail dropped her bundle of clothes and knelt beside the man.

"Don't touch him," Scrooge said. "He might be contagious."

"Oh bother." She gently turned the man onto his back, revealing the shirtless, uncovered, raw skin of his chest to be almost blue. "He wears no shirt. See? His wooden crucifix hangs about his neck over mere ribs. There's no muscle on him at all." Tears came to her eyes.

"My word, he compares markedly like a Pharoah's mummy recently retrieved from its burial vault. He's more dead than alive." Scrooge pulled his eyeglasses from his forehead and placed them on his nose and bent to peer closer. Automatically, his mind took in details of the man's appearance. It was a new, powerful habit of his, and he could not shake it. He captured in his mind the Irishman's pocked-scarred face, his dirty hands with the fingernails almost gone from his fingertips, the multiple wounds on his face and body. Scrooge quietly surmised, *This man's had smallpox, digs in the ground for food, and has been in many a brawl.*

The Irishman turned bloody eyes towards Scrooge, and he wheezed so his bones rattled under his skin. "The banshee's here, ya know. She's warnin' us all that me soul 'tis to be gone. For sure."

"Banshee!" Scrooge exclaimed, stepping back. He knew well of the Irish lore, and his mind flowed over his knowledge learned from an Irish acquaintance of his youth. The banshee was a different type of spirit, a foul one, bent on pulling souls from bodies before they were fully dead. Or so he had heard ....

Of a sudden, the air felt tight to Scrooge and seemed to dry up in his lungs. Grabbing his cravat, he sought to loosen it from around his neck.

A harsh wind whipped into the alley, blowing dust in volumes and flipping the clothing that hung above them on clotheslines stretched from building to building. A dense mist then flowed up from the darkening street beyond and into the far reaches of the shadowy rear building. Scrooge peered into that dark region, from whence came a low, warbling moan. He crouched down.

"She comes!" the Irishman cried mournfully. "Send 'er away!" His eyes squeezed shut.

Scrooge looked down at the struggling man then again at the pitch-black wall, pulling his spectacles down from his nose. He thought, *Is that a woman standing there?* He squinted and could just make out, in the swirling mist ... *Is that the face of an old hag wearing shreds of a black dress?*

Abigail was too busy caring for the man to notice. She had taken her cape and wrapped it around his chest. Attempting to get him to sit up, she was without success. He could not even rise up on his elbows.

"Oh, so there you are!" came a familiar voice.

Scrooge spun around to see Bob Cratchit, his fellow detective and loan officer and boon companion, striding up to them. Arriving at a brisk clip, he looked past Scrooge, and with amazement, at the derelict man. "What have we here, Ebenezer?"

Scrooge hmphed then sighed. "We have a poor Irishman, probably here because of the potato famine, and he has fallen on hard times." He looked again to the opaqueness of the far wall. He saw only a formless shadow.

"So, you and Abigail are seeking to help him?" Cratchit asked. He took off his tall hat and brushed his long black locks back from his forehead. "What do you hope to do?"

"I was just going to say—" Scrooge began.

Abigail interrupted him with a glare. "You were fully disposed to leave the man here to die of starvation in the alley."

"What?" Bob asked, incredulous. "Come now, Ebenezer. You're not slipping back into your old, uncaring manner, are you?"

Scrooge held up his hands, palms out. "I was only considering all the options in light of ... Oh humbug! Who am I kidding? I needed your arrival here, friend Bob, to remind me of my earnest quest. You see, I have no trouble being kind to friends like you and Miss Jiggins and our junior partner, Lockie, and his wife, Lucy. And to my nephew, Edmund, and his family. And I donate to the church and worthy causes for the poor. But I find any charity in situations such as this to be anathema to me. It's a fault, I know."

He stuck his hand in his jacket pocket and searched for his pipe. He had taken up the pipe at the behest of a doctor who had told him it was extremely healthy for the lungs to smoke. And he wished to be healthy, else he would die too soon before accumulating more wealth.

"Ebenezer," Cratchit laughed. "You'll be the death of me." He squatted beside the ailing, starving man. "I don't believe he can even walk. Come, Abigail, help me hoist him on my shoulders. We'll take him to a Quaker soup kitchen and get some food in him."

Abigail helped place the thin man over Cratchit's bulky shoulders and arms.

Scrooge noticed the muscular vigour of Cratchit. "How is it, Bob, that you have grown your physique so much larger in the past two years?"

"Come now, friend, you know I took on additional after-hours work down at the wharf. Lifting and toting barrels and crates will build the muscles of any man."

"So I see." Scrooge pinched his own arm muscle, felt its flaccidity, and then frowned.

After Abigail quickly changed into more womanly attire, the friends journeyed to a soup kitchen, Cratchit carrying the man across his shoulders like a milkmaid's yoke. Abigail carried the shillelagh against her side under her cape so as not to draw attention to it. She did not want askew glances thrown at her.

At the decrepit soup hall, used as a sort of feeding trough for the starving masses, the four settled into an empty booth. The man, with trembling hands and Abigail's assistance, picked up the metal spoon that was chained to the table and ate the weak corn porridge and bread and then drank a glass of milk. "There be no way to repay ye. I've not a farthing to ma name."

"Not to worry, sir," Abigail said.

"Thank ye kindly, lassie."

"What's your name?" she asked.

"Why," he said, wiping his lips with his sleeve, "'tis Seamus O'Boyle." He paused, looking piercingly at each of his hosts. "When 'twas lyin' there in the streets, I heard the banshee wail. 'Twas a terrifyin' sound. I was wont to bat my ears."

"Banshee?" Scrooge leaned back against the booth wall. "Hopefully not. I've had enough ghosts in my life."

"'Tis not a ghost," Seamus said, "but far worse. And there's more and more of 'em roamin' about Ireland with the *Great Hunger* goin' on."

"Interesting you should mention a banshee," Cratchit said. "Just today, our firm received a letter requesting our assistance in solving a murder of his brother. In the letter, an Irish businessman by the name of Mr Byrne alluded to a banshee."

Scrooge's heart raced. He wanted no more to do with ghosts or anything like them. He found it difficult to breathe, and his heart pounded hard.

"Oh," squeaked out the poor Irishman. "I've a family here in London a-starvin' too. Have ya a few coppers that I might fetch them some vitals?"

"Where are you staying?" Abigail asked.

"My wife and five kids are bunkin' in an alley not a stone's throw away. In some open crates."

Cratchit, Scrooge, and Abigail looked aghast at the man.

STAVE THREE
THE GREAT HUNGER REVEALED AND SCROOGE'S NEW HABIT

Sending Scrooge and Abigail back to the office, Cratchit helped the weak man limp along to the alley where he could gather his family. Arriving at the hodge-podge of crates that served as the family's home, Cratchit hoisted three of the smallest children who were too weak to walk while the man leaned upon his wife in order to tread. Ultimately arriving at a sordid but generally clean inn, Cratchit plunked down a crown to the innkeeper and insisted he provide clean sheets for the beds and meals for the entire family. He told the innkeeper he planned to return in a day or so after finding a job for the father.

Scrooge, on the other hand, was glad to be rid of the burden of the man as he and Abigail strode back to the office. His walking cane clacking on the boardwalk, he pretended to listen to Abigail's comments on the whole affair and how she would be gathering used clothing for the family.

"Think of that man when he was a child," she said, being careful to keep her stout weapon hidden under her cape. "He was once, like all of us, a babe sucking on his mother's breast and smiling, and she glad he was alive and not stricken with some disease, and her thanking God often while she rocked him, and him falling gently asleep, and then in later years, him growing into a rambunctious child. I'll bet he was a wild one once. And then his growing into a man, filled with hope in his heart and marrying for love. I can see their simple, joyful wedding in a small church." She went on in that manner about the Irishman and his little family all the way to their office of business: *Scrooge and Cratchit, Detectives and Money Lenders.*

Scrooge almost passed his own door, his mind so occupied initially with the dire situation of the man and banshees and starving Irish people but then with his recently hired employees. First, there was Abigail, the fast-thinking, agile fighter, who had saved the day against Ginny Wheeler's kidnappers then against the vile criminal Blackmun. She now was an apprentice in the detective trade, letting Scrooge off the hook for researching clues so he could focus on making money with the loan function of his business.

He quickly felt abject concern about the two other new employees who had been in his and Cratchit's employment barely one month: the bookkeeper and the scrivener.* A new concern rushed upon him—one of suspicions. He thought, *That scrivener had better have copied the contract by now. I'll not tolerate idleness.*

He burst into his office, Abigail at his heels. On the left perched Bob Cratchit's high desk by one window, clear of any item save his pen and inkwell. Scrooge's own desk on the right squatted like some old sea-chest. It was clear of anything save a stack of documents. A robust man, tall hat on his lap, whom Scrooge had failed to notice, was sitting opposite it. Beyond the entrance area and the desks and the safes and such, in the newly expanded back office, the two new employees worked, heads down—noses to the grindstone, as it were—penning and tabulating and completing business for their employers.

Scrooge marched up to the bookkeeper and leaned over his shoulder, his eyes tight upon the numbers in the ledger. He started to point at a particular set of numbers then saw the bookkeeper's tabulations were correct. "Hmph," he said. He turned to the scrivener. "Is that contract copied yet, Penman?"

"Yes, sir," replied the skinny man with a jacket too large and sleeves too long, the cuffs of which he kept tied back with twine behind his wrists. "I finished three copies an hour ago. They're on your desk. I'm working on the next contract."

Scrooge wheeled around and saw the pages on his desk. He rushed there and perused the documents for errors, still oblivious of the man sitting across from him.

After a moment, the man cleared his throat. "Ahem."

Scrooge looked up. He also noticed Abigail standing behind the man with her hands on her hips, tapping her foot and frowning. She mouthed the words, *Say hello to the client*.

The man was stout, about five-and-a-half feet tall, with a rosy complexion and a gleaming shock of auburn hair. Scrooge immediately began sizing him up. *By his dress with refined cloth, he is probably of aristocracy.* He further noticed that the man's cravat, though silk, had a splotch of tea on one corner. *Perhaps he drank the tea in haste.* The hat was well-brushed and shone, another sign of wealth.

"I beg pardon," Scrooge said. "As you can see, it is a busy office. I've just come back from a … demonstration of … pertinent elements of our trade."

Abigail's frown deepened.

The man stood and extended his hand. "My name is Reginald Byrne."

Scrooge shook his hand. "Pleased to meet you. Are you here for a business loan or personal one?"

"Neither." The man sat and leaned across Scrooge's desk.

Scrooge slid forwards in his chair, for he could see the man wished to speak confidentially.

Byrne fiddled with his hat. "I believe my brother has been murdered. I tried to get the local police to help, but their hands are full with the potato famine problems taking up all their time. After checking around, I heard on good account that your firm was the best in the English isles." Though his speech indicated he was highly educated, his accent was markedly Irish.

Scrooge had little fondness for the Irish class. He had once wished a new king in the vein of James II and Charles I or the Parliamentarian Oliver Cromwell would sell the whole rabble of Irish—every man, woman, and child—to the Americas as slaves, just as those three rulers had done in years previous. He sighed. "Murder, you say." He looked up at Abigail. "Find a seat, Miss Jiggins. Take notes."

She leaned her sturdy shillelagh against Cratchit's desk, took pen, ink, and paper, and sat in a nearby chair.

Byrne began telling the tale of how his brother's body had been found dead by a farmer of potatoes and peat on the moor in central Ireland near Kindlestown Castle. He said in earnest, "Ireland has turned into a wicked place since The Hunger began. Folks stealing, betraying, absconding, abandoning, and ultimately dying. My brother, Sean, was a healthy farmer of wheat, not potatoes, with a good head on his shoulders and dreams in his pockets."

While taking notes, Abigail looked up. "Why would someone wish to kill your brother?"

"That's the mystery," Byrne said. "He was well-liked by all in the hamlet of Wicklow where he lived. He often shared the flour he had ground from his own mill with the poor and starving neighbours." He paused. "Recently, he came upon some, shall I say, *items of interest* to him." Almost at once, his whole demeanour began to turn bleak, his face pale. "I believe a dark force was at work in his demise."

"How so?" Abigail was not allowing Scrooge to question the man, though the former miser was now studying every aspect of the man's appearance.

While Abigail gathered information from the man of his family, Scrooge observed various aspects of the man's attire. There was a maroon stain on the man's jacket lapel. *Possibly blood, but from what?* He further noticed the man's fingernails were chewed down to the quick. *Nervous sort, or perhaps having a recent cause to be nervous.* His palms were calloused. *He's accustomed to strenuous work, unnatural for a man of nobility.* The man's eyes were purest blue, but dark circles lay around them. *Not much sleep of late.* The most important aspect Scrooge noticed was a circular, metal pin of green and gold secured to his visitor's vest. On it read the words, *Erin Go Bragh.* He knew enough of the turmoil of recent times to recognise the Irish sentiment of "Ireland till Doomsday." He knew well that no man would dare to wear such a pin in London were his sentiments not firmly connected with the on-and-off rebellions of the Irish-against-British rule. *Perhaps he's a fool looking for a fight. When will the Irish learn?*

Byrne continued with details about his brother's life and the whiskey bottle and small wooden box found on his body. "My brother has no family left," he said. "They all died of the colic. Oh, he does have one son who he believes sailed to Mexico, but none of us have heard from the young man in years. Beyond that, I need your help. I'm here in London to purchase grain and sheep to take back to Ireland."

Scrooge folded his hands and leaned across the desk. "Is there anything else you wish to say?"

"Other than asking when you can journey to Ireland to solve the crime, I've no other comments. Additionally, I will pay your way via my own ship and your daily rate allowances while you are there, abiding in my manor home. I so hope you'll take this concern of mine."

"Concern. Yes, to take the case. Hmm." Profound hesitation was in Scrooge's voice. "I will consider it. Good day, sir. My secretary has taken notes. We have a busy docket, as you can see."

All that sounded in the office was the scratching of pens on paper by the bookkeeper and scribe.

"How will I know if you accept?" Byrne stood and put on his hat and gloves. "My ship leaves in two days. I can delay a day if need be."

Scrooge looked hard at the man. "As I said, we'll let you know. No need to call again."

"If you are willing to take the case, I'm staying at the Holcomb Arms. You can message me there."

"Good day, sir." Scrooge swivelled his chair around, his back to Reginald Byrne.

"Good day." Byrne exited, an exasperated expression on his face.

Furious, her dark eyes glaring, Abigail spoke to Scrooge's back. "Why did you *not* say we'd take his case?"

Before Scrooge could answer, Lockie exploded through the door, which was the typical nature of his entry almost anywhere. "Mr Scrooge, I've got good news!"

Scrooge turned his chair back around. "And what would that be, friend Lockie?"

"At last, my bride of ten months and my adopted child and newly born baby will have a real 'ome. As you know, the morrow is Saturday, and neither Bob nor I will be here working. It's moving day! Bob and his family have a new 'ome, as befits his rise in the world, and Lucy, our son Mycroft, our newborn baby Sherlock Jr, and I will be moving into Bob's former abode."

Scrooge's voice rose as he spoke. "You know, of course, there will be no pay for your cutting work." He attempted to pound his fist on his desk, but the swoop of his hand ended with him only tapping a finger on the desk.

"Yes, Mr Scrooge. We 'ope to 'ave it all moved in one day. We daren't work on the Lord's day." Lockie swept off his cap and pushed his blond locks back from his face.

"Yes, that means the rest of us will have to work extra hard," Scrooge pronounced angrily.

"Don't be put out, Mr Scrooge," Lockie said, twisting his cap in his hands. "It's a great opportunity. Besides, come Sunday, I plan to bring Lucy's and my new baby around for you to see. He's a winner. Born just two weeks ago and bright as a button." His enthusiasm for his new son was unquenchable.

Scrooge tried to look irate for all of a minute. The eighteen-year-old man had saved his life and Cratchit's and been definitively instrumental in solving major murder crimes. He almost wished Lockie was his own son. Finally, his demeanor softened, and he smiled. "So, his name is Sherlock Jr. A fine name. I hope he grows up to be just like his father."

"He'll be better, and I'll wager he'll become well-known in London and the whole world."

Abigail said, "Don't get your hopes up too much, Lockie. He's still got to survive more than ten years, not die like so many children do here in London. No sunlight through the clouds. Too much smoke."

"Oh, he's a strong one." Lockie waved at the two new employees, tipped his cap to Abigail, and bowed to Scrooge. "I'll work all the harder next week, sir." He bounded out the door, slamming it behind him.

Abigail turned to Scrooge. "You *will* take this murder case."

"Not likely," Scrooge replied.

STAVE FOUR
CORDIALITY OF KITTY CLUTTERBUCK

After Scrooge dismissed Abigail's entreaties, she stood tapping her foot loudly, her lips pinched. Scrooge ignored her and commenced to soundly admonish the new men—Arthur Penman, who was the experienced scrivener, and Fabio Fibonacci, the bright-faced Italian bookkeeper—about his expectation that they arrive earlier than usual the next day, ready to increase their work output.

With a scowl on his face, Scrooge departed the office. *The wages I pay them better be a sound investment, or ...* He shuddered to a stop and looked back over his shoulder at the establishment, wary that Abigail might not lock the doors securely, which was her duty. It did not matter when he left the building, day after day, he always hid himself to watch her lock every lock on the door, put the keys safely in her apron pocket, and then secure the pocket with a pin. This evening, Abigail hurried the new employees out then painstakingly secured each of the three locks.

Scrooge hastened towards his home, satisfied his business was safe but worried about his costs versus his revenue. Having hired the scrivener, Penman, at the behest of his friend, Hiram Grumbles, he could not say he was satisfied with the man's work. Then again, he could not find a reason not to be satisfied. Fibonacci was detail-oriented, quick, and cordial. Despite himself, Scrooge could not find a thing wrong with the accountant either.

Although it was the middle of October, a few flakes of snow drifted about in the gloomy, smoky air. Trudging along the same dark streets and alleys he always walked when heading home, he happened upon some street urchins sticking out their tongues to catch a flake or two, laughing, and being wholly delighted with so simple a pleasure.

Scrooge, for a reason he could not fathom, stuck out his own tongue and collected two flakes. The tiny ice filaments melted immediately, and Scrooge caught himself smiling. Then, when the street boys began pointing at him and snickering, the sourness overtook him again. "Humbug."

❧

Arriving at his warehouse home, he plunged his key into the keyhole and found the door unlocked. Rushing inside, he bellowed, "Kitty, what is the meaning of this? The door is unbolted. Why? Any thief could creep in and steal me blind!" He sped up the stairs to his large flat above the old warehouse, holding a hand on his heart. The door to his flat was wide open as well. Inside, he heard Kitty clanking away at some supper pot or pan, and smelled the rich aroma of roast goose, spicy gravy, and boiling cranberries. The odours flooded his nose, and his stomach immediately growled with pleasure, and his mouth watered.

Again, he barked, "Kitty Clutterbuck, what is going on? You know how dangerous it is to have the door unsecured. You may be serving as my maid and bodyguard, but carelessness like this will not be tolerated!"

Kitty, her bulky muscles bulging under the sleeves of her dress, strode in from the kitchen, carrying a bowl of steamed vegetables and mushrooms, the aroma of the dish flowing stoutly into Scrooge's nostrils. "Hello, Ebenezer, and would you not have your door open for our guests tonight?"

"Guests? What guests?"

"Why, Sergeant Eugene Hart of the Metropolitan Police and his fiancé, Ginny Wheeler, of course! We are celebrating their engagement. With all of Ginny's family at Tamperwind Mine, who else could celebrate the announcement of their forthcoming nuptials? Personally, I would feel sorry for any thief coming in and having to face Eugene Hart, one of the finest police officers in all of London. He would surely give the thief a good thrashing. You did not forget, did you?"

"Of course not." He lied then gleaned a tepid smile of sorts. Turning so she could not see his face, he thought, *Fine thing, spending my hard-earned money on supper parties. Yes, I know Kitty has a becoming face, but I don't know why I put up with her.*

The woman in question cocked her head, listening and smiling. "Well, who would that be coming up the stairs?" She, of course, knew exactly who was making their way up the stairs.

Scrooge heard the footsteps on the stairs too, and knew immediately who was ascending the stairway. One pair of heavy, street-tough boots, the other pair a dainty, almost slipper-like affair. He had heard the footsteps of Sergeant Hart often enough to know his scuffing tread. He also knew the light footfalls of Ginny Wheeler—the petite stride akin to a faery's dance.

Scrooge took off his overcoat and hat, hung them on the hall tree, loosened his cravat, and turned just in time to shake hands with the Metropolitan police officer Eugene Hart, recently promoted to sergeant. Ginny, who often went by the nickname "Snow," had done up her dark hair in a bun, covered with a snood. Her blue eyes were shining, her skin as white as drifting snow, her cheeks rosy as cherries. She was dressed in an elegant, silvery gown, and her silver shoes were almost akin to slippers, rather than the typical high-topped laced shoes worn by most women. She clung to Eugene's arm.

"Oh, Snow!" Kitty said. "That dress looks gorgeous on you."

"Thank you," Snow said. "My father purchased it for me for just such an occasion."

"How is old Bobbie Wheeler?" Scrooge inquired.

"I believe your bosom friend, who is the best father anyone could ever have, along with my uncles and the rest of the family, are faring well. The menfolk are helping Samuel run the Hopworth and Tamperwind mines. They have their hands busy."

"Supper will be ready soon," Kitty announced. "I've a few more things in the oven. Make yourselves at home and have a goblet of smoking bishop* there in the bowl."

Walking into the newly furnished sitting room of Scrooge's flat, one would hardly recognise it from what it had been before Kitty redecorated it. Plush armchairs now surrounded the fireplace which had a warm fire glowing. New brocaded curtains hung over the several tall windows where no bothersome wind leaked in, for Kitty had repaired the leaks around the window edges with grout and fixed the latches. A fine set of braided rugs were laid dramatically over the floor, and paintings of various bucolic scenes adorned the walls.

Scrooge served himself a cup of the purple brew from the bowl and plopped unceremoniously in the chair Kitty had assigned to him. Sipping on the mixture of port, red wine, and squeezed oranges, he could not enjoy its luxurious taste, for all he thought of was the capital his live-in maid was costing him. *Smoking bishop*, he thought. *Why not a cheap wine?*

Ginny and Eugene each took a cup of the savoury concoction. She then sat demurely in one of the plush chairs, and he leaned on the chairback. "'Tis fine for me to stand, dear one," he said to Ginny. "My new job as police sergeant has me sitting on my bum in the station for aeons."

Just then, Abigail Jiggins appeared at the doorway. As she had become wont to do, she had practiced pacing so softly, few could ever hear her approach. It was part of her training from Mister Wang.

STAVE FIVE

A CALAMITOUS CASE IN THE CHANCELLOR COURT

Abigail appeared distraught. "I'm sorry I'm late," she admitted. "I had to return home for more appropriate garb." She swept into the room, her fists clinched. "I'm dreadfully torn. I just received a wire from Samuel. It seems the civil court case is proceeding dismally." She gave the telegram to Scrooge.

When Scrooge finished perusing its contents, he then put his hand to his brow in annoyance. He had invested heavily in the Tamperwind and Hopworth mines, seeking additional wealth, but he could not stir that pot in front of his friends and employees. He spoke, instead, of Abigail's and her brother's dilemma. "So, the law firm of Cragle, Pincher, and Schleege are proceeding and appear to have the judge's ear?"

"Not so much, Mr Scrooge," Abigail said, untying her bonnet then removing her cloak and hanging both on the rack beside Scrooge's coat and hat. She removed her elbow-length gloves and slapped the pair against her palm. She pronounced, "The firm claims they have true ownership of the mines because my uncle Erasmus took out a loan against the mine, and they say he failed to pay the remuneration. Their suit claims he defaulted. Our attorney has them beat at every step, but it's the bureaucracy of the tedious court. As long as new papers are filed, and suddenly found claims by the firm keep being presented, the trial flounders." She succumbed to her worry, collapsed into one of the plush chairs, and began to weep.

Ginny rushed to Abigail and attempted to comfort her with a hug. "There, there," she said.

Kitty, unaware of the sad news Abigail had shared, emerged from the kitchen, rang a small bell, and announced, "Supper is served. Please repair to the dining hall."

Scrooge and the three guests made their way to the small hallway off the sitting room Kitty had chosen to deem a dining hall. At each end of the hallway, she had lit two dozen candles in standing candelabras. Scrooge had never once required so much light while living alone. The rest of the candles glowed in three ornate, standing candelabras stationed in the corners of the dining hall. The crowded room seemed bright with joy and celebration. Scrooge remembered the visits from two different Ghosts of Christmas Present and the astounding spread of food they had set before him in that very room.

This slender table somewhat mimicked those festive tables filled with tasty fare of his Christmas past. An Irish linen tablecloth covered the short, narrow table. Fine, porcelain plates and serving dishes were positioned beside polished silverware set on fine napkins. Kitty's face beamed when she brought the platter of roast goose and placed it on the table in front of Scrooge. His mouth watered so much, a drip of saliva spilled from his lower lip onto his cravat.

The companions sat, and Abigail admonished them all not to speak of the trial until after the meal was finished.

On the table was a large bowl of boiled cauliflower, piled high, all white and glimmering with melted butter in little lakes atop it. A dish of steamed corn, peas, and carrots sat beside it. At several places, mincemeat pies of dried currants, raspberries, walnuts, and a smidgeon of lamb meat were twinkling with a sugar coating and drenched in honey. Warm, crusty, twisted rolls were bound in a napkin in a basket. The goose, its skin browned to perfection, awaited Scrooge's action, for Kitty had designated him to carve it. She handed him the knife and fork. After staring at the challenge before him a moment, Scrooge opted to let Eugene have the honour of dismembering the fowl.

Then the napkins were applied to the collars or laps of each person, and knife and fork laid hold of, but only after Ginny led a gracious prayer, and they all ate and chatted of small affairs as if nothing of serious merit had occurred in the previous twenty-four hours. When all had thoroughly complimented Kitty on the fine supper and wielded their culinary weapons and filled their bellies and let the silverware, when they felt pleasantly full, clack upon the empty plates in repose, a solemn silence fell over them all.

After a long moment, Abigail threw her napkin on her plate and rose unsteadily to her feet, tears flooding her eyes. "W-what are we t-to do?" she stammered. "It's all that Samuel can do, along with Ginny's father and uncles, to keep the mines operating. I'm quite sure the rancorous rumour being promulgated about the mines being haunted was initiated by either Cragle or some cretin on his behalf. Good workers refuse to apply there, leaving only the dregs to carry forth the effort. Samuel refuses to hire children under a dozen years of age, as is done in so many mines, so our costs are higher. Cragle and his cohorts are lawyers and incur no costs to themselves, but we must pay our lawyer and spend a fortune defending our inheritance. Where is the justice?"

Scrooge's mind immediately flashed to the Jarndyce versus Jarndyce* civil trial, which had been proceeding doggedly for six months with no end in sight. Its tawdry filings and counter-filings and suddenly discovered papers and reports continued ad nauseam. He hoped the Tamperwind trial would not become like that case, which was posted about regularly in the newspapers and had become the joke of the courts. While London laughed, the family's will and testament hung precipitously over a chasm of debt. *It may not ever end*, thought Scrooge. *I can only hope the Jiggenses case does not go down that road.*

He was unable to pay attention to what Ginny, Eugene, and Kitty were saying in support of Abigail. He knew not of their advice or consolations nor of Abigail's entreaties and elaboration of her fears.

"I have decided!" Abigail exclaimed, which brought him back from his far-away thoughts. She pounded her fist on the table. "Samuel is coming to London this evening for the trial that has been going on for three months. He needs to confer with our attorney, Abel Leggitt."

"Ah, yes," Scrooge said, remembering his dear friend. "Good old Abel."

Abigail drew a long breath. "I have decided I must spend tomorrow with my brother at the lawyer's office and encourage him. Further, come Sunday, my cousin Lucy must be told of the severity of this lawsuit. With her newborn son, I do not wish to cause alarm, but I must convey to her the seriousness of it."

"Are you saying you will be with your brother all day tomorrow?" Scrooge inquired. "You have your duties at the office, you know, and—"

"I must appeal to you, Mr Scrooge," Abigail pleaded. "I also hope to go with him to court on Monday then do whatever he asks of me. If need be, I shall make travel arrangements to the mines in Cornwall."

Scrooge stared at her tear-filled face. "Let me think on it. You have my permission to confer with the attorney tomorrow and attend court on Monday. Beyond that, I may have a greater need of you here in London."

Scrooge went back to existing in his own world while Abigail, Ginny, and Hart discussed the various ups and downs of the mine, about which they knew only some aspects. The tin mine was producing little. They needed to strike a new vein. The silver mine was barely getting by. Five workers had walked off the job and just vanished. Ginny wished that she, too, would be going by coach to Tamperwind but could not, for she had a job as a tutor and had to prepare for the wedding. She was concerned for the welfare of her family who were working and living there now.

For Scrooge, something was stuck in the back of his mind; something Mr Byrne had said about the murder of his brother in Ireland. *"A dark force." What did he mean?*

STAVE SIX

SHAMUS SHACKLE AND SORCERERS

That night, Scrooge had awakened twice from torrid dreams of being chased by shadowy women in ragged, black mourning dresses. Having heard his screams, Kitty rushed from her bedroom down the hall of the warehouse and did her best to calm him until he fell asleep.

Now, in the dark, pre-dawn Saturday, awake and dressed, Scrooge trudged out of his home against a blustering, sharply cold wind towards his workplace, fully aware that three of his employees would not be there. "I'm always first there and tired of always carrying the load," he quietly complained. His thoughts were entirely crusty, just as his shoes crunched on crusty ice left by the previous evening's bleak weather. Though he had enjoyed the previous evening's elaborate supper, he was unhappy about the expense of the meal, not to mention Kitty's burning of so many candles. *What a waste!* He then patted his jacket, wondering about the bulge there, and quickly remembered Kitty had placed a thick, gooseflesh sandwich in his inside pocket. He was glad for that, at least.

A sudden movement in the alley shadows caused him to convulse to a halt, trembling. His remembrance of the shadowy form he had seen in the alley with the Irishman raced into his mind. It seemed as if this shadow itself had taken form and curled like a serpent ready to strike, yet it was unlike any living being he had ever seen. He had no means to defend himself, for he kept his pistol in a drawer at the office, knowing all the ill feelings his detective firm had created; he had received threats of bodily harm delivered to him thrice. When, at last, the shadow was revealed to him to be only a feral cat perched on a barrel, the creature waving its tail like a snake, he relaxed. He watched the feline hop down from the crate. It suddenly turned its cat eyes towards him, staring. It was completely black, save a white mark on its nose in the shape of a heart. It slinked away.

Taking a deep breath, he treaded onwards. Besides the threats he had received, he had grown weary of being in the detective business *entirely*. After winning the acclamation and awards of Queen Victoria, his and Cratchit's detective business had swelled but almost entirely due to callous husbands wishing to have the detectives tail their wives whom they expected of philandering, or suspicious wives speculating on a similar notion about their spouses. This new business of uncovering such hidden affairs had involved Scrooge and his team in the tawdry underside of London's life. Though the money pouring in was pleasing, he cared not for the humdrum and monotonous reports from, primarily, Lockie who performed the lion's share of uncovering evidence of individuals' poor choices. This new avenue of income had brought about the downfalls of several marriages.

Knowing he could almost predict the outcome of the aforementioned sleuthing of anxious spouses, Scrooge found himself wishing for a more mentally intriguing challenge. Not a single complex mystery had come to them. In opposition to such a desire, he found himself caring more and more about the loan business which also had been a boon for several months due to the firm's notoriety. He felt at odds with his own ambitions.

Exiting the alley onto the street in which his business stood, he immediately saw Chief Inspector Shamus Shackle standing on his porch. The burly man with plentiful grey hair on both his cheeks, yet none on his chin or upper lip, did not look pleased. A strong-looking, young policeman with a full head of brown hair stood beside him, his tall hat in his hand.

When Scrooge drew near, Shackle barked, "I thought you would have been open hours ago, Scrooge! Why the delay?"

"I've not delayed. In fact, I'm arriving earlier than usual." Scrooge checked his pocket watch to be certain.

"All right then. Let us go inside. Ebenezer Scrooge, this is the new recruit taking the place of Officer Hart, who, as you know, has been promoted to sergeant. This young officer's name is Devland Blevins."

Scrooge shook hands with the cheery officer, who smiled abundantly and gave a firm grip.

"Extremely pleased to meet you, Mr Scrooge," Blevins said in a marked Irish accent. "I've heard so many good things about you."

"Yes, well." Scrooge butted past both officers and began unlocking the three locks to his office door, keeping his back to them so they could not ascertain which of his abundant keys undid the locks.

Once inside, Scrooge lit the oil lamps and two candles. He opened the curtain to the window beside his desk. The morning sun was burning through the eastern clouds, tossing stripes of sunbeams into the office. He dropped his keys in a desk drawer and sat in his chair. Shackle took a seat opposite. Blevins stood at a sort of relaxed attention behind the chief inspector.

"Mr Scrooge," Shackle began. "I'll not beat about the proverbial bush. I've need of your services in Ireland. A particular case for a Mr Byrne."

Scrooge was astounded. "Surely not. I daren't go to Ireland. Why, 'tis filled with goblins and demons. And you, Shamus, are certainly privy to the elements of the night, having experienced the dark malevolence of only this past January."

Shackle sat back in the chair. "Ahem. I'm unsure that event was not just some malfunction of the foul criminal's electricity and lighting. There's always a scientific explanation."

Scrooge coughed. "Excuse me?"

Shackle adjusted in his seat again then leaned across the desk. "Let us talk in private."

Scrooge's eyes grew wide.

Shackle dismissed Officer Blevins to stand outside. After the young officer had closed the door, Shackle led Scrooge to the back of the office to stand by the bookkeeper's desk. "I'd hoped you hadn't brought up that event, but here is the honest truth. I have many experienced officers, excellent at following orders, halting crimes before they occur, guarding important locales, and hunting down the common criminal. The list goes on, and though there are other chief inspectors in other parts of the city, they don't have the background or acumen you and Cratchit have."

"I and Cratchit have?"

"Quite right. You and he, along with that young fellow that works for you …?"

"Lockie Holmes?"

"Yes. You've solved two of the kingdom's most baffling crimes. Therefore—"

"Why not go to Ireland yourself?"

"Ebenezer, I would, but I have another pressing matter in Manchester upon which I must intervene at the Queen's request, God save her." He pulled Scrooge by the jacket collar to draw him close. "In Manchester, a rebellion is stirring. A man named Engels is firing up the workers there, saying they deserve better pay and working conditions. And that's all fine. Perhaps they should be paid better. But he claims the only solution is through violent rebellion. Kill everyone who is not with the rebels."

Scrooge gently pushed Shackle back a foot, though the inspector still clung to the detective's jacket lapels. Scrooge asked, "Why not allow me to do the digging and detective work in Manchester while you go to Ireland?"

Shackle released his grip and turned towards the dark corner of Scrooge's office, facing the warehouse door through which Marley's ghost and the dark malevolence had passed on that fateful night Scrooge was almost killed. He shook the locked doorknob. "Where does this go, Ebenezer?"

"Uh, only to an abandoned warehouse. I have no use to access it." He trembled in his remembrance of that horrid night.

"Very well, here is the bottom line. You, being a thrifty loan businessman, will surely understand this. I have no choice but to do the bidding of the Queen. You and Cratchit and that other young fellow, the one we arrested and then found was not guilty …?"

"Lockie?"

"Yes. You three have experience with those beings of the grey parts of our world, whereas I do not. You three have the expertise. And it is our conjecture, both mine and Sergeant Hart's, that you should go to Ireland. The case there may involve beings who exist beyond our pale. I have no one else to send. Furthermore, Queen Victoria suggested I send you."

"Her Majesty is aware of the issue in Ireland?"

"She knows only a little, and Ireland is part of her domain. Reginald Byrne is an acquaintance of some of her husband's cousins. I believe you've already spoken with him. Did he tell you much about the death of his brother?"

Scrooge shuffled his feet. "Honestly, I sent him away before he could say much. I care not for travelling to Ireland. Of all the places on this globe, why there?"

"I cannot force you to take the case, but I can send Officer Blevins with you. His parents are from Ireland, and he knows the country well. He can be a guide and an intervener with anyone who does not know your intentions."

"If Bob Cratchit and I both go, who will run my loan company? I have considerable business now, and—"

"I am confident you will find someone. There is a great deal more at stake than the demise of one man out on a moor. Have you ever heard of two Biblical sorcerers named Jannes and Jambres?*"

STAVE SEVEN
THE LOATHSOME LAW FIRM, THE DIRE PREDICAMENT

"Oh, Lockie," Lucy said while sitting at her new vanity desk and mirror in the late Sunday afternoon.

"Yes, my fondest love?" Lockie responded.

"Wasn't it delightful, moving into our new home this morning? And did our sons not behave admirably? Not a peep from either of them."

"Indeed," Lockie said.

"Do we not have the most wonderful sons?" She smiled down at the sleeping two-year-old and the newborn, both lying side by side in a cradle, which she rocked with her stockinged foot.

"Yes, we do. Mycroft, the son I gained when I completed the adoption papers just a month ago, is forthrightly loving towards Sherlock Jr. Look how he cuddles the baby."

"Their breathing is so soft, I sometimes worry they have stopped altogether. Then, when I touch either one, they gently turn towards my hand and smile in their sleep. We are so blessed."

Lockie rose from their new bed in their new home once owned by the Cratchit family and strode over beside the cradle. He took over the rocking of the cradle with his foot, allowing Lucy a respite. All the while, he gazed at Lucy, admiring her strawberry-blond hair falling in ringlets, the freckles across her nose, and her trim, petite figure. While watching her smudge her cheeks and forehead with a gooey concoction, he asked, "What is it you do there, dear one?"

"I've been reading a column lately in a woman's magazine. It's all about how to make one's face more beautiful. Though I don't consider myself ugly, I do not wish to become that way. The article offers 'hints for the toilet' and methods to make a woman more attractive."

"But you are far more attractive than any other woman on Earth."

"I know you feel that way, Lockie, and I want to remain so. This white face paint is made from ammonia and some white paint with lead in it. The article says it is sure to keep a woman's skin glowing white, which is the fashion now. I want to look my best for you." She turned towards him.

Lockie could now smell the ointment, and it made his nostrils burn. He flinched. "Lucy, you are beautiful enough. And were you to ever turn ugly, I would still love you. I married you for life."

Lucy curled her pink lips into a smile.

"Now wash that off right now."

Lucy took a cloth and began removing the white paint from her face. "But the woman in the store says it is the best thing to maintain a porcelain white skin."*

"I don't want you to have porcelain skin. I want you to have your glowing pink skin."

"How about opium? One article said rubbing the drug on your skin at night does wonders. Could you go to an opium din and pick up some for me?"

"I wouldn't step foot in one of those dins of iniquities unless it was part of my detecting work."

Lucy, having removed the cream, dropped her head and pouted her lips. "You mean you don't need me to try to be more beautiful?"

Lockie knelt on one knee and peered up at her, taking her hand in his. "Lucy, you are the prize of my life. No woman could ever compare to your beauty."

Lucy brightened and stood. "I was just testing you, silly. I had no intention of using that filthy smelling mixture. Nor ever using opium for any reason. This facial brew was given to me free, as a sample. I prefer to get out in the countryside and let the fresh air and sunshine bathe my skin. Now, kiss me, my brave detective and loan scrounger." She pulled him up to embrace him.

Lockie took the cloth from her hand and wiped a small amount of the white goo from her upper lip, and then they kissed with utmost passion.

After the kiss, Lockie asked, "And do you like our new home?"

"I love it. And Mister Scrooge is allowing us to buy it in instalments at no interest."

He chuckled. "And he makes certain he gets the payment by deducting it from my salary."

Lucy dressed and joined Lockie at the kitchen table beside the hearth, which held a brightly glowing fire. They sat beside each other on a wooden bench in a fond embrace.

A knock at the door broke their shared reverie. Lockie rose and opened it to reveal Abigail standing in the doorway. "May I join you?"

Lockie invited her in and took her cape and bonnet.

Abigail rushed to Lucy's side, and they hugged. "Dear cousin," she said. "My brother and your cousin, Samuel, has arrived and informed me that we are in a dire predicament. The loathsome law firm—Cragle, Pincher, and Schleege—are proceeding with their suit to steal the mines that Uncle Erasmus bestowed to us in his will."

Lucy responded, "I was aware of something troubling Samuel in his last letter to us, although he did not intimate what it was about. I thought the lawsuit had been dropped."

"No. Despite the best efforts of our attorney, Mr Leggitt, the suit is going forwards. Samuel arrived last evening by coach and is resting in my flat. We both met with Mr Leggitt yesterday. I am joining him in court on Monday. I hope you can find a way to attend, Lucy."

Lucy looked at Lockie. "Mrs Goodman can watch the boys for the brief hour I'm at court. I'll send a note to her now." She scribbled a message and went outside in search of a ticket porter.

After she hollered for one several times, a fashionably dressed man appeared next to her. "I'm your message deliverer, ma'am." His tone was like a growl.

She looked him up and down. "Where's your apron and badge?"

"Oh, I just got off work, and after seeing you, I thought I'd do you a favour. 'Tis getting late." His language seemed all too formal to her, and there was something off about his toothsome smile. "To whom goes this message?" He extended his hand, still smiling.

"Oh, never mind. I've decided to do something else." She hurried back inside. When she peered out the window, the man was nowhere to be seen.

STAVE EIGHT
ONLY ALL CIVILISATION IS COUNTING ON YOU

Saturday evening, Scrooge fairly dragged his weary body towards home after a rushed business day at the office. The uneaten sandwich was still in his coat pocket. He had not benefited from Cratchit being there to keep an eye on the bookkeeper and scrivener, so he felt compelled to do so himself. All the while, a steady flow of loan payers had come in to make their weekly payments. He had always counted on Abigail to keep the crowd maintained, but she was not there. So, disorder reigned. Lockie, who had been assigned to a particularly sticky investigation of a wayward wife, was not present either. He was moving into Cratchit's old house. Scrooge's encumbrances had exhausted him.

I'm to turn fifty-five soon, he thought while slowly making his way home. *Fine day for a birthday. On the eve of all hallows. Humbug.*

Scrooge made it home ready for a hot supper. Upon hanging his hat, comforter, and coat, he realised it was Kitty's day off. He would have to provide sustenance for himself. Too weary to even look for something to eat, he collided with his chair and collapsed into it. The hearth was cold, but he had not the energy to build even a small fire. He gathered a blanket from the floor and pulled it over his body. Before falling to sleep, he mumbled, "I'm not going to Ireland. I care not about what Shackle demands. I am *definitely not* going." He lifted a foot in order to stamp it in his determination but only allowed it to lightly touch the floor. In two minutes, he was sleeping.

The cold night drifted into London town, and smoke poured forth from the chimneys across the city. Some men spent several hours in pubs, and some prostitutes prowled the streets where the cats and dogs did the same. And for a short time, a myriad of stars shone in the night sky before the smoke and an evening storm's clouds veiled them all.

Scrooge awoke with a start. The room was completely dark. He fumbled for the candle and matches on the side table. He found both and lit the candle. A small flame threw tiny glints at the room's shadows. Scrooge held the candle up and looked about the room. The shadows fled but a little. "What was that?" he whispered.

He hoped he had not heard the sound he remembered so well: chains dragged upon stairs from deep below in the old wine vault. He listened, straining to hear. He heard the rain slamming against the window. After looking about the room thoroughly, he sighed with relief. "Ah, 'tis nothing."

Just then, through the window, he witnessed lightning flash across the sky. And in that brief moment of light, he beheld the ghost of Jacob Marley standing before him, transparent as always. The ghost was attired as before—the old waistcoat and vest, the britches and tall stockings, the shoes turned up at the toes. Around the phantom's head was the same cloth used to tie his jaw shut when he had died. Of course, he was restrained by chains around his shoulders, waist, and legs, and heavy lock boxes drug along the floor. Standing there, he had his hands folded, and the look on his face appeared as if he were pondering some vast question.

The thunder from the previous lightning crashed, and Scrooge flinched. The lightning flashed again, and he bolted up. Taking his one candle, he went about the room, lighting several more. After lighting the six candles of the standing candelabra, he slowly turned. He had hoped all the light might have driven the ghost away. It did not.

Marley's ghost was still standing and pondering. "Why am I here?" he asked. His fathomless eyes pierced Scrooge. "Do I know you?"

Scrooge set down his candle, breathed a sigh, and walked towards the ghost of his former partner in his past business: Scrooge and Marley—Money Lenders. Drawing within a few feet of his visitor, he stated, "I am Ebenezer Scrooge, your partner when you were alive."

The ghost's face showed sudden recognition. He breathed his fetid, dead breath in Scrooge's face. "Ah, yes. I have something to tell you." Then he put his hand to his chin, and his eyes darted about the room, a puzzled look on his visage. "But what is it?"

"I had hoped," Scrooge said, "I had seen the last of any ghosts after the last series of incidents." He opened his mouth to say something else, but then fear overtook him, and he looked around to see if any vile creature from the darkest realm had accompanied Marley's ghost. He saw nothing. The light was sufficient throughout the room.

At last, the ghost snapped his fingers. "Ah, yes. I must tell you that you are to travel. Yes, yes. To go forth to burn, burn, burn."

"Burn? Are you saying you are taking me to *hell*?" Scrooge wailed. "I've been trying to be a better man! Is there no mercy?"

Marley's ghost gave Scrooge a bewildered look. "Whatever are you talking about? I've not come to tell you you're about to die. As far as mercy is concerned, in the abode in which I dwell, such a word is never mentioned and is, in fact, forbidden to be spoken. Mercy comes from another source, whose name I am not allowed to mention."

Scrooge collapsed to the floor. "So, I'm not due to die yet. Praise God."

"Careful now. Don't say his name too loud."

Scrooge pulled himself into his chair. "Then what did you mean by 'burn, burn, burn'?"

"Certainly not that you are supposed to burn. At least, not yet. Hmph." Marley's ghost crossed his arms and stuck his nose in the air. "I haven't the faintest idea as to why my curse in this eternity is to come to the dwelling of a man I hated so much while alive. Why should whatever you do matter to me?" He stomped about the room, dragging the loathsome chains and metal boxes and creating a horrendous noise. He stopped suddenly. "I don't recognise your flat."

Scrooge sighed heavily. "It's been decorated. Albeit against my will, but it is tidied up a bit."

"I see." The spirit barked his next words. "To address your confusion, I was not speaking of anything to be *burnt*. I was speaking a name. A Mr *Byrne*. You are to go with him to Ireland and solve the murder of his brother. But there is more. A calamity is about to occur. The prevention of this great catastrophe is contingent on you and your companions, shall I say, *saving the day*. What little I know of what you're up against, I am quite certain you will fail, which would bring me great pleasure. Were I a praying man, I would pray for you to fail miserably."

"Well, that's a fine attitude, Jacob, after I've been nothing but cordial to you during your visits."

"I care little for your kindness, Scrooge. Remember, it was I who saved your life from the malevolence. I feel relieved neither of us has to deal with that entity again."

"I cannot agree more."

Suddenly, Marley's ghost grabbed his throat and uttered a choking sound. He was being dragged by the neck across the floor, his feet stumbling along. Then the strangling stopped. "I must go," he said, gathering himself and straightening his cravat. "I stayed far past my allowance. Remember, you must go with the Irishman. 'Tis but a small matter. Only all civilisation is counting on you." He slowly began backing towards the door which swung open long enough for him to exit before slamming shut. The ghost was gone.

Scrooge sank into his chair. "I'm too tired to worry about it now. I'm too tired to deal with any more ghosts. Dear God, please release me from this travail." He folded his hands and spoke a silent prayer. Then he looked up. "Nothing, not even a ghost, can make me go to Ireland. Tomorrow is Sunday. So, a good day to figure out how to avoid going. What could possibly happen if I decide not to go?" He fell asleep with the candles still burning brightly.

STAVE NINE

BURN, BURN, BURN

Scrooge was certain he was in hell after all. Surrounding him were deep-red walls covered in flames hot to the touch. The heat seared his skin. *Burn, burn, burn* kept running through his mind. Then, someone was yelling his name and reprimanding him.

"What have you done, Ebenezer?" Kitty screamed.

Scrooge awoke from his dream to see one of the window curtains ablaze, the flames licking the ceiling. Aghast, Scrooge leapt from his chair, staring at the fire. *What has happened? Why? What?*

Now fully awake, he saw Kitty rushing from the kitchen with a pail of water and sloshing it on the burning curtains. She then reached up with a broom and knocked the curtains, rod and all, to the floor. "Quick, Ebenezer, help me stomp it out!" She was already pouncing on the curtain whose flames had abated some.

Scrooge followed her admonition and took frequent stabs with one foot at the flickering elements. Smoke had filled the room. Scrooge coughed and crumpled to his knees below the smoke.

Kitty stomped out the final flame then raced to the window and fanned her apron, sending the smoke outside. Finally, only a few glints of cinders glowed in the blackened, ashen fabric. "Oh, my poor curtains. I worked so hard to find just the right ones." She blubbered into her hands.

Scrooge rose and gazed in shock. He searched for the cause of the blaze and spotted his candle holder against the wall where the curtain had hung. "I must have knocked the candle over while I slept. I had placed it on the side table when ... Never mind." He kicked the ruined curtain a little and observed the scorched floor. He then scanned the blackened wall and sighed in disgust. His first thoughts went to the cost of repairing the damage. Then he chastised himself for even thinking of that issue. "I am lucky to be alive."

Kitty was still bawling and occasionally stomping the last cinders. Scrooge kicked the destroyed curtain once more. It still held heat.

Lockie arrived at the door. "What ho, Mr Scrooge, 'appy Sunday! Your front door was open, and ... My word! What 'appened here?" He came forwards and stared down at the fire-spoiled glob of fabric.

Scrooge rubbed his brow. "I'm lucky to be alive, Lockie. Were it not for the fortuitous arrival of Kitty, I'm afraid I would be heading to my grave."

Lockie turned to Kitty. "Are you all right, ma'am?"

Kitty raised her moist, reddened face. "For now, yes. Give me a moment." She stumbled into the kitchen and sat in a rail-back chair with her back to them.

At that moment, Lucy arrived with Sherlock Jr in her arms, bound in a warm blanket, and she was holding the hand of young Mycroft. Her face sank. "Oh, my dear."

Lockie went to her. "Sweetheart, our benign Mr Scrooge has suffered through a terrible accident. He and Kitty both are fortunate to be living still."

"Oh, Mr Scrooge," Lucy said. "I'm so sorry. We came here to share the joy of our new son but, instead, find you dealing with a terrible, chaotic event." She coughed from some remaining smoke in the room and pulled the blanket over Sherlock Jr's head. "We'll come back another time."

"No, no," Scrooge said. "Please stay. Let me see this newborn child of yours, but don't ask me to hold him. I fear dreadfully I would drop him." He strode over to Lucy and patted Mycroft's head. Ignoring Scrooge, the young lad seemed enthralled by the ashen display on the floor before him.

Lucy pulled down the blanket and showed to Scrooge her sleeping, newborn son. Her husband's employer smiled in approval. "Well done, Lockie and Lucy."

"Before we leave, Mr Scrooge," Lockie said, "at least let me remove this burned mess."

"I'll accept your offer. Down in the old wine cellar, I believe you'll find a large scoop shovel. That should make it easier."

Lockie hastened down the stairs and returned with the scoop. In short order, he had removed the debris to outside and returned the scoop from whence it came. "Well, sir," he said. "We will bid you adieu and share the joy of our children another time." He and Lucy turned to leave.

"Wait," Scrooge said. "Have you been to church yet?"

"Not yet," said Lucy. "We were on our way when we stopped here."

"Please." Scrooge bowed his head and gave the most pitiful expression. "May I join you at the services?"

"Of course," both Lucy and Lockie said together.

"Don't ask me to attend!" Kitty called over her shoulder from the kitchen. "I'll be saying my own devotions and petitions right here in this chair."

Mycroft, who had been perfectly quiet and calm the entire time, was lifted into his father's arms and carried as the little family and Scrooge departed to St Paul's.

Scrooge thought hard about what Inspector Shackle had asked about. *Do I know who Jannes and Jambres were?*

When he returned after the church service, he found Kitty still sitting in the same kitchen chair with her back to the door. She called over her shoulder, "You needn't see me now as I'm wholly unbecoming!" She glanced back at him then immediately turned away and hid her face in her hands.

STAVE TEN

THE FOG OF WIGS

In the dismal grey hallway of Chancery Court, Samuel Jiggins, his hands visibly shaking, stood beside his sister Abigail and their cousin Lucy. They had halted just behind their short, trim barrister Abel Leggitt outside the large, black double-doors of the Chancery Court in Lincoln Inn, Old Hall. Court was held daily there, except Sundays. The heavy leather chairs in the hall and the oft-lacquered doors held a smell of legitimacy but also of dread. Whole fortunes were lost there.

Leggitt, whose height mimicked that of a horse jockey, wore his flowing, black robe and the standard, powdered-white wig for court proceedings. He held his pinched nose high, clutched his portfolio tight under one arm, and occasionally nodded at other barristers waiting for the doors to open. Had he a rooster's red comb for a headdress rather than the wig, many might have referred to him as a fighting cock, one never once defeated.

A clock on the wall struck nine in the morning. The doors were swung wide open by guards in officious-looking black uniforms. Leggitt marched in with the Jiggins siblings and Mrs Holmes close behind. The other barristers and clients followed.

After the Jigginses and Lucy found a bench just behind the respondents' table, Samuel pointed out barrister Al Cragle, their adversary. "I've never seen the other two members of his firm," Samuel said. "Though Abaddon

Cragle is always surrounded by several assistants." Four clerks took seats behind Cragle, who stood at the table designated for the plaintiffs in the suit.

Leggitt took his stance at the table for the respondents. He lightly waved a hand, and seven clerks and scribes filed in and took seats near him. Lucy saw him smirk at Cragle. Then, the crowd that loved to watch court proceedings raced into the large upper seating gallery, shoving and squabbling over seats. As was usual, many were forced to stand.

Leggitt, before taking his chair, turned to the gallery and was greeted with several whistles of approbation and a few polite applauses.

The court sergeant, bearing a large staff with a jewelled mace at the top, struck the floor with the bottom of the staff. "Hear ye, hear ye! His honour, the Lord Chancellor."

Everyone rose. The chancellor took his seat on the judge's bench the trial began, and Cragle and Leggitt came to legal blows. Cragle would present a document, and Leggitt would present the sworn affidavit of a witness verifying the document was false. Cragle would question the veracity of the witness, at which point Leggitt would produce further documents verifying the honesty and high stature of the witness. Cragle would then cite some legal precedent, at which one of Leggitt's assistants would peel open the law book to the appropriate page, and Leggitt would then read aloud the counter argument to Cragle's assertion.

At the appropriate point, Leggitt would bring in the aspects of the murder of Mr Tamperwind and its impact on the case, where Cragle would claim that contracts always take precedence, at which Leggitt would plead several aspects of law which applied counter to Cragle's assertion. Thus, the hearing went on for two hours. Every so often, the crowd above would "ooh" and "ah" at some legal point Leggitt would make. Occasionally, an unknown person in the upper chamber would "boo" some comment by Cragle, at which the Lord Chancellor would bang his gavel. After an extended length of time, the Lord Chancellor drew the hearing to a close, stating he would confer with the chancellors in his chambers and see if a decision could be made or if further evidence was required.

When the courtroom cleared, Attorney Leggitt sat with his clients, who were also his friends. "The system is set up for abuse," he said. "When you have twenty-odd men in wigs debating over even an uncontested case, too many objections, a plethora of points of order, and all the rigamarole of men who deem themselves of high stature, you get a fog that pours out of this institution into the streets, filling all of London."

Samuel asked, "Is there nothing we can do to hasten the outcome of this travesty?"

Leggitt drew a long breath. "In trickery, evasion, procrastination, spoliation, botheration, under false pretenses of all sorts, there are influences which can never come to any good.* I wish there were more I could do."

"Then, we shall proceed to Tamperwind," Samuel said, "and entrust ourselves and our family's legacy to your wise judgement, Abel."

"I will do all I can." Leggitt affixed the straps of his legal valise, and they all left. Though he gave no indication, he was not confident of a quick end to the case.

STAVE ELEVEN

MINDLESS MINDFULNESS

"Oh, Lockie, what is my family to do?" Lucy lamented. She sat at their new home's kitchen table while Lockie started a fire in the hearth. Mycroft played on the floor nearby with some toys.

Lockie blew on the small flame, which burst abundantly, and turned to Lucy. "I've thought about what I know from researching the Cragle law firm. It is a vicious group, tireless in their strivings to remove people from their rightful properties. The law is their battering ram."

"I don't doubt a word you say, dear husband. Oh, look, we've awakened Sherlock Jr. He's whimpering and needs to be fed." Lucy picked up the baby and undid the necessary buttons of her dress and corset stays and nursed him.

Lockie finished stoking the fire and pumping the bellows. The Cratchit's former home was not built entirely to plumb, and the night air leaked in at several cracks by the windows and doors and even at cracks in the walls, adding to the cold feel of the house. After the fire was sufficiently warm, Lockie lit another candle on a stand. He sat at the table, set his elbows on it, and leaned his chin on his folded hands. "You wish to go to Tamperwind, Lucy. Am I correct?"

Lucy looked lovingly into Lockie's eyes. "Yes, love of my life. I fear if we don't all pull together, we could lose the mines."

"Yes, their income has helped us with the moving fees and the midwife's fees for Junior's birth and such. It is not much though."

"It won't be until Samuel sells the forthcoming load of tin next month. Then we should have quite a bit of money."

"Then we'll be as rich as Mr Scrooge?" Lockie guffawed, and Lucy giggled.

Little Junior had fallen asleep, and Lucy gently put him back in the crib then scooted closer to Lockie. "Abigail is returning with Samuel to Tamperwind Manor on Wednesday. I want to go with them, but I don't want to leave you. I'd have to take our new baby and Mycroft by myself on a dangerous journey and … I just don't know what to do. Poor Samuel. Poor Abigail."

"Then you won't have to go alone. I'll go with you. How long could it possibly take? Two days there, help Samuel for two days, and return. Mr Scrooge can survive without my help for one week."

"Lockie, that is wonderful! Are you certain Mr Scrooge will let you go?"

"If he dismisses me, come November, the mine will sell the tin, and we'll all be rich." He smiled broadly. "And now I have skills to gain employment perhaps even in a bank. Mr Scrooge would be making a foolish error to dismiss me."

❧

On the next day, when Lockie told Scrooge his plans, Scrooge issued a solemn scowl. The former miser had too much else on his mind. A police detective and a ghost were coercing him to go to a land he fairly loathed. He had already made arrangements with Hiram Grumbles to oversee the running of the office. "Send a telegram from a nearby town when you arrive at the mines," Scrooge told Lockie. "Give my well-wishes to brave Samuel. I already knew Abigail was leaving the firm to go there. You must go with your wife." Then he turned his back on Lockie and walked away, buried in his worries.

After the workday ended, with the day drawing to a close, Scrooge seemed to be moving as a clock might function, a steady tick-tock followed by an hourly chime of a bell. He felt as if he were one of those wooden characters that moved around the animated clocks, a meticulously carved figure with tiny nails pinned in his shoulders and knees to allow his arms and legs to move. He was planning to go to Ireland. *To Ireland, for goodness' sake!* He made a plan, forfeited it, and then commenced a new one, all while walking in a sort of zigzag fashion through the London streets, near where he abided. His plans did not include going home to his warm hearth. Instead, he could only think of little Mycroft and Sherlock Jr. He found himself plodding up to Tackleton's Toyshop.★

"That old ogre," he whispered while he peered in the shop's window. "Tackleton is an ogre, and yet, he manages to produce some of the finest toys for children anywhere. He must employ some fine workmen." In his stupefied state, he gazed first at one toy. "No, that's not for a boy." Then another. "That one is for an older boy." He looked at cricket bats and a wind-up, dancing clown and jack-in-the-boxes and various toys that would magically move when a spring was wound tight by a key. He felt as though he himself had been wound with a key and set in motion to venture forth on this journey to an isle surely filled with goblins and creatures of the night. He imagined he would zip around like an out-of-control, spinning-top to crash into a wall of danger and death.

Being thus fraught with fear, he found himself gawping at a puppet in the corner and imagined himself as a puppet where Jacob Marley's ghost, Shamus Shackle, and Reginald Byrne pulled his strings. He sighed and opened the shop's door. He went to the clerk and purchased a ball for Mycroft and a velvet-covered, stuffed lamb for the baby.

Along the way home, he made one more purchase at a cart, more automatically than due to any deep feeling. He just did it. *So, there!* he thought.

ꙮ

"Oh, Ebenezer! They are lovely! Wherever did you get them?" Kitty clutched the bouquet of flowers Scrooge had purchased from the flower cart for her. He had absent-mindedly laid them on the kitchen counter, still in his muddled state of mind. Kitty had just arrived from her bedroom down the hall. Her room had once been an office of the warehouse, but she availed herself of the handy salary Hiram Grumbles paid her on Scrooge's behalf and outfitted the room to be a comfy haven in which to retire each evening. The sweet-faced, stout woman found the flowers and looked around to see who else might be in Scrooge's apartment. Seeing no one but Scrooge, her joy abounded.

Scrooge had sunk into his stuffed chair in his parlour, now completely oblivious to her presence. He fumbled with the gifts for Lockie and Lucy's children. Kitty rushed to him, threw her arms around his neck, and gave him a peck on the cheek.

Brought back to reality, he turned to look into the beautiful, expressive face of the sturdy, plucky woman who worked for him, primarily as his maid, but hired originally by Hiram Grumbles to be his bodyguard. She was definitely tough enough to take on several men and had done as much often in her lurid past. Kitty had sought to tell him some of her past, but when she arrived at a particular sordid juncture, he called a stop to her elaborations and said, "I care not to know."

Scrooge blushed at her attention. "Yes. There you are. I never thank you enough, and since I'm going to be gone for some while—"

"No need to justify your generosity, Ebenezer. The gesture is explanation enough."

Scrooge handed the toys to Kitty. "Here. You must wrap them and somehow get them to Lockie and Lucy Holmes. Call it a house-warming gift. But, mind you, spend nothing on fancy paper and bows. Newsprint and string will do fine." Before Kitty could respond, he said. "I'm going to bed. I've much to attend to tomorrow before I leave for that infernal place."

"Ireland?"

"Yes."

"Ebenezer! I hear the country is like a treasure of emeralds as far as the eye can see."

Scrooge turned towards his bedroom. "Emerald treasure! Bah! Humbug!"

STAVE TWELVE

THE TINKER, THE THIEF, THE MURDER

In her fashionable but moderate brick home in the middle of the village of Wicklow on the edge of the Wicklow mountains, Gwendolyn Kelly, the mayor's wife, worked in the kitchen. She was a tall, big-boned woman with grey hair and rough but rosy skin. She was busy kneading bread for upcoming meals when she heard a loud rap on her door. "Don't worry, Sally!" she called to her maid. "I'll get it."

When she opened the door, before her stood a short, broad man buried in a heavy coat, the high collar up to his ears, almost hiding his face, and he was standing sideways to her rather than facing her. In a barrow behind him, he had an assortment of pots and pans and looked to be a tinker. "Any pots or kettles, ma'am, with rusty holes to block?" the man asked in a meandering stream of words. "Any pots that be rusted? Your sink got a hole? I'm your man to fix holes. Got me tools right here." Though never looking straight at her, he shook a pouch with tin snips and tin patch pieces jingling.

"My goodness. I might have one pot." Gwendolyn turned and called over her shoulder, "Stay right there!" She reached inside her cupboard and pulled out a small pot.

When she turned around, the man stood before her, this time with a mask over her nose and jowls. Only his fierce eyes showed. "Now, you'll tell me where *it* is," he growled.

The mayor's wife backed against the sink, dropping the pan, which clattered and rolled. "Whatever do you mean?"

"G'won. Tell me where it is!" He moved closer to her, looking into her frightened eyes. "I mean it."

"If you mean to rob us, I shan't tell you where we keep our valuables. My husband would be too upset."

"I ain't lookin' for no valu'bles. I want the treasure. I know you got it 'ere."

Just then, the maid, Sally O'Neil, came down the stairs, stopping on the last step. "Is everything all right, ma'am? Shall I send Billie for the constabulary?" A teenaged, tow-headed boy peeked out from behind his mother. Both son and mother were as freckled as any two people could be.

"You call the law, and someone's gonna die!" The short fiend pulled a pistol from under his coat and cocked the hammer, aiming it at the maid and then the mayor's wife.

Sally and her son shrank back. The invader, tired of waiting for an answer, ploughed around the kitchen and parlour, opening drawers, and spilling them. His actions were like a wild animal's. Sally scooted her son upstairs, but no sooner had she done so, the man stormed after him and could be heard rummaging through the bedrooms, crashing and banging. Some glass breaking.

Sally called after her son, but he had adeptly climbed out a window and leapt to the ground. Both women watched as Billie raced by the window. "I'll get help!" he called and was soon out of sight.

The boorish man clomped down the stairs. "Where is it? I demand to know!"

Gwendolyn raised herself and took on an air of authority. "If I knew what you wanted, I'd tell you, you brigand. My husband is the mayor, and you shall be held accountable."

The pretender snarled. Then he heard the crowd of people striding up the street and yelling. He looked out the window. "I'm not done with you yet!" he claimed then raced out the door.

The crowd of townsmen led by Billie arrived and filled the parlour, where they questioned the mayor's wife and maid. A few men went outside to see where the man had vanished, but they saw nothing. The man had left his barrow of cookware behind.

That evening, Mayor Timothy Kelly returned home from a journey and was appraised of the events by the would-be robber. He thanked the maid and her son and told his wife he would contact the Dublin authorities in the morning. As was his habit, he took his long pipe and went outside to smoke it.

Standing and looking at the stars, he heard footsteps behind him. He turned and saw a man in the shadows, holding a lantern. The light shone upon Mayor Kelly, but he could not see the man's face. "I'll have the box now, Kelly," the man said in a sombre tone.

"The box?" Kelly smiled, not intimidated by the man. "What box do you mean? If you mean to box with me, I'm a renowned boxing-ring fighter. I doubt you'd have a chance against me."

"Your arrogance doesn't impress me, Kelly. I want the box." He stepped closer, and Kelly made out that the man wore a tall headdress which emulated a cobra, not unlike one a pharaoh might wear.

The mayor snickered. "It's not Halloween yet. You must be part of a jest." Suddenly, a stout arm grabbed around Kelly's chest, and a knife was held against his throat. His pipe fell from his lips. "What do you want? I have money."

The man gripping the mayor scraped the knife gently along the mayor's neck and clinched him tighter.

The man with the pharaoh's headdress moved closer, his face still in shadow. "You know what we want. Tell us now."

"And if I don't?" Kelly asked.

"We'll kill you." The pharaoh man turned and walked away. "In fact, we'll find it another way. Kill him now."

The second man sliced open Mayor Kelly's neck, the blood spilling forth, and the poor man collapsed.

When the mayor didn't return inside, his wife went out to call him in. Instead, she found his dead body.

STAVE THIRTEEN
MUDLARKS, NIGHT SOIL MEN, AND THE CRATCHITS

"Dear Ebenezer," Hiram Grumbles said, "although I cannot speak to the detecting side of your business, I can assure you your loan business will be well taken care of while you're away in Ireland. You have the two employees you hired to write the contracts and keep the books. I believe I've had enough experience in business to keep things afloat." Hiram Grumbles stood head and shoulders above Scrooge. He was indebted to Scrooge and Cratchit and Lockie since, by their intrepid detective work, they had saved him from hanging for a murder he had not committed. He was broad and strong, and his face always beamed of bright youthfulness, though his age was near fifty. As big and proud as he was, he would be beholden to Scrooge for the rest of his life. "Besides, I can contact your nephew, Edmund, to assist, should it be warranted."

"Thank you, Hiram." Scrooge looked upwards at the friendly colossus. "It's generally not too complex to operate the loan applications, fees, and collections. However, Abigail Jiggins will not be here to oversee the clients. She left yesterday to go to Tamperwind in Cornwall. And Lockie is going there too. I worry most about those scallywags who fail to pay on time. Scallywags! Like useless farm animals. I heard an American use that term. I feel it is an accurate appraisal. Usually, Lockie takes care of that angle of the business. You'll have no one to collect on delinquent accounts."

"Then, they shall wait upon your and Lockie's return and be charged interest thereon."

After the two men bid farewell with firm handshakes, Scrooge flung his comforter around his neck and exited his office with his portmanteau in one hand and the other clutching his jacket pocket where he usually kept his keys, for now Grumbles had total ownership of them. "I feel naked without my keys," he mumbled.

On this early morning, with the last night stars still twinkling somewhere above the fog, London had become more vapor than air. The fog was dense, it hid from view the man walking in front of Scrooge. He only heard footsteps ahead and did his best not to step on the fellow pedestrian's heels. The misty clouds concealed even the buildings across the street from where he trod. This chilly October air was cruelly pinching his toes and fingers, and it dwelt in his eyes and throat, and he knew such was the case of probably all people across England. The costermongers★ would sell little this morning, for the punters★ doing their shopping would pass them by, unseen. They would holler about their wares into a vast nothingness of grey and white, and no one would respond.

Scrooge knew the old folk would be wheezing by the firesides of their humble dwellings; and fog would settle in the stem and bowl of the city's labourers pipes.★ He wished to smoke his own pipe but was wary to pull it from his pocket lest he drop it into the miasma at his feet and never find it. He strode past a shivering, little ticket porter who was hugging himself with his arms and stomping his feet to stay warm. Passing over Blackfriars Bridge on his way to the ship that would carry him to Dublin, he noticed people on the bridge, peeping over the parapets into a nether sky of fog, and he wondered what they were seeking.

In his portmanteau, he had a change of clothes, several logs of his accounts, investments, fees due from loanees, and the like, as well as his pistol and a bag of ammunition. Two money sacks hung on leather straps around his neck, hidden under his shirt.

Arriving at the assigned pier, with the sun gleaming through the now-much-thinner fog, Scrooge strode tenuously along the long boardwalk until he located the schooner barque, *The Intrepid*, tied fast in its berth. The tall, two-masted ship rocked in the mellow current of the Thames River, the boards of the vintage vessel creaking either in pain or to mimic a sad "hello" to him. Seamen and dock workers were trundling huge sacks of corn and wheat up the gangplank onto the deck and then down into the hold. A herd of complaining sheep huddled in a corral on deck.

With the fog cleared now, the ship's captain—with bacca-pipes* on his face, wearing a dark-blue jacket with gold-filigreed sleeves, a flouncy cap, and white breeches tied at the knee with blue ribbons—stood spread-legged on a lower mast spar, shouting orders in a voice that demanded a great deal of room.* Each member of the crew hastened to do his bidding.

A man in a shabbier uniform who appeared to be the first mate snarled at every seaman and squinted one eye in reproach at each one who passed him. "Be quick about it!" he barked.

Mr Byrne, the owner of the vessel, was nowhere in sight. Bob Cratchit, surrounded by his entire family, hovered close to the edge of the pier, just past the ship's bow. Scrooge came up behind the group, unbeknownst. Not a single board creaked under Scrooge's weight, yet there he stood, with his attentive face and hat and walking stick in his hands and his hands behind him, a composed and quiet listener,* gazing at the family he loved so well.

Tim, who seemed (according to Scrooge) to grow taller each day, was pointing at the sandy beach running alongside the river. His sisters and older brother, Peter, hovered around him. "Look!" Tim shouted. "There's several more mudlarks."*

"It appears to be an entire family," Peter said. "I thought mudlark people worked the riverbanks closer to its outlet to the sea."

"I believe you are right," Bob's wife said. "That's where most of the lost items wash ashore. Perhaps the group feels this area has not been scoured enough for river treasure."

Cratchit held tight to his wife's hand. "Alvina, dear one, I've been told some make a pretty penny from their finds. In the days when I worked the wharf farther along the Thames, I saw whole mudlark families combing the banks for whatever prize had washed ashore."

Belinda looked puzzled. "Why do they call them mudlarks, Papa?"

"Well, my dears," Cratchit said, "these poor creatures, the poorest of London's poor, find this is the only way they can eke out a living. Scrounging in the riverside mud, they may find a trinket or other valuable object and sell it at a pawnshop. Many have a disability, a lost arm or leg, or a severe illness like tuberculosis; or they've lost their jobs and must scavenge to make ends meet. Say a prayer when you think of them."

"Amen," Scrooge said. He shuddered at the thought of being so poor.

Cratchit turned and beheld his friend. "What a great surprise! Here is Ebenezer. Here to join me on our first ever voyage!"

"Hello, Bob. Hello, Alvina. Bob is a lucky man to have such a lovely wife."

"Thank you, Mr Scrooge," Alvina replied.

"My second father!" Tim rushed to Scrooge and gave him a tight hug. "We have a new home now, Mr Scrooge. It is *much* larger."

"As are you, my dear Tim. You seem to grow taller and more rugged every time I see you." The much-healthier Tim was only a head shorter than old Scrooge now. "And all of you are here to see your father off on this perilous journey. Perhaps you could talk us out of going."

"Not so perilous," Cratchit said. "What could be so dangerous about sailing around our island home just long enough to land on our neighbour island, Ireland? Why! Ships do it all day and night. Many's the time when Tim, Peter, and I have built paper boats and sailed them in the gutters after a rain. I'm sure this large vessel is up to the task."

Scrooge looked at the sky past the masts, the sails still furled. The fog had ebbed considerably, revealing a blue sky but with a vast array of dark clouds off to the east. "I hope so."

"Papa!" Belinda exclaimed.

"Yes, daughter?" Cratchit stroked her long hair.

"Who are those men on that low cliff above the beach? They are dumping basket after basket of dark dirt into the river."

Cratchit and the others came beside her to witness the not-too-distant activity. A half-dozen, burly, black-shirted men were emptying baskets of viscous muck into the Thames. Cratchit explained, "Those are some of the night soil men.* Their jobs are to dig out the human waste—"

"Feces," added Peter, trying to sound learned.

"Yes," his father said, "the human feces from the thousands and thousands of cesspools of London. The stalwart men, like those on the cliff, work at night, going under houses and apartments, digging out the human waste and hauling it away."

"I've read," Peter said in an erudite manner, "that generally, these night soil men take the waste to farms to use as fertilizer."

"That's correct, Peter," his father replied.

"Do the men stink?" Belinda asked.

"I should think they would!" Peter exclaimed. "I'm amazed, from the ammonia in the waste, they don't sometimes spontaneously combust!*" Peter, the oldest boy in the family and about fourteen years of age, had found a subject of which he was thrilled to expound.

"Spontaneously combust?" Scrooge echoed. "Is that possible?"

"There are educators who validate its reality," replied Peter, somewhat full of his perceived scientific knowledge. "There are known cases where those who drink alcohol all day or work around volatile chemicals, such as chemists, have been known to explode spontaneously." He raised his eyebrows as if he had proven his point. "The evidence is insurmountable."

"Why, then," queried Belinda, "would any man find satisfaction in such a task as the nightly cleaning of human waste? Why would he not do such a job as you, Papa?'

Cratchit put his hand to his chin and conjectured. "A wonderful fact to reflect upon is how every human being is constituted to be a profound secret and mystery to others."

"Let us change the subject." Alvina gave her family gentle nudges to move away from their position at the edge of the pier, closer to the sailing vessel's gangplank, thus obstructing the view of the beach and cliff.

Tim interposed a new subject. "Later today, I'm going to watch Mr. Charles Green sail into the clouds on one of his gas balloons at Lord's Cricket Grounds.* He's flown aloft at least one hundred times."

Alvina shook her head but smiled. "Our youngest son has taken quite an interest in ballooning. He reckons he can recall as much as is known on the subject."

"'Tis more than a subject, Mum. 'Tis a sport, where more and more people are travelling about the country with no impediments of traffic, observing the land, the farms, and the cities like a hawk or sparrow might. It sounds glorious. Mr Green and others have sailed across the channel to France and Germany. I wonder what those countries are like."

"Just don't be thinkin' you'll be ridin' up in one of those balloons," Alvina said with intense fervor. "'Tis too dangerous for a young lad."

"I'm almost ten, Mum," Tim replied. "Come All Saints Day. If I can work in the boot-blacking factory* Papa arranged, I am almost a man."

"What's this about him working in a factory, Bob?" Scrooge asked.

"Ah, for only two days a week," Bob replied. "If that much. He'll fill in if a worker is absent. Never more than six times in a month."

"As long as he's not worked too hard like the poor young boys in the coal mines."

"It would never happen, Ebenezer," Cratchit explained. "My Tim wants to earn some of his own money. This way, he can work, and I can keep a keen eye on what goes on. Halloo! On a different subject, here comes Mr Byrne and Officer Blevins."

When Scrooge turned to see the men, he remarked, "Byrne doesn't seem at all happy."

Byrne hustled up to the group. He briefly introduced Officer Blevins to the Cratchit family. Blevins smiled broadly, and after shaking Cratchit's hand, he kissed Alvina's hand. "I am honoured to make your acquaintance. I've heard much about the accomplishments of your brave husband. I feel as though I know Bob well already." He even made polite bows to each of the children. Belinda smiled bashfully at so handsome a man.

Mr Byrne could wait no longer, his face tense. "Mr Scrooge, Mr Cratchit, might I have a word?" He led the two men away from the family. "I'm sorry for my tardiness. I just received a telegram saying the mayor of Wicklow has been murdered. His throat cut."

Scrooge and Cratchit gawped.

"I'm afraid our task to unearth the cause of my brother's murder has become more complex. You see, my brother was good friends with Mayor Kelly, who had knowledge of my brother's recent exertions in the Wicklow mountain area. I trust you are still up to aiding my cause."

"Of course," Cratchit said.

After a moment, Scrooge mumbled, "Of course." And he looked at the gathering storm over the ocean, into which the ship would be sailing.

The ship's captain called from his perch on the mast, "All aboard, all passengers! We set sail on the tide." He then began shouting orders, as did his surly looking first mate who seemed to prowl rather than stroll about the deck, sneering. Several sailors quickly scaled the masts like jungle monkeys, while other seamen set about untying the ropes that tethered the ship to the dock.

After giving many hugs to his family, Bob Cratchit boarded the ship first, followed by Byrne and Blevins. Scrooge hesitated at the foot of the gangplank and twice turned as if to leave. At last, closing his eyes and arms outstretched, he ventured onto the gangplank. Two burly seamen took hold of his arms and fairly dragged him aboard.

The ship lightly drifted away from the dock. Lightning flashed in the dark clouds. Scrooge ducked down and only peeked over the ramparts at the wharf slowly sliding farther away.

STAVE FOURTEEN
A CODED MESSAGE

Riding in the stagecoach bound for Cornwall where lay the Tamperwind and Hopworth mines, Lucy held three crumpled letters from her friend in one hand while she rocked Sherlock Jr. Worry spread over her face.

Sitting next to her, Lockie held Mycroft on his knee, jouncing him up and down to mimic the bumpy ride. "Ride the horsie, don't fall down," he chanted to his smiling, adopted son. Mycroft was Lucy's son from rape by a villainous man who had been supposedly seeking the hand of her widowed mother. Lucy had raised Mycroft well, and after she and Lockie married, Lockie adopted him.

"Lockie," Lucy said, "I'm so grateful you're allowing me to visit my dear friend, Hortense Cherry. Her last letter, though filled with glowing comments about her new living arrangements at the Abode of Love,★ concerned me. I fear she feels she is facing danger. Reading between the lines, I sense she feels she is being kept prisoner there. In one letter, she says the community has a twelve-foot-high wall around it and guards and dogs at the gate. Though she describes it as a community of love, the people seem to be very tight and unimaginative, though she never speaks ill of them. She speaks highly of the leader, Reverend Henry Prince,★ who insists that all his congregation live lives of chastity and abstinence."

"I don't see what her worries might be," Lockie said. The coach suddenly hit a pothole in the road, and he clutched Mycroft tight. "Whew! This road is in need of repair."

"That's something else she mentions. Nothing gets fixed in the complex where one hundred members share a living space. Now, let me read this to you. She wrote, 'The reverend said something odd to me. He told me he had been absorbed into the personality of God and become the embodiment of the Holy Spirit.' What do you say, dear husband?"

"I think you may be concerned over nothing. Isn't the name of the church 'Agapemone'? *Land of Brotherly Love*? Besides, Hortense has a right to make her own decisions."

Lucy looked out at the scenery of Somerset County. The land was a patchwork of lush green, rust, and golden farmland, for the weather was changing. Here and there, farmers trod through their field, turning up the soil with ploughs. She tired of the monotony of the view. "Lockie, I know something is wrong. Hortense wants to leave but cannot. She's given all her money to the community, *all her money*, and now has nowhere to go, except as a beggar in the streets or to a workhouse." Lucy dug a letter from her reticule. "Look at this last sentence ... a postscript to her last letter."

Lockie read the following sentence to himself, *Here Everyone Loves Puppies. I Am Merry. Truly Reminded About Perfect People Every Day.*

"Can you see it?" Lucy asked, her tone fervent.

"Yes, the sentence has the first letter of every word capitalised. Taking just those capital letters, the sentence of the coded message then reads, 'Help. I am trapped.'"

"So, do you now understand my concern?"

"Indeed, I do, dear Lucy. We will investigate this matter and help Hortense as best we can."

"Thank you, Lockie. I'm so worried."

"We'll be arrivin' in the town of Spaxton★ soon, dearest. You'll see all is well." Lockie had not been fully honest with his wife. His keen detective sense was on high-alert. He knew of secret slave societies. *Perhaps this is one,* he thought. He also noticed that the final three sentences in the missive was in a different hand. He noticed something disturbingly unique about the way the letter M was written in the word *Merry*.

STAVE FIFTEEN

A MERCY ERRAND AND AN UNSEEN GUEST

Lockie, holding Mycroft in one arm, helped Lucy down from the coach at Agapemone Estate in Spaxton. She then picked up Sherlock Jr, who was bundled in his small wicker basket. Lockie carried a single, small portmanteau. He called to the coachman, "Come 'round here tomorrow morning by nine, and we will continue on our journey."

The coachman waggled his head, his appearance vexed. "We'll see about that." When Lockie closed the coach door, the coachman popped his whip and slapped the reins of his coursers. "Let me away from this place!" The coach careened away, out the gate.

"Why would he behave that way, Lockie?" Lucy asked.

"I'm not sure, but this place does appear foreboding." Both gazed upon the dark-brick, two-story manor, the windows all shuttered. Without saying a word, both further noticed two large, black hounds chained to a nearby post, their bloodthirsty eyes following the couple's movements.

Lockie acknowledged, "Although, there is a decent chapel off to the right and stables and even a gazebo. Perhaps we've come upon a true place where love abounds." He snickered, and Lucy held her hand to her lips to cover her smile.

With their boys in hand, the couple walked along the stone pavement to the door, which suddenly opened wide. A pregnant woman of about thirty-five years greeted them. "Welcome to the Abode of Love!" she cackled, though it was not an ominous laugh. "Come in, come in." She motioned them inside as if she had been expecting them for some time, leading them into a parlour. "My name is Agnes Nottidge. Welcome, welcome. I see you have children. I'm to have one too. Of course, everyone here is celibate." She blushed and rubbed her stomach then walked with great haste into the next room, calling over her shoulder, "Be seated! The lamb will be here soon to share the blossom of love."

Lockie and Lucy sat with Mycroft between them. Lockie held Junior. Lucy asked under her breath, "What did she mean by 'the lamb'? Are we to have mutton tonight for supper?"

In a moment, they heard a gaggle of giggling females approach from whence Agnes had gone. The group of happy women surrounding one man in a protestant pastor's regalia burst into the room as if prizes were to be awarded. The Holmes couple stood. Lockie extended his hand to the man, who took a handkerchief from his sleeve, wiped his hand with it, and then shook hands with Lockie. "Welcome, welcome, new lovers," said the man. He tugged at his pastor's collar. "The Abode of Love is always ready to invite newcomers to share in our bliss."

The women tittered softly then took positions around the room, all of them smiling. Lockie noted how they seemed a varied lot of young, middle-aged, and old; one of them tottering along with a cane. Their dress was generally drab, but all wore some sort of jewellry.

The man wiped his hand again and put the kerchief away. "I am Dr Henry James Prince. Called by God and filled with the Holy Spirit. In fact, I have been absorbed into the personality of God. Hence I am *love itself*." He smiled demurely and cocked his head a little. "And may I know your names?"

"My name is Lockie Holmes. This is my wife, Lucy. Our two boys—"

"No matter their names now," Prince said. "We are delighted to receive you. We are a communal parish here. Though still on the earth, we live in the spirit. We contribute to the whole and pray generally all day long. Perhaps that's why you're here. To enhance your prayer life."

"Not exactly," Lockie said. "We're honoured you have shared these gladsome tidings with us, but we are travelling on an important journey and wish only to visit with one of your women staying here."

"Hortense Cherry," Lucy added.

"Well, I think that can be arranged," Prince said. "I'll have Louisa Nottidge show you around and set you up in your love chamber. I believe you met her sister, Agnes, when you arrived." He pointed at a willowy woman with a gentle brow and deep cow eyes. "I assume you are staying for a week or more."

"No, sir." Lockie smiled. "Only the one night. We brought a single, small bag and will be leaving tomorrow morning. Thank you for your kind offer. Is there a charge for staying?"

"Not at all. Most visitors leave a donation. We are always glad to receive support for our community. You will be pleased to know a woman and her boy arrived today, also in order to determine if they wish to live here. Louisa, please show them the grounds and set them up in the far cottage yonder." He pointed out the window towards a row of cottages. He departed with his entourage just as two older, finely dressed men sauntered into the parlour and sat and lit up cigars. Two of the women who had been following Prince returned with brooms and began sweeping the floor. Another dusted the furniture.

"This way, please," Louisa's timid voice sang.

"Before we begin our tour, Louisa," Lucy said, "when may we visit Hortense?"

"I will take you to her soon. She stays in one of the cottages on the backside. Not in the big house where most of us share the twenty bedrooms. It's most delightful." Her smile was genuine. "Isn't the Lamb wonderful? He is the epitome of God on Earth. So kind. So generous." Chattering gleefully all the way, she led Lockie and Lucy with the boys out into the well-maintained garden, then to the chapel, and finally to their cottage for the night. "I will alert Miss Cherry of your presence," Louisa said when she departed.

Lockie and Lucy failed to notice a boy of medium stature of about thirteen years watching them from an upstairs window of the estate house. Upon his face was a scornful look, his eyes squinted in hatred. He then gave a snigger of delight.

Two hours later, it was getting dark outside, and supper was about to be served. The Holmeses had still not been permitted to see Hortense.

STAVE SIXTEEN
THE LASCIVIOUS LAMB

The supper bell rang, and Lucy and Lockie hurried with the boys to the dining hall in the main house. Sherlock Jr slept comfortably in Lucy's arms, and Mycroft locked his arms around Lockie's neck and hung on to his father. Upon entering, the couple saw roughly sixty women and one man seated at several long tables in two rows. Louisa met them at the door. "Sit here at the end. You are our guests. The hall is only so large, so in order for everyone to be fed, we need to have three rounds of supper. This is the first round. The second and third shifts come later. Everyone is fed and of good cheer." She hurried away with what looked to Lucy like a forced smile.

"Her demeanor does not seem genuine," Lucy whispered.

She and Lockie sat at the end of the table, their boys on their laps, and Louisa returned and stood just behind them. "Oh, I don't eat until the second round. Hortense, your friend, eats during the third round."

Several women carrying heavy iron pots and ladles exited the kitchen and dished a dark broth into bowls, but no one lifted a spoon. A fierce-looking woman wearing a shabby bonnet and soiled apron brought three bowls with a hearty venison stew and large slices of brown bread to the Holmeses. Mycroft began nibbling at a chunk of the bread.

When the last of the broth was served, Prince entered at the head of the room, opposite the Holmeses. "As I am your father in the spirit," he

began, "I am both appalled and gladdened by today's revelations. First, I
am appalled and saddened. God has given a warning. He told me to be on
the lookout for nefarious individuals, ones who would undo the good being
done here." He stopped and stared at the Holmes couple. Then looking at
the women, he smiled, and his voice rose in a commanding baritone. "And
I have had a revelation from an angel. Considerable good tidings are to be
bestowed on certain individuals here. I will tap the shoulders of those who
are to receive the brilliant news I received straight from Heaven. After this
sumptuous meal, you are to come at once to my chambers to hear the word
of God and more." He then gave a prayer and blessing for the meal that
lasted five minutes. Mycroft continued to eat the bread.

While the sixty women and one man slurped their broth, and the
Holmeses ate their stew, which had grown tepid during the wait, Prince
went round the tables, tapping the shoulders of four of the comeliest young
women. Each one blushed and hurried to finish their broth.

Lockie leaned towards Lucy and whispered, "I'm uncertain what great
news he has to share with those women, but I fear it may not be Godly."

"I agree." Lucy finished helping Mycroft with his small portions from
her stew. "Lockie, I must go nurse young Sherlock. He has been ever so
patient. Will you join me at our cottage?"

"I think not. I plan to find Hortense and gain more knowledge as to
whether her plight is as much as we perceive."

"Good idea."

When Prince released all to "go to your prayers," as he called it, the four
young women followed him out and up the stairs. The other women set
about cleaning their bowls and spoons and cups at a communal washtub and
then dried the items on their aprons. In a few moments, all had left the hall,
the tables spotless. The fierce woman arrived and took the Holmeses's dishes.
She glowered at them, never speaking.

Louisa, who had been seated against the wall behind them, called out, "I
am hungry!" The Holmes couple turned to look at the woman, whose eyes
were turned towards the ceiling, her expression as if in ecstasy. "Yet, I feel so
spiritual, I may not eat. I've not eaten for three days. Isn't that wonderful?"
She lowered her large eyes to look at Lockie and Lucy. "Go now. I'll attend

to Hortense." Before the couple could respond, Louisa hurried away up the stairs.

"Did you find it odd," Lucy asked her clever husband, "how she boasted about not having eaten in three days? Why would she do such a thing?"

"It is a puzzle. Further, she made no mention of bringing Hortense to us. And did you notice the reverend—if that is what he truly is—called the simple meal of broth, bread, and water 'sumptuous'? Things are not necessarily what he says they are."

"I'm even more worried for Hortense," Lucy said.

"Now that it's dark, I'll escort you to our cottage then see if I can find Hortense's cottage. I'm keen to ferret out this situation. The game is afoot."

Sherlock Jr smiled at his father. Lucy said, "If you say those words enough times, I'll bet they will be the first ones spoken by our baby."

After ensuring Lucy and the boys were settled in their assigned cottage, Lockie lit a lantern and ventured across the grounds.

STAVE SEVENTEEN
MEETING THE SNAKE AGAIN

A heavy cloud carpeted the sky, blocking all starlight. Nor had the moon risen. Carrying a bullseye lantern, Lockie strode quickly along the walkway, passing the outer cottages. He saw two women and a man exit one abode and rush to the dining hall. They appeared wholly solemn. He began calling Hortense's name at each cottage, hoping she might hear him. "Hello, the house!" he called. "Is there a woman named Hortense inside?" Having reached the end of the outer cottages, he turned around and, this time, knocked on each cottage door while hollering for Hortense and announcing himself as Lucy's husband. Those who answered claimed to not know Hortense's whereabouts.

When he reached the cottage nearest his and Lucy's, Hortense, a woman of medium stature and with a fine curve to her body, slipped out the door before he knocked, shut it, and leaned against it. She put a finger to her lips and whispered, "Please be quiet. My roommate is very suspicious. She drinks a lot, and fortunately, she's asleep. I'm Hortense Cherry. I overheard you say at the cottage next door that you're Lucy's husband?"

"Yes."

"I'm grateful you've come," she whispered. She had a full face with dark eyes and black hair and appeared to be ten years or more older than he. "We must be quiet. I believe the reverend assigned the woman to watch me, lest I escape."

"I understand."

The third supper bell sounded.

Hortense whispered, "I must go to the hall. Many are watching."

"Wait! Lucy and I can help you escape. We have the means."

She leaned close to Lockie's ear. "I believe you, but we must be cautious. When can we leave?"

"As soon as I make arrangements. Perhaps this very night." Lockie snapped his fingers. "Stay here a moment. I'll be back."

Hortense bit her lip, dread filtering through her entire being.

Lockie, hurrying along the pathway to the entrance, hollered back to her, "I'll be right back to lead the way for you. I have this lantern." At that moment, an intense wind slammed into the estate grounds, the trees whining a lonesome wail and bare limbs racking against others, sounding like the rapid drumbeat of a warring army.

Lockie returned minutes later, and the two paced into the gale across the grounds towards the dining hall. He called into the windstorm, "By the gate, there are two large, snarling dogs. I am fortunate they were chained, for they lunged at me several times."

"Yes, when I attempted to escape once before, the dogs and a vile man, one of the reverend's servants, barred my way. I was terrified then. I am still."

They arrived inside the hall, leaning on the door to shut it against the wind. Lockie rubbed his eyes, for his sight was blurry from the wind and blown dust. Finally, his eyes cleared, and he scanned the room. Louisa Nottidge was standing near the massive fireplace, the wind howling down it like a haunting ghoul. Her back was straight, her hands clutched behind her.

Mostly women sat at the tables, just as before, but three men were in this group rather than just one. Each was beefy and wore a foul expression as though they were searching for someone with whom to brawl.

Then Lockie noticed someone he never would have expected to see. Seated at the far end of the farthest table was James Moriarty★, a little taller than last when Lockie had seen him at Tamperwind. The boy, wearing a suit and shirt with a high collar about his neck and a red ascot, smiled, but it was not a pleasant one. His gaze was on the crowd, not Lockie. Lockie's first impulse was to throttle the cruel boy, but he realised his greater concern was to help Hortense escape.

When the servers brought forth the pots of broth, Hortense took a seat at the nearest table. Lockie moved to stand in a shadow, hoping Moriarty had not seen him.

The moment when Reverend Prince entered the dining hall, as he had done during the previous meal, a great commotion arose in the building's outer parlour. Each person looked towards the sounds of male voices shouting and furniture being shoved in violent fashion. The three stout men rose and rushed to the door leading to the parlour. They halted when three finely dressed gentlemen entered, each one carrying a walking cane and being quite strong of arm in their own way.

The one in front raised his hand and waited for all to quiet. When the noise subsided, and the three toughs lowered their fists, the leader announced, "I am Edmund Nottidge, brother of Louisa Nottidge. I see her there by the fireplace. I am joined by my cousin, Edward Nottidge, and brother-in-law, Frederick Ripley. Louisa's mother fears for her well-being in this insubstantial excuse for a domicile of peace and love. I spit on it. Now, at the behest of Louisa's mother, we are here to bring her home." The three men strode around the tables and encircled Louisa.

"*No!* I don't want to go!" Louisa screamed.

Immediately, the three ruffians attacked the Nottidge men, and the fracas began. All the women, save Hortense, sprang from their chairs and fled in every direction. Prince's three guards were throwing punches, and the Nottidge men were making excellent use of their sturdy canes, knocking the large men multiple times about their heads and bodies. Lockie saw Hortense gazing upon the event as if watching a play.

When the fight ranged to the far end of the hall, Lockie moved to Hortense and bade her stand. "Quickly," he said. "Go to our cottage, the one next to yours. Tell Lucy to bring the boys and meet me at the outer wall gate as quickly as you can. Here, take this lantern. Make haste!" He handed her the lit lantern, and she rushed out the door which, clattered against the wall when she opened it. The storm wind was too fierce to close the door, and the force of the gale threw napkins about, turned over vases, and sent bowls of soup sliding along the table. Hortense ran out under the sky now glimmered with starlight and moonlight, for the wind had blown the clouds into another county.

Lockie kept his eye on the slowly fading battle of the six men. Edward Nottidge held his female cousin while Edmund and Frederick finished pummeling the oafs who had tried to stop them. The three massive boors rose from the floor, holding their heads and bloodied faces, and stumbled away into the kitchen. Reverend Prince was nowhere to be seen.

Edmund and his relatives took Louisa in hand and gently escorted her out of the dining hall, through the parlour, the entranceway, and thence into the night. She was wailing a lament the whole way, claiming she did not want to leave, when Lockie heard the great front door slam shut. They were gone.

Throughout the melee, one other person had remained in his seat: James Moriarty, a gloating scoff upon his face. Lockie watched him, waiting for his chance to advance upon the criminal and strangle him. However, before Lockie could take a step, Moriarty turned his black eyes towards him and said, "I see you there, Sherlock Holmes. Do you still go by *Lockie*? Don't even think you can accost me or even get close to me." He pointed at the array of overturned chairs and crockery lying about the floor like a maze. "I can easily elude you, just as I have before."

"Why are you here, you little snake?" Lockie demanded.

"Oh, *snake* is it? How droll." He snickered, rose, and stood on his chair. "You see, when I stand on this chair, I'm taller than you. And in a few years, I will equal you in height and far surpass you in abilities. I don't care what you do, I can always outthink you, mislead you, and thwart you at every turn, just as I did at Tamperwind Mine. I know you're going there now. Be sure to take in the local folklore while your wife's mining business goes broke." His disgusting laugh rang like a thousand arrows slicing through the air.

"Answer my question! Why are you here?"

"Oh, I suppose I can answer your query. As it happens, upon my return to England from the Baltic region, I heard of the incredible sway this ostensible reverend has maintained over these dreary, tedious people. I wished to observe him and perhaps imitate his techniques. Lonely, bored people make excellent fodder for a host of engagements, especially the rich ones. Holding sway over large numbers of people is one of my goals, you see."

"I do see." Lockie began weaving his way through the overturned chairs. "I'd like to get closer to you so you can further explain your reasoning."

"I think not." Moriarty snapped his fingers, and the three toughs who had been beaten by the Nottidge family men, re-entered the hall and stood beside Moriarty. "You see, Lockie, you inferior creature, these men now work for me. Of course, they did what they could to stop the young woman from being taken, but I've convinced them to sign on with me. The remuneration is far greater than the reverend's. I pay quite well by virtue of my adoptive mother. She's not here now but will arrive shortly with a number of bobbies to arrest you. The four of us will give our word that you were the instigator of this unfortunate riot. I'm quite certain the good parson will agree. You will be imprisoned for kidnapping and disrupting a house of the Lord. My goodness, I predict you will never again see the light of day."

Lockie eyed the three large men, bloodied but with their meaty fists clinched, and he evaluated if he could take on all three and still grab hold of Moriarty. Then he remembered the reason for his and Lucy's journey: to help Hortense escape. "Then I bid you adieu, pitiful slug. I've got better things to do." He glided swiftly out the door and hurried to reunite with Hortense, his wife, and the boys.

STAVE EIGHTEEN
THE EXTRICATION

With the wind increasing to a tempest and the temperature quickly dropping, Lucy and Hortense were struggling across the lawn towards the front gate. Lucy held Junior in one arm, keeping a blanket tight around him against the wind with the other. Mycroft walked beside her, clinging to her dress with his tiny hand. Hortense carried their portmanteaus. They bent their heads against the gale. Lockie met them and hoisted Mycroft into his arms, and the group hastened along in the black-as-coal night.

"I do so hope," Lucy called into the wind, "the driver was careful! I worry for my trunk of lab equipment atop the coach. I do not wish for broken test tubes, beakers, or pipettes. They're difficult to obtain."

"We'll worry about that later," Lockie remarked. "Right now, we flee for our lives."

Just as they reached the gate, like shadows in the obsidian night, the two black, sentinel hounds lunged at them. Lockie instantly swept between the dogs and the women and children. The dogs leapt into the air at him, their jaws wide, snapping at his throat as he raised his arm to receive their tearing bite. But the hounds fell to the earth just shy of Lockie. Their chains held them fast, inches from him. Still, they snarled and lunged repeatedly.

Wiping his brow, he turned to see the coach career from the road through the gate and shudder to a stop. The same stout driver who had brought them here now wore a long, black coat against the gale wind. He pulled tight on the reins of the four well-bred horses. A small boy jumped from beside the driver and stood before Lockie with his hand out, palm up.

Lockie place five shillings in the boy's hand. "Thank you, my fine ticket porter. You did precisely as I instructed. Now, get you home lest the storm catch you."

The boy scampered off. The driver stepped down, loaded the portmanteaus atop the coach, and stated to Lucy, "I took special care with your trunk, ma'am."

Lockie gave the man half a crown and helped his family then Hortense into the carriage, all the while making sure they were not followed, and then he slid inside. When the coach sped away, Lucy saw three huge men burst through the front door and shake their fists at them. "What will those men do?" she shouted.

Lockie looked out the window at the rapidly vanishing Spaxton Hall and grounds and could make out Moriarty's three new employees standing in the glaring lamps of the front porch. Then the carriage rumbled into the tree-laden lane, hiding all vestiges of the unholy facility.

Speeding along in the dark night, Lockie's thoughts rumbled around in his head as to why James Moriarty was at the Abode of Love. He felt Moriarty's explanation was not entirely forthright. *What else might the conniving beast be doing?*

Lockie rapped on the coach roof. The driver halted, and Lockie requested he return in a stealthy manner to just outside Spaxton. The driver complied and soon had the vehicle stationed in the shadows of the forest a good distance from the open gate. Lamps glowed all about the front of the hall and gate.

Lockie and Lucy peered out the coach windows despite the biting wind and waited a good long while.

At last, their patience proved fruitful. A Police Black Maria wagon rumbled up to the Abode of Love. Several bobbies dismounted and rushed inside the main hall. A small cabriolet carriage came to a halt beside the police wagon, and the driver helped a woman dismount. In the dismal light of the porch, Lockie and Lucy recognised James Moriarty when he rushed from the main building into the arms of his mother, Evangeline Peabody, née Moriarty.

Then a thin man, wearing a tri-cornered hat and swallowed in a cloak with a high collar, emerged from the carriage. In the glaring light, they could make out his black hair and starkly pale complexion. His lips appeared blue. Like a passing breeze, the three vanished into the hall.

Lucy gasped. "That thin man looked near death, and his eyes looked vile."

"Moriarty is plotting something far eviler than he admitted." Lockie clinched his teeth. "However, figuring out what that is will have to wait." He rapped again on the roof. "Drive on."

The coach slowly departed into the pitch-black night towards western England and Tamperwind Mine, which was shoved against the stormy, rocky coast.

STAVE NINETEEN

AT TAMPERWIND, THE MYSTERIOUS DISCOVERY

When the coach arrived at St Austell, Lucy gave Hortense coins for the train fare back to London, and Lockie gave her the address of Scrooge's nephew, Edmund Nuckols, telling her he felt certain Edmund would find her employment. After saying their goodbyes, the couple continued their journey to the mines of Cornwall.

Arriving two days later in the mid-afternoon at Tamperwind Manor, Lockie and Lucy emerged from the coach with their two boys. Abigail raced down the manor's long steps to greet them, running the entire eighty yards to where they were retrieving their luggage from atop the vehicle. When she arrived beside them, not even a tad out of breath, the three adults shared hugs, and she gently stroked the hair of Mycroft and Sherlock Jr. "I think they both look like you, Lucy," she remarked. Lucy smiled, and Lockie bobbed his head in agreement.

"I'm astonished by your manner of dress, Abigail," said Lucy.

Abigail was outfitted in trousers, a man's shirt with a cravat tied at the collar, and heavy workman's boots. She explained, "I've made it my business to observe the mineworkers to assure myself they are not shirking their duties. Hence, I must dress for the mine. It is dirty work, and a dress hem could catch on a jagged rock or even a pickaxe and send the workers to fetch a doctor."

"Ah, that is true," Lockie said.

"I agree," said Lucy.

Abigail's demeanor changed suddenly into a sort of sadness coupled with fury. "I know you wish to greet Samuel, but he must not be disturbed. He is at this instance dismissing two men who were caught pocketing some of the silver-ladened rocks from Hopworth Mine. In addition, the situation is quite grim in the minimal production in Tamperwind Tin Mine. I am quite certain some of the workers are either thieves or drunkards ... or even murderers." She pounded her fist on her palm as if indicating there was no doubt of her supposition.

"That is dreadful, Abigail!" Lucy said.

"We have much to talk about, but for now, come." Abigail picked up Mycroft. "Let's get you settled. Then, I must go to Bobbie Wheeler and his cousin, Barnabas. They are overseeing Hopworth Mine, which is where the silver streak produces. How those diminutive men inspire the workers is beyond my comprehension. And they are experts at the business of mining. Thankfully, the other Wheeler cousin, Angus, is a hard taskmaster in Tamperwind Mine. He is so cordial to me and Samuel, but despite his being a dwarf, he is a hard driver to the workers. They flinch when he barks orders at them, and they do as he says. He is a blessing."

With a coachman carrying their luggage and two mine workers carrying Lucy's trunk of books and chemistry laboratory items, the cousins walked up the steps of the manor. Halfway there, they passed two shabbily dressed men hastening downwards, cursing and complaining. When they had passed, Abigail whispered, "Those are the two miners Samuel has dismissed."

Lockie commented, "They were certainly unhappy. On another subject, when will we be able to visit Samuel? We want him to know we are here to help."

Abigail sighed. "I don't know. He stays locked in his office, dealing with the books, ordering supplies and food, and paying bills as best he can, and he seldom comes out. I fear for his melancholia. His old back injury has returned. The best chance to see him will be during tea this afternoon. He never misses that."

Abigail spared no effort in affording Lockie and Lucy and their boys every comfort. Bobbie Wheeler's wife, Cora, was working as a temporary housekeeper, and her children cavorted about the large manor rooms like they had found a hidden castle.

After unpacking and putting the boys down for a nap, Lockie and Lucy quickly surmised that the diminutive Cora Wheeler had arranged a comfortable tidiness to the manor.

The grandfather clock chimed four o'clock. Teatime had arrived, and Cora had all in order. Every piece of furniture had been shaken and dusted, the paintings wiped, and the best tea service set forth. An excellent provision made with dainty new breads, crusty twists, cool fresh butter, thin slices of ham and German sausage, and delicate little rows of anchovies nestled in parsley.*

Samuel plodded down the stairs with one hand on the rail and one on his back. He winced at reaching the bottom step. Seeing the visiting cousins, he put on a brave smile and strode painfully towards Lockie, hand extended. "My dear Lockie, how good to see you." They shook hands. Samuel then hugged Lucy. "Before coming down, I made a point to look in your room at your two handsome babes sound asleep. You must be so proud."

Seating themselves in the parlour, the foursome made polite conversation and drank their tea and nibbled on Cora's excellent fare. Mrs Wheeler doted on them and poured new cups of the brew for each one, even before they had emptied them.

At last, Samuel sighed and frowned. He could wait no longer to bear his concerns regarding the mines and the cousins' ownership. "Our situation is dire. I had to dismiss two more miners today whom Bobbie Wheeler caught stealing some of the silver ore from Hopworth Mine, and of course, Tamperwind Tin Mine is barely presenting itself to be a mine at all. Unless we find a new seam of ore soon, it will quickly become a burden just to keep open."

The three listeners did their best to commiserate while Samuel explained Barrister Leggitt's regular messages from the civil trial at London's Lincoln Inn Chancery Court.

Samuel was in mid-sentence, elabourating about the death of one of the horses that hauled the tin wagons, when a sudden whooshing wind buffeted the house with one loud knock after another. Abigail hurried to the window to search out its cause. After watching outside for a period, she turned to the others. "I see no evidence of wind blowing. The trees are almost motionless."

The front door banged open. "We've uncovered a riddle!" Bobbie Wheeler announced, striding quickly into the room. He was followed by Pudge who waddled along, holding a wooden, hinged box of a cubic foot in dimension. Wayne—or Dimsight as the eleven-year-old boy with shaded glasses was nicknamed—was last to arrive. The three marched up to the tea table, and Pudge gently placed the box in the centre of it.

Bobbie pointed at the plump young man with thick fingers and an overround belly, and who had been alive on Earth about a dozen years. "Pudge here stumbled upon this in the mine. He had dropped his pickaxe into a narrow crevasse."

"That I did," Pudge said and reached for a crumpet, popping it quickly into his mouth.

Using arm motions and bending down as if pantomiming the incident, Bobbie explained, "With a lantern, he peered down into the crack and set eyes upon a small cave room. The one thing he and the rest of us could make out by looking into the room was a wooden table. I put everyone to work, searching for the entrance to the room for the better part of the day." He pointed at the small, thin boy. "Dimsight here, being slight in build as he is, volunteered to trek down the narrow creek running through the main cavern hall. The creek flows between two walls, slowly ever downwards. No one had gone down it, at least, not that we know of. He was the only one slim enough to fit between those walls. About twenty yards from where it flows along between the walls, the creek ducks under another cave wall and empties somewhere out into the ocean." He drew a long breath.

"By the grace of God," Dimsight said, "when the aisle between the walls became too narrow, and the water was up to my chin, I decided to hold my breath and go under, leavin' my lantern behind. After a minute of swimmin', I came up in the dark. I could hear the roar of the waves, and I was most afeared. The water was pullin' me hard towards that sound. All was dark, but I reached up, and my hand found an iron ring handle protruding from a portion of the rock wall. I grabbed it to help me climb onto a narrow ledge. Once I was on the ledge, the cave ceiling was so low, no one, save a wee child or dwarf or myself, could stand upright. I was trapped!"

"How could you see?" Samuel asked in wonder.

"I'll get to that. I took ahold of the ring handle as big as a big man's fist and yanked on it. Nothin' happened despite my best efforts. Then, I decided, for no good reason, to twist the thing to the right. When I did so, the rock wall to the side of it slid open like a door to the room. Lantern light filtered down through the crack above the room, where Mister Bobbie and the others was waitin'. I showed my face up through the crack, and Pudge handed me down a lantern to use."

Pudge stuck his thumbs in his suspenders and stuck out his chest. "That I did."

"Lookin' around with the lantern light," Dimsight continued, "I saw the room was about shy of six feet in each direction. On one wall, a small, silver cross hung on a nail. I took a moment to kiss it then went to the table with *this box* upon it." He tapped the lid. "The room held naught else, save dust. There was pieces of wood lyin' on the ground that might have been a chair. I stood on the table and pushed the box through the crack above, and then I slid into the stream in the dark and swam back the way I came. And here I am!" His smile beamed.

"You are so brave, Dimsight," Lucy said. "But in what manner is this for it to be so well-hidden?"

"Indeed," added Abigail. "What sort of man or being would go to such lengths to secret this box away to remain hidden perhaps for centuries?"

"It is boggling to consider," said Samuel. "This much I know. The criminals that killed our uncle and pretended to run the store that fronted the opening to Hopworth Mine were after what they believed was some sort of treasure. But I always assumed it was only the silver lode in the mine."

"I thought the same," said Abigail. "But perhaps they were after whatever is in this box."

The group fell silent.

Bobbie cleared his throat. "We've not opened it. I felt it best to bring it here first."

"Well, open it!" Lockie finally exclaimed.

Each one drew nearer to watch Bobbie lift the lid and reveal the box's contents. It creaked a little, and one rusty iron hinge fell loose upon the table. When it opened, a clap of dust flew from the box. Each observer recoiled.

"It smells ..." pronounced Lockie with a cough, "somewhat like blood."

Inside were three black, tapering bars, each shaped like the letter J. The bars were roughly eight inches in length. Beside them were three black, flat iron pieces about the size of a crown coin, each one about an inch across.

"A collection of rusty metal!" Pudge exclaimed.

"They look heavy," Lucy said.

"Perhaps these were part of an ancient coat of arms," Abigail offered. "Or some sort of pry tools to pull rocks loose."

"Or maybe a sort of weapon," Dimsight said. "Like part of a trident spear."

Lucy looked closer. "What is that cloth beside the nails?"

Shoved against the edge and bound by rotting leather twine was a tightly rolled sheepskin scroll of ten inches in length.

Bobbie undid the twine and opened the scroll. "'Tis several odd markings. Perhaps it is a language of a sort, though not the good King's English."

At that moment, another great wind shook the house, causing the teacups to clatter.

STAVE TWENTY

"I HAVE BEEN BENT AND BROKEN—
BUT I HOPE INTO A BETTER SHAPE."
—GREAT EXPECTATIONS

The storm slung daggers of icy sleet onto the ship. Scrooge cowered under the gunwale, his teeth chattering with each sudden, bitter blast of wind and rain. He would, by turn, peek over the gunwale to watch the roiling sea with high, frothy waves before ducking back down to observe the swarthy first mate direct the seamen to tie down the sails and secure the battens over the hatches. Three sailors hammered the wooden stakes to hold the tarpaulins over the hatches and prevent water from spilling down below. The storm sloshed about like a pot of water slung around and around, the waves spilling over into the boat and splashing on the already wet-as-a-drowned-rat Ebenezer Scrooge.

The first mate seemed akin to an ogre from a faery tale. The man's back was hunched and seemed to have a vertebral column poking through his shirt, narrow enough to imitate a dragon's spine. He had a piercing eye that searched tirelessly about the vessel while the other eye remained squinched shut. His teeth showed when he barked an order and were fouled brown and chipped, though his canines were sharp as knives. A grizzled beard around his jaw was like a scouring brush. He wore a broad red-and-white striped shirt over white trousers tied off below the knee. His black, crumpled shoes resounded on the deck like thunderclaps. When the last batten had been driven into place, and the seamen braved the storm to attend to their sailing duties about the barque, the first mate paced up to the former miser. "What be ye doin' up 'ere on the deck, ye sloppy piece o' meat? Get ye below!"

"I ... don't wish to go below. You see, I've been in several mining caves and grown quite wary of such darkness, and being below is too much like being in a cave. I fear it more than I fear this storm. I hope to beg lodging with the captain and—"

"Ye what? Ye 'ave the gall to make such a request? Ye be braver than ye think! Come wit' me."

Scrooge fell in behind the first mate, skirting the tarped-down hatches and wobbling along the pitching deck, to the captain's cabin. The mate gave a quick rap on the door, and the bearded captain appeared. He was a robust man with a large frame and even larger belly. His pate was bald. "What will it be, Thrusher?" he bellowed.

"This man be in want of shelter from the tempest, Cap'n Thorn." He leaned to the captain's ear as if to whisper, but Scrooge heard every word. "He be afeared of below deck."

The captain pursed his lips and turned to Scrooge. "Have you half a crown to pay for your improved lodgings?"

Scrooge was almost tossed from his feet when the ship crashed down from a high wave. He took no time to dicker on the price. "Yes. May I stay above deck in your cabin?"

"I don't see why not, sir," said the captain. "Name's Thorn. Laslow Thorn. My friends call me Land Ho." He tugged Scrooge into his cabin, slammed the door shut, and directed him to sit on a settee screwed to a wall. Thorn walked to a small keg filled with green limes, took one out, and offered another to Scrooge, who abstained with a shake of his head.

While tossing the lime from one hand to another, Thorn said, "One must make a repast of limes if one cares not for scurvy. I hope you get your share of the fruits ... er ... What be your name?" He sliced open the lime with a heavy knife and squirted the juice in his mouth.

"Ebenezer Scrooge." He trembled from the wet cold which had dove down under his skin.

"Here. Take this and bind yourself." Thorn threw Scrooge a blanket, who graciously wrapped it tight about himself, then pulled up a chair in front of Scrooge and shoved a smoking pipe in his lips and lit it. "Do you afford yourself the luxury of baccy?"

Shivering and tumbling about on the settee like a wobbling top, Scrooge stuttered, "I-I hav-hav-have a p-pipe in my po-po-pocket. I'm afraid my tob-b-bacco will be all wet."

"No call for worry," said the gentleman amiably who seemed to never budge from where he was lodged in his chair despite the rocking of the storm-battered ship. "You must try some of this tobacco. It's chock full of flavour." He opened a metal cannister taken from his pocket and shoved the item beneath Scrooge's nose. "Smell."

Scrooge took a deep whiff of the black leaves and smiled. "May I?"

"Of course."

With shaking hands, Scrooge withdrew his pipe from his inside coat pocket and plucked some tobacco into his pipe and tamped it down. Thorn was quick with a flaming match to light the pipe. Scrooge puffed and inhaled twice, and the little bowl glowed, and smoke filled his lungs. He blew the smoke out to mix with Thorn's fumes. Both men smiled.

After a few minutes, full of smoke and warmth, Scrooge said, "If I understand correctly, you are hired by Mr Byrne to captain this ship."

"The *Intrepid*. Yes. I steer the *Intrepid* back and forth from England to Ireland."

"Yes," Scrooge said. "But I wonder why he takes corn and wheat with him to Ireland. Surely, if he owns a vessel such as this, then he is wealthy enough to not be in need of the grain. I'm aware he has quite an estate."

"As did his brother who grew wheat when he was alive. Byrne buys the wheat in London, which has been sold by Irish landowners to the English, and further buys the corn which has been shipped from the American colonies. He does so to give it away to starving Irish families. Costs him upwards of two hundred pounds, but he renders it to them entirely without charge." Thorn blew a long stream of the aromatic fumes.

Scrooge almost spit his pipe from his mouth. "Renders it free? He gives all this wheat and corn away at no cost?"

"That's correct."

Scrooge had the oddest explosion of emotion, as though his inner being was stretched in two different directions. He had learned over time since that particular Christmas to, somewhat begrudgingly, share his wealth in regular small portions. Nevertheless, he was mystified by Byrne's extending such a large sum of benevolence to his fellow man and was perplexed by how he could do so without expecting a farthing in return. Why! Even ministers sought donations to buy bigger churches or build a new wing to the seminary school or purchase a new organ and new hymnals or pay the organist. And the churches were alive in munificence. That a single individual could be so generous was confounding. Scrooge knew his friends, Grumbles and Leggitt, regularly collected from himself and various businesses for some worthy cause, but each benefactor gave a particle of a sum that the whole of which did some good. But Byrne's extravagance baffled him entirely.

"Yes." Thorn stood, went to the door, opened it, and yelled, "Avast there! Make secure the jib boom." Scrooge heard a couple of "aye-ayes." Thorn returned to his seat, never troubled in his stride by the pitching and jarring movement of the ship. "Now, Mr Scrooge, the storm is abating. I've got some work of my own to do, so I'll have that half a crown now."

Scrooge lifted his cloth money pouch from inside his shirt, undid the knots of the leather binding, and withdrew the coin, handing it to the captain. He attempted to smile. "Thank you for the baccy. Will you be going ashore in Dublin?"

The captain rose and walked to his cabin door and stopped before exiting. "Nah! I'll never set foot on Irish soil. I let my first mate, Isiah Thrusher, do the business at the custom house. Then I sail the ship back to England. There is no reason I can think of for stepping foot in a land filled with vile, mischievous ghoulies, fairies, and sorceresses. I'm fully aware of the tribe of Tuatha Dé Danann. I had an uncle who faced some of their ilk on the marshes. 'Twill set your teeth on edge to hear of them. Nah! Curses on the Irish."

Scrooge gulped. His fears had become intensified. The storm calmed, but Scrooge's fears did not. Even after his clothes had dried, he continued to tremble.

STAVE TWENTY-ONE
RUSTY METAL AND LUCY'S DILEMMA

Lockie had removed the rusty J-shaped bars from the wooden box and was fingering them. Lucy peered at the scroll she had extended on a side table. Samuel had gone back to his office, and Abigail had departed to the mine to check with Angus on the day's efforts. Bobbie, Pudge, and Dimsight had returned to Hopworth Mine.

"They look like the pins to hold a large door hinge in place. Or, more likely, they are pry tools." Lockie pronounced into the air. "Why would a miner hide his tools in a box in a secreted away spot?" He clanked two of the spikes together. Particles of black and maroon rust fluttered to the floor.

Lucy sighed. "Lockie, I believe I may be able to uncover the message written on this scroll. My father, before he died, had become an expert in several languages including Greek and Latin. He was also an archaeologist and Egyptologist and had once travelled there on an expedition to the pyramids. He took copious notes in several journals. I have a feeling I might find something in his journals to help me decipher these markings. I believe they might be Arabic or Hebrew."

"But you left most of your books at home. Why would you bring any of his journals here?"

"Lockie, there is something you must know about me. I often surprise even myself in what I pack for a trip. I get distracted and don't always know what

I put in the chest. Besides my science and philosophy books, I recall bringing along some Latin and Greek volumes and two of my father's journals."

"I know enough about Latin from my days in the Ragged School to know none of those scribbles are in Latin."

"I agree, dear husband. They could be using the Greek alphabet or a derivation of the language. I'll study right now." After giving him a quick peck on the cheek, she headed upstairs to open her travel chest. When she returned to the parlour, she found Lockie napping with one of the bent spikes lying on his stomach. He snored only a little. "Lockie." Lucy shook him. "I hate to wake you."

He turned in his sleep but did not waken. The rod tumbled to the floor, and some of the rust flaked off. Lucy sighed, gathered the scroll from the table, and carried it along with her father's two journals she bore to the dining room table. Seating herself, she spread out the scroll, placing a sugar bowl at one end of it and a salt bowl on the other end to keep it flat. She then opened her father's journal entitled, *Travels to Syria and Judea.*

After reading several pages, she referred to the other book, which was really a stack of pages loosely bound together with a heavy cowhide cover and twine. Each page held markings similar to those in the scroll plus what appeared to be translations into Latin. Some pages bore her father's scrawled notes in English in the margins.

Cora came into the dining room and set a lighted lamp beside Lucy who smiled and thanked her. Lucy bent over the writings, scanning first the intricate markings on the scroll, searching for similar markings on the stack of journal pages, and trying to find a match for the markings in Latin. For the two hours she worked, she mostly felt despair. Nothing made sense to her.

The night moved in like a slow sludge, turning all outside elements of trees, fences, and the shacks of the miners first grey then charcoal before making them vanish completely, except for occasional glints from the moon gliding amongst low-hung clouds. While Cora Wheeler shuffled about the downstairs with a box of lucifers to set the lamps aglow around the parlour and dining room, the lamplighter lads outside went around the miners' village, lighting the handful of streetlamps. Farther down the hill at Tamperwind Mine, agile young men climbed ladders to light the taller lamps outside the cave opening. The night-shift workers were treading their way to the mine while the day-shift workers headed for home.

Lucy stole upstairs and brought her two boys down to the dining room. She gave Mycroft some soft toys to play with beside her, which he eagerly did. She began nursing Junior and continued perusing one of her father's old journals of his travels in Syria and Judea. Despite her uncanny ability to concentrate on the task at hand, she felt she was not making any headway with her father's translations of the ancient text. She thought, *This is Hebrew, and the alphabet is daunting to learn.*

She took a moment from her studies to look out one of the tall manor windows. She observed the smoke rising from the many chimneys of the miners' homes and knew the women were cooking the evening meal. Most of the women and the older, more sturdy girls worked outside the mines for several hours during each day, save Sunday, in the effort of sorting, cracking, and then pummeling the rocks into finer pieces so the tin could be extracted. Each day, they left earlier than the men to prepare the meals and care for the younger children at home who were watched and sometimes taught in a makeshift school run by a schoolmarm.

Lost in thought of the perilous events of a year earlier at the Tamperwind and Hopworth mines, she was alerted by Mycroft making a babbling sound over and over. She realised he was repeating a Latin word she had read aloud several times from her father's writing. She quickly returned to the scroll and her father's Latin translations. Amazingly, the babbling of her son had given her a unique understanding. She recalled how, when she was ten, her father had told her he was speaking Hebrew. She had noticed he was tracking his finger across the words from a Bible tract from right to left, rather than left to right. *Maybe …*

Lockie arose from his nap and began playing with Mycroft on the floor. He was alarmed when Lucy exclaimed loudly, "I've deciphered some words!"

STAVE TWENTY-TWO
THE FACTS AND THE FAMINE

Scrooge walked tentatively down the gangplank onto the dock beside the immense Dublin Custom House. The *Intrepid* rocked gently at the dock on the River Liffey. The storm had fled, and blue sky glistened above, but Scrooge could not help feeling that a different sort of storm cloud hovered over him. He stopped by some crates, taking in the bustling port. Ships were being unloaded and others being loaded. Dockworkers and sailors and numerous well-to-do families crowded about, looking for relatives and friends disembarking. The women waved their handkerchiefs. The men stretched their necks to see.

A second ship, nearer the *Intrepid*, was unloading large wooden grates and bales of cotton. Scrooge thought, *Must be a vessel from the Americas.* On the periphery of the dock was a cordon of peelers spaced a few yards apart from each other. On the other side of the line of bobbies, Scrooge saw perhaps hundreds of drastically thin and horridly dressed people, whole families, watching the dock with vacant eyes.

When the dockworkers opened the port storage door of the *Intrepid*, revealing the flock of sheep to be unloaded, the crowd yelled as one voice, begging for food. Their voices rose again and again like waves breaking on Scrooge's ears. "Food! Have pity!" Then, as a whole, the crowd began pushing against the bobbies, and the English policemen held firm for a brief moment. Only a few small boys broke past the cordon.

Byrne called to Scrooge, "It's liable to get chaotic quite soon!"

Scrooge backed closer to the ship. The clamour of hoarse voices kept calling for compassion, for a decent ration, for any handout. The new storm of a human origin grew to fever pitch.

A portly customs official, who was folding up his chin in his fat smile* and wearing a long, blue coat with gold, brocaded sleeves, wrote on a form attached to a thin board. He was tabulating the number of sheep being unloaded. A handful of shepherds began driving the herd along the dock towards a holding pen to the right of the huge custom house. The bleats of the sheep added to the cacophony of yelling policemen and the desperate pleading of the crowd of farmers.

Suddenly, the throng surged as one and broke through the police line. They raced towards the sheep. Scrooge wondered at first if the people sought to kill and eat the sheep raw. The sheep stampeded in every direction, with people tripping over them as they spilled onto the docks. Several men tried to grab the fleeing creatures but to no avail.

Then a group of men and women, all of whom looked like death itself with their skin stretched over bony arms, veered from the main crowd and broke towards the ship. They carried woven baskets. "Get the grain!" the one in the lead called. "No one can stop us!"

He was wrong; three bulky dockworkers stepped between the group and the crates of grain, each wielding a heavy cudgel. The smaller group split and attempted to evade the big defenders of Byrne's grain. Half scrambled left, half broke right. Scrooge suddenly realised a sizable number were headed straight towards him in their attempt to flank the defenders. He would be knocked down and trampled. He turned towards the river, preparing to jump in.

When the crowd came within a few feet of Scrooge, Officer Blevins arrived, holding two pistols. He fired one in the air and aimed the other at the crowd. The crowd halted, their gaunt, grey faces like the stone statues Scrooge often saw in cemeteries. Byrne came up right beside him. "Many will be fed!" he hollered at the crowd. "But not in this way!"

Bob Cratchit arrived just behind Byrne, bearing two pistols of his own. Officer Blevins put his pistols in his pockets and began thumbing his nightstick Billie club hanging on his belt.

Though standing, the group appeared lifeless with their empty, staring eyes. Scrooge stepped behind Byrne, remembering his own pistol was in his portmanteau, unloaded. "Thank you, Byrne," he mumbled to the man's back. "I don't know if I could kill a man who seems mostly dead."

Byrne stepped towards the band of ravenous people and lowered his voice. "Dear farmers, dear Irishmen, food is coming! My gift to you all. But it will be prepared and cooked. Mutton and bread for as many as I can feed tomorrow at the Quaker kitchen. For now, return to wherever you're staying, as I know many of you have been turned out of your farm homes by your English landlords. So, go be with your families here in Dublin until tomorrow. A notice will be posted in the morning, where you can receive one meal and some bread and a little meat to take home. I beg of you, please be patient."

The dockworkers, now joined by other hefty men, had forced the breakaway group to succumb. The emaciated, ragtag people backed away, forlorn, like a defeated army. The bobbies, joined by other officers on horseback, gained control of the remainder of the crowd and forced them back into the thoroughfares behind the custom house. The shepherds hunted down the sheep and secured the herd into the holding pen.

Byrne turned to Scrooge and Cratchit. "There you have it, detectives. The dire circumstances of this isle. Most of the nation's potato crop is largely ruined, especially in western Ireland. It's what most of the farmers' families subsist on. We are living in a time correctly called in our papers the *Great Hunger*. These dear Christian people, all of them potato farmers, have come to Dublin in hopes of finding a job or a little sustenance just to stay alive. There are a few Quaker soup kitchens but not enough to feed them all."

"I had no idea," Scrooge said. "The *London Times* and *Evening News* make only trivial remarks about the goings-on in Ireland."

Cratchit tucked his pistols away inside his long coat pockets. "How did they know the *Intrepid* was arriving at the dock today? Or do they come here every day to find a scrap to gather and eat?"

"Word on the docks flies like eagles," Byrne replied. "These people have seen what happens here and at other smaller ports. Ironically, they watch the Irish-grown wheat and barley and the cattle and sheep always being loaded onto ships to be taken to England and other parts of Europe. Seldom does any ship bring foodstuffs here."

"I don't understand," Cratchit said.

"You see, for the rich and London economists, it's all about laissez faire.* The highest pound rate is paid by English purchasing agents. Farmers of wheat and barley are primarily absentee landlords who live in England and have no interest in feeding people at little to no cost. For them, the realm's coin is all they wish to obtain. There are Irish wheat farmers too, but none willing to sell low. They wish to do more than simply survive. Thus, grain, beef cattle, and mutton make their way to England and abroad."

"Wouldn't it be best to keep some of it here?" Officer Blevins pursued.

"Indeed, Blevins. My murdered brother was a wheat farmer and used to sell the grain locally or milled it himself at his own mill, even before the potato blight. However, a year ago, when he ventured into his perplexing, wild passion, which he never completely conveyed to me, he let his fields go fallow and allowed a neighbour farmer to let his sheep graze there."

"What could have taken hold of him?" Scrooge asked.

"That is what I could not determine nor even fathom. And it's part of the reason I have summoned you here. To uncover his murderer's identity, and what my brother was seeking."

"And now the mayor is murdered as well," Blevins added. "Chief Inspector Shackle will expect me to get to the bottom of this."

STAVE TWENTY-THREE

THRUSHER—WHAT DOES HE KNOW?

Byrne led Scrooge, Cratchit, and Blevins to a nearby inn so they could freshen up and have something to eat. He bade them to remain there until his return from seeing to the expense he had to pay at the Dublin Custom House and ensuring the grain was safely loaded on wagons to head west to his brother's mill.

While he was gone, the three men dined on braised haddock, dark rye bread, and cabbage. Blevins explained his upbringing in the same county in which Reginald Byrne resided. His father had been moderately well off, and his parents had sent him to Oxford to gain a broader education than Ireland could offer. Despite his Irish heritage, he had fared well in the sciences. "But," he said with great alacrity, "my heart was with the law. Wealth would come, but the law needed to be maintained, so I set about becoming a policeman."

"It is a noble employment," Cratchit said. "You have my admiration."

Blevins smiled.

The moment they finished their meal, the first mate Isiah Thrusher entered the inn with several sailors. They sauntered to the bar and ordered a bottle of whiskey to share. The keep filled their glasses and handed the bottle to Thrusher, who upturned the bottle and emptied it down his throat.

The bunch of them wandered around the inn, gawking at the handful of women in attendance and generally acted in an obnoxious fashion.

Thrusher made his way to the detectives' table. Scrooge immediately noticed the haversack the first mate had slung on his shoulder. In it, three books poked out the top. Thrusher pulled up a stool and sat down, plunked the empty bottle on the table, and glowered at the three men. "So, one of ye be a peeler, an' you two," he said, pointing at Scrooge and Cratchit, "be the fearless detectives that solved the dog-men crimes in London. Is 'at so?" He guffawed, stuck out his tongue at both Scrooge and Cratchit, and then burped a long gaseous stream of air.

Blevins said, "See here, old fellow, old seadog, what business do you have accosting these fine gentlemen? You are acting completely out of line."

"Out o' line?" Thrusher chortled and beckoned some of his sea mates over to the table. Three came near and bent over the seated men. "Ya see, officer, I ain't accostin' no one. I'm 'ere only conversin'. This be the third inn we been in since we come ashore, an'—"

"That explains a good deal," Scrooge said. "You're drunk."

"Ye be right. I am," Thrusher admitted. "An' so be these other blokes."

The three seamen weaved and laughed and swallowed more of their whiskey.

"Well, is there something you wish to say to us?" Cratchit asked.

Scrooge could tell his partner was losing patience.

"Say ta ya?" Thrusher took hold of the sleeve of one of the seamen and laughed and choked and coughed. The three attending seamen rocked back and forth, laughing. One fell on his backside and passed out. Wiping his eyes with his cap, Thrusher finally gained his composure and grew serious. He opened the lid of the eye he kept squinted, revealing it was made of glass. "I know ye be goin' ta Kindlestown Castle in the Wicklow moun'ains. An' I know a lot more than ye will e'er know about what be goin' on. An' it be goin' ta change the world." He burped and lay his head on the table.

Byrne entered, almost tripping over the passed-out sailor on the floor and was surprised by the entourage. "Misters Scrooge and Cratchit and Officer Blevins, I have a carriage arriving soon, so let me fill you in on what I've arranged. I've sent the wagons of grain on to my deceased brother's mill. I secured a troop of soldiers to escort it. With the help of the Quakers, I've arranged for the herd of sheep to be slaughtered and cooked into stew for the starving poor. They have butchers on staff. I left some of the grain to be milled here in Dublin for bread. That's all I can do."

Officer Blevins said, "That is magnanimous of you, sir. I'm sure they'll be grateful."

The three rose and walked out. Scrooge looked back at Thrusher who now seemed to be snoring. Laying in the first mate's half-open haversack were three books, one entitled *Two Years Before the Mast*, one a poetry book of Keats, and one a book of maps. In his mind, Scrooge could not help but rummage over the details about each of the sailors he had observed. He knew little of the sailing lot, but he committed to memory the appearance of each one, considering he might encounter them later. He was most interested in the first mate who appeared to be more learned and astute than he put on.

Byrne directed the men to follow him for a short tour of Dublin. "Thomas, my stableman, will not have the carriage here until later in the hour. Let me show you something of what Ireland is all about." He began walking down the fashionable streets with Scrooge and Cratchit close on his heels.

Blevins noticed a tall man in a long coat and sock cap following them. He stopped and watched the man who also stopped and seemed to be lighting a pipe. Blevins made no mention of the man—who was, in fact, someone he knew—to the others but kept a wary eye on him.

Byrne pointed to Dublin Castle just across the river. "Therein lies the government that rules Ireland. The Lord Lieutenant, the office of the Poor Law Commission and Relief Commission, as well as the officers of the crown." The men walked into the major shopping district, and Byrne pointed out the shops of the well-to-do: Piggots and Pims, Cranefields, and Andrews. "Dublin's population is over three hundred thousand, and it is growing daily with the arrival of the starving masses."

Turning the corner, they found the entire street filled with poor families, some sitting anywhere in the middle of the street, others meandering aimlessly, still more sleeping, huddling under a makeshift covering of a single blanket. A farmer, with splotches all over his face and hands, limped towards them, holding out a tin cup. Each man dropped a coin in the cup. Scrooge unknowingly gave the coin of largest amount.

The man said, "Thank 'e. God bless 'e."

"With the famine," Byrne explained in an angry tone, "butchers and bakers are charging what they call 'famine prices,' though they have no shortage of meat or milled grain here in the city. They are squeezing every penny they can."

When the group passed a workhouse, Scrooge slowed to a stop. He heard the grinding work going on inside. The others watched as he walked up to a window and witnessed emaciated individuals, those who could find no way to earn money for food, labouring at menial and backbreaking tasks. He stepped away, his eyes downcast. He did not look up but said, "I'll never forget what I said to Grumbles and Leggitt when they came asking for a donation for the poor on that windswept Christmas Eve. I asked, 'Are there not enough workhouses?'" A tear slid down his cheek. "And here they are still."

Byrne's personal landau carriage arrived, and Scrooge's thoughts slid precariously back to the admonition about Jannes and Jambres and who they might be and what their connection was to the murders. He stepped into the carriage.

When all were seated, Byrne said in a low tone, "Before the mayor was murdered, there was a break-in at his home. And … there has been one more murder in Wicklow."

STAVE TWENTY-FOUR

TIN ORE, TREASURE, AND PIRATES

B ack at the Tamperwind and Hopworth mines, Lockie accompanied
Abigail and Bobbie and Angus on journeys to the mines, and Cora
Wheeler played with the young boys. Sensing some foreboding
message within the scroll's words, Lucy plunged into deciphering the old
parchment. She sat at a small desk in her bedroom. The document was
ragged on all edges, and portions of it had deteriorated, leaving holes in
much of the writing. Undaunted, she compared the scroll's letterings with
those outlined in her father's journal and painstakingly found coinciding
markings here and there. The meanings of those markings were obscure.

She had studied Latin as a girl and knew it well but would never accuse
herself of being a scholar. Her father had insisted on teaching her Latin and
some Greek before he died, but he had also insisted she be humble in all ways.

Cora, the kind-hearted wife of Bobbie Wheeler, came into the bedroom,
carrying both boys. Sherlock Jr was fussing some, and Mycroft was rubbing
his eyes and pouting.

"This man was a tin merchant!" Lucy suddenly exclaimed, surprising
Cora. Lucy looked up. "Oh, Mrs Wheeler, I'm sorry. My deepest appreciation
for your monitoring the boys while I work on this confounding scroll."

"I'd watch them longer," Cora said, "but it's obvious Junior is getting
hungry, and Mycroft needs a nap."

"Bring them here."

"Ya know, Lucy, should your wee one take to bein' too fussy, there's always Godfrey's Cordial★ that will quiet him right up. The cordial's called the 'Mother's Helper,' ya know."

"I don't think I should ever use it." Lucy unbuttoned her blouse and corset and began nursing Junior. "I've heard stories of too many infants never opening their eyes again after taking the cordial. I'll simply deal with a few tears and crying. No dram of opium tonic for my boys."

"Suit yourself." Cora turned to leave then returned. "And I'm sure you've noticed that in between kickin' a ball around and stackin' wood blocks, Mycroft can talk up a storm."

Lucy smiled. "I'm quite aware. He often sits near me and watches when I do my experiments. He comments in his own sweet way and even pretends to read the science books with me."

"He's a bright one, all right. Why, just a while ago, in perfect, clear phrases, he pointed out to me how the light gleams through the window and dances across the floor and furniture. He used those very words. *Gleams* and *dances*. Of course, it was only phrases, but how young to be noticing such details!"

"Cora, he's amazed me a few times too."

"I wonder should his younger brother take to bein' so observant of the smallest details when he grows up. Might serve them both well when they reach manhood."

"I would hope so." Lucy looked at Mycroft who had lain down and curled into a soft slumber at her feet. "Ah, my poor little one. Falls asleep so easily."

"Then I'll let you and your sweet family be. I've got supper to prepare, and that Mycroft is a good eater."

Lucy finished nursing Junior, placed him asleep in the wicker basket, and lifted Mycroft onto the bed where she lay down beside him, and she, too, fell asleep.

A few moments later, Lockie slipped into the room, followed by Abigail. He whispered, "Abigail, I must find where you get those special shoes with rubber soles. My old clodhoppers make so much noise. It's quite difficult to sneak up on anyone."

Abigail laughed gently. "I'll tell you later where I got them. But look at your lovely family, fast asleep. My cousin and your two boys, my nephews."

She turned to leave when Lucy bolted upright in bed and exclaimed, "Yes, that's it!" Checking first to see she had not woken her sons, she sped to the scroll and journals on the desk and ran her fingers several times across the scroll while turning the journal pages several times. "Yes, yes." Her eyes glowed with excitement. She stopped and gave Lockie a big hug and kiss while Abigail looked on, amazed.

"What have you discovered, sweetheart?" Lockie asked.

"With the help of my father's intensive work on translating the Hebrew writings, I believe I have made a great discovery." She tapped the sheepskin scroll. "Whoever this man may be, he is a tin merchant who buys from miners in Cornwall and elsewhere on the coast of England and then sails back with the load of ore to the harbour city of Tyre in the Holy Land. *Stannum* is the Latin word for tin which my father had noted in one of his journals. *Navago* is Latin for 'I am sailing.' I deciphered the Hebrew letters based on my father's translations of other Hebrew writings."

"A tin merchant. Hmm," Lockie said.

"What has occurred with this man, I believe, is he was carrying a treasure. *Gazae* in Latin translated from the Hebrew. At some point, after sailing from Cornwall, he sees a *pirata vexillum*—a pirates' flag. Rather than sailing headlong towards the pirates, he bids the ship's captain to reverse course and sail to *Hibernia*, which is the Roman name for Ireland." She looked between Lockie and Abigail who were blinking and nodding. "Don't you see?"

"I think you've explained who this man is," said Lockie, "and his predicament with pirates chasing him."

Lucy twirled one of her long golden locks and pinched her lips. "But I've not discovered the meaning of this box and the crooked iron door hinge rods, or whatever they are, yet."

"Yet," repeated Abigail. "*Yet* is the key word, my brilliant cousin." Abigail's brown eyes flashed with fervor. "I know you can solve it."

"I agree," Lockie said. "Simple deduction."

Lucy grimaced. "I've more research to do." She plopped into the chair and began perusing the Hebrew scrawls again. "I will find the answer."

While she again plied her acumen to the task, Lockie lay down next to Mycroft and soon fell asleep. He was awakened when a new violent wind shook the manor house.

STAVE TWENTY-FIVE

TO DIE ON HOLY GROUND

Scrooge rode in Byrne's landau carriage with Byrne, Cratchit, and Blevins along an eastern coast road of Ireland, south of Dublin. With the full moon shining brightly above, he looked out the window at the white-capped waves crashing on the rocky coast. The waves rose and plummeted in long lines and made a sort of vibrating grumbling that mingled with the steady rumble of the carriage wheels. The sea breeze felt good on his face, and he took a moment to gaze up at the vast arrays of stars like glittering diamonds spread on the black fabric of the sky.

He recalled briefly when, almost three years ago, the Ghost of Christmas Present had carried him across land and over the sea and shown him the sailors on a ship far out on the briny deep who still felt the joy of Christmas and sang and danced as if they were at a ball in an extravagant palace. A lump rose in his throat.

He held a blanket across his legs, as did his companions, the weather crisp but not unbearable. Cratchit's head was bobbing, his eyes closed, a slight snoring whistle peeling from his lips. Officer Blevins sat opposite Scrooge and also looked out the window at the endless grey sea. To Scrooge, the officer appeared to be the hallmark of manliness—calm, confident, and a gentleman. "It's quite beautiful when seen from afar," Scrooge remarked to Blevins. "The surf, that is."

"'Tis true, Mr Scrooge, but be wary if you go down on the beach."

"Wary of what?" Scrooge was alarmed.

"Of the merfolk. The song of the mermaids will enchant you, and they will take you prisoner in their abode in the deep."

Scrooge considered pulling down the window curtain lest he see a mermaid and hear her song. He chose not to but instead gazed at the frothy, churning beauty of the waves.

Sitting beside Scrooge, Byrne studied a ledger using a small bullseye lantern. Scrooge wondered if this beneficent man was worrying his own funds might be in jeopardy because of his charity. The man's face was creased in a frown.

Suddenly, Scrooge's thoughts jumped to the fact that there were now three murders in a small village, not one. *Are they connected?* he thought. He further struggled with what angle the seadog had taken in saying he *knew* things. *What are those things?* His mind then ranged through his recent visit from the ghost of Jacob Marley and to the shadow being he had seen in the alley where Abigail and he had found the starving Irishman. That shadow had seemed to possess the form of a frightful hag. "I am coming undone," Scrooge mumbled aloud.

"Beg pardon?" Blevins said.

Now aware he had spoken aloud, Scrooge said, "Oh, I believe my vest button has come undone." He began fiddling with a button.

Byrne snapped the lantern door shut and spoke into the dark. "It is too late in dangerous times, and there have been highwaymen oft times on this road. Starvation makes for desperate men attempting desperate courses. We will stop tonight at an acquaintance's estate." He rapped his cane on the roof then leaned out his window and shouted to Thomas, his driver, "Take us to Kilruddy Estate." He turned back to the three. "We'll sleep there tonight. Vitruvius Chichester owes me a favour."

In a quarter mile, the coach turned inland, and the ocean and its symphonic roar slowly faded away. The road immediately began to ascend. Through the tall trees, Scrooge could just make out lights glowing in the distance.

"Ah," Byrne said. "It's as if they've expected our arrival. Old Vitru should be glad to see me since I saved his life in that hunting accident."

In the moonlight dancing through the trees, Scrooge saw a quaint church, its steeple bent slightly at an angle. Candles were lit in the church, which sent out a dreary glow onto the adjacent cemetery graves.

When the coach slowed for a sharp turn beside the church, Scrooge became aware of bodies lying on the ground among the graves. Some lay perfectly still, others were moving, barely perceptible, and some were crawling towards the church steps where several individuals, scarcely visible in the shadows, moved listlessly. He distinctly heard a sharp wail, sharper than the howl of the wind, and he immediately knew it was a banshee. When the coach completed the turn, the scene was out of sight.

Scrooge felt faint. He thought, *What land have I journeyed to? Are the dead rising from the graves?*

STAVE TWENTY-SIX
GREAT POMP OF RICHES, DISDAIN OF THE POOR

At the Kilruddy Manor, Scrooge and Cratchit were amazed at the imposing manor building and the grounds, laden with numerous reflecting ponds and fountains. The carriage pulled up to the two-story edifice with a cupola and tall clock tower near the door. Scrooge, Cratchit, and Blevins made remarks about the long horse stable with cupolas, gleaming its white paint in the moonlight. The manor house lights shone through soaring windows.

A slender, bewhiskered man—obviously a stable hand by his soiled clothes and leather apron—rushed to the carriage. He kept bowing at regular intervals and welcomed each man with a somewhat toothless smile and offered to help each one step down from the carriage. When the driver began handing down the luggage, the poor fellow could not wield even one of them, his bony arms shaking when he received them, and almost dropped each one on the ground.

"Faith and begora," the little man said in a bright Irish tenor. "You are welcome here, fine gentlemen. I am off to get some help to carry in your bags." He fled quickly to the stable where two equally emaciated men came forth, each looking somewhat like a replica of the first.

Byrne crossed first over the footbridge across a narrow moat then to the door and knocked. "Hello, the house! Hello, Vitru! It's me, Reginald Byrne."

In a moment, a petite Irish maid, her dress and apron twice-turned, opened the door. She courtseyed and announced their arrival in a tiny voice.

Vitruvius Chichester, balding and pot-bellied and with astonishingly wide thighs, sauntered down the stairs. The whiskers on either side of his jowls were grey and bristling. His clothing was impeccable—clean, starched trousers, a scarlet vest, and a bleached-white shirt with a gold pin on the chest pocket from which an elegant gold watch chain hung. His hand sparkled with jewelled rings on five of his fingers. "Ah, Reggie," Vitru said in a staunch English accent. He extended his hand. "The only Irishman I know for whom I give a rat's behind."

After Byrne introduced his companions, and all had made polite comments, Vitru extended his arm. "Welcome to my humble home."

Cratchit gazed up towards the high ceiling, bedecked with Renaissance-style paintings, and said, "Hmm."

Suddenly, Vitru yelled at the petite Irish maid, "Get thee hence, you pitiful animal! I'll not have my wife cast eyes on you. And bolt the door, you worthless pigswill. Do it quick, or I'll dock your food allowance."

The little maid courtseyed and quickly bolted the door and ran away into the adjacent music room and took a seat in a shadowed corner. Though Byrne looked deliberately at the ceiling, as if admiring it, Scrooge and Cratchit were alarmed, their eyes wide. Blevins appeared angry enough to assault the man.

Oblivious of the expressions of disgust on his guests' faces, Vitru pinched some snuff from a small ornate box he had pulled from his trouser pocket, and he shoved the potent tobacco in each nostril. In a moment, he sneezed, drew a handkerchief from his sleeve, and blew his nose. He dropped the handkerchief on the floor, and the maid rushed to pick it up then escaped to her shadowed cove. Vitru sighed then bellowed, "I cannot stand the Irish, but they are cheaper to keep and feed than a good English butler or maid." A knock on the door sounded. Vitru hollered at the little maid, "For the love of our gracious queen, you foolish wench, see who's at the door at this hour!"

The maid rushed to the door and unbolted it. The three thin stable hands and the carriage driver stood there. "Your bags, sir," said Thomas.

Vitru was turning red. "Reggie, please have your man bring in your items." Then he strode vehemently towards the stable hands, pointing at the stable. "Get thee back to your duties! You smell like manure!"

The stable hands hurried away.

"Shall I set these here inside the door?" asked Thomas. "Until you're ready to retire?"

"Yes, Thomas. Thank you."

Thomas, a stout man of near six feet in height, set the bags inside then closed the door behind him and left to settle the team of carriage horses in the stable.

Vitru, still completely unaware of the shock on his guests' faces, said, "Come, let me show you my water clock tower." His guests followed him a few dozen feet to a short stairway leading to a landing on the backside of the imposing tower they had seen on arrival. Looking up, they saw a large clockface about a yard across, and below it ran four pipes and two metal reservoir tubs. They could hear the water running through the pipes and bubbling in the tubs and heard the clock tick. "Now, watch." Vitru pointed up.

They looked and saw the minute hand click forwards. "Runs entirely on water pumped from the moat. As accurate a timepiece as you'll ever find. The clock on the front of the tower and this one here keep perfect time."

Each man voluntarily took out his pocket watch to compare.

"Indeed," Scrooge said. "It's right on time."

"I believe it's time," Vitru said, "for you to meet my wife."

The four men followed their host into a large gallery with numerous animal heads mounted on the walls. Vitru gestured to the second floor at a hallway running along one wall. It was abutted by a heavy railing. A portly woman in an elegant scarlet dress with black lace about the bosom and sleeves stood at the railing holding a slip of paper. She let it fall, and it fluttered to the floor.★

"Ah, there is our breakfast menu for our cooks," announced Vitru.

Scrooge asked, "Why did she drop it and not give it to the cooks?"

Vitru turned to his guests. "My wife has one personal English maid and wants no call to ever interact with the Irish staff whatsoever, much less even put her eyes on them. The cooks come out a little later and pick up the menu. They prepare the meal per her orders, set it out for us on the table, and then we eat it. After we've dined and departed the table, they enter and clean.* My poor wife would faint should she have to deal with these rabble. She sees them as rats and earnestly bids me to dismiss them and pay for more expensive English staff. I refuse out of love for her."

Scrooge and Cratchit looked aghast. Byrne maintained a neutral expression. Blevins fumed.

Barely able to imagine what the host was describing, Cratchit asked, "How does she go about the house with the staff doing their chores?"

"Oh, that's easy. In almost all cases, the staff must pass through a tunnel under the house.* They labour at night, so we seldom see them at all, save the maid who keeps the door or the stable hands when I go for a ride."

STAVE TWENTY-SEVEN
BALEFUL DISCOVERIES AND BRIGHT HAPPENSTANCES

The meal extended to Chichester's guests was extravagant, expanding to four courses, with a great variety of fare including roast duck, roast boar, and a multitude of vegetables swimming in butter, but no potatoes. Once everyone had eaten, and the matron had chosen to retire to her bedroom, and Vitru had coaxed the men into the parlour where he partook of a pipe, Cratchit mentioned to Scrooge, "In a moment, Blevins and I are going to take a walk to see these Irish 'rats,' as Mrs Chichester calls them."

Seeing Vitru smoking, Scrooge felt compelled to take out his own pipe and smoke it, which he did. While the men sat, talking and coughing, they could hear the tiny clattering of dishes and silverware coming from the dining room where the kitchen help were quietly clearing the table. After a few minutes of listening to the boorish monologue of Vitru, Cratchit excused himself. "After all this travel, I need a walk before I turn in."

Blevins joined him, and they exited the front door. The little maid hurried to secure it upon their departure.

"Come, Officer Blevins," Cratchit said. "Let's go find these Irish workers."

The men journeyed first to the stable where eight sleek thoroughbreds and Byrne's carriage horses were in stalls. "I guess the stable hands have turned in for the night," said Cratchit.

The pair then headed back, all the time discussing the plight of the Irish farmers and the potato blight. Deciding to see more of the grounds, they rounded the corner of the manor. Quite by accident, Blevins found the tunnel the workers used to travel under the house. A single torch sputtered in a wall. They ventured through the dank, moldy tunnel and out the other side and discovered, some fifty yards from the manor, down in a vale, the dwellings of the Irish staff.

Three whitewashed houses with roofs in need of repair stood in a row. When they knocked on the door of definitely the noisiest one, a young lad in ragged clothes answered, and he invited them to enter. Inside, they beheld thirty women and men, including the manor's farmhands and the three stable hands, all of whom kept bowing and lowering their eyes. "You're welcome here, sirs. What work can we do for you?" asked a timid fellow, holding a small drum.

Another said, "We are at your service, lords." A fife protruded from his a pocket.

"We are not lords," Cratchit said, smiling. "We are but humble workers like you, but we are from London. I am Bob Cratchit, a detective." He gestured to the officer. "This is Officer Devland Blevins of Her Majesty's Metropolitan Police."

"We've not stolen anything," growled an elderly man with a long white beard extending almost to his knees. Cratchit thought it the longest beard he had ever seen. "I'll have you know, we're good Catholics here. We steal from no one. T'would be a grave sin."

The small group murmured "Aye's" and nodded over and over.

"What business have you with us here, sirs?" the long-bearded man asked, a scowl on his face. He poked a crooked walking cane towards them.

"We're not here to arrest anyone or even bother you," Blevins answered, his Irish tongue evident. Then he spoke some Gaelic words, at which the entire group smiled.

"What did you say?" Cratchit asked Blevins.

"I said I saw all the instruments they were hiding, and I knew they were setting to start a dance. I asked if we could join."

The wan and dishevelled Irish people began smiling, their humanity shining forth. In a twinkling, several men and women produced fiddles, pipes, drums, and one bagpipe. Young boys and girls and teens, who had been hiding before, suddenly emerged. Thomas showed up at the door and joined in the celebration. In no time, the young and old were dancing a jig so fast, Cratchit could barely believe his eyes.

When the first song ended, Cratchit said, "I've never seen feet move so fast."

"You've not seen nothin' yet," announced the little stable hand who had first met them. He marched forth to the middle of the floor and stood perfectly still. With a slight wave of his hand, the makeshift band began an even faster trill, and the thin man danced his legs rapidly while his upper body remained erect and still. He was soon joined by the bonnie lasses and lads, their complex stepping all aligned far better than any marching army.

Cratchit admitted to himself he had not seen such abundant joy in so many faces since Christmas time.

STAVE TWENTY-EIGHT
THE VAMPIRE WOMAN

Inside Chichester's home, Byrne had grown tired of debating the merits of the Irish with Vitru, though the manor owner seemed thrilled with the deliberation. Listening to their banter, Scrooge had mixed feelings about the qualities of the Irish and wondered, based on Vitru's comments, if they had any moral values at all. The London papers certainly wrote ill of them, painting all of them as drunken brawlers. He was, however, impressed with Byrne, and he did not appreciate the way Chichester spoke of his own staff. He thought back to when Abigail, Cratchit, and he, on that cold afternoon, had helped the poor, starving Irishman. He thought, *It's befuddling.*

Suddenly, Byrne invited Scrooge for a walk. "It's warm in here. Let's view the grounds before all the moonlight is gone." The two excused themselves from Vitru, who struggled to stand when they left towards the front door. When they arrived at the door, the little maid hurried to unbolt it. When she did, Byrne gave her a coin worth five shillings. She merely blushed and whispered a thank you.

The full moon was directly above them, and the light from the house windows shed ample light.

"Let us look at the horses in the stable," Byrne said. "See? There are lanterns aglow there."

The two strode towards the stable. They quickly became aware of the horses stamping their feet and neighing in a startled fashion. "I wonder what has the animals so agitated," Scrooge remarked.

Striding along, they stopped when a black cat crossed their path. It halted a moment and turned towards them. Scrooge noted the white heart-shape on its nose before it slipped into the darkness. He wondered, *Did the cat I saw in the alley in London stow away on the boat when it sailed?*

When they entered the stable, they both stopped short. At the far end open door of the long stable stood a beautiful woman in an almost threadbare nightgown. She had dark, flowing hair that spun and danced in the wind, her skin was as pale as moonlight, and her lips were deep red. She began beckoning to the men with soothing words, almost melodically. "Come hither, fair gentlemen. I have need of you. I yearn for you."

Though the horses continued neighing and stamping their hooves, even rearing, Scrooge could only hear the woman's voice. He was immediately enthralled with her beauty and began walking towards her while Byrne stood stock-still. She kept up her entreaty, now calling Scrooge by his name. "Ebenezer," she crooned, bending towards him so her lowcut gown showed ample cleavage. Scrooge had never been intimate with a woman, not even with Isabelle, his long ago fiancé. The only intimate contact with a woman he had experienced of late was when Kitty, his maid and bodyguard, gave him a peck on the cheek when he had brought her flowers. His thoughts flowed back to his days as a young man, remembering holding the hand of Isabelle, his betrothed, before he lost her because of his miserliness.

Now, the woman of pale skin and red lips looked longingly at him. He quickened his pace.

Suddenly, a horse in a stall directly beside Byrne reared and screamed violently. Byrne broke from his hypnotic stare. "Scrooge, go no farther!" he yelled. "That is no woman! It is the Dearg-Due!"*

Scrooge stopped and looked back momentarily, though his face showed no interest in Byrne who was now sprinting towards him. Scrooge continued towards the woman with his arms outstretched. She was just beyond the door. Soon, he would be in her embrace.

"Scrooge, halt!" Byrne yelled. "She wants only to drink your blood." Byrne tackled Scrooge to the dirt, just at the alluring woman's feet. They both looked up, and she appeared so pitifully sad. Then she opened her mouth, her sharp incisors evident, and her eyes flaming red with snakelike pupils.

Byrne pulled Scrooge to his feet. "Run! And don't look back."

While Scrooge raced to the opposite door in full panic, Byrne stood before the fiend shouting words in Gaelic. A great gust of wind blew up around the woman, and then she was gone. Byrne rushed back to Scrooge who was bent over panting just inside the stable door.

The two next attempted to head towards the manor house. When they looked back, the vile creature was chasing them across the lawn, and she was gaining. As if by lightning strike, a tall black stallion appeared between them and the Dearg-Due, and reared, flailing its legs in striking motions towards the evil creature. In a grey mist, the Dearg-Due evaporated. The stallion galloped into the deep dark.

"Come," Byrne said. "Let us head to those lights there in the vale. I believe that the despicable being has business here at Kilruddy Manor. Those lights must be the homes of the Irish workers. We'll be safe there."

With Byrne fairly pulling Scrooge along, the two quickly made their way to where the Irish families were holding their party. Byrne threw open the door and brought Scrooge in with him. The music stopped, the dancers quit their jigs, and all eyes turned on the out-of-breath pair.

Byrne closed the door. To the astonished crowd, he exclaimed, "We just escaped the Dearg-Due."

A vacuum of sound. Not one person spoke or even breathed. Finally, Cratchit, who was sitting by the door, asked, "What is a Dearg-due?"

The entire Irish people shrank back while Cratchit looked about in wonder.

The old Irishman with the beard almost to his knees came forwards and planted himself with one foot in front of the other, hands behind his back. His voice rang. "That specter ye encountered, whose name we dare not mention aloud, be fully dead but thrives still on the blood of unsuspecting men. She be coy and enterprising, but her heart be filled with rage, so she yearns to strike down anyone she feels be unworthy and devour them by drinking their blood. That be all ye need know."

"But why is she here?" Cratchit asked.

"Some boundless, sordid deeds have been done here by someone," Officer Blevins said. "She roams Ireland for revenge against anyone she considers wicked. She is of the spirit world. Lost in the very same time when she broke free from her grave. So, she knows not where she is. Only her bloodthirst and desire for revenge."

A quaking Scrooge asked in a quivering voice, "But why was she after me?"

"Probably, she was not after you," said the wise, bearded Irishman. "Because you are *new here*. She is after someone else who lives here or nearby. You were simply unlucky."

The party rejoined. After staying another hour, the visitors, including Thomas, left and hurried to the manor house. Scrooge, Cratchit, and Blevins entreated Byrne that they leave as early as possible in the morning. Way ahead of them, he had already made arrangements with Thomas to have the coach ready, and they left before dawn and before Vitru or his wife had arisen.

While they drove away in the starlit morning, Blevins said, "A curse on his house."

Scrooge, for his part, had not slept the entire night, and he still shook from fear. He thought, *So, Ireland has its own share of malevolent beings. What will I encounter next? And still ... why was the cat I saw in London there last night? And where did the brave, black horse that drove the creature away come from? I hope I shall never see the blood-sucker again.*

STAVE TWENTY-NINE

FIRST ENCOUNTERS

With the sun rising steadily in a clear sky, the four men journeyed in the carriage via a circuitous, hilly climb to Byrne's estate, located in the foothills of the Wicklow Range. Jouncing along on the bone-racking road, Scrooge kept his teeth clinched. His wariness had not abated. He expressly sensed some unknown evil was plotting and labouring against him in this green island.

Byrne's two-story manor, though large, was not presumptuous on the outside, save the statues of cherubs above the front door. Inside the manor, the walls were lined with stained oak panels, the old floorboards creaked, and the furniture was far from up-to-date. The home had a comfortable feel to it.

When Byrne's guests were seated in the parlour, sipping tea with biscuits, he said, "I'm sorry if you have to fend for yourself often enough here. A neighbouring landowner offered more pay to my staff, including the farm hands, and most of them took him up on it. Now, for the house staff, I've only got one housemaid, the butler, and his wife, who is the cook. The butler sees to the overall running of this house, which has twenty bedrooms, and he takes on such tasks as he deems necessary. Our little maid is busy all day either in the kitchen helping the cook or in the scullery washing clothes or dishes and pots. She has the duty to empty the nightjars of the house, including when I have several guests spending the night. There is no way she could have the time to dust and sweep as well. Fortunately, I was able to employ some new farmhands. For the house, I figured that I could get by well enough with a minimum staff. But you won't find much dust anywhere, and the floors are always swept. Let me just say we have some new welcome guests."

"Are we to meet these guests?" Cratchit inquired.

"Not likely," said Byrne. "They arrive surreptitiously each night, perform a myriad number of tasks, and only ask for a few bowls of cream. Each morning, I find the house spic-and-span."

"So, you have Brownies!" Blevins exclaimed.

"I think it must be a whole family, for this house is so large," Byrne replied.

While Blevins and Byrne nodded knowingly, Cratchit smiled. He said, "I hope I see one."

Scrooge merely grumbled. He had quickly hypothesized Byrne had reduced his staff to save costs. *Brownies! Humbug! There's no such thing. That is his excuse because his philanthropy is most likely more than he can afford while still trying to maintain the estate.*

"Things are dourer lately than in recent years." Byrne looked up at the ceiling as if pleading to God. "Parliament keeps raising taxes, and I am forced to collect from my tenants on their homes as well. I've told the tenants they need to seal one of their two doors and one of their two windows so their tax is not so high.*"

"I've often wondered," said Blevins, "why the Parliament charges tax on a home based on the number of doors and windows it has. I would think it would be based on total square footage of the building."

Cratchit asked, "Why do these people need two doors anyway? The huts I've seen on our journey here seem almost too small for any family to dwell."

"You may have noticed," Byrne explained, "that these poor farmers have no barns on the property. Each family tries to keep a cow for milk, butter, and cheese. And when the weather turns bitter in the winter, they bring their cow inside the hut through one door to keep it from dying. When the weather clears, they pull and push the cow out the other door."

"I've lived in Ireland most of my life," Blevins said. "My family's condition was not impoverished, for my father and his brother made a good living in legal advisement. Lawyers." His face turned sorrowful. "However, our neighbours did not fare as well. I witnessed so many cases where the families were so large with eight or ten kids and perhaps a grandparent living in the same household, so I'm sure bringing a cow inside must make for horribly crowded conditions."

"I'm amazed!" Cratchit exclaimed. "I feel blessed to live with my family in London."

Byrne's butler, a thin man with grey, short-cropped hair, entered. His sallow face, bearing a pencil-thin mustache, seemed to hold a permanent grimace, and Cratchit thought the man's lips never moved when he spoke. "Mr Byrne, supper is served." Then he harrumphed, turned on his heel, opened the door to the dining hall, and stood at attention, shoulders back.

"Thank you, O'Malley," Byrne said and rose.

Byrne and his guests filed into the dining hall. Cratchit, last in line, heard O'Malley mumble, "Don't know why I work here with the pittance I'm paid."

Cratchit showed no response, kept going, and took a seat at the long, polished table.

A slight, young woman in her mid-twenties with a myriad of freckles on her face and arms stood prepared to serve soup from a toureen on a cart. Bright, fiery scarlet ringlets hung down under her maid's cap, and her hands appeared red-raw from considerable labour. She curtseyed and beamed a wide grin. Beside her stood a grey-haired woman with grey eyes, wearing a grey apron over a grey dress. Scrooge, who sat nearest her at the table, perceived that even her lips were grey. She perched by a sideboard, ready to carve a pork roast.

"Gentleman," said Byrne while seating himself, "may I introduce my esteemed butler, Herbert O'Malley; his wife and excellent cook and herbalist, Grizelda O'Malley; and our only maid left in the house, Miss Bonnie Jean Goodacre."

Herbert and Grizelda smirked with a nod. Bonnie said, "I'm pleased to make your acquaintance, gentlemen." She courtseyed again.

The meal was delivered by the three servants who coordinated all three of the meal courses and never spilled a drop of food nor a drop of wine in pouring it. At the end of the meal, the cook and maid removed all the dishes, and Herbert sauntered off.

Byrne leaned forwards. "I tell you, gentlemen, something is amiss."

STAVE THIRTY
GOLGOTHA'S DROPPED TREASURES

While her two children slept on the bed in the warm sunshine that was dancing through a window, Lucy Holmes set down her pencil. She had finally deciphered the entire text of the mysterious scroll. The writings exhibited several sayings from the Jewish Torah and prayers to a person the author called, "The Great Teacher."

When she had deciphered all she could, she lay her head onto the desk and frowned. She muttered to herself, "Well, Lucy, you know he's a merchant from northern Judea and a member of the Jewish Sanhedrin and travels to Cornwall to obtain tin, probably for the manufacture of bronze. You know he sought to escape pirates, and he had some sort of valuable item or items with him, though it never says what this treasure was. I cannot gather who he is calling a great teacher who is also his relative."

Lockie slipped into their bedroom. "Don't be glum, dear one. I've got some good news."

"Yes, dear husband?" Lucy raised her head, though her frown remained long.

"Samuel reports a new vein of tin has been found and he's quite optimistic about it."

"Such wonderful news! But I worry still, for the civil trial goes on. Has Samuel said any more about it?"

Lockie sat beside his wife. "Yesterday, he commented about a wire from Abel Leggitt. It said Cragle continued to *paper the argument* so the court officials would 'take it into account.' According to Leggitt, that means the officials will retire to a chamber to mull over the new 'so-called' evidence for hours and come *to no conclusion*. I almost didn't share that news with you. It's so troubling."

"It seems the Chancery has nothing better to do than hold counsel and never accomplish anything." Lucy tapped the scroll. "Lockie, I've learnt all this scroll has to offer. We still don't know the meaning of the box or the iron bars or the round, iron pieces."

Lockie could not stop smiling. "I actually have some even better news. I was rather bored this afternoon, so I began studyin' the iron bars and the box, tryin' to figure out their purpose, when …" He paused to be sure Lucy was looking at him. Her eyes were bright upon him. "Lucy, I discovered a hidden panel in the box bottom."

Lucy gasped. "And?"

"I jimmied it a little, and it slid open." He pulled three flimsy, yellowed parchments from his jacket's inside pocket. "Before I hand them to you, I must tell you that in my days of learnin' in the Ragged School, I picked up quite a bit o' Latin. Though I cannot read it as well as you, I read enough on the first page to believe it has the answers we're lookin' for."

Lucy threw her arms around him then pulled back and lightly lifted the fragile documents from his hands. Her face glowed with anticipation. The rest of the afternoon, Lucy poured over the new pages and often shouted comments of surprise. Finally, at suppertime, she emerged from the bedroom, carrying her two boys.

She had sent word through Lockie to have the entire Tamperwind and Wheeler families present in the dining room, along with Pudge and Dimsight. Lockie had placed the box with the iron rods atop it in the centre of the table. Cora saw Lucy descending the stairs first. "The supper's stayin' warm on the oven, and everyone's here."

Lucy handed Junior to Abigail and let Mycroft wander around amidst all the people he had come to know well. No one said a word, and all were attentive to Lucy.

She began. "What I have to tell you has incredible bearing on us and, perhaps, on the entire world. This box we found was hidden by none other than a man named Joseph. Though he did not mention his hometown, I believe he is *the* Joseph of Arimathea mentioned in the Bible. On the first page, he explained he was an uncle to Jesus and a relative of Jesus's worldly stepfather, St Joseph. Yes, this tin merchant of the town of Arimathea *had* to be a relative of Jesus. Otherwise, Pilate would not have released the body to him. As the Bible tells us, Joseph was a secret follower of Jesus. In these pages, he refers to Jesus as the 'Great Teacher.'"

By this time, everyone in the room was in total wonderment.

Lucy paused, fighting back tears. Finally, she whispered, "The iron rods in the box are not the tines of a trident nor hinge pins from a door … but *they are the nails that nailed our Lord to the cross*. I conjecture that over time, the heads of the nails rusted loose and fell off. The round coin-like pieces are the nail heads. Joseph's writings say the nails are bent at one end because after the nails were driven through Jesus's hands and through the crossbar, the soldiers bent the nails to hold His hands tight against the wood."

Her words fell on her listeners like a hammer on an anvil. Abigail and Cora gasped aloud. Pudge was turning his floppy cap in a twisted knot. Dimsight removed his dark glasses and wiped his eyes. Each of the men held dumbfounded expressions on their faces, and tears welled up in their eyes.

Bobbie Wheeler and his cousins, Angus and Barnabas, folded their hands and began to pray silently, their eyes towards heaven.

Lucy calmed herself and said, "The final explanation for why the box is hidden is because of what happened when Joseph and Jesus's mother, St Mary, and St Mary Magdalene, and St John were busy caring for Jesus's body when it was taken down from the cross. I can only surmise they were wiping as much blood from his body as they could before the body was to be loaded into a cart to be carried to the tomb." She took a deep breath. "Joseph explains how, as they were hurrying to carry the body to Joseph's tomb by sundown before Passover, he caught sight of two sorcerers *from a cult* which he did not name. They were bargaining with a Roman centurion to possess the nails. His writings said he knew they would try to use the nails and the blood on them for dark, evil magic."

"Perhaps," interjected Samuel, "they were of the cult of Jannes and Jambres. Remember, they were the Pharoah's sorcerers who disputed with Moses."

"The Bible recalls," said Angus, "when Moses' staff turned into a snake, they used magic to turn their staffs into snakes as well."

Bobbie stopped praying. "Yes, I remember those sorcerers are mentioned in St Paul's letter to Timothy. The cult still existed then."

The room fell quiet, save Mycroft pattering around and smiling at the adults.

"But what dark magic would they engender?" Abigail asked.

Lucy, trembling, was now beginning to understand more deeply the raw significance of what they had in their possession. Lockie rose and stood beside his wife, placing his arm tight around her waist.

Finally, Lucy choked out the next words. "This humble tin merchant who claims to be an uncle of our Lord knew he had to stop the sorcerers. The last page says he rushed forwards, grabbed the nails from the centurion, and pulled a knife on the sordid necromancers. The centurion fled in panic because of the earthquake. Joseph says the storm and the dark at that time were incredible. The ground was constantly shifting and shaking."

Abigail rose, handed Sherlock Jr to Cora, and then hugged Lucy.

Samuel had maintained enough wherewithal to ask, "Was there anything else?"

"Yes," Lucy said. "He said he picked up the head of the spear which had pierced Jesus's side. It had broken loose from the lance. He wrapped the nails and spearhead in his tunic and carried them away. His final sentences explain how members of the sorcerers' cult had been stalking him for years. At that point, the document became unreadable."

"I have a feeling," Lockie said, "he realised the pirate ship was one belonging to the cult."

"But," said Angus, "the first document said Joseph's ship turned to Ireland. These nails have been hidden here in Cornwall. If the nails are here, where is the spearhead?"

"I have a strong feeling I have to do some strident investigating about the history of Cornwall," said Lockie. "I will find answers. The game is afoot."

Lucy gave him a slight smile. "I knew you'd say that."

In the next two days, Lockie rode one of the Tamperwind steeds up and down the coast of Cornwall, stopping at each town and at several farmhouses. He discovered most everyone knew one story or another they swore to be true, one which had been handed down by their forefathers, that Joseph of Arimathea *had journeyed along the coast, bartering for tin and other ores.*

He returned to Tamperwind Manor and called his wife and relatives together in the great dining room. He said, "I learned a great deal from the good people in this country. I heard from almost every inhabitant of Glastonbury that, accordin' to them, Saints Joseph of Arimathea and Mary Magdalene and other early Christians escaped the first great persecution in a small boat, floatin' across the Mediterranean first to Marseille, France, then travelling by foot across France, then by boat once more to Cornwall. These individuals adamantly claim he and the others established the first Christian church in England in Glastonbury before returning to Judea."

"Be it legend or imagined stories," Lucy said, "I think, if they did escape the Jewish persecution, Joseph would have brought them to Cornwall to be among his known friends."

"That makes sense," Abigail said.

"Finally," Lockie said, "several persons claimed that Jesus, when a young man, had accompanied Joseph at least once on his voyages. Perhaps, one day, someone will find the complete truth."

STAVE THIRTY-ONE

TIM CRATCHIT, HIS FRIEND, AND THE HOT AIR BALLOON

In a damp, early morning, Tim Cratchit raced along with wild abandon on his strong legs, waving his cap and shouting, "Hurrah!"

Step-for-step beside him ran a boy whose skin was cocoa brown, wearing a nice suit made to order, who also hollered his loudest, "Twiddle um day. Twiddle um day!"

They were going to Vauxhall Gardens to watch an unscheduled launch of Mr Green's lighter than air balloon. Tim's good friend, Rick Canby, was a freeman's son and a free boy himself and proud of his state in life. Tim was taller than Rick, but they had struck up a friendship while Tim had been coming to watch the regular launches of the balloons. Rick's father was a worker, indeed a scientist, who helped concoct the chemicals in the boiler that produced the hydrogen gas fed into the balloons to make them rise.

Turning a corner after crossing Westminster Bridge, Tim almost collided with a street performer holding a squeezebox, rendering a song. Tim shuttered to a stop.

"C'mon, Tim!" Rick shouted. "We'll miss the launch."

"Wait a minute, Rick," Tim said. "This bloke's singing my favourite song. 'Hot Codlins.'* I must listen to it a bit."

Rick strode up beside Tim and put his arm about Tim's shoulder. "Very well. For a bit."

The performer, now aware he had an audience, for a young adult couple had stopped to listen too, sang with great gusto the popular tune, all the while nodding at his tin cup for contributions at his feet. Here were his lyrics:

> A little old woman her living got
> By selling hot codlins—Hot! Hot! Hot!
> And this little old woman, who codlins sold,
> Though her codlins were hot, thought she felt herself cold;
> So, to keep herself warm, she thought it no sin
> To fetch for herself a quartern of ... rye!
> Ri tol de rol, ri tol de rol.

Tim and Rick joined in the song and sang it by heart through two more verses then Rick said, "That's enough. Let's go. My papa will be wantin' me around to 'elp."

The two boys sped away and soon arrived on the wide open, lush green surrounded by groves of trees. The balloon was being rapidly filled with the hydrogen gas, and Rick's father, seeing his son, called for him to carry some gear to Mr Green who stood beside the basket inspecting it. Two men were busy at various tasks about the balloon. Four more sturdy men held the balloon in place from floating away by holding heavy ropes wound about tall, heavy posts. Other men were helping with the banging, clanging machine producing the hydrogen gas. One watched a gauge, another poured carboys of iron into the heavy bronze vat of sulphuric acid in the machine that rattled and hissed. A skinny fellow stood inside the balloon's basket, arranging equipment and the like, and then he stepped out.

Rick's father, a dark-skinned man of fair features and a winning smile, was busy overseeing the work of the others.

Tim went up to Rick's father. "Hello, Mr Canby."

The scientist smiled then went back to observing the dials of the hydrogen making machine. Tim strode up beside Rick who stood next to the aeronaut.

"'ello, Mr Green," Rick said.

"Hello, Rick. Good morning," Mr Green said. "I see you brought your friend with you. Hello, Tim Cratchit."

"Top o' the mornin' to ye," Tim said. "I said that because my father has journeyed to Ireland. They talk that way there, you know."

"I believe you are right, son," Mr Green responded. "Ah, the balloon 'tis about filled and ready to take off. You boys best stand a good distance away."

Rick backed next to his father standing beside the rattling machine slowly quieting down. Tim leaned against one of the tether poles.

"I don't know if I like this east wind," Rick's father called. "An ill wind blows no good."

"I hear you, Able," Mr Green said. "I would prefer a western one. But I didn't want any crowds onlooking today like we usually have. I just want to go up, take some measurements, and come back down."

"But the wind's really picking up, Mr Green," Able reiterated.

The trees were shaking loose the last of their red and brown leaves and the limbs were rocking raucously back and forth.

"What's that you say, Able?" With the noise of the machinery and the increased wind, he could not hear his scientist. He climbed into the basket, released the rubber hose that fed the hydrogen into the balloon, and then tied off the cords holding the opening to the balloon, thus securing the hydrogen inside it.

Six men strode quickly forwards and held on to the basket. One of the ropes around a post slipped loose, and the basket tilted some. A helper raced back to grab it and fell across another rope which then released itself from its tether pole. The basket began twisting around with Mr Green inside it. The remaining men holding the basket lost their grip and fell, tumbling down the embankment.

Then a heavy gust lifted the balloon. The last two men holding tight to the ropes on the posts did all they could to hold on, and the ropes burned their hands, dragging through their grips. The other ropes used to secure the balloon to the ground dangled and twisted in the sudden gale. The wind threw burst after burst which kept the balloon rising and descending, and the basket bumping up and down across the park lawn.

Mr Green almost tumbled from the basket. Finally, he yelled, "Let her go, Able. I'll bring her down later!" The two men at the posts released the ropes which then dragged along the ground, following the balloon, which was rising steadily.

Tim was smiling, watching the balloon ascend in a haphazard fashion. Suddenly, a rope dragging along the ground twisted around his ankle, and he was lifted into the air, hanging upside down.

The balloon sped upwards, climbing above the trees with Tim trying to reach up and untangle his leg. Caught in the rope, he was slung into the branches of the trees where rough limbs raked his skin. With great effort, he raised himself and grabbed hold of the rope with both hands just when the tangled rope fell loose from his ankle. He was now swooping along barely above the treetops, the balloon racing west, blown by the vicious eastern gale.

"Help!" he called. "Help, help!"

STAVE THIRTY-TWO

TIM CRATCHIT AND THE AERONAUT'S PLIGHT

His arms tiring, Tim looked down. *If I let go, I'll surely die.*

Below him spread the great city of London. Buildings, roads, parks, creeks, and streams. There, Westminster. There, a church and banks. He even spotted costermongers hustling along the streets. Looking back into the vanishing distance, he made out the launch area of Vauxhill Gardens where Rick and his father stood with the other men. His arms were aching. "Mr Green, I'm down here!"

Mr Green's voice rang out. "What're you doing down there, Tim?" He was gazing over the side of the basket at the boy. "I knew you wanted a ride, but that's not the easiest way to do it."

Tim felt the rope he was hanging onto being pulled up, and then a strong hand grabbed hold of his jacket and hauled him into the basket. Tumbling into a corner, out of the wind, Tim panted hard. *I can't catch my breath*, he thought. He looked up into the eyes of Mr Green who was stooped over and smiling, their noses almost touching.

"Well, Tim," said the aeronaut, "I hadn't planned on a partner for this quick voyage, but as long as you're here, I'm putting you to work. These balloon rides aren't free, you know."

"Yes, sir," Tim gasped. He struggled to his feet and immediately felt the stiff breeze blowing across the basket. He looked up at the balloon itself, which fully blocked his view of anything above it. He could not help himself from turning in a circle. "I can't believe I'm actually flying in a balloon!" He spun around and around. "I'm flying. I'm flying."

"There, there now, Tim." Mr Green placed his rough yet gentle hands on Tim's shoulders and brought the boy to a halt. "I need you to do something for me."

"Yes, sir."

"Take hold of that sling psychrometer by the chain and swing it around so I can get some temperature and humidity measures."

Tim picked up the two-sided thermometer.

"One bulb thermometer is wet, the other dry," Mr Green said. "When you twirl it around, I can gauge an accurate measurement of humidity and temperature."

"I'm sorry, sir, but I can barely hear you with the wind." Tim leaned forwards, and Mr Green repeated his explanation.

The aeronaut turned to observe his aerometer spinning violently. The simple weathervane spun as well, though it mostly indicated the wind was coming from the east.

Tim began twirling the psychrometer. After a moment, he handed the device to Mr Green who was now seated, entering the findings in a log. He looked up. "Goodness, my intrepid partner, we are certainly moving along swiftly and gaining considerable altitude." The ropes which held the balloon were clacking in the wind, and the easternmost side of the balloon was trembling with the wind gusts.

Tim had taken a position facing towards the western horizon. He looked down at the rapidly passing panoply of forests, farms, and small villages, and roads that looked like pencil markings, and even a passing train, its stack pouring out smoke. "This is glorious! Wait until I tell my friends and my family." He stopped, his face taking on deep worry. "Oh, no. What will my mum say?" He turned to Mr Green. "I've got to get back. My mum specifically forbade me riding in a balloon. Yet here I am."

"Not to worry, Tim. Let me take a few more readings on my equipment. Perhaps rise a bit higher, and ..." He glanced back towards London. "Uh-oh. We may need to do some quick descending, Tim. Look at that bank of storm clouds coming our way from the east. It seems the wind earlier was just the harbinger of a rather big storm."

The thunderstorm, despite how fast the balloon was speeding along, was gaining on them. Lightning flashed its jagged fingers across the clouds. Mr Green took some last-minute measurements and recorded them in his journal. "All right then." He reached up and began loosening the straps of the balloon in order to release the hydrogen gas.

Tim felt a jolt.

"There you go, Tim. We'll be descending faster than you can imagine."

"I can imagine my father being quite upset and the same with my mum."

"Not to worry. I'll get you home." The aeronaut pulled the straps together, thus tightening the outflow of gas to a measured amount. "Don't want to descend too fast. Now, where's that anchor?" While holding the cloth strands, he scanned the interior of the basket. "Where's the anchor? Was it not loaded?"

"What's the anchor for, sir?"

"It's quite important when we get close to the ground. I use it, when we are near hitting the earth, to snag a tree and thus hold us in place so we descend slowly to the ground. Without it, we could go bumping along over some rough ground, even smash into boulders and buildings." He frowned and bit his lip. He looked again at Tim. "Not to worry, young man. I'll figure this out." He smiled then looked back at the storm. "We've got to get above it, or there'll be hell to pay. Quick, Tim, unfasten those sandbags. Let them drop."

"What if we don't go higher?"

"We could be electrocuted inside the storm. Quickly now!" He re-tied the strands holding the valve tight and began releasing the sandbags that plummeted down. Tim untied two that directly fell.

The balloon shot upwards. Tim immediately felt the deep cold of the higher altitude. He dropped down to be out of the wind and drew his knees up to his chest, his arms bound around himself.

Mr Green ducked below the edge of the basket, rose just a little, and peered back at the angry storm. His brow furrowed, he turned towards Tim. "It's out-pacing us." Thunder growled with several lightning flashes. "Tim, I have to release the last sandbags. Get ready." He reached in a small basket, pulled out a thin blanket, and tossed it to Tim who wrapped himself in it. Then Mr Green untied the last two bags.

Suddenly, Tim was aware of almost blinding sunlight, for they had risen now above the clouds and were still ascending. He inched towards a small crack in the basket weaving and stared down at the horrendous, black storm cloud below with arrows of lightning slashing through it.

Mr Green crouched down behind him and turned the brave lad towards himself. "We're taking a much longer journey than I anticipated. We may ... we may be soon approaching the ocean."

"The ocean?" Tim shivered at his own words.

"Aye. But if I can get us down earlier, I will. We're above the storm for now, and that's good. I only wish I had the anchor stowed. When we do land, it might be a tad bumpy." He tried to smile.

STAVE THIRTY-THREE

BYRNE'S STAFF AND THE DETECTIVES

When the soft evening sun sat low, Reginald Byrne called his entire staff and farming crew into the manor to meet the detectives and the bobbie. Cratchit, who had been touring the big house on his own and admiring the paintings and art objects, caught sight of the butler, Herbert O'Malley, who was making sure each worker was presentable. Before lining them in the main hall, he made the farm workers wash their hands and face in the kitchen and tie their kerchiefs neatly around their necks. He had the dairyman remove his filthy apron and comb his hair. The final staff member to arrive was a hunchback, the gardener. O'Malley merely *hmphed* at the bent man who took a position beside the pretty maid, Bonnie Jean Goodacre. O'Malley stood to the side by his wife, Grizelda.

Byrne arrived with his guests and began the introductions. "Misters Scrooge and Cratchit and Officer Blevins, may I introduce my staff. You've already met the O'Malleys. God bless them. And the maid, Bonnie Jean." The young, cheery woman courtseyed. He walked down the line and shook hands with the hunchback gardener, a man of around fifty but fairly spry-looking despite his disability. "This is my magician with plants of all kinds. I give you Rian Simple. He waves his magic wand, and the fruit trees produce abundantly, as does every vegetable and flower in the garden."

"I've been planting the autumn cabbage, Mr Byrne," said Simple in a gravelly voice. "We should have quite a good crop."

"Splendid, Rian." Byrne patted the gardener on the back then proceeded to shake hands with his farming crew. Each man, with some measure of red hair, wore a worn leather vest over a cotton shirt. The belt loops of their trousers were strung with rope, their brogans dirty and ragged.

Byrne tapped the arm of the first man. "This here is Barry Lowe, as mild-mannered and hardworking a man as you'll ever find." Lowe was quite tall, over six feet by several inches, and abjectly thin. He bore an old scar on his left cheek, running over his eyelid onto his forehead, so his eye was bleary red. He bore a pleasant smile under a bushy mustache. Scrooge particularly noticed his large ears protruding from his head.

"Pleased to meet you," said Lowe, his voice a resonant bass.

"And this smiling man," Byrne said, referring to the next squat man who seemed as round as tall, "is Simon Crimp, as hard a worker as you'll ever find."

"Thankee, sir." Crimp took off his chequered cap and bowed.

Byrne shook hands with the next man. "Here is our accomplished dairyman who cares for twelve cows and keeps us and the surrounding homes with milk. The man deserves applause." He shouted, "Hurrah! Lorcan Duffy." He gave a brief clapping, and all the others made a pitiful attempt at applause to the square-shouldered, balding man whose face beamed pink.

Byrne came last to a man who bore no smile. He was tall and the only man with black hair, and he looked like a scowling human mountain. He wore a black suit, though a dusty one. "Gentlemen, I give you my accomplished overseer who has been at the estate for nigh on thirty years. Though other manors try to steal him away, he has chosen to remain at Byrne Hall. My overseer deluxe, Darragh Lynch."

Byrne then introduced his guests to his staff. Each member of the staff gave pleasant approbation statements to the detectives and bobbie.

Cratchit took it upon himself to go and shake hands with each man. He even shook Mrs O'Malley's hand, but when he came to Bonnie Jean Goodacre, he feigned a kiss on her wrist, at which she blushed. Blevins followed suit with handshakes and kind words, but Scrooge hung back and merely nodded. He was too busy taking in details of each person and remembering their names and duties. He thought, *I hope to speak with the dairyman. If he delivers milk for the surrounding farms, by his travels, he may offer some clues. Perhaps a dropped word here or there.*

Cratchit was using a different approach. Though he had no reason to suspect any of the household or farmhands, he wanted a chance to look closely into the eyes of each one. He even shook hands with the cook in order to inspect what herbs might be on her hand. Putting his hand briefly past his nose, he used his strong olfactory sense. He smelled coriander and thyme … and something else. Something sweet like a flower. When he bent to feign the kiss on Bonnie Jean's wrist, he did so in order to perhaps ascertain why her hands were so raw. He would share his thoughts with Scrooge later.

After making a few more positive remarks, Byrne dismissed the staff and farmhands.

When evening closed its doors on the sun, and the wind began howling around the corners of the house and banged often against the windows, Officer Blevins retired earlier than usual. "I didn't sleep much last night. I have much on my mind. I'm anxious to begin investigating these three murders."

"And a break-in," said Byrne.

"Yes. Good-night. I shall be refreshed in the morning."

STAVE THIRTY-FOUR
THE LATE NIGHT DISCUSSION

Scrooge, Cratchit, and their host sat together long into the night. Cratchit asked Byrne, "Were you close to your brother?"

"As close as brothers could be. If I'd known he was in some kind of trouble, I would have immediately come to his aid. He often came round to visit me. Our farms are adjacent. He would share good news of his crops, his workers, or a new maid he wanted to marry, though he never did. He was an idealist, always wanting the best for everyone. Then, some six months back, after a trip to Dublin, he took on a different air. He seemed distracted. Suddenly, one day, he dismissed several of his house staff, even his cook, and then all the farmhands, save Malachi, his overseer of some twenty years. There was no one to harvest the crop, and the land is now fallow and the wheat overrun with weeds." Byrne drew a deep breath.

"That is a sad loss," Cratchit said.

Byrne turned his face from his guests and looked out at the dark sky where the wind blew turbulent clouds about. "Sean began talking about a treasure he hoped to find every time he came to visit. When I would take my walks, I twice watched him wander around the old Kindlestown Castle sitting astride his land and mine. He would dig in the soil with a small spade near a wall, then race inside the building, then come out and look fervently at some scrap of paper, then move on to tapping various stones of a wall. When I joined him, he was as cordial and sane as always, and our conversation was genuine enough, but … now, he's gone." He turned back to Scrooge and Cratchit, his visage morose, his eyes downturned.

"Ebenezer and I are so sorry for your loss," Cratchit said.

"What can you tell us about the death of your brother?" Scrooge asked.

"I was away in France when his body was found on the moor by a poor tenant potato farmer, a neighbour of ours. Sean's body was hauled into Wicklow to the constable who simply pronounced him dead. Since we have no other relatives in Ireland, as the rest have emigrated to America, the constable gave the body to the priest who arranged a wake for him in the church rectory and sent word to me. I hear large numbers of folks who knew him came and prayed. Many rosaries were prayed. I heard his farm's caretaker, Malachi Doyle, made a fine eulogy at his funeral. 'Twas printed in the paper."

Scrooge leaned forwards in his chair. "You told me, Reginald, that Sean was found holding a small box on his chest. Any idea what was inside?"

"Nay. All I know is the constable received the box from the farmer who had discovered Sean and then gave the box to the mayor who gave it to Malachi to hold for me. However, he didn't wish to have it, so he gave it back to the mayor. I've seen the box. It's locked with no key and made with fine workmanship, filigree gold inlaid along with sapphires and abalone. It is a simple jewellry box. Nothing more. Having no use for it myself, I left it with Mayor Kelly."

"Has anyone opened it?" asked Scrooge.

"Not that I'm aware of," said Byrne. "It's just a pretty box."

"And the mayor's been murdered?" confirmed Cratchit.

"Aye. His throat cut." Byrne sighed. "He was a good man."

"Does the wife have an idea who might have done it?" Scrooge asked.

Byrne rubbed his chin. "I know not. I only received word of his murder from a friend in Dublin. I don't even know if the constables have made any effort in the cause. The police are English, not Irish, and seem to have only disparaging opinions about the Irish, which they often expound upon in the ale houses."

"Hmm," Cratchit said. "I think Mr Scrooge and I would like to have an interview with the mayor's wife and Malachi Doyle tomorrow, if possible."

"And the neighbour tenant farmer," Scrooge added.

Byrne agreed. "We'll go early in the morning."

Scrooge and Cratchit bid good evening to their host and retired to their rooms. Scrooge did not put on his sleeping gown, for he knew Cratchit would soon be arriving, and he did. Cratchit slipped quietly into Scrooge's bedroom. He sat in a plush chair across from Scrooge who settled on the edge of the bed.

"Ebenezer, what are your thoughts?" Cratchit began.

"I took note of each staff member and farmhand and was just committing them to paper when you arrived. Firstly, I don't immediately believe any of Byrne's staff would have cause to kill their benefactor's brother, unless there was a squabble that turned violent. Most seemed congenial and pleased with Reginald and their station at the estate. All seemed happy and smiled abundantly, save his overseer, Lynch, who appeared stoic or maybe even bothered by having to stand and be introduced. If anyone looked to be a pugnacious criminal, he would fit the bill."

"As we both know, however," Cratchit said, "a sour face does not a criminal make, and smiles can often hide a foul intent."

Scrooge agreed. "As I have seen many times by those who make stories as to why they cannot produce payment on their loans."

"I made a point of standing close to measure the men, plus the two women, on Byrne's staff. Each man gave a firm handshake, though the dairyman's felt soft. Too much time with milk, I conjecture. Mrs O'Malley's hands smelled of cooking spices but also of some sweet flower. Perhaps she has been making an arrangement of flowers, though this late in the fall, I doubt it."

"Yes." Scrooge smiled. "I saw you kiss the hand of the young maid. I'm not sure your wife would be pleased."

"Just a courtesy. I only pretended a kiss, as I love my wife far too much. I wanted to feel why her hands were so rough and raw. Simply washing dishes would not be the cause of that. She winced a bit when I took her hand."

"Well, raw hands are hardly suspicious, nor is the smell of flowers."

"You're right, Ebenezer. Perhaps I'm overthinking this. My first thoughts are that some other criminal of the town or fields is our murderer."

"I concur. Let us speak with the constable tomorrow as well."

"Agreed."

When Scrooge turned in, his mind was occupied with thoughts of his loan business and what funds he might be losing. He thought, *Yes, Hiram Grumbles is a capable businessman. Still ...*

STAVE THIRTY-FIVE
MORE QUESTIONS, NO ANSWERS

Byrne's landau carriage drove into the small community of Wicklow. Byrne pointed out to Scrooge, Cratchit, and Blevins the ruins of the Dominican Monastery where the priests were working in the garden of the town's Catholic church, and the gaol where Billy Byrne, a relative of Reginald, was hanged during the Irish 1798 rebellion.*

"The Presbyterians didn't approve of the overbearing attitude of the Anglican church," Byrne explained, "and being inspired by the American and French revolutions, they conspired to break free from England's iron grip. They were joined by various Catholics, but the British brought in their fine, cruel army and easily quelled the rebellion. What can farmers with rakes do against a well-trained army with muskets? My distant relative was caught, tried, and hanged."

"What was the big black rock castle we passed?" Scrooge asked.

"'Twas built by a Fitzgerald after the Norman invasion of England and has always been called the 'Black Castle.' In 1641, during one of our many Irish rebellions, my forebears and the O'Tooles held the castle. The English general, Sir Charles Cootes, arrived in Wicklow with his army and drove them out. He then turned on the town and essentially annihilated the entire population, engaging in savage and indiscriminate killing. He ordered his men to shove a good number of the poor farmers and townsfolk into a building, locked the doors, and set it ablaze.* He hated the Catholics and only stopped killing them when he realised that if he killed them all, he'd have no one over whom to rule."

"Ireland has had its share of tragedy," Blevins said mournfully.

The carriage rolled to a stop. "Ah," Byrne said. "Here's the mayor's house, now a house of sadness. The windows are still draped in mourning black."

After Byrne banged the door's knocker several times, and Blevins rapped his nightstick on the same door, a dowdy, teary-eyed woman finally opened it.

"Ah, Mrs Kelly," said Byrne. "We are all pleased to see you but, at the same time, overwhelmed with grief for the loss of your esteemed husband, our Mayor Timothy Kelly."

Mrs Kelly, with abundant wrinkles on her face wherein the tears trickled, snuffled and bade the men to enter. "I've put the kettle on," she said.

After introducing his companions, Byrne explained how they were there to gather facts with which to bring the murderer to justice. They took seats around her, and a maid, dressed in a bright, clean dress and smock, brought in tea for everyone. Scrooge unconsciously observed every detail he could of his surroundings and the appearance of the mayor's wife and the plain-faced maid, being neither pretty nor ugly. He took note of each aspect and tried to remember them. The maid gave polite smiles to each gentlemen. Then she gave a wink and knowing look to Cratchit, which did not go unnoticed by Scrooge.

After all the company had sipped some of their tea, Mrs Kelly turned directly to Scrooge and Cratchit who sat next to each other on a settee. "I know of ye detectives. The story o' the roundin' up the dog-men and the rioters by ye made the papers 'ere. 'Twas quite the tale."

"Yes, well," responded Cratchit, "we really had little to do with rounding up the criminals. That was more the work of our fine Metropolitan, of which Corporal Blevins is part."

She turned to Blevins. "Yes, what 'ave ye to say?"

Blevins cleared his throat. "I am here at the behest of Her Majesty to uncover all we can regarding these murders. I hope to know all you can tell us."

Her eyes darkened. "I should think the Crown would be more concerned about the thousands of Irish dyin' from starvation 'cause of the potato blight.

There is the real murder." Her face grew fierce. "I'll 'ave ye know, me husband, Timothy, was doin' all he could to 'elp the poor starvin' farmers. He further was tryin' to get to the bottom o' who killed our good friend, Sean Byrne. A fine lot the English policemen were; them makin' no attempt to look into it at all. No one from Dublin or our own county has even asked a single question."

Scrooge noted her lilting Irish accent, a stark difference from the tone of those persons with whom he was in contact in London.

"Very well, what can you tell us?" Blevins took out a small notepad and pencil.

"About the break in and the demise of your husband," said Scrooge.

"Well, first," she said then wiped her runny nose and eyes, "there was the break-in. A fellow came to me door, claimin' to be a tinker an' askin' about 'oles in me pots an' pans that needed blockin'. I told 'im I 'ad no 'oles fo' 'im to fill in me cookware and was closin' the door when he burst in and began demandin.' He yelled, 'Where is it?'" She paused.

"Where was what?" Cratchit asked.

"Why! I knew not what he wanted, but he was most insistent. He stormed 'bout the house, frightenin' me maid and 'er child, pullin' open drawers, goin' in the bedrooms, and ploughin' through our clothes. I tried to stop 'im, but he kept demandin'. I tell him whatever he was lookin' fo' was 'id. Since I didn' know what he wanted, I couldn' tell 'im. After he made a mess o' the place, he stomped out."

"What did he look like, Mrs Kelly?" Scrooge asked.

"Like a tinker. He 'ad a hammer on 'is belt and a bag o' pieces o' tin clankin' 'round."

"Yes, but was he tall? Short? Thin? Any marks about his face?" Scrooge pressed for more details.

"Oh," Mrs Kelly continued. "He was movin' so fast. I would say he was 'bout me 'eight. Sort o' round. Lots o' energy. He wore a leather apron. I think he may 'ave been bald, but he wore a cap. Filthy shoes. I remember those. Walked all o'er me carpets."

After her last remarks, the group fell silent. The maid appeared at the bottom of the stairs and beckoned Cratchit with a head nod then returned upstairs.

Cratchit arose suddenly. "May I look around?"

"I suppose," Mrs Kelly said.

Cratchit departed into the kitchen briefly then made his way upstairs to the bedrooms. Though Blevins and Byrne and Mrs Kelly were engaged in a discussion of the woman's future, Scrooge could nominally hear his partner having a conversation with two persons, a woman and child.

Byrne patted Mrs Kelly on the hand. "There, there, Gwendolyn. You have been most helpful. I know Mr Scrooge and Officer Blevins want to know what you can tell them about your husband's murder."

The matronly woman drew herself up. "It was the night o' the tinker throwin' things about. Edgar came 'ome at twilight and went 'bout settin' everythin' aright. Then he stepped outside to smoke his pipe like he always did. He said he would contact the police in the mornin'. When he didn't come back after an 'our, I went outside and found 'im dead wit' his throat cut from ear to ear. All his jacket and trouser pockets were turned out. He looked so peaceful and pitiful, both. My maid and 'er boy and I were able to bring the body inside. Then the rain broke. It poured. The next mornin', neighbour men took his body to the church. The priest 'imself cleaned the body and made 'im presentable fo' the wake." She burst into tears, putting her face in her hands.

"Did the police find anything?" Scrooge asked.

"They didn't show up for two days. They ne'er asked a question. Said they'd seen the body at the church. That was 'bout all they did."

After a few more questions from Blevins and Scrooge, Cratchit returned from upstairs. The men offered condolences to Mrs Kelly, bade her farewell, and departed.

Before getting in the carriage, Cratchit showed Scrooge a pretty jewellry box with a round, hinged lid. Weathered wood with inlaid abalone and chips of sapphire; the box was locked with no key. "The maid gave me this," Cratchit said. "She said she knew the thief was looking for it because it had been valuable to Mayor Kelly. She kept it hidden in her apron pocket."

"That's amazing. And she never told his wife she was keeping it?"

"No. Apparently, the mayor had reason to keep it secret from his wife. That's what she intimated. The maid, a widow named Sally O'Neil, said the mayor told her it had been found on Sean Byrne's dead body."

Scrooge's eyes grew wide. "Could she tell us anything about the man of the break-in?"

"No, but her son said the man, when he first came to the door, was speaking with an Irish accent, but as he roamed about the home, his accent changed to English. He was certain of it."

"Hmm. An Englishman pretending to be Irish." Scrooge stepped into the carriage. "Interesting."

Once everyone was inside, Byrne directed the driver to go to the farmer who had discovered the dead body on the moor.

When Cratchit shared with Byrne and Blevins about the jewellry box, Byrne exclaimed, "That's the one I saw! It's fetching but looks weathered."

Cratchit handed him the box. He turned it over and over. "And it's locked with no key."

When Cratchit shared about the intruder's changing accent, Blevins became visibly upset. He asked to see the box, and Byrne handed it to him.

Blevins looked long at the box in his hands. "I have an ill feeling about this box. This does not bode well. Her Majesty will want to know of it."

"When we return to my estate," Byrne said, "we'll find a way to open it."

"We mustn't damage it," Blevins said and placed it gingerly on the seat beside him.

STAVE THIRTY-SIX
THE POTATO FARMER'S RENDITION OF FACTS

Byrne's carriage halted in front of a home with rock walls and a thatched roof. A single window was covered with a shutter, and the thin wooden door hung on rope hinges. A grey, muley-horned cow chewed its cud not twenty feet from the hut. Blevins announced, "In Gaelic, that cow is a Maol."

Several small, freckled children played a game of spinning-tops in the dirt yard. Scrooge attempted to number them, but they moved too quickly, and he lost count. An older lad was repairing the roof, patching a hole in the thatch. Two young maidens with red hair tied with ribbons worked at a washtub, scrubbing clothes on a washboard then hanging the clothes on a line. The mother, a slim woman with a soft, gentle face and a few grey strands in her red hair, was mending a torn pair of trousers. None of the family's clothes were without patches.

The four men stepped from the carriage and bid "good mornings" to the family who waved back and sang "hellos" cheerily.

At that moment, the husband of the farm family came strolling in from his potato farm, whistling an Irish tune and bearing a sack of potatoes on his back. Beside him walked the largest hound Scrooge and Cratchit had ever seen, its head almost even to the man's chest. It was shaggy and bluish-grey-haired and barked twice at the newcomers. A bundle of twigs was tied on its back. Scrooge moved behind Officer Blevins, who was also astounded by the size of the dog.

The farmer ambled up to the four visitors and bade them, "Top o' the mornin' to ye." Then he called to his wife, "Who be these guests?"

She merely shrugged and kept at her mending.

The children yelled in a disjointed, discant chorus to their father, "'ello, Da!"

The farmer placed his sack on the ground and spat. He patted the dog who had sat with its tongue hanging out in a sort of grin. Then the man washed his hands in a bowl of water atop the small rock wall before turning to the four men. "Well, I'm guessin' ye'll have to be tellin' me who ye be. But make it quick, I ain't got donkey years★ to listen to some tale o' woe by lost travellers." He dried his hands on his filthy trousers then removed the bundles of twigs from the dog and handed them to two of the young boys. "Run 'em inside fo' the 'earth, wee ones." The boys scampered away with the hound on their heels. The hound's shoulders were even with the boys' towheads.

Byrne spoke first. "Mister James Callahan, you've a fine family here."

"Like as not." The wry man of about forty years spat again and turned a burning blue eye at the detectives.

"Kind sir," Byrne began again, "my name is Reginald Byrne. I live in the estate—"

"Aye, I knew 'tis ye. I knew yer ole fella and ole wan, Malcolm and Sarah. Fine couple and fine parents. If somethin' was done arseways★ anywhere, Malcolm fixed it plumb right. That he did."

"Thank you, Mister Callahan. Those are kind words about my parents. May I introduce my friends, all of whom are adept at solving crimes." After he had introduced the detectives and officer, and all had shaken hands, Byrne continued, "We are here to gain what knowledge we can regarding the death of my brother, Sean. You found him on the moor not far from your farm."

"That be true. But I be knackered★ now from all me work, and me wife be wantin' me to fetch in the taters fo' supper, so I'll speak quickly." He rubbed his jaw then flicked his fingers, beckoning them closer. Blevins took out his pad and pencil. Scrooge, Cratchit, and Byrne gathered around the farmer. He began in a whisper, "Me wife don' take to me carryin' on 'bout no death. She claims it invokes the banshees o' which too many o' 'em be roamin' 'bout all o' this emerald isle. I be fortunate in that I 'ave a few acres and not just a plot o' land like so many poor Jacks. And I be far enough east, away from where the potato blight be ruinin' everythin' out west and south. I only hope it don' make its way 'ere. St Patrick, pray fo' us." He looked up at the sky and made the sign of the cross. "Now, where was I?"

"Getting to the part where you discovered my brother's body," Byrne said.

"Ah, the weather was awful good but was a-changin' rapidly. Storm was a-makin' fo' a strong brew. I was headin' fo' 'ome wit' a load o' peat fo' the fire, and a recent rain 'ad washed out me usual path, so I takes off o'er the peat fields and the swampy areas, pickin' me feet up and bein' extra careful where they landed. Suddenly, I sights the quarest* thing. There was this man laid out on 'is back. Naturally, I launches forwards to see to 'is 'ealth. He's got a bottle in one 'and, so I first thinks he's fluthered.*"

Scrooge held up his hand. "What does *fluthered* mean?"

"It means he looked like he'd 'ad a whale o' a time and got too many drinks in 'im," said Callahan. He snickered. "'appened to me many's the time. So, I examines Sean's body and finds he be ready for a wake at the church. Dead as a rock."

"Was there any evidence of foul play?" Blevins asked, tapping his pencil on his pad.

"Foul play? Not that I could see right aways, but ..." Callahan paused. His listeners bent forwards as he whispered even softer. "I've lived 'ere me 'ole life, and if a man gets unsquared, he don' take off into the moor, especially not that one. He sleeps outside the pub or stumbles 'ome. I don' care 'ow drunk ye be. And the bottle still sloshed. I be advisin' that some sleeven did 'im in." He hmphed and crossed his arms.

"I'm guessing," said Cratchit, "a *sleeven* is your term for some underhanded person."

"Right ye be."

"Did you see anyone else nearby?" Blevins asked.

"No ... wait. I did see a man, but he was far off, too far fo' me to 'oller at 'im or fetch 'im. He was headin' aways from there. 'Twas just me."

"Could you show us exactly where you found him?" Scrooge asked.

"As long as ye'll be joinin' me at the pub down the road a piece, and ye buys the first two rounds." Callahan smiled a toothy grin through his grizzled beard.

STAVE THIRTY-SEVEN
THE SCENE OF THE MURDER

After Callahan took the potatoes to his wife, he led Byrne, Blevins, Scrooge, and Cratchit on a half-mile jaunt to where he had discovered Sean Byrne's body. At the point where they left the road, they found themselves stepping into swampy pools which rose past their ankles. Scrooge was careful to follow last in the line, hoping to avoid treading in the goo where the others had walked, but it was of no use, for he twice floundered in the murky puddles. He shook himself after each dousing and muttered, "Why am I doing this?"

At last, they arrived at the death scene. A small patch of rough peat spread before a remarkable tumble of boulders of diverse sizes. Cratchit began examining the ground in a wide circle for any clues while Scrooge peered at the grey boulders laden with moss, lichens, and vines. He quickly noticed various graffiti etchings had been made upon the rocks. He guessed travellers who had ventured there over the centuries had felt compelled to leave a remembrance. Some markings were symbols, some were representations of animals, and some appeared to be whole sentences carved in an ancient tongue. The detective spirit in him surged forwards. "What do you suppose this row of markings means?"

Byrne and Blevins came closer. "Why, it's Gaelic words," Byrne said. He moved closer to decipher them. "This string of markings—a sentence,

in essence—say these are the stones hurled here by St Patrick himself."
He brushed away some hanging vines. "Look! Here is more. It's not just
a sentence but a whole paragraph." While Blevins began jotting on his
notepad, Byrne ran his finger along the Gaelic words. "Roughly, it states,
'Herein lies the remains of the stone statues of the temple of the god,
Crom Cruaich.'"

Byrne turned to Blevins, Callahan, Scrooge, and Cratchit. "In Irish
lore, Crom Cruaich was the demon god of fertility who required sacrifices
of cattle and, sometimes, people. According to legend, he was brought to
Ireland by one of the early high kings, King Tigernmas." He turned back
to running his fingers along the markings. "Some words have worn away
with time, but it seems to detail how Tigernmas and his whole army were
worshiping this false god one day and were suddenly removed from the
world. It says the date was Samhain." He faced the four men again. "That
day is now our Christian eve of all hallows. It was on Halloween, which
comes in a few days."

"Well, I'll be," Callahan said, rubbing his whiskers. "I ne'er knew such a
tale 'bout this spot. Guess I ne'er went out o' me way to get 'ere, 'cept when
I found the body."

Scrooge began trembling. He thought, *"Removed from the world"? A whole
army just vanished? What kind of power could do that?* He gulped.

"What does this line say?" Cratchit pointed at words much lower than
the rest. "Is this Gaelic also?"

Byrne bent down. "I can barely make out what it says." He ran his fingers
over the etched markings several times. "I believe it is relating to how St
Patrick stood on a hilltop opposite Magh Slecht. I learned from my da that
it was the temple of the dark god of fertility. The writing explains how
the saint cast his famous staff, Bachul Isu, at the temple, which caused the
golden god to melt and the twelve stone statues on Magh Slecht to be flung
here." He stood. "I must surmise that St Patrick turned the statues into
these boulders."

Though Scrooge was wary of what he had heard, and his mind raced to
wondering what form of witchcraft surrounded the place, he joined all the
men who set about counting the stack of boulders, jumbled together, some

lying atop others, and of various sizes. One was as big as an Irish hut, but most were about the size of a small cart.

"I count twelve," Cratchit announced.

"As do I," said Blevins.

Scrooge pointed at the boulders. "It is indeed twelve."

Byrne and Callahan agreed.

Byrne returned to where he had just read the words and strode to his left towards a smaller stack of three boulders. "Look here," he said. The other men drew near, leaning over his shoulders. "There is a St Patrick's Celtic cross etched above this spot where these two boulders sit atop this lower, flatter one. Where the three boulders meet, there is a triangle-shaped opening. Below the cross are words which are absolutely in Latin." He lowered to his knees and examined the words more closely. He released a long sigh and leaned his head against the boulder.

"What does it say?" Scrooge asked, worried the spot was home to an Irish demon covered by a Latin incantation.

"It says, 'Hic est gazae.' It translates to, 'Herein lies the treasure.'"

All the men took on grim faces. At that moment, a wild wind whipped around them, tearing Cratchit's hat from his head and sending him chasing after it. Off to the west, an immense, dark storm cloud grumbled with lightning hurling towards the ground.

Byrne called into the wind while the others bent against the gale, "That's why my brother was here! He found what he had been looking for!"

STAVE THIRTY-EIGHT

THE DEAD MAN'S FOREMAN

After speaking with the Wicklow constable, who offered nothing in the way of clues, the men returned to the manor, where Blevins offered to hold on to the box for safekeeping. "I've learned a few tricks at opening locks. I have tools in my bag." He shook the box. "It appears to have nothing inside, but I'll give it a go."

The others approved of his attempt, so he headed upstairs to his room. Scrooge sat down with a pen and some foolscap and scribbled several notes. He remarked to the others, "The constable gave us nothing. What exactly is his job if he does not investigate a murder?"

Byrne agreed. "Tomorrow, we'll talk to Malachi, the only man left on Sean's estate. Now, I'm going to see what great supper Grizelda O'Malley is preparing for us." He headed for the kitchen.

Cratchit drew close to Scrooge and whispered, "Have you noticed Reginald has said nothing about a will from Sean who has been dead for over a month?"

"That is a good point. Perhaps one was never made, or it's not been located."

"It would be good to know who was listed as beneficiaries and discover if they had a reason to cause his demise."

"And Reginald has not explained why he was in France," Scrooge added. "What business would he have had there?"

The butler, O'Malley, strode into the room. "Supper is served."

Scrooge pushed his notes into a jacket pocket as he and Cratchit went to supper.

Blevins came down shortly and shrugged his shoulders. "I've tried some key tools on the box, but nothing yet. I daren't break it."

At supper, a thought which had been riding in Scrooge's mind finally bubbled forth, and he said to Blevins and Byrne, "You Irish know a great deal about the spirits and such in your isle."

They laughed, nodding their heads.

Scrooge frowned. "Then tell me this. In London, a particular black cat ventured near me. I know its appearance well, for it gave me quite a start. At first, I believed it to be a serpent in the shadows of an alley. Then it emerged from the darkness, and I saw it was an all-black cat, save for the white mark on its nose, shaped just like a heart. That *same cat* crossed my path and yours, Reginald, the night at Chichester's home when we made our way to the stable. Moments later, we faced the foul dead thing that sucks blood, and while we were escaping, we were fortunate enough to be saved by the huge black horse driving the ghoul away. What is all that?"

Grizelda put down her serving spoon. "Ye see, Mr Scrooge, ye surely faced the dire evil of the creature whose name I will not mention. Now, on the other hand, that cat ye saw was a pooka, a shape-shifter. That same pooka was there to keep an eye on ye. When the foul one chased ye, the pooka changed into a stallion. Almost all pookas are black. They generally mean no harm and can be of aid when most ye need it. But don't fail to believe in 'em, or they'll pull some scary mischief on ye." She took up her spoon and kept serving vegetables on the plates and handed them to Bonnie Jean who set them at each man's place.

Byrne said, "That pretty much sums it up. You had a pooka looking after you. At first, it sought to put a scare in you when it took the form of a serpent. Pookas enjoy playing tricks on folks. It then changed into a harmless cat. For some reason, it decided to help you. But *don't dare* refuse to believe in them. That would surely bring bad luck. We'll seek out a four-leaf clover for you tomorrow. You can keep it in your pocket for further good luck."

While they finished their meal, Scrooge was not entirely certain of the explanation given him, but he decided, based on all the experiences he'd had so far in Ireland, he would definitely believe in pookas.

⁓⊗⁓

The next day, after Byrne had found a four-leaf clover and given it to Scrooge, the four men journeyed to Sean's manor. Malachi Doyle, Sean's foreman, met them at the door. He was a man in his late forties and had sunburned arms and face. His hair was the brightest red Scrooge had ever witnessed.

Scrooge noted how tidy the home was, despite Malachi being the only man there. They had barely sat down to discuss the matter of Sean's death and how Malachi had been maintaining the estate when a becoming lass pranced down the stairs. She wore a light-yellow dress with a pretty lace shawl around her shoulders. She was about twenty years old with dark-black hair. Each man was surprised to see her and taken by her good looks. Malachi, smiling abundantly, introduced her as Matilda, the love of his life. She shook hands with each of the men, gave Malachi a peck on the cheek, and flounced to the door. "I'll be back soon, my darling. Don't fret." She made a pouty face at him then exited, closing the door softly. Through the windows, the men could see her skipping down the road.

Malachi sighed blissfully. "I've not expected such a gift in my life. Although she does cost me a pretty penny. She loves to shop, and I cannot deny her. Despite my strong denials, she always convinces me, and I buy what she wants."

Scrooge had noted the many rings on her fingers, and he wondered if the necklace around her neck was made of gold.

"I take it," said Byrne, "that since my brother's death, you have not received any wages. Surely, you're not allowing her to plough through your savings."

"Not at all," Malachi said. "When Mister Byrne set about his treasure huntin', as he called it, he told me to help myself to whatever funds I needed to keep the house runnin'. I've done so now for all the time he was off on his hunt and for this time whilst he's been dead. I figured I should uphold the place as best I could until the will be read. If I'm about the place, I imagine I am keepin' the thieves away. That's my own thinkin'. You're his brother, Mister Byrne. If you've a mind I should leave, I'll pack up right away." The whole time of his monologue, he was smiling.

Byrne reflected on Malachi's words. "No, no. Stay here for the time being. I've got a lawyer out of Dublin trying to find the will. I would imagine he has left you something in exchange for your loyalty and valuable service."

Malachi beamed.

"Do you know," Scrooge inquired, "why he would dismiss all his staff and farmhands, especially in these troubled times?"

"I do," answered Malachi with further smiles. "He told me he didn't want anyone seein' what he was a doin'. No one was to know of his efforts. He gave each of his workers, when he let them go, a small sum and a letter to take to other future employers. After they all left, I've not heard from a single one of them. So, I'm bidin' my time, keepin' everythin' tidy, maintainin' his horse and cow, hoein' the garden, and such." He made a movement like he was hoeing some weeds then chuckled.

Cratchit wondered if the man's ebullient attitude was because he was hiding something. "Is there anything we should know about Sean which might help us discover who murdered him?"

Malachi looked surprised. "I didn't know he was murdered. I thought he just died of a bad heart. He drank a lot, you know."

"It is my opinion," said Byrne, "that he was murdered, which is why I have these detectives and the policeman with me."

Blevins now took a turn at questioning the man. "What can you tell us about the days before he died? Anything unusual? Did he eat? Did he sleep?"

Malachi had finally dropped his smile and rubbed his chin. "Come to think of it … Well, I couldn't cook an egg, much less a meal for him, but fortunately, neighbours came to look in on him. They were all concerned. Even Mrs O'Malley, Mister Byrne's cook, brought him fresh baked bread and some home-brewed beer every day. He was never wantin' for food, but I took to worryin' for his health. I encouraged him to eat more. However, for the last two weeks before he died, he ever so often took to doin' the never-endin' jig dance and fallin over in a heap on the ground. Twice, I had to carry him in the house, and he was babblin', and his eyes were all starry-like. I became worried for his mind. I've seen that sort of thing from a man who drinks too much. He had 'drunken fever.'"

Byrne became visibly upset. "I wish you had told me earlier. Perhaps he died of some illness, or ..." He sobbed, his body shaking. "Or he drank himself to death from loneliness."

"Or a witch's curse," Malachi said flatly. He squinched an eye at each man. "If 'twere a curse, it didn't hold. He seemed to recover a few days before his death. As a matter of fact, one night, two days before he passed, he told me to come to the window. We both seen some shadowy men with torches up on the hill, pokin' around the old Kindlestown Castle. It had him quite upset. We couldn't tell what they looked like. He headed out to the castle, but when he got there, they were gone. He swore he didn't like anyone pokin' around up there."

"So, he never uncovered the men's identities?" Cratchit said.

"No, he just kept studyin' them books with strange writin' in them that I ain't never seen before. Ate very little, just the bread and beer, kept searchin' most of the days, always carryin' a small shovel with him."

"May we see the books he was reading?" Cratchit asked.

"Well, you're welcome to look in his library. It's full of his books."

Blevins rose and quickly made his way to the library. He lifted and looked at a handful of books on a table, slapped the opened ones shut, and then returned. "I don't think there's anything there to help us."

"I think I'll take a look," Scrooge said. He walked into the library and first inspected the shelves for several minutes. He could hear Blevins and Cratchit attempt to console Byrne, and Malachi chatter about his young lover and how he intended to marry her. After examining the shelves for quite some time, Scrooge finally stopped at the stack of books on the table. One book lay open. He could make no sense of the scribbles on the page. He recognised the markings as not being of the standard European alphabet. He returned. "I don't see anything of use."

Matilda burst through the door as happy as a lark, holding a basket of bread and greens, and threw herself into Malachi's arms. The four visitors excused themselves from the couple and departed. The lovers bid them happy farewell and waved after them.

On their way to the carriage, walking well behind Byrne and Blevins, Scrooge remarked to Cratchit, "I sorely wish Lockie was here. I have a task only he can do."

Cratchit replied, "There are too many unanswered questions in this string of murders. We could certainly use an extra hand, specifically Lockie's. At least we know there is a will, and Byrne has someone looking for it."

Once the men were in the carriage, Byrne had his head down as he mumbled, "Maybe Sean wasn't murdered but died of drinking too much."

STAVE THIRTY-NINE

ALL THE CLOCKS ON THE WALLS STOPPED

In the late afternoon, Scrooge and Cratchit strode briskly from the manor to the small house of the farm overseer, Darragh Lynch. Though the sun was setting, and Lynch was finished with his farmwork, they found him in his shed, toiling away at an anvil and hammering a bent plough blade straight. Even when the detectives approached, he kept hammering, never looking up.

In between the hammer blows, Cratchit cleared his throat, and Lynch eyed the men but kept at his labour. Finally, Cratchit hollered, "Mr Lynch, if you please?"

Lynch halted, set down his hammer, and wiped his hands and brow with a dirty cloth. "What'll it be, gentlemen?" He turned away from them to a bucket of water and splashed his face.

Scrooge cocked his head, and Cratchit shrugged, neither having been able to hear him.

With his back turned to them, Lynch bellowed, "What'll it be, sirs?"

"You call us gentlemen," said Cratchit, "but you don't treat us so. You won't even face us."

Ever so slowly, the huge man turned, rolling up the sleeves on his strong arms. "I'm listenin'."

"We hope you can tell us anything that might help us ..." Scrooge gulped, seeing Lynch's eyes glaring, "in our investigation of the murder of Sean Byrne."

"Who said he was murdered?" Lynch picked up the hammer and tapped it in a steady rhythm on the plough blade.

Cratchit stepped forwards, hands on his hips. "We don't mean to take much of your time. Just answer some questions."

"Very well." Lynch put down the hammer and sat on a tree stump. "Ask away."

"Where ... where were you when he died?" Scrooge asked timorously, for though Cratchit seemed to be acting bravely around the big man, he felt intimidated.

"Nowhere in particular since I don't know when he died." Lynch then spoke a phrase in Gaelic. "*Ar uair an bháis.*" Then he translated, "At the moment of his death, me neighbours all said the clocks on their walls stopped. That is, those few neighbours who have a clock at all." He leaned over, grimacing, and rubbed his backside. "I work too hard, saints preserve us. *Is fearr lúbadh ná briseadh.*"

Cratchit shook his head. "I'm sorry, what did you just say?"

"I said, ''Tis better to bend than to break.'" Lynch sighed.

"All right," Cratchit said. "What have you *heard* about his death?"

Lynch again spoke in Gaelic. "*Bás a raibh baint ag alcól leis.*" Then he said nothing but turned towards the setting sun, still rubbing his back.

A moment passed. "Which means?" asked Cratchit.

"That he died of too much alcohol. *Méala mór a bhás, drochscéal ceart a bhás.*" A tear showed on one eyelid. "In your English tongue, that translates to 'his death was a great loss.' To me, his death was a travesty." The man appeared to be ready to break down in tears.

"Mr Lynch, sir," Scrooge said in a conciliatory tone, "I know you work for Sean's brother, Reginald, but were you close to Sean?"

"Aye, you could say that. He was engaged to me sister and devoted to her, he was. You could see his love for her. But she died out on the moor, just like he did. I believe that's why he drank so much." The tears trickled down his cheeks. He wiped his eyes with his palms. "What else, Misters Scrooge and Cratchit?"

"Tell us about the two farmhands. I believe their names are Barry Lowe and Simon Crimp."

"That's right. Two fine labourers. Generally, they work hard, though sometimes, I have to teach 'em a skill or two. Lowe and Crimp came on after the previous farmhands were found drunk by Mr Byrne. He dismissed 'em immediately. I was plum worried 'bout bringin' in the fall crop meself when Crimp and Lowe showed up lookin' for work the next day. Mr Byrne hired 'em. They're quiet types. Never begrucchen* nothin'. Not into drinkin'. No mots* hangin' 'round. Turns out, they're brothers by different das. Once in a while, Mr Byrne lets 'em ride his thoroughbreds into Dublin to visit their ailin' mother and visit the graves o' their two das in Donnybrook cemetery. They always come back appreciative, and they ask what work I have for 'em."

Cratchit asked, "Can you think of what cause they would have to murder Sean Byrne?"

"I can't. They told me they only arrived from western Ireland where the potato blight is ruinin' every spud in every farm. I doubt they even knew Sean."

"Anything else you can tell us?" Scrooge asked.

"Nay. They go to church on Sundays. Always sit in the back. I think they might've had some schoolin'. They don't talk like a typical, uneducated Irish potato farmer. More formal-like. I guess the hard times is hittin' everyone, not just the farmers."

That evening, Byrne did not join his guests for supper but stayed in his room. When Cratchit walked by, he heard Byrne sobbing.

STAVE FORTY

TIM, THE AERONAUT, AND A SAD OUTCOME

Racing along in the lighter-than-air balloon, propelled by a stiff wind, Tim Cratchit looked down through breaks in the dark storm clouds. He scanned the craggy coast of western England and guessed they were above Cornwall, for he saw two pump towers for some companies' mines and two small miners' towns. Beyond the coastline was the grey ocean, stretching to what seemed like the end of the world to him. He felt both amazed and frightened.

Mr Green stood beside him. "Looks like we're going to sail over the ocean, Tim. The way this gale is driving our balloon, you'll get to see Ireland where your father has journeyed."

"It should be delightful," Tim replied and pulled the blanket tighter around him.

"Are you warm enough?"

"I guess I'll have to be. Might we ever be away from this storm?"

"My guess is it will diminish once we're over the ocean."

Within minutes after the balloon glided over the ocean, the temperature dropped precipitously. Frost immediately started gathering on the balloon fabric, and Tim began shivering in the salty breeze. His hands and face hurt from the icy blasts the sky was throwing at him. He ducked down in the basket. Mr Green pulled a heavy coat from a sack, along with a woollen cap and comforter. He put on the coat and tossed the hat and comforter to Tim who quickly donned the apparel, but he still shivered, drawing his knees up close to his chest. Mr Green plopped down next to Tim and put his strong arm around the boy to share warmth.

After a half hour, ice was forming everywhere on the balloon and basket.

"Tim," said Mr Green, whose teeth were now chattering. "We must be over a mile high. I've got to take the balloon down so we won't freeze to death." He rose onto his knees and peered over the side. "It looks like the storm has drained itself out over the ocean." He stood and undid the secure ties of the release valve to let the hydrogen gas begin to release. While the inflatable let out its gasping sound, he gathered the barometer and estimated their height.

Tim's ears began popping unmercifully, and his teeth still chattered.

Suddenly, they were surrounded by light-grey clouds laden with moisture. "Get ready, Tim, I believe we're going to get a little wet. The lightning is gone, but there is still some moisture."

In a moment, a gentle rain surrounded them, leaving them soaked. Mr Green stood again and again and tightened the straps holding the valve then loosened and tightened them once more, attempting to control their descent. "I don't want to land us in the Irish Sea. I'm not sure how well this basket floats," he said, attempting to lighten the mood.

Tim gave a bleak smile, for he felt miserably cold. His clothes clung like plaster to him, and water dripped from his wool cap in streams down his face. He snuffled.

Then, as quickly as it had begun, the rain stopped, the clouds quickly drifting away and disintegrating like the smoke in a magic act. Bright, azure sky surrounded them.

"My Lord!" Mr Green exclaimed. "I see the coast of Ireland." He dropped to one knee and gave Tim a hug. "We're going to make it!"

Tim truly smiled for the first time in hours. He rose a little and peered over the side. There it was … a green land like no green he had ever seen. Green upon green. "It's like God spilled a bag of emeralds," he said wistfully.

Beyond the reach of the waves pouring rhythmically onto the beach lay some rolling, verdant pastures and low hills. With the clouds lifted, Tim could even see the sun setting in a range of low mountains farther inland.

"Tim, turn around," Mr Green announced, pointing. "Just there, you can see the Snowdonia Mountains of Wales."

Tim turned, and the intrepid pair gazed a while at the barely visible snowcapped peaks, rising high into the blue-grey atmosphere.

"I'd say this has been quite an adventure," Mr Green said. "What say you, young aeronaut?"

"I'm thrilled." Tim ducked his head. "But I'm bothered for my mum and brothers and sisters. They'll be mighty anxious."

"Indeed, they will be." Scanning Ireland's coastline, Mr Green pointed once more. "Look! We seem to be heading straight for that small harbour, and there's a town. If we land near there, I'll bet I can dispatch a message by way of a packet boat or sloop to your mum in London. She'll know you're fine in a twinkling."

"How long is a twinkling, Mr Green?"

Mr Green rubbed his chin. "Well, that's hard to say. Less than a fortnight but more than two days. Oh dear. I'd best get us down quick, or we'll sail right over Ireland."

In a jiffy, he had released enough of the hydrogen. By leaning to and fro and tugging on the lines of some ingenious flaps attached to the balloon's outer walls, he had manoeuvred the exhaling balloon over the waves. It floated just above the rooftops of the town. "Steady now!" he called mostly to himself. "Hang on, Tim. There will be quite a jolt." The balloon fabric was collapsing about them, one side slumping, and the basket was swinging wildly. A herd of sheep scattered, baaing in alarm. "Hang on! Here we go!"

No sooner had Mr Green yelled the words than the basket lurched hard onto the ground, with the fabric of the balloon being driven by the wind over grass and rocks at a breakneck pace. Tim flew from the basket and tumbled over and over, landing face-first in a small stream. He shook his head and looked around.

At last, the basket slammed to the ground and was crushed against a rock wall the height of a man. The empty balloon fabric flapped gently over the wall, its ropes hanging on the craggy rocks.

Tim ran to the basket and found Mr Green lying out on the grass, unconscious, and one leg bent terribly awry.

STAVE FORTY-ONE
SCROOGE AND THE NIGHT STAFF

At night in Byrne Manor, Scrooge could not avail himself of slumber. He tossed enough times to become entangled in his sheets. The autumn weather had grown considerably colder, and though a pleasant fire glowed in the fireplace in his room, he was terribly uncomfortable.

He sat up in bed and shook his fist at the enfolding darkness. He said aloud, "Jacob Marley, why did you send me here? I'm getting nowhere with this mystery, and I'm surrounded by all manner of ghouls and odd creatures. There are three murders, the third of which we haven't even learned anything. My mind toils back to those poor humans in the graveyard, clawing their way to the church door. What is wrong with this country? Perhaps Prime Minister Peel was right when he said the Irish are generally vile creatures and getting what they deserve." He stopped speaking, suddenly realising he may have spoken too loudly. He whispered, "I'll go downstairs and get some warm milk. That may calm me."

He put on his robe and slippers, took a punk from the holder, and lit it from the fireplace's flames, and then he lit a large candle. He opened his door, peered out, and then began making his way down the hall to the stairs. Every third floorboard creaked, and he thought of turning back.

Reaching the top of the stairs, he peered down. There seemed to be numerous small lanterns, like fireflies, glowing throughout—in the parlour, the main hall, the dining room, the kitchen, everywhere. Tiny sweeping noises and clattering sounds fell upon his ears. *Whatever is this?* he thought.

He ventured onto the first step. It creaked. The little noises stopped. He held his breath. Shortly, the noises began again. *I hope it's not the pooka cat.* The remaining steps were more forgiving until the last one snapped like a gunshot. He froze. He definitely had his mind on a cup of warm milk, but he had no desire to encounter some ghastly beastie tonight.

Just as he stepped onto the hall floor, several minute lights brightened. Then, one tiny fellow, no taller than a foot high and dressed in the most sordid clothing and shoes, jumped into the room not three feet away, facing Scrooge. He held a teeny lantern and a broom the size of a twig. "Who goes there?" he squeaked. "Friend or foe?" He cocked his head and squinched an eye.

Scrooge was so surprised, he scarcely could draw words from his mind down his throat and out his lips to answer the tiny man.

"I say," the wee man demanded. "Who art thou? And what is thy business?"

Scrooge stuttered. "I'm a guest of Mr Byrne. I couldn't sleep ... and ... and—"

"And what?" The fellow raised his broom as if he might strike Scrooge, though the blow would likely only reach his knees.

Suddenly, close to a dozen similarly dressed beings emerged from all corners, some smaller, some larger, both male and female, yet all about a foot tall. Each of them wore only brown, black, or deep-maroon clothing. One in peculiar, who bore a round belly and wore two hats, one hanging off each ear, hopped onto the banister post beside Scrooge's head. He beamed a smile then stuck his finger in Scrooge's ear and tickled it. Scrooge giggled and pulled away. Chuckling, the little person jumped down.

Scrooge then noticed all the little persons, had expressly long, pointed ears. Scrooge shrunk back, his eyes wide. He further saw each lantern bore a bevy of fireflies for its radiance.

"What be thy name?" asked the one who had first addressed him and was obviously in charge, his tone becoming more benevolent.

"Ebenezer Scrooge," the miser peeped.

"Oh, well then," the miniature man in brown clothes said. "I'm King Aldus of this tribe of Brownies." He doffed his feathered cap and made a low bow. A small maiden stepped up next to him, and he hugged her to his side. "This is my queen, Ailil."

Though she was so petite, Scrooge was struck with her beauty. Besides the barely seeable crown on her head, she, too, wore the shabbiest brown apparel, her dress torn and patched.

King Aldus commanded congenially, "Come forwards, fine guest, Mr Scrooge. The O'Malleys wrote me a note sayin' ye were visitin'. We know of the prowess of ye and Mr Cratchit. Ye be the ones who halted the vile dark malevolence in London. We read the papers, ye know. Come hither, man."

Scrooge slunk forwards while all the Brownies skipped and cavorted around his ankles.

When they arrived in the kitchen, two female Brownies had lit a lamp, and the room glowed beneficently. One Brownie, with amazing skill, leapt from the floor to all the way atop the stove, struck a match, and lit the wood then turned and said, "Thou will be havin' some warm milk for ye in no time."

Two other Brownies brought forth the crock of milk and ladled it into a pan. One more pushed the pan over the burner.

Queen Ailil invited Scrooge to sit. He did so, and then she clapped her hands, and several of the Brownies went back to their chores. She and King Aldus sat cross-legged on the floor in front of Scrooge. In a short while, the three of them were sharing stories. The royal couple were amazed by his ghost stories, and he by their stories of wild faerie folk and pixies riding birds and insects and certain ones pulling pranks on unsuspecting mortals.

Two Brownies brought him the cup of warm milk, each holding a side of the cup, while a third heaved mightily on a metal stove plate and snuffed out the fire.

An hour slipped by as Scrooge sipped the milk and became completely relaxed. Finally, he yawned, stretched, and wished the king and queen and all the Brownies a good night. "Is there anything I can do for you?" he asked.

"Yes," said King Aldus, "leave a note to the cook each evening to be sure to leave us a saucer o' cream before she goes to bed. Two saucers would be even better."

"I'll do my best." Scrooge yawned and trooped back to his bedroom for a good sleep.

When he awoke and was getting dressed, he looked in the mirror and wondered if his ears had become slightly pointed.

STAVE FORTY-TWO

THE BOBBIE RIDES TO WICKLOW, THE FOUND GLOVE

In that time of day, when it is neither night nor day, but the sun is hinting of its arrival, Tim stood near the bedside of Mr Green at a Wicklow inn.

The aeronaut's leg was laid in a wooden box, the plaster around the leg still drying, and he had a bandage around his head. The only light in the room, save the hint of the sun through the inn window, was a single candle on the aeronaut's bedstand.

"Well, Tim Cratchit," Green said. "I won't be flying any balloons for a while, but you'll be sailing home to your mother and family soon. The innkeeper is allowing me to recuperate here for free and said a ship is sailing to London this morning to fetch someone from your family hither to gather you. Here is a crown and a dispatch of two letters to give to the captain of the vessel called the *Fair Wind*." He placed the coin and envelope and another page with instructions in Tim's hand.

The young lad shoved the coin in his pocket and clutched the missives tight.

Mr Green winced in pain then took a breath. "The captain is to deliver the message to my chemist in London, Abel Canby, who will then know I am safe. He will pass the second letter along to your mum. Save for five shillings, that crown is the last of the coins on my person for the fastest ship available, the *Fair Wind*, to sail to London, thence the letters to your mum.

She will soon know you are in fine shape. Had I enough funds, I would send you back on a ship myself, but I rarely take my wallet when I'm aloft. So be patient, young man."

"Thank you, Mr Green."

"Thank *you*, young man, for you so quickly sought help for me in my injured state, and the fine farmers brought me to this inn where the doctor from Dublin set my leg and bandaged my wounded head. I bless you more. Had you not been aboard the balloon, I might have died in the collision with the rock wall, being left in the middle of nowhere for who knows how long for some beast or Irish ghoul to find me."

"No thanks needed. I had a fine run to a farmhouse, and I thank God I now have the full use of my legs."

"Yes, I know Mr Scrooge provided for your care and recovery from rickets."

"God bless him."

"Daylight has come. The tide will be up. Make haste, Tim. Deliver the crown and message and envelopes. Then take these two shillings and find us some fare before I starve." He gave Tim the coins. "The innkeeper says there is a café which serves fried fish down by the docks. Go to the dock, give the crown and the letter to the captain of the *Fair Wind*, and you can watch the sloop depart to London. Hurry now."

Tim sallied forth onto the streets of Wicklow, two shillings in one pocket, a crown in the other, two important letters in his grasp, and deep homesickness for his mum and siblings in his heart.

Before the sun had decided to rise and shine on the world, and the farm's cock was crowing vociferously atop the chicken coup, Scrooge and Cratchit traipsed downstairs together in the manor house, fully expecting a bounteous breakfast. Instead, they found Blevins and Byrne seated in the parlour. Byrne was still in his robe and declined to eat the simple breakfast of bread, butter, and marmalade set upon the dining room table. Both Scrooge and Cratchit perceived that the manor lord looked too upset to be involved in any detective work.

Byrne groaned while tamping tobacco into his pipe. "I have to come to grips with the fact that my brother may have drunk himself to death. But I still encourage each of you to look for any clues in all three deaths. How was your interview with Darragh Lynch last evening?"

"Scrooge and I could ferret little," Cratchit responded. "You are probably right. Perhaps your staff had nothing to do with Sean's death. Darragh said he believed your brother died of too much alcohol."

"Sadly, it could be the reality I must face," Byrne reflected. "Did he say anything else?"

"Only that Sean was to marry Darragh's sister," Scrooge said. "And Sean loved her very much."

"I'm sorry to say Sean did not love her but couldn't find the words to tell her. He told me his proposal to her was an error. I believe he felt great guilt when she died on the moor a year ago. I admit it was when he took to drinking more than he ever did before."

"Do you know her cause of death?" Blevins asked.

"Nay," Byrne said. "She was found dead, but no one could say if it was a suicide or some other cause. A doctor from Dublin ruled it a heart attack."

Scrooge placed his chin onto folded hands. "Do you suppose if Darragh found out she committed suicide because Sean told her the engagement was off, would he then have had cause to kill Sean?"

Each man reflected on the premise.

"Nay," Byrne said at last. "I believe Sean fully intended to follow through with the marriage and make a go of it."

Scrooge considered describing his visit with the Brownies, but something else gnawed at him. *Three deaths*, he thought. *Two of them undoubtedly murders. And the warning about Jannes and Jambres. I cannot shake that admonition.* He chose to say nothing.

Just then, a spear of sunlight pierced through the window, and Blevins abruptly stood. "Gentlemen, as you know, Inspector Shackle has made it incumbent upon me to convey our findings to him regularly. I feel I have been somewhat remiss in my duties. Therefore, Reginald, may I borrow one of your thoroughbreds to ride into Wicklow and remit a quick post via a fast ship to him in Manchester? I know the address of where he is staying, and I feel he should be glad to have some tidings, bleak as they are at the moment."

"Of course," Byrne said. "Have Thomas saddle the grey gelding, Swift Fire. He's a safe ride. Not easily spooked. Tell Thomas to allow the workers to ride to Dublin today to visit their mum on any other two horses, if they wish to do so. Is there anything else you need?"

"No, Inspector Shackle gave me funds to pay for just such a situation. I shall take my satchel and return forthwith." Blevins slung the leather satchel on one shoulder. "Farewell, gentlemen. I know the Queen will be pleased when we solve this case. Er, I should say *cases*."

He hastened to the stable.

When Byrne and the two detectives walked to the door to see him off, the mayor's maid, Sally O'Neill, paced rapidly across the gravel drive towards them. With her hand on his back, her son of twelve years strode bashfully beside her. He, like her, was freckled splendidly across his face and hands. They halted in front of the three men.

"Top o' the mornin', Mr Byrne." She courtseyed.

"Yes, Mrs O'Neill." Byrne extended his hand. When she offered hers, he gave it a kiss. "What can I do for you and your son?"

"This is my son, William, or Billie, as most call him," she said. "He has somethin' to show ye." She gave him a slight shove.

Never looking up, Billie cleared his throat. He mumbled, "When the tinker, er, the criminal came into the good mayor's home, he dropped this glove. I know ye gentlemen are detectives and look for a cause, and such an item might be important in solvin' a crime. Me ma thought I should give it to ye."

Cratchit took the soft glove. "Thank you, Billie and Mrs O'Neill."

"Go on, Billie." Mrs O'Neill nudged his back. "Out with it."

"Aye, and," Billie blurted, "the tinker's apron had milk stains on it. I know what milk stains look like 'cause I milk the mayor's cow." He looked at his mother to see if he had spoken correctly.

She smiled.

When the men said nothing more, the woman blushed and took her son's hand, bidding good day, and they departed.

"That's quite a walk from town to here," said Cratchit. "At least five miles."

"Yes," Scrooge said. "And I feel we may have our first important clues. This morning, I shall do some investigating." Scrooge was astonished at himself. He had so despised the idea of travelling to Ireland and even begun wishing he was not in the detective business at all. But, now, with an intriguing murder case before him, he felt rejuvenated.

Then he thought, *Three murders. Unless, of course, Sean Byrne was not murdered and died of drinking too much.*

STAVE FORTY-THREE

THE BOBBIE TO DUBLIN, CRATCHIT TO A PUB

Blevins arrived in Wicklow, trotting Byrne's horse along the cobblestone main street, and rode to the dock. Reining the gelding, he saw only small fishing vessels tied. A tall schooner with half its sails unfurled was just passing the bar, thence towards England. Tim Cratchit emerged from a café beside the dock, holding fried fish wrapped in newspaper in both hands.

"Say there, young man!" Blevins called to Tim, whom Blevins did not recognise, though he had seen him at the dock in London when he had boarded the ship with Byrne, Scrooge, and Cratchit.

"Yes, sir." Tim strolled up to Blevins, who still sat on his horse.

"Are you from around these parts?"

"For the time being." Tim was worried the greasy, cornmeal-coated fish would grow cold before he could take it to Mr Green. Neither had eaten since breakfast the previous day.

"I can't see any seamen about. This *is* a dock for larger sailing vessels, is it not?"

"I believe so. Say, I remember you. You're the bobbie—"

"Sure, you do." Blevins kept scanning the surrounding town streets for an adult. Finally, he looked down at Tim. "Do you know if a schooner or packet is due? Or is there another seaworthy vessel about? Not one of these fishing skiffs."

"No, sir." Tim's stomach was rumbling. "There were three ships earlier. They all left on the tide. That last one sailing away is the *Fair Wind*. I just placed a letter to my mum on it, and—"

"Confound the luck! I'll have to ride to Dublin." Blevins said nothing more to Tim, just turned his horse and galloped away.

Tim hurried back to Mr Green, and they both ate their fill. After the meal, Tim said, "I wonder where my pa is."

❧

Scrooge opted to use the day to talk to the farmhands and house staff while Cratchit chose to walk into Wicklow to ascertain anything he could about the death of the third person, a pubkeeper. While Scrooge spent the morning studying his notes and preparing a message to Cornwall to request Lockie's help, Cratchit hiked his way to Wicklow, five miles away. He did not mind the jaunt, for often he walked so far in London on tasks for Scrooge. After visiting several wrong pubs, he strolled to the pub with the name Byrne had jotted on a piece of paper. The pub—The Flying Corsair—had a closed sign in the window, but the door stood ajar. Inside, a middle-aged woman was busy polishing the bar, and a second younger woman entered from the back, carrying glass mugs.

"Hello," Cratchit said.

Both women looked up, and Cratchit noticed the marked resemblance, for both had coal-black hair and emerald eyes. The older one said, "We be closed. Come back tomorrow."

"I understand you're closed, however, I'm a detective assigned to investigate the death of ..." He looked at the page in his hand. "A Mr Freddy McDevitt."

"That would be me husband, recently deceased. Killed by an assassin."

The younger woman stopped setting the mugs as she began to cry, bent over, and buried her face in her apron.

"There, there, darlin' daughter," said the mother. "Shoo now! Take yer tears to the kitchen and be about preparin' fo' business 'ere tomorrow."

The daughter exited, and Cratchit strolled to the bar. "My name is Robert Cratchit." He handed her a card, and she glanced at it. "I'm working on behalf of Reginald Byrne and Her Majesty's Metropolitan police."

The woman slapped her bar rag over her shoulder. "Well, the English constable came by and asked questions, shuffled around where me husband lay dead, told the locals to take the body to the undertaker, and that's all I know that any police did. I don't know what else ye could do."

Cratchit smiled. Sadly, he had figured there was no reason to question the English constable. "May I ask you some questions?"

"Go 'head." The woman took on an indifferent air.

"Were you close to your husband, Freddy, uh, Mrs McDevitt?"

"We were married, if that's what ye mean."

"How did he die?"

"Throat was cut." She poked a finger at one earlobe then traced the finger under her chin across her neck and stopped at the other earlobe. "Sliced clean ear to ear. Now I 'ave to run the place all by meself and with me daughter."

"I'm sorry for your loss."

Mrs McDevitt shrugged.

"And you saw his dead body?"

"He was found by me daughter, Abby. She told me, and I had 'er run fo' the constable. The blood made a terrible mess. We spent days cleanin' it up, but we can't survive if we don't open soon. The fellas will go elsewhere for a drink and forget 'bout this place. We were their 'ome fo' some o' 'em."

"I understand. Do you know of anyone who would wish to kill him?"

She shrugged again. "There be many a sot he's had to throw out o' the inn. That makes a lotta 'em that would want 'im dead."

"Did he have any unusual dealings with anyone in the previous days or weeks?"

The woman looked at the ceiling. "None I can think of."

"No one? Not someone who was an unusual visitor?"

"I said no. See 'ere, laddie, I got to get this place ready fo' this evenin'. Lotta men be countin' on us. No one unusual came by."

Cratchit turned to leave, and the daughter burst from the kitchen. "I know someone unusual came by a lot."

"Now, Abby," the woman said. "Don't be botherin' this gentleman."

"I'm sorry, Mama," Abby said. She turned to Cratchit. "Three times over about a month, a woman came by, or at least, it sounded like a woman. Or maybe a man with a 'igh voice. I ne'er saw who it was. The person asked me da fo' bottles o' whiskey. All I know is he sold it to whoever it was."

"But you never saw her?" Cratchit asked.

"Like I say, it sounded like a woman. Kinda 'igh voice. Might've been a man."

"May I see the whiskey he sells?" Cratchit asked the older woman.

"I guess it won't 'urt," Mrs McDevitt said. "Follow me."

On a shelf in the back room, Cratchit saw the bottles. "May I purchase one, please?"

With the whiskey bottle in hand, Cratchit headed back to the manor.

STAVE FORTY-FOUR
QUESTIONS FOR MISS GOODACRE
AND MRS O'MALLEY

While Cratchit was winding his way through the town of Wicklow, Scrooge finished his notes in late morning. He returned downstairs, intent on questioning the house staff, beginning with the maid, Bonnie Jean Goodacre. He stopped her from polishing the silverware. She wiped her hands. "Yes, sir," she said, smiling unabashedly.

"Miss Goodacre, have you any knowledge in regards to the death of Sean Byrne?"

"No, sir. He was a good man, and I can't imagine anyone wantin' him dead."

"Did you know about him hunting for treasure?"

"Oh yes. He spoke of it often, tryin' to impress me." She blushed. "I believe he had an interest in me. I didn't take to him right away, plus I'm just a simple maid. He is of aristocracy."

"I see. What did he say about the treasure?"

"I thought it odd. He said it was not somethin' of this world. But it was like ... let me think. Oh, he said it was like *a pearl of great price*."

"A pearl of great price?"

"Aye. He even told me one evenin', when we was sittin' on the settee in the garden, he would sell all he owned to have enough to buy it." She giggled. "If he had found this pearl and asked me to wed him, I'm sure I would've."

"What do you know of his offering to marry Darragh's sister?"

"Oh." Bonnie Jean looked down. "I guess it was all right."

"Were you friends?"

Bonnie Jean shrugged.

"Did you two get along?"

She shrugged again and looked down.

Scrooge changed his tack. "Did Sean speak to you about her?"

"Of an occasion once." Her eyes were turned down.

"What did he say about her?"

Her face reddened. "I can't remember. He just thought she was pretty and had asked for her hand. Do you mind? I've got chores."

"Do you know how she died?"

"Nay. She just died. Why would I know how?" She began rubbing her raw hands.

Scrooge looked at her red, inflamed hands and wrists. "Miss Goodacre, have you some ointment for your hands? They look to be in atrocious shape to me."

"They hurt somethin' awful right now." She rolled her hands round and round.

"What work do you do around here to cause them to be so inflamed?" Scrooge began, worrying her ailment might be catching.

"Just daily chores. Washin' the pots and pans and dishes, scrubbin' the floors, dicin' the vegetables, carvin' the venison Mr Lynch brings in after a hunt, tendin' the herb garden for Grizelda, pickin' the herbs and flowers and such."

Scrooge's eyes grew wide. "You do all that?"

"Most days, even more." She continued to scratch at her hands. "I can't stop their itch." Her eyes filled with tears.

Scrooge then noticed even her cheeks appeared raw. "Well, I won't take any more of your time." He rose. "Where might I find Mrs O'Malley?"

"She's at the worktable in the herb garden, preparin' remedies."

Scrooge was glad to be away from Bonnie Jean, concerned he might catch her skin disease by being close to her. Just outside the back door of the kitchen, he found himself strolling, despite it being autumn and the weather chilled, in a luxurious garden. Amongst the flowers were short, wooden stoves, some with low fires burning. Flowers of every colour spread like something he would imagine being in the gardens of the royal palace.

His thoughts rushed to the remembrances of the assassination attempts on the Queen's life. *Four,* he thought. *One by Edward Oxford, one by the hunchback, John Bean, and twice by the bedevilled John Francis. The court ordered him to be hanged, drawn, and quartered. Whyever would our dear queen commute his sentence to life imprisonment?*

The pathway curved through the garden for forty yards and ended at a small, opened shed, outfitted with glass windows. To the side of the shed grew what looked like a golden glade of wheat, flowing gently in the wind. Standing at a tall worktable was Grizelda, a bonnet on her head, a heavy apron around her, and garden work gloves on her hands. A tall vase held several brightly colored flowers. Smaller medicinal bottles sat on a tray.

Scrooge called, "Hello, Mrs O'Malley!"

After a brief moment, she turned with a bright smile. "Hello, Mr Scrooge! Come, I'll show you what I'm working on."

He walked up beside her. On the table were finely chopped flowers and stems. A few small pails held sundry herbs. "See here," she said. "This is my joy. I have learned the art of remedies. I mix just the right amount of specific herbs and then laden the mixture with whiskey." She laughed. "Of which there is no short supply here in Ireland."

Scrooge smiled. "So, I've heard." He reached to touch the petals of some tiny, white flowers.

"Goodness, gracious, Mr Scrooge. Please don't touch the flowers! You might ruin their potency."

He drew his hand back.

She chopped a few more times on the plant pieces, swept the tiny bits into her gloved hand, and placed them on a scale. It tipped, she eyed the measurement and ultimately poured the contents of flower parts through a funnel into a small medicine bottle already sloshing with an alcohol brew Scrooge could smell. She held the mixture in the sunlight then smiled at him. She bragged, "Here you have a remedy for gout and headaches. I've learned from the best herbalists. Do you have gout?"

Scrooge was surprised by her question. "Why, no!" Just the words of a disease made Scrooge anxious he might have the early stages of the malady and wish to own the concoction for later in his life. Despite trying to become a better man and Christian, he often found himself slipping back into the cruel nature he had possessed for so many years. With so many ghoulish encounters of late, plus with the ghosts from beyond the grave, the idea of falling ill and thence dying wore heavily on him. "That's amazing, Mrs O'Malley. I applaud you. But what do you do with the remedies?"

She hmphed. "I give them away at no charge. But honestly, I hope to start a business with these cures, sell them from a store. My husband approves of the idea."

Scrooge could not hide his surprise.

"We can't live here for much longer, not with the way the master spends his money feedin' all the poor, starvin' rabble. He's goin' broke, if you don't know."

Scrooge's surprise intensified. Finally, he found his words. "How do you know this?"

"Oh, he was borrowin' from his brother, to the point that his good brother had to discharge all his help 'cause he couldn't afford the costs either. That's why he went crazy, lookin' for that magical treasure, and ..." She stopped and turned to begin chopping on a purple flower.

"I've come to ask you if you know of anyone who would have wanted to kill Sean Byrne."

"I've no idea. But he was spendin' time where no man should ever go." She grimaced.

"And where was that?"

"Up at that rundown castle. It's haunted. I'd never go near it. That's probably why he had the hallucinations and the jitterin' dance." She gripped her mouth shut. "I've said too much already."

"I understand. You've been very helpful. How do you keep the flowers growing, even past the summer?"

"It's the hot pots. Stokin' the fires in the small ones keeps the air warm, and Bonnie Jean and I tend the garden daily, bless her. Of course, Mr Simple, the gardener, does the majority of keepin' everythin' proper and pretty."

"Oh, I do admire how you even have a crop of wheat. How is it growing this late in the year?"

"'Tis a winter wheat. I like to make bread from freshly ground wheat when I can. I hand grind it into flour. I'll be baking some loaves this evenin'. Oh, look at me." She dropped her tool, took off her gloves, and tore away to the kitchen. "'Tis almost time for the midday meal."

"Thank you, ma'am!" Scrooge called after her. He could not remember when he had ever called any woman "ma'am." When he was a money-lender, he never extended the courtesy. Each person, male or female, was merely fodder in his barrage of fiendish methods to extract as much money from them as possible. He cared not for their feelings nor their problems. Their coin was his pearl of great price.

STAVE FORTY-FIVE
TAILING THE RUTHLESS TYRANT

Blevins rode the thoroughbred hard into Dublin, thrilled with the rapid pace of the sterling animal. Arriving about midday, he quickly made his way to the dock. In short order, he found a brigantine bound for Manchester and gave the details of the investigation in the Byrne murder case in a sealed letter to the first mate who was to insure it would be delivered into the hands of Chief Inspector Shamus Shackle. Blevins waited until it sailed, and then, leaving the horse at a livery, he hurried into the city shop areas, seeking a particular item.

He searched up and down the streets. Though some of the people walking along the avenues were fashionably dressed, the destitute farmer families roamed the street in little, despairing bands. Such threadbare coats and trousers, fusty gowns, squashed hats and bonnets, and boots and shoes were never seen in a rag fair.

When Blevins stepped out of a pawn shop, holding the item he had sought in a sack in his hand, he ran directly into Chief Inspector Shamus Shackle. Both men almost took a spill in the collision.

"Sir," Blevins said, his eyes wide. "What are you doing in Dublin?"

"Shhh!" Shackle put a finger to his lips. He was breathing hard, and sweat poured from his brow despite the chilly weather. He pulled Blevins behind a skinny lamppost, though it did little to hide either of them. He peered out. "I've followed Frederick Engels here. He is on a crusade to tear down our country. Stay close to me."

Blevins placed his parcel in his jacket pocket and followed on the heels of his immediate supervisor. They traversed the Dublin streets, stepping around numerous corpses lying untended on the streets, many of them blackened by the disease that killed them. Beggars held out cups to the two men, but they were ignored. Seeing one dismal woman as thin as a fence rail, Shackle dug in his pocket and dropped a shilling at her feet. She merely looked at it, so the policemen continued on their way.

"There he is!" Shackle exclaimed in a whisper. He and Blevins halted. "The one in the grey jacket and bowler." He pointed at a man standing between two women. They appeared to be chatting. "I would love to hear what corruption he is spewing at those poor ladies."

Blevins studied the man not thirty feet away with his back turned towards them. "So, this is the man the Queen has bade you to research?"

"Yes, and if necessary, incarcerate him."

"What is he doing here? I thought he was in Manchester."

"He *was* there, stirring up immense trouble. He counts himself a journalist. He writes for several horrid tabloids. Let me think." He pulled Blevins into a narrow alleyway then began enumerating the periodicals on his fingers, all the while whispering, "He writes for the *Northern Star,* and for that immoral sycophant Robert Owen, the *New Moral World*, and the *Democratic Review* newspapers."

Blevins peered around the wall at the man but said nothing until Engels began walking again. "Shouldn't we let him be? I'd hate for him to realise we're in pursuit."

Striding rapidly, Shackle called over his shoulder to Blevins, "Oh, I believe he already knows he's being followed. I've been to several of his meetings with the so-called labour parties and a Chartist group.★ He's seen me but doesn't care … for the time being. He knows I know he intends to start a bloody revolt."

They reached a point in their traverse where hundreds of the starving Irish farmers lay in small groups along the sidewalks and streets. The lane through them was bedevilling with each man being careful not to step on some poor wretch's hand or even a baby's foot. Still, the two kept close behind their mark. Ultimately, Engels went inside a large pub.

Shackle and Blevins entered a moment later and slid along the wall in the shadows of the particularly dark pub overflowing with Irishmen, some with a pint, others with nothing but air in their hands. All looked like famished wolves to Shackle.

By the bar, a sort of spotlight shone on a rotund man who bore a scowl like a shrunken apple with angry, black whiskers and large lips. He chewed on a cigar, and his dark eyes scanned the audience who were all turned towards him. His attire was clean and maintained, unlike the other men seated. The scowling man clapped his hands, and his voice growled, "All right, men! Ye've come 'ere 'cause ye wants a choice. Ye wants a say, and ye wants the lousy English gov'munt to rot in 'ell."

The crowd of men began pounding applause on the tables and hooting and cheering.

The angry man held up his hands, and the crowd quieted. "We be in luck tonight, fo' luck be a peculiar gift to the Irish." He took off his bowler and held it over his heart. "But don't think I'm gonna be praisin' the Lord, for if there was one, we wouldn' be in this predicament right now. This plague be not the wrath o' any god. It be the wrath of a cavern of a gov'munt filled with snakes!"

More applause echoed in Shackle's and Blevin's ears.

The ovation ended when the heated man barked for silence. Then he set about introducing the guest speaker. "This man," he said, "comes from Germany and has worked in England in manufacturing." He spat on the floor. "But his heart be not black like those in the English parl'ament and the English landowners who parcel out land to us good-hearted Irish. He might as well be an Irishman 'cause he speaks our thoughts. He knows our pains. He 'as a great plan to change the 'ole world. I give you Mr Frederick Engels."

Engels emerged from the shadows into the spotlight. After the polite applause, he looked slowly about the room, even walking a few feet one way, a few feet the other. He halted and looked down a long time as if he were searching for something. He raised his head. "I won't find a four-leaf clover anywhere I look in Ireland, for Ireland's luck has run out. However, I can offer all of you something better. I give you the offer of action! No more waiting for the English to do something decent about the plight of the Irish."

Blevins was feeling uncomfortable. "Let us depart. This crowd looks ready to kill."

Shackle waved at him to be quiet.

"I wish to offer a proposition," Engels said, his voice rising. "Would you like to hear it?"

Many men in the crowd voiced loud yeses.

"Here it is. What if we all shared what the rich have? What if they no longer owned all the land, no longer lived alone in great houses, and no longer had a single say in our lives? Would that be to your liking?"

The crowd roared, "*Aye!*"

"What if the deaths the rich have caused for us poor instead became their lot in life? What if they forfeited all their lands, money, and power to all the Irish to be shared *equally*?"

Many in the crowd were on their feet, shouting approval. Other men sat quietly, much more subdued with frowns on their faces. *Perhaps,* thought Blevins, *some men are not so naïve as to blindly believe what Mr Engels is saying. Interesting.*

The crowd quieted a little, though private conversations still existed at some tables. Suddenly, Engels slammed a pint glass on the bar. It shattered to hundreds of pieces. He glared long and hard at the surprised crowd then pronounced, "*That* is what we must do. We must shatter the rich and mighty. And that means blood! Yes, take their blood until they're all dead. Only with a revolution will all be set right. Make plans, gentlemen, make plans. Don't waste time praying to a god. Instead, make plans. I bid you good day."

First, there was roaring applause and shouts from the crowd. The men in the room then erupted into vicious arguments; the movement of the men was like a swirling eddy of branches and detritus. Some men waded in bellowing a rant with one group then dove into another. Almost all the men were shouting.

It was then Blevins noticed the two farmhands from Byrne's estate: Simon Crimp and Barry Lowe. They sat quietly at a table in the deepest corner, watching the turmoil and occasionally shaking their heads in a disapproving manner.

Blevins was unsure of what to do. He thought it best if Shackle and he escape. After all, he was in his Metropolitan uniform. He could become an object of derision or even an attack. "I'm leaving," he told Shackle and walked outside.

"Very well." Shackle followed him out into the uncountable throng of poor, dying farm families who had come to Dublin to plead for food and help. He stopped. "I'll wait for Engels to leave. He'll surely come out this way and speak to these farmers too. By the way, how is your investigation of the murder going?"

Blevins responded, "I just sent a missive to you, explaining our progress and frustrations, on a ship to Manchester, thinking you were still there."

"I would have been, but this Engels fellow has been traversing northern England, inciting folks to violence. I barely discovered he had taken a ship to Ireland. He seeks to start a revolution, and he's deathly serious about it."

"I'm not convinced these weak people could lift a finger to fight for a revolution, much less wield a musket." Blevins pointed to several families huddled like sheep on the walkway. "I don't believe his rhetoric is anything to concern ourselves with, Inspector Shackle."

Shackle sighed. "I suppose you're right, Officer Blevins. It's not as though England hasn't dealt well with rebels in the past."

"He's merely just an attention-grabbing loudmouth. Ironically, like some of our representatives in Parliament."

Shackle turned towards him and frowned, and then both men broke out in laughter. The chief inspector abruptly halted. "Very well, what are the current findings in your investigation?"

"So far, very little has been uncovered. If I had any specific ideas of where to look, I'd do so. Scrooge and Cratchit have been thorough, but some evidence now points to his drinking as being Sean Byrne's assassin. Either his heart or liver could not withstand the burden."

Shackle rubbed his whiskers and looked long at the pleasant-faced, physically fit young man, remembering back to his own days as a new officer. "Be that as it may, Queen Victoria will want a thorough report. The Byrne family has close relations with the Queen. Gather every piece of evidence you can find, no matter how trivial. Your report *must* be accurate."

"Yes, sir. I shall return to Byrne's estate now."

"And I will obey my orders to follow and record everything about this vile man and his new friend, a German by the name of Karl Marx. They are like cousins in the same despicable design. Two peas in a poisonous pod."

The men shook hands and parted.

With the evening and a storm closing fast upon him, Blevins rode the thoroughbred at a steady gallop. His mind was on Crimp and Lowe and the fact that they were at the same pub as the revolutionary. Was Shackle aware of any connection? *I have more work to do*, he told himself. He would speak with Scrooge and Cratchit and Byrne upon his return. Urging his horse faster, he shouted into the wind, "Things are going awry!"

STAVE FORTY-SIX
SCROOGE PURSUES THE GLOVE CLUE

At the noon mealtime, Byrne did not show once again. Sitting alone at the long table, Scrooge ate a plate of boiled cabbage and sausage. He realised having a great deal of wealth and a fine house did not necessarily make a man happy. Though Byrne had it all, he, like Scrooge who had lost his sister years ago, had lost his brother. *Sorrow seems to be the regular burden of the lives of all people*, Scrooge thought. When he finished the meal, he set his knife and fork lightly on the plate. The small clatter was all Bonnie Jean needed to hear. She rushed from the kitchen and lifted the plate from the table. She smiled at Scrooge and courtseyed and then was gone.

Scrooge wanted to help the suffering maiden, but time was not on his side. Solving the murders was taking longer than he could afford. There were no telegraph wires from Ireland to London, and he wished desperately to ascertain how his office was faring. The more he thought, the more he became convinced his money-lending business was on its last legs, despite Grumbles being a capable businessman and able to ask Scrooge's nephew, Edmund Nuckols, any question. Scrooge's stress still catapulted, and he began to have indigestion, belching a bitter volume.

He listened a while to the low rumble of the storm then said to the vacant room, "Enough of this. I shall talk next to the dairyman. Perhaps he knows something." He pushed back his chair and rose. Suddenly, he felt woozy.

"Perhaps I ate too much or stood too quickly." His equilibrium rushed back to him, and he strode to the hallway, retrieved his tall hat from the rack, and then walked through the kitchen where he saw both of the O'Malleys, along with Darragh Lynch and Bonnie Jean. Each one exchanged polite acknowledgements, wishing him an Irish blessing.

Lynch asked, "Have you found any evidence?"

"Nary a thing," Scrooge responded. He stopped. "Mr Lynch, I should like to question your farmhands. Where might I find them?"

Lynch said, "I'm afraid today is the anniversary of their dear ma's death, so they're ridin' to Dublin to visit her grave and place some flowers. They'll be back before dark, so you can speak with them then."

"Thank you."

Scrooge walked out the kitchen door and wound his way past the garden and the flower shed and then through a meadow where a flock of sheep grazed. He heard cows lowing. Turning past a copse of trees, he came upon the dairy barn. Inside, milk pails, rakes, ropes, cowbells, and such lay strewn about without a care. He tripped on a bucket and almost fell. At the far end, he recognised Lorcan Duffy pouring a pail of milk into a twenty-gallon tin can sitting in a cart. A sleepy-eyed, grey donkey stood in the cart traces.

"Good afternoon, Mr Duffy!" Scrooge called.

Duffy set down the pail, brushed some milk splotches from his leather apron, pulled off his gloves, and tossed them on a shelf. Scrooge immediately saw the gloves were very much like the one Billie O'Neil had found after the tinker's search of the mayor's home. The dairyman paced rapidly to Scrooge, his hand extended. "Welcome," he said. "I was wonderin' when one of you would be along to question me."

"We've had a number of persons with whom to speak." They shook hands, but Scrooge's eyes remained on the gloves.

"Come, have a sit on these milkin' stools."

They sat, and Scrooge marveled at the man's ebullience.

Duffy took off his cap and stroked his sweaty, bald head. "It's been a corker of a day, Mr Scrooge. I believe one of my cows has taken ill, for she gave very little milk, despite my talkin' kindly to her and rubbin' her belly and utter with my fine, soft gloves." He pointed to the shelf above their heads.

"I expect the soft cotton gloves are much appreciated by the cows."

One of the cows let out a long moo.

"I'd say she agrees," Duffy said. "And the gloves are woven with silk and cotton, makin' them amazin'ly smooth and durable."

Scrooge asked him similar questions he had asked Bonnie Jean and Grizelda, but the man could offer little more than they. Scrooge then asked, "Have you been into Wicklow recently?"

"No, sir. I've not a reason. I've got everythin' right here. My wife used to live with me in the cottage yonder, but she died last year. 'Twas mysterious to me, but the doctor Mister Byrne paid to come from Dublin said she had a failure of the kidneys. Likely, it had been gettin' worse, but she would never complain."

"I'm sorry for your loss."

"Thank you kindly, sir, but I have my three boys who are off workin' in Dublin. They come 'round to visit often enough. They were good friends with Sean Byrne before he died. I think they came to visit him as much as me. They were often takin' in the sights and pubs of Dublin, the three of them and Sean. They came to his funeral and looked most melancholy." Duffy sighed.

"Excuse me for asking, but do any of your boys have financial difficulties?"

"I would wager that, as much fun as they're havin', they've either struck it rich or are in debt up to their ears." He guffawed at his comment then wiped the tears of joy from his eyes. "Why do you ask?"

"It's my job to ask questions, no matter how private. One last question. Have you recently misplaced a pair of your soft gloves?"

"Not to my knowledge." Duffy walked over to a shelf and lifted a paper box filled with the fine, white gloves. "I have plenty. Wouldn't care if a pair did get lost. I'm somewhat forgetful, so I often lose things. A glove, a teacup, my cap, my apron, even the milking stool." He chuckled then put his hands to his cheek. "Where is my lunch pail?" He began pawing through his shelves, and the cows mooed noisily the more he prowled around the barn.

Scrooge excused himself while Duffy continued rummaging. He next sought the gardener. He looked around the flower garden and the vegetable garden but could not find him. He did see Bonnie Jean weeding the garden. "Shouldn't you wear gloves?" Scrooge asked her.

"Oh, the gloves just make the itch worse." He inquired about Rian Simple's whereabouts, but she did not know. "I believe he's gone to Dublin. Said he was doing research on his flowers."

The storm slowly rolled in, and great drops of rain began falling. Heading inside, Scrooge spotted Blevins at the stable, however, he was not in the mood to discuss anything with Blevins or anyone else, for that matter. He was actually feeling unusually tired. *Strange*, he thought. *I never need a lie-down. Must be from living in the fresh air of the countryside.*

STAVE FORTY-SEVEN
STILL MORE QUESTIONS AND NO ANSWERS

The *Fair Wind* schooner docked early evening in London. The first mate handed the envelope with two letters marked "urgent" to an older ticket porter and gave him two shillings. The man hurried away to deliver the envelope. Within an hour, a younger errand boy—none other than Abel Canby's son, Rick, who was also Tim's good friend—raced through the streets, ducking around pedestrians, and arrived at the Cratchit home.

Belinda Cratchit opened the door. "Welcome, Rick, dear friend of Tim and our family. What brings you here?"

He smiled and handed her the letter. She passed it to her mother who read it then grasped a hand over her heart, dried her tears from her eyes, and relayed the joyous message to her children: Tim was alive. She hugged Rick and sent him on his way.

Alvina turned to her oldest boy, now fourteen years old. "Peter, we can't afford passage by ship. You must journey to Cornwall … to Tamperwind. Tell the Holmeses and Samuel and Abigail Jiggins. They will know how to obtain passage on a ship to fetch your wayward brother."

Peter beamed with the opportunity to do something brave. "I will not fail you, Mother."

With the moon rising, Peter Cratchit rode in a stagecoach, paid for with what little money Alvina Cratchit had hidden away over the years, and headed for Cornwall to inform Lockie and Lucy and the Jigginses couple of Tim's plight. In two days, he would arrive in Tamperwind. Peter thought to himself, *Surely, Tim will be safe until help arrives.*

⁓⊙⁓

Scrooge spent the next two days in bed, feeling ill in his very bones. Though Mrs O'Malley, when she held her hand to his head, felt no fever. And despite Bonnie Jean fetching him some hearty soup and fresh-baked bread both days, he still felt nauseous and dizzy each time he attempted to rise. He could scarcely listen to Blevins telling of meeting Shackle in Dublin and how the chief inspector had urged them to continue their search for evidence and the murderer. Nor could Scrooge pay any attention to his boon companion, Cratchit. He did, however, share with both men some of his findings from questioning Lorcan Duffy and Bonnie Jean Goodacre.

The late-October weather had turned bleak, and the wealthy farmers of Ireland had finished covering their haystacks with tarps against the elements for their cattle and sheep herds to eat during the winter. The wheat, rye, and barley farmers had bundled the last of their crops off to Dublin to be sold and quickly shipped to England. The potato farmers throughout the western and southern parts of Ireland sold their cows and furniture and even some clothing so they might obtain a few paltry coins in order to purchase morsels of food for their families.

Many estate homes and those abodes of the wealthy had jack-o'-lanterns carved from turnips on their doorsteps while harvest parties were celebrated indoors with plenty of ale and feasts of venison and duck and boar. Folks danced and sang then sat around a roaring hearth while old codgers with ample grey locks and long beards and beady eyes told stories of macabre and ghastly creatures. The womenfolk put their hands to their cheeks in amazement at each turn of the tale, and the wee children closed their eyes and covered their ears so as not to hear more of the scary events. The menfolk who stood about listening, a pipe of tobacco in one hand and a pint of ale in the other, did their best to look nonchalant about the yarns but still felt a pinch of dread in their stomachs.

When the festivities were long over, and the fires had burned low, the revelers piled into their carriages or mounted their steeds to head out into the relentless, encompassing dark surrounding them like a cloak. The joy of the evening they had felt when departing was met with a howling wind and blowing leaves turning round and round, crackling like skeleton bones. Eerie sounds no one could hear during the day rose, as though night creatures were emerging from their graves. Thence, the brave revelers hurried to their homes and beds and pulled the covers over their heads. Outside, the wind kept howling and buffeted their windows. Strange noises sounded and bounded through the halls and stairways. Those deep under their coverlets had chills running up their spines.

Halloween was coming soon.

Cratchit, for his part in the two days of Scrooge's illness, went about questioning anyone he met at nearby farms, searching for clues. Scrooge had made him aware of his findings in the interviews he instituted. So Cratchit, in between interviewing local farmers and townsfolk, wondered about the dairyman, Lorcan Duffy, and the milking glove dropped by the thief in the mayor's home. *Was the thief also the murderer? Furthermore, what is so special about the little jewellry box? Similar to the faux tinker, Duffy wore a leather apron stained with milk. Did he kill the mayor?*

He wondered also about the potato farmer, Callahan, the man who claimed to have discovered Sean Byrne's body. *Would he have had a cause to murder the man? Was it a disagreement over land? Was finding the man an attempt to cover up the foul deed?*

Then he conjectured about Darragh Lynch. *Did he realise Sean had killed his sister rather than marrying her and, thus, took revenge? And what of the innkeeper's demise? The man's wife showed no indication of fondness for him or sorrow for his death. Could she have killed him?* However, the daughter had claimed a woman, or a man who had sounded like a woman, surreptitiously purchased several bottles of whiskey from the innkeeper. *Who might that have been? Would they have cause to kill him?*

He considered Malachi Doyle. He had been closest to Sean Byrne in many ways, being the foreman of the estate. Cratchit thought hard about the man. *Did he know of the will and how he was to inherit a tidy sum and, thus, have ample means to impress his much-younger lover? And where is the will? Finally, are the three murders related?*

After a day, Byrne emerged from his room, having abandoned his melancholy of consideration that his brother had died the death of a drunkard. With new vigour and purpose, he twice joined Cratchit at Scrooge's bedside, and the three discussed and formulated cause-and-effect, yet nothing came of their conversations, save frustration.

At the end of the second day, Scrooge asked Cratchit, "Have you had a chance to interview the gardener, Rian Simple?"

"No, I thought you had."

"No, he was not available the day I took ill. The maid said he had journeyed all the way to Dublin to research plants."

"Hmm. That's interesting. I will find time today to question him." Cratchit turned to Byrne. "I've put off asking you, and I hope you don't think me impertinent, but has the will been located?"

"It has. I received a letter today from the lawyer. He has invited me to Dublin to review it before the formal reading."

STAVE FORTY-EIGHT
THE ATTACK ABOARD SHIP

After the two-day journey, Peter arrived in Tamperwind and delivered the message regarding Tim's whereabouts, and Lockie and the Jiggins siblings quickly formulated a plan.

The next day, Lockie Holmes strolled beside Abigail Jiggins and Bobbie Wheeler along an unremarkable, short dock in Tamperwind Cove that was adjacent to the rocky coastline of Tamperwind Mine. It was the dock used by the mine to ship out its ore. The three examined the lugger* ship tied to the dock they were about to board to sail to Wicklow, Ireland. The ship was stained black, as were its sails.

Lockie pointed. "Everything is black on this ship because it was once used for smuggling, primarily rum and whiskey."

"Is it safe?" Abigail asked. "I should hope we won't be pulled over by a revenue cutter and placed in manacles because illegal goods are on board. Or worse yet, run afoul of pirates."

Bobbie chuckled. "There you are, holding that stout shillelagh like it was your child. I wholeheartedly believe any pirate boarding the ship would have to deal with your skill and quickly sail away in embarrassment."

"Yes, well ..." Abigail held a portmanteau in one hand and had planted the sturdy, four-foot-long staff on the dock boards.

"I spoke with the captain," Bobbie said. "He told me there's few pirates anymore. Too many revenue cutters and marines with muskets aboard, patrolling the seas and keeping a sharp eye on sailing commerce. He admitted his own smuggling days are over. It's safer and more profitable just to carry small amounts of *fine goods* such as silk and jewellry and the occasional passengers like ourselves. He cruises along the western coast of England and the small harbours of Ireland."

"We were lucky he docked here," Lockie said. "Though I don't know why he did."

"And my brother, Samuel, God bless him," Abigail stated, "put up the funds for our safe passage. He is confident of Captain Thorn and spoke with him when he was taking on some additional crew. Captain Thorn said he needs more hands because he is retrieving a great number of barrels of Irish whiskey, as it turns out, in Wicklow where Tim abides, hopefully safe. He plans to load the whiskey to bring back to London."

Lockie sighed. "I already miss my darling wife and my sons but it is vital we locate Tim in a lamb's shake."

"And I shall miss my family." Bobbie looked at his taller-than-he companions. "But I have some special friends in Ireland whom I've not seen in ages. They are roughly the same height as myself, yet they be not dwarfs. It will be good to see them again."

The captain called, "All aboard!"

The three made their way up the gangplank and onto the deck. The captain waved at them from the foredeck.

Bobbie pointed at two burly men, each with scarves tied around their scalps, who were carrying a long crate down to below deck into the hold. He said, "I don't recognise those men as being from any village around the mines, and they certainly are not former workers at either Tamperwind or Hopworth. Hmm ..."

Bobbie and Abigail walked up the short stairs to the forecastle to speak with the captain. The master of the lugger vessel was a tall, stout man with auburn hair and whiskers with streaks of grey. He had a look about him of being a lifelong seafaring man. He appeared happy to speak with his passengers as he smoked a pipe. Lockie strolled the main deck, attempting to analyse how the exact rope knots were tied to the various stays and hooks. The captain turned his attention to the sailors in the masts who were scrambling like monkeys among the rigging in order to set sail.

Suddenly, the two burly fellows who had earlier descended below deck sped from the hold, malice on each of their faces. One toted a foot-long rubber club in his hand, the other held a short length of chain. They headed straight towards Lockie. Not knowing their intent, he did not expect it when they rushed him. In moments, despite his acute combat skills gained during his time on the streets of London, the one with the rubber baton began beating Lockie about the ribs and head. Soon, the other man swung the chain around Lockie's neck in a choke hold. They began pulling him to the ocean side of the ship and quickly had him halfway bent over the rampart. Lockie saw they were attempting to dump him into the sloshing waves.

Then, like a lightning strike, Abigail arrived and swept into her well-learned stance. Feet apart. Elbows out. One arm stretched forwards while holding the shillelagh high. With her sturdy staff, she slammed the chain man in the ribs. He collapsed, loosening his grip.

Lockie removed the chain from his neck and righted himself onto the deck. He quickly elbowed the second man in the stomach, who buckled, but not for long. The foe with the chain flung a fist into Lockie's groin, but before he could take another swing, Abigail knocked the assailant hard in the head. The muscled man fell hard but adroitly rose, holding one hand on his noggin. Then, in a smooth motion, he grabbed a sturdy oar extending from the lifeboat. Abigail and the assailant circled each other, the man taking numerous swings at Abigail, which she easily blocked. He raised his oar high to smack her head, but Abigail was too quick. She plunged the end of the staff into his stomach then swept it up against his chin. He fell unconscious.

Lockie was now using quick footwork in a fisticuff duel with the rubber-baton man. He landed two sharp blows to the bloke's face and then was able to grab his wrist and yank the rubber club loose, and it fell to the deck. Abigail stepped towards the assailant with graceful, gliding steps and thrust her staff hard into the man's ribcage. He yowled in pain.

Before she could land the felling blow, a third man of enormous size, his chest looking as broad as an oxen's girth, grabbed Abigail from behind, knocking her shillelagh to the deck. She glanced at his immense biceps and thighs. Struggling to break his hold around her waist, she found her attempts were to no avail, for he was too strong.

Bobbie, despite his short legs, had raced from the front of the ship and gripped the man tight around one enormous thigh. Seeing the effort did nothing to stop him, Bobbie began kicking him with his iron-toed mining shoes. The giant now moved one hand to Abigail's throat, choking her. Gasping for air, Abigail struggled to gain release from the villain's grip while Lockie fought hard against his own assailant.

Recovered somewhat from his blow to his ribcage, the baton attacker pulled a broad blade from his belt and attempted to slice Lockie. After blocking three swings from his attacker, Lockie landed two powerful left jabs to the man's jaw, causing him to drop the knife and stumble backwards. Lockie tackled him, and they rolled in fierce combat about the deck.

When the huge man, who was now dragging Abigail to the side of the ship, swatted at Bobbie who was repeatedly kicking him, Abigail used the opportunity to free herself. Using her training from the Chinese master, Mengzu, she took hold of the man's arm around her neck, bent in one smooth motion, and flung him over her back. He landed on his rump with an amazing *thud* which echoed like thunder on the deck boards.

He leapt up, but Captain Thorn and two more sailors arrived with pistols trained on him. Bobbie had retrieved his own loaded pistol from his portmanteau and pointed it at the man's private parts, smiling sardonically.

Lockie sat astride his attacker and was pummeling his face when he saw two sailors arrive and poke whale harpoons into the man's cheeks. The man stopped struggling. Lockie rose and stood beside Abigail.

STAVE FORTY-NINE
MORIARTY, HIS MOTHER, AND A DARK SECRET

"My deepest apologies," Captain Thorn said, his eyes still focused on the immense man. "I hired these men as workers, not true sailors. They were supposed to help load a hundred whiskey barrels when we arrived in Ireland. Do you know why they would attack you?"

Abigail retrieved her shillelagh and shrugged her shoulders. Lockie held a hand to his chain-injured neck and shook his head no.

"Well, I have no reason either, except I consider them reprobate criminals. I have ways of dealing with these sorts." He turned to two of his sailors. "Run out the plank on the starboard side." In short order, a board plank extended out through an opening in the ramparts and over the ocean. The captain put his pistol to the biggest man's ear. "Walk it."

The man, with fear across his visage, walked slowly towards the gangplank. With two sailors pushing him, he stepped on the plank and walked timidly out to the edge. He turned. "Don't make me jump. I can't swim."

"It's time you learned," Abigail announced. She put one foot on the plank and extended her stout stick. She pushed the shillelagh against his torso, and he fell backwards into the water with a loud splash.

Lockie smiled when a cranky-looking, older sailor with a squinted eye, apparently the first mate, ordered three sailors to pick up the unconscious man. They did so and flung him into the waves, where he awakened and began swimming to shore. The third man willingly walked the plank and leapt into the ocean. He, too, swam hard. The big man kept floundering and splashing along but eventually was washed by the waves onto shore where he collapsed beside the other two.

"It's a shame none of them drowned," said Captain Thorn.

When the ship's real sailors returned to their duties, and the lugger set sail, Lockie, Abigail, and Bobbie sat beside a rampart and ducked out of the wind. Lockie looked dejected.

"What's the matter, Lockie?" Abigail asked. "We defeated the villains." She rubbed her raw neck but looked at the chain marks on Lockie's neck and the bruises on his cheeks. She felt regret for asking.

"Do you miss your sweet bride?" Bobbie added.

Lockie turned his tear-filled eyes towards them. "Yes, of course I miss her, but there are two more factors. I believe there are rogues who are searching for the nails in the box we found. If they discover Lucy and Samuel have it, I fear for their safety and for my boys."

Abigail gasped. "I hadn't thought of that. I was on this trip to see a land I had never seen. We've barely begun and already faced great danger." She bit her lip and tightened her grip on her shillelagh.

"I am so grateful you came." Lockie rubbed his sore head.

"What is the second thing that bothers you?" Bobbie inquired.

"I don't know how to swim. And I don't know who knows that, for those men were trying to throw me into the ocean to drown. Who would know that about me? I've never told a soul."

If Lockie Holmes knew who had travelled in the single cabin below deck in the same ship to Ireland, he would have been filled with anger. James Moriarty, the boy of fourteen, waited until he was certain Lockie and his companions had departed after the lugger arrived in Wicklow harbour. He and his mother, Penelope, then sauntered onto the deck. The two criminals had watched through a peephole the attack on Lockie and his friends. Moriarty had contracted the job with the attackers. Once again, however, he was confounded that his plan had not been successful. He had a vague remembrance of the woman, Abigail Jiggins, and the meddlesome Wheeler dwarf. He thought, *Oh, well, a loss of a few coins.*

The three victims of the attack had left the ship and now walked the streets of Wicklow, heading for the address of the inn given by Mr Green's letter. Moriarty watched them go then sighed. *There will be another time to remedy myself of Lockie Holmes. I feel it in my bones.* He was surprised to see a stout but wizened sailor stealthily tailing them. "Who might that fellow be?" he asked, pointing him out to his mother.

"I believe he is the first mate," said Penelope.

"I see." Moriarty strolled down the gangplank. Finding the single livery in town, he rented a team of mules and a wagon with a long bed, and he found the specific man he knew would be waiting for him to drive the wagon team. The sailors carried his and his mother's luggage and the long, narrow, heavy crate to place in the wagon bed.

With the crate and trunk loaded, Moriarty rode, seated on the front bench of the long, supply wagon beside his mother. Penelope was a woman whose last name changed so regularly, she often forgot which name she was using as her current alias. Her auburn hair fell to her neck and was twisted into a delicate braid. Her alabaster skin gleamed in the sun; her cheeks rosy. Beside them, the driver flicked the reins. He was a dark man, his skin the color of lignite coal, and he had narrow eyes, almost like a cat's, peering under a wide-brimmed, black hat, one similar to those worn by the American cowboys. He wore a long, black coat, and his shirt was black, as were his coarse, patched trousers. He stared straight ahead at the mules pulling the wagon.

Moriarty began chuckling to himself.

"What's so amusing, my son?" Penelope asked.

"I was thinking about the surprise the captain will have when he finds the two corpses of his sailors in the below decks."

"Surely, the bodies have been discovered by now." Penelope could not hold back her own joy and began to titter. She could barely utter her next words. "He will first be shocked, and then he will wonder. Then he will be searching for reasons, accusing the rest of his entire crew. He will never guess at who might be the mountebank."

"I only wish I could have had a hand in it personally!" Moriarty exclaimed gleefully. "What a thrill it would have been!"

The wagon waggled over a deep rut in the road and bounced as each set of wheels hit the indention. The driver whistled and clucked at the mules. Then the three heard a loud *thump* behind them. When the driver halted the mules, Penelope and her son looked back at the tarp covering the long crate. They waited, but there was only silence. After several minutes, the driver resumed driving the horses more slowly.

STAVE FIFTY
THE WHISKEY BOTTLE AND A NEW QUESTION

While Blevins journeyed to Wicklow to ask around town for anyone who would know of why Sean had died, Cratchit left the house in a mild drizzle to find the gardener, Rian Simple. He found the hunchback man seated in the middle of a flowerbed of the wide garden, his cap pulled low and his leather-aproned lap filled with bulbs. "Hello, Mr Simple. May I have a word with you?" Cratchit squatted next to the man.

"Ye most certainly can, laddie." His tone was cordial, but his voice sounded like a saw scratched across fiddle strings. He kept brushing each bulb one by one then held them up for examination.

"I don't believe anyone has asked you about Sean Byrne's death."

"Nay." Rian rubbed his stubbly grey beard. "Don't know what I'd tell 'em if they did."

"Let me ask you this. Do you know of anyone who would want to have him killed?"

Rian rubbed his beard. "Can't say I do. He was a kind man, gentle to all, a lover o' life, ne'er touched a drop o' alcohol."

"Wait. You say he never drank?"

"Not whiskey nor beer. He was a borin' sort. He would carry a bottle 'round for show, ne'er to drink. If he drank anythin', it was buttermilk. He said it was 'God's true gift.' Why, if I weren't so busy 'ere, I'd spend me life bein' drunk on good Irish whiskey." He grinned with a mouth missing teeth. "I keep a token o' the strong stuff with me." He lifted a half-full bottle of whiskey from his apron pocket. "I use it if the moment calls. Settles me nerves. Helps me see straight."

"See straight?" Cratchit remarked. "Most of the men I've ever known who've drunk too much have trouble seeing anything and often see double."

"You mistake me meanin'. With me bent back, I need a way to see the world sunnier than it really is. The whiskey helps me do that. The world takes on a rosy glow. In the other times o' the day, I surround meself with these flowers so I be part o' the beauty o' the world." The drizzle had increased, and rainwater dripped from his cap. He looked with caring eyes towards Cratchit. No disdain for the world showed on his humble face.

Cratchit bowed his head then looked squarely at the gardener. "I think I understand. Tell me, though, I heard you journeyed to Dublin. How did you go? I can't believe you rode a horse."

"Nay. I 'ave me a friend. Malachi Doyle from Sean Byrne's estate. Once a month, he brings a carriage and takes me to Dublin to the library and to the gardens so I can learn."

"And what do you learn about?" Cratchit was liking the man.

Rian puzzled a moment, his hand on his chin. "Let me think. First o' all, do ye see these brilliant flowers and shrubs?" He pointed at several flowering plants. "They grow in me garden 'cause I keeps the small hearths burnin'. There be larkspur, foxglove, lily of the valley, and mountain laurel. Me favourite be the oleander."

Cratchit was almost incredulous at the beauty of the flowering garden. "Quite pretty. And to look so brilliant this late in the year."

"It won't be for much longer. The November frost will come." Mr Simple frowned. "Anyway, to answer your question, this last time, I went to Dublin at the behest o' the good lady, Grizelda O'Malley. She wanted to know the medicinal aspects of certain herbs and in what quantity they were most useful. Which ones could cure. Which ones can calm a wayward spirit. Which could bring restful sleep. She be quite the chemist."

"Mr Scrooge told me she appeared to be an accomplished herbalist."

"I wish I knew what she knows. I just know me flowers and me veg'tables."

"Thank you, Mr Simple." The drizzle had turned to rain.

"Can ye 'elp me up, sir? Gettin' down for me be fairly easy but risin' be a difficult task."

Cratchit helped the gardener to stand. The little man, bent through no cause of his own, gave Cratchit a brilliant smile then toddled off to the servant's entrance to the manor. It occurred to Cratchit that it might be propitious to search the rooms of the staff and the cottages of the farmers. He immediately thought of Lockie. *He would be the one to find clues no one else could.*

Cratchit slipped inside to the kitchen where Mrs O'Malley was stirring a delicious stew. It smelled a good deal like a stew his wife often cooked, and his feelings for her swelled. He missed all his family. Of course, he was not aware that five miles away, Tim Cratchit stayed at an inn with Mr Green, who was struggling to stand with his leg in a cast up to his hip.

❧

Scrooge was feeling better, less tired and nauseous. He and Cratchit and Byrne sat for a delicious midday meal of stew and bread. Blevins arrived from Wicklow and began explaining how he had uncovered nothing new. Then they heard a knock on the front door, and Bonnie Jean appeared in the kitchen entrance. She announced, "There be a farmer at the door. I believe it be Mr Callahan from the farm one over."

All four men went to the door. Callahan, wearing a coat so long, it dragged on the ground, held his hat in his hands. "I was 'bout to tell ye when we was at St Patrick's tumble o' stones out on the marsh. Ye know, the place where Mister Byrne died, and we read the words scratched on the rocks." He fumbled with his hat.

"Hello, Mister Callahan," Byrne said with formality. "'Tis good to see you. What brings you here?"

"Well … ye see. Me wife's got a way 'bout her. She owns me heart, she does. But when she catches wind o' somethin', she won' let go."

The four men looked with eagerness to ascertain where the man was heading with his talk.

"At any rate," Callahan continued, hemming and hawing, "she finds out that when I discovered poor Mister Byrne's body that he 'ad a whiskey bottle in his hand. I picked it up and could tell it still had somethin' in it. Me thinks, 'Praise God. Free whiskey.' So, I slips the bottle in me pocket and spirits it home then hides it for a special day. Well, me wife won' 'ave the devil's drink in our 'ome, and she finds the bottle. She opens it to smell it, but it ain't whiskey. She gives it to me to smell, and it reeks to rotten Hades, not anythin' like whiskey. She demands I give it to ye. So, 'ere it is."

Callahan produced the small brown bottle from a deep jacket pocket and handed it to Byrne, who opened it to take a whiff. He made a disgusted face and quickly plugged the cork in the top. "It smells of rotted cheese."

"That be right, it does," said Callahan. "I'm glad to be rid o' it. I don' know why he 'ad it."

Byrne handed the bottle to Cratchit who turned it over and over.

"Interesting," Cratchit said.

Byrne shook hands with Callahan and thanked him, and the farmer wished them all an Irish blessing then, with his coat sweeping the ground, he strolled away, whistling a jaunty tune.

Cratchit announced, "I believe there is a connection with this bottle to the death of Sean. When I went to the Flying Corsair pub where the owner, Mr McDevitt, was murdered, the man's daughter said, in the three weeks before Sean's death, what she assumed was a woman came three times to buy bottles of this sort. This was done in the early morning, and she said the buyer wanted the purchases kept secret. Wicklow has a large number of pubs. Having gone into several of them before I found the one where McDevitt was murdered, I can clearly state none of them had bottles of this size and color. I purchased a bottle, brought it here, and even sampled it. It's a hearty brew."

"Why do you see a connection?" Scrooge asked.

"For some reason," Cratchit replied, "this mysterious woman, or a man with a female's tenor, brought the bottles to Sean on at least three occasions. What ended up in this bottle is not whiskey. Someone placed something else in it, and whatever it was probably hastened his demise."

"Could it be poison?" Byrne asked.

"One might come to such a conclusion," said Cratchit.

"But who would ever imbibe something so revolting?" Blevins asked.

"Therein lies the question. And why would Sean have this bottle in his hand when he died?"

"Furthermore, why was he at the pile of boulders in the middle of a marsh?" Scrooge added.

"I believe we have more questions for Malachi Doyle." Cratchit opened the bottle, smelled its contents, and turned up his nose.

STAVE FIFTY-ONE

LOCKIE, ABIGAIL, AND BOBBIE WHEELER
ARRIVE IN WICKLOW

Lockie was the first to arrive outside Mr Green's room at the inn. He knocked vociferously. When Tim Cratchit opened the door, their joys exceeded all evaluation. They hugged and smiled, and then Lockie gave Tim a gentle push into the arms of Abigail who handed her shillelagh to Lockie. Tim and she hugged, and Abigail said, "You are a brave fellow, Tim." Next, Bobbie Wheeler shared hugs and pats on the backs with him.

Tim introduced Mr Green who sat in a straight-backed chair with his leg in the cast extended onto another chair. In short order, Tim explained his entire ordeal and adventure and admitted he was substantially ready to return home to his mum and siblings. "So, what is the plan?" he asked.

Lockie addressed his question. "We sent word to Mr Canby, the chemist for Mr Green, saying we would see to the aeronaut's safe arrival back in London. Samuel has supplied enough funds for all of us to return. However, I should like to look in on Misters Scrooge and Cratchit and see how their sleuthing is proceeding. I would imagine they have solved the case by now."

Tim remarked, "Two days ago, I saw the officer who sailed with them. He didn't remember me. He was riding a strong horse and in a big hurry."

"Ah, yes, Officer Blevins. Seemed like a competent law officer," Lockie said.

"My guess," said Bobbie, "is if he was riding through here, then Scrooge and Cratchit are staying somewhere nearby. Would Byrne Estate be nigh?"

"As it turns out," Mr Green said, "I've had several conversations with the innkeeper. He told me there have been three deaths in the area. He claims the mayor was tragically murdered, and a pub owner by the name of McDevitt was also killed. He said Sean Byrne, who owned an estate about six miles away from town, may have been murdered as well about six weeks ago."

"Byrne! That's the name," Lockie said, not wanting to discuss murders in front of Tim. "If the estate is close, I must visit Misters Scrooge and Cratchit. What do you think, Abigail and Bobbie? Should I share news of our discovery in the mines?"

Abigail shrugged, and Bobbie nodded.

"Then it's agreed," Lockie said. "We will visit my employers and see what they need."

"But what of young Tim?" Mr Green asked. "I believe he's inclined to hurry home to London. I admit, I wish to return to my family as well."

"I will take Tim home," Abigail said, "and escort our injured Mr Green home too. One should never journey alone with a broken leg. We'll leave on the next available packet."

"Before I return to my mum," Tim announced, "I would like to see my father, especially if he's a mere five miles away."

"Very well," Lockie said. "Tomorrow will be a quick visit for you, Tim, and then it's back to London."

"I'll remain in Ireland a while," Bobbie said. "I specifically came to visit my friends. That is, if I can locate them. They're an elusive sort." He chuckled. "Might get a new pair of shoes from them."

"Are your friends cobblers?" Abigail asked.

"You could say that." Bobbie smiled broadly then looked down at his well-worn shoes.

The sun was sinking over the Wicklow mountains in a spilled butter and marmalade sky. Abigail paid the innkeeper for two rooms, one for herself and one for Lockie, but Bobbie said he was going on a hunt in the surrounding forests. "Some old pals of mine used to live around here. If I find them, they'll put me up for the evening. If I'm not back, don't fret. I'll see you in the morning." Twirling his pointed cap around his finger, he pranced out the inn's door like a cat who had found a mouse and was proceeding to play with it.

By the window in the pub next door, Isiah Thrusher bent his good eye to watch the dwarf cavorting his way out of town towards a dark, emerald-green forest. He considered following him but was still formulating his plans. He had treasure on his mind and would not be dissuaded until he had it in hand.

At the inn, lying on the less-than-comfortable bed, Lockie's mind raced. *Three murders, not just one.* He yearned to know more, his acute senses alert. *Is someone on some sort of killing spree, of which Sean Byrne was an unexpected victim?* He looked out the window at the full moon with a ring around it and sat upright. *Something's wrong. I need to find Bobbie Wheeler.* He leapt out of bed, drew on his trousers and shoes, and bolted down the stairs.

STAVE FIFTY-TWO

FIRST MATE THRUSHER AND THE ENCHANTMENT

Brilliant stars shimmered and winked over the little village of Wicklow. *Which way did Bobbie go?* Lockie thought.

"Lookin' for yer wee friend, are ye?" The voice came from behind him.

"Aye." Lockie turned to look at the wizened fellow dressed in a seaman's garb—blue trousers tied just below the knee, a heavy wool shirt, and a blue vest tied with leather laces. High buckled shoes were on his feet. The man with sea-wind-raw skin strode up to Lockie and squinted his eye at him, giving a somewhat smile.

"Aye," Lockie said again. "Do ya know which way he went?"

"I do." He pointed. When Lockie turned to go in the same direction, the man grabbed his sleeve, bringing him to a halt. Lockie faced him again. "Name's Isiah Thrusher, late employed on the very sea boat ye sailed on. I was first mate and ordered the men to throw the unconscious brigand into the sea."

"Yes, I remember you."

"Well, let me tell ye. It be more 'elp than findin' him you'll need." Thrusher grimaced.

"What do ya mean?"

Thrusher pointed to the sky. "Do ye see that full moon with the ring 'round it."

"Yes, I saw it, and it gave me a strange feelin' like someone I know was in danger, and I figured it must be Bobbie, my friend."

"The dwarf, right?"

"Aye."

"Then follow me, for yer friend be in dire peril." The man raced away, and Lockie flew behind him. Soon, they were running side by side. "This way!" called Thrusher, and he angled towards a tightly grown copse of trees.

Drawing closer, Lockie heard the voice of Bobbie. *Yes, definitely Bobbie,* he thought.

"Help me!" Bobbie yelled from somewhere in the knot of trees. "For the love of our dear Saviour, help me! I'm trapped." His pleadings peeled like bells in the leafy cavern.

The moment Lockie reached the outer trees, just ahead of Thrusher, a limb seemed to reach down and smacked the young detective hard against his chest.

"Hold!" Thrusher called, coming up beside Lockie, who was gasping for air. "Ye mustn't run in there, for this forest be enchanted."

Lockie looked at Thrusher with surprise. Unlike his two employers, Scrooge and Cratchit, he had not ever encountered the elements of the world.

"Stay still," Thrusher whispered. "Look, even now, the trees be bendin' and sweepin' their lowest limbs across our path."

"What do we do?" Lockie could hear Bobbie's yells for help growing more fervent.

"We must pretend. Follow me lead. Ah, 'tis the excellent-tasting walnuts ye be wantin'?" He whispered in Lockie's ear. "Say 'aye.'"

"Aye," Lockie said. "And with those walnuts, I shall make the most wonderful pie—"

"No, ye idjit. Say ye wants to plant them in yer garden and have a grand tree for shade."

Lockie reworded his remarks. "Ah, yes. To plant those nuts in my vast estate and have the grand trees growing everywhere. Here a tree. There a tree."

Both peered into the gloom and could just see the trees relaxing the sweeping of their limbs as they creaked and moaned.

"Now," Thrusher whispered. "And keep talkin' at a nice easy stroll."

The two men ventured along a seldom-trod path, overgrown with weeds and with numerous patches of mushrooms along each side. Lockie kept announcing his intent to find walnuts. All the while, though their path parted barely in the continuous gloom, they could tell they were edging closer to Bobbie's voice. They rounded an especially large walnut tree, and there in a circular, wide, grassy glade lay Bobbie on his back. Directly overhead, the moon, with its uncommon ring, shone all its brilliant light specifically on the grassy plot.

Bobbie turned his head towards Lockie. "Oh, there you are. Help me, please! They have me. I am powerless."

At first, Lockie marvelled at Bobbie's predicament and then further wondered who had him so secured, for he saw no one and no ropes around his friend. Yet, Bobbie struggled as if he were tied down with strong bindings. Then, the first faerie mounted on a dragonfly flew by Lockie's face. Other faeries, too many to count, with wings on their shoulders, flitted and zipped about. One stopped in front of Lockie's nose, the little creature staring and smiling at him then zoomed away. Some larger faeries in red caps and jackets danced along the ground, and they yodelled in tiny voices, sounding like pebbles rolled around in a can. The taller faerie folk, obviously elves, dressed in brown-and-yellow-striped clothes, did cartwheels into the grassy stage made brilliant by the moon's beams of inordinately bright light. Soon, a miniature orchestra plinked, and a chorus of faeries broke into song. He could make no sense of what they were singing.

"They be speakin' and singin' Gaelic," Thrusher said, his voice hushed. He gripped Lockie's elbow. "Do not rush to 'elp yer friend. He be trapped in a faerie ring. They 'ave enchanted his bein'. You don' want to become enchanted too."

Lockie noticed Bobbie lay within a circle of about three yards in diameter, surrounded by tufts of grass and mushrooms. No sooner had the old seaman spoken than a host of faeries of all shapes and sizes and numbering in the thousands invaded the glen. Some beautiful and petite, others of them ugly as ogres, some as thin as saplings, a few as squat as toads. They all came in, prancing together in a march of sorts. Next, a troop of elves, dressed in brown and green and numbering in the hundreds, emerged from the far end of the glade, pulling the ropes of a sledge with runners, the length of Bobbie's body. They pulled the sledge directly beside Bobbie whose face was now white with terror.

Bobbie turned away from the sledge and looked piercingly at Lockie. He said, "The faeries started singing, and I went to hear their beautiful melody. Then they invited me to come watch them dance and perform, which I did, then they invited me to sit here on this very spot. It was all so beautiful, and their performances were so enticing. I felt love in my heart for them. Great beauty. Great peace. Then I felt like I was not here but somewhere else, in a beautiful place. Finally, I remember feeling sleepy. Then I wake up, and I'm unable to move." He struggled with all his might but could not escape his ethereal bindings.

Lockie took a step forwards, but Thrusher pulled hard on his arm, and he halted. To their right, tiny trumpets sounded, and teeny drums beat a solemn rhythm. All the faeries and elves fell quiet and turned their heads towards an opening in the trees to Lockie's right.

In the same manner as horses would, a team of eight crickets pulled a diminutive, gold-laden coach, the size of a large melon. The carriage rolled to a stop in the centre of the glade. The coach had a driver and two footmen dressed in white-and-gold clothing. While the band of trumpeters blared their pretty tune, and the drummers beat their drum cadence, the coach was stationed not far from where Bobbie lay.

When Lockie looked closer, he saw the restraining bands running across Bobbie's body and holding him to the ground were no more than gossamer filament. "Why can't he move?" he whispered to Thrusher.

"Because he be under an enchantment. He believes he be tied down by 'eavy cords. What he believes be his reality."

Lockie felt total astonishment. He wished to save his friend, but he had heard of faerie magic, and now he was actually seeing it. One of the footmen stepped down from the back of the gold coach and set the steps and opened the door. An elegant, beautiful queen, scarcely ten inches tall, dressed in a brilliant white-and-silver gown, wearing a gold crown, and holding a sceptre, stepped from the carriage. Lockie was taken by her ravishing splendour.

"Be wary," Thrusher warned. "The faerie queen be powerful. She can enchant ye in a thrice if she wishes."

Lockie sighed heavily. "What can we do?"

"We'll 'Ave to barter."

"Barter?"

"Aye. 'ave ye anythin' of value on ye?"

Lockie shrugged. He peered quickly at the queen who appeared to be blessing the entourage of admiring faeries. He worried a host of the small creatures would roll Bobbie onto the sledge and cart him off, never to be seen again. *I have to save him.*

Several faeries mounted on various insects suddenly buzzed around his head.

Thrusher saw them. "Don't be thinkin' of savin' 'im. Some o' the faerie folk can read yer thoughts."

Lockie brushed the bothersome beings away. "What do we do?"

"If ye want yer friend released, ye must offer somethin' o' value to faerie folk. What 'ave ye in yer pockets?"

"I've got a few coins of the realm. Even a crown."

"They 'ave no need of coins. They find those lyin' on folks' night tables and lost in the gutters o' the streets. How do ye think the queen has all that wealth?'

Lockie looked at the queen's carriage which indeed looked to be solid-gold plated. He patted his pockets and looked at his worn shoes. "I have my pocketknife."

"A pocketknife! We be in luck." Thrusher sauntered close to the crowd of faeries and elves. "Pardon me, dear queen." He doffed his cap and bent a low bow, followed by a lower bow, his nose touching the ground.

The queen looked askance at him and pointed her scepter to a dozen tall elves who immediately surrounded the seaman, each elf holding a sharp pike.

Looking up, Thrusher said, "With yer permission, yer 'ighness," he bled out the *s*'s in the expression, "I should like to barter fer yon dwarf." He knelt, his head tilted downward and eyes barely up.

The queen waved for the elves to stand down. They did so but remained close to Thrusher, their pikes at the ready. Lockie stepped forwards and bowed to the queen. He, too, knelt and bent low to the ground.

The queen clapped her hands, and four elves rushed forwards with a sort of ladder platform. She mounted it. Thrusher was bending so low, she stood at the level of his head. "All right, mortal," her skinny voice squeaked. "You have one minute." She looked about. "Where is this item with which you wish to barter for this … oh, dear … what do you call it?"

An elf in a grey robe stepped up. "A dwarf human, your majesty."

She cocked her head at Thrusher. "Your time is passing quickly."

"Aye, yer majesty. Indeed. Me companion offers just the sort o' thing that would serve ye and yer subjects well." He snapped his fingers at Lockie. "The pocketknife. Quick."

Lockie, with one hand on the ground in his kneeling position, dove the other hand in his pocket and retrieved the knife. He opened it and gave it to Thrusher, who then set it on the ground before the queen.

Bobbie was looking on in dismay and terror. "Why would you give them your knife?"

The queen beckoned an elf who looked like a silversmith or blacksmith. He strutted up to the knife, bent his wee head close to the blade, examining it. He plucked a hair from his head and slid the hair across the blade. The strand split in two. "'Tis a fine piece, your majesty," said the smithy and backed away.

She turned to the grey robed elf who nodded. "Very well. The trade is made."

Thrusher and Lockie began to rise.

The queen said, "One thing more completes the deal."

Lockie's mouth dropped open. Thrusher rolled his eyes.

"I should like a lock of hair from that young creature." The queen pointed her scepter at Lockie.

"A lock of my hair?" Lockie exclaimed. "Whatever for?"

"That is the business of my realm. Either I have a lock of your hair, or your dwarf friend is ours." Without looking at Bobbie, she waved her scepter at him, and he felt his bindings tighten. He hollered in pain.

Three stout-looking elves were carting off the knife.

"I'll need my knife to cut the lock of hair," Lockie said.

The queen folded her arms. "Very well." She snapped her fingers, and the elves laid the knife at Lockie's feet. When he stooped down, he saw movement in several spots within the trees just beyond where Bobbie was tied down. He gave a head flick towards the trees, and Thrusher looked that way then smiled.

A long, narrow, grey cloud was gliding across the sky. While Lockie began stalling for time by fiddling with his knife, the tip of the cloud pierced the face of the moon.

"Now!" came a call from the woods. Immediately, a host of short men, perhaps twenty in number—some dressed all in green, some in red, but all with tall pointy hats—dashed from the trees. Several bore bullseye lanterns, which shot brilliant spears of light into the entire glade.

"To arms, me hearties!" one of them called.

"'Ave at 'em!" another's voice rang.

Soon, the short men, even far shorter than Bobbie but taller by six inches than the tallest elf, leapt into battle. They swung miniature shillelaghs and batted the elves and faeries like balls, sometimes knocking several of them into the trees. The melee grew fierce as elves with pikes stabbed at the little men in green and red, while faeries, riding winged bugs, dove at their opponents, tossing acorns and pebbles at their heads. The faerie queen was hurried into her coach by her attendants, and the coach was driven sharply away.

With no hesitation and his knife in hand, Lockie vaulted to where Bobbie lay and sliced through the gossamer bindings with great ease. When Bobbie was freed, he jumped up and began dancing a jig, despite the battle going on.

In another minute, the elves and faeries had retreated and were lost in the gloom. The grey cloud covered the centre of the full moon. Much of the glow faded from the glade.

The entire troop of small men gathered around Lockie, Thrusher, and Bobbie.

STAVE FIFTY-THREE
LOCKIE JOINS THE HUNT

Bobbie began introducing several of the leprechauns that he knew, and each one made a polite bow. "There is Andrew, the troop commander. And this is Cillian. Meet my dear friend, Conor and his cousin, Dale. I don't know the rest, but all of 'em are members of the Leprechaun troop number 12327, better known as the Wicklow Lowlanders."

The bright-faced half mortal, half faerie beings beamed with pride.

"But don't try to catch any of 'em," Bobbie warned. "They're one of only two troops of fighting leprechauns. And, also, I'll admit, they make fine pairs of shoes."

Lockie took note that every one of the leprechauns wore a leather apron and had a small hammer hanging from a loop of the apron.

The leprechaun, Andrew, stepped forwards. He was the only one with tufts of grey hair sprouting out below his cap. He spoke in Gaelic. "Fan san áit a bhfuil tú. Which for you mortals means, 'Don't be ever tryin' to snatch one of us. If ye do, the whole troop will be upon ye.'" He turned a warning glance at Thrusher, who backed up a step.

Andrew put a hand to his ear. "We were surprised to hear our boon companion, Bobbie Wheeler, yelpin' like a kitten stuck in a crack in a wall. And surprised more were we to see him bound in a faerie trance. But t'was little trouble to drive the connivin' spirt folk away. Bobbie, we'd love to stay longer with ye, but we're behind on our shoe order. There's lots of poor, starvin' Irish, with this famine, what needs a pair."

"Ah, 'tis a shame, Andrew. I wish we had more time," Bobbie said.

"Perhaps another time."

Leprechaun and Bobby shook hands. In a brief display of twinkling lights like so many fireflies, the entire troop of leprechauns vanished.

Thrusher muttered, "I should like to 'ave bound one o' 'em and get me three wishes."

Bobbie, after a big sigh, said, "Lockie." He pointed at Thrusher. "I don't know who this gentleman is, but I am grateful to him."

Lockie said, "This is Isiah Thrusher. He led me to you and seems to know a lot about faeries and elves."

Thrusher and Bobbie shook hands. Bobbie said, "Thank you from the bottom of my heart."

Thrusher growled, "Well, let it be a lesson to ye to neer venture out at night when a full moon be encircled by a ring. That be when faerie magic be at its strongest."

"A good point to remember," Bobbie said and wiped his brow.

Thrusher said, "Ye'll probably not see me again. I've business to attend to."

࿐

In the bright morning, Abigail skipped down to the docks to find a vessel that would take passengers to London. Her search was short in that not a single vessel was bound for London. All were sailing only to the western coasts of England and Wales. She returned to the inn.

Lockie slept well, dreaming of faeries, elves, and leprechauns. He had heard so many tales in his life of those sorts of folk. He awoke feeling such exhilaration. *I can't wait to tell Lucy.*

Bobbie slept late.

Lockie bounded down the stairs to the pub area of the establishment and found Mr Green, with his leg up on an ottoman, speaking to the innkeeper. Tim was the only other person in the room. He jumped up when he saw Lockie.

"Lockie!" he exclaimed in a full run and then collided with the detective. Backing up, he said, "Let us go to Byrne Manor. I wish to see my father."

"And I," said Abigail, "should like to speak with my employers. I, too, have an interest in this crime."

"Well, if we can get a carriage, I think that can be arranged."

An hour later, Tim, Abigail, and Lockie rode not in a carriage but in the back of a farmer's wagon loaded with hay and chickens. The amiable farmer was the only transportation available for them. Arriving at the manor house, Lockie paid the driver a tuppence and gave him a hearty handshake. Brushing straws and feathers from their clothes, the three travellers walked to the heavy door, and Tim slammed the knocker a few times. He could barely contain his excitement.

When O'Malley answered the door, he frowned and said, "We have no positions. If you're looking for a handout, we've none to give. Good day." He began closing the door.

Lockie stopped the door with a strong arm. "We have business with Mr Robert Cratchit. This is his son." He pointed at Tim. "This is Abigail Jiggins, secretary to Misters Scrooge and Cratchit, and I am Misters Cratchit and Scrooge's business partner. I am Sherlock Holmes Sr."

The stuffy butler allowed them inside. "Wait here." He strutted off to the library. When Cratchit came to the front door, he was at first amazed, and then his face filled with sorrow. "What grievous news do you bring me? Has your mother or a sibling died, Tim?"

"No, sir," Tim responded. His voice turned repentant. "I accidentally boarded a hot air balloon with Mr Green. The balloon was caught in a storm, and we floated across the sea to here. We crashed in a farm, and I ran for help for Mr Green who was injured. I've been in Wicklow at an inn with Mr Green for five days."

Cratchit bent down and hugged his son. "Dear Timothy. I almost lost you years ago to a foul illness. Don't let me lose you to an accident. You'll have to tell me all about your—"

"Adventure, Papa. It was a true adventure. I recommend everyone should take a ride in a balloon. The world is so beautiful from up in the air."

Scrooge arrived, and Lockie shook hands with his two employers. The two loan officers and detectives extended polite remarks to Abigail who did the same.

Lockie explained to his superiors how Peter Cratchit had relayed the message from Mr Green, which had arrived via a fast ship, of his and Tim's aerialist sojourn and how he, with Bobbie Wheeler and Abigail, had sailed directly to Wicklow harbour, later to locate Tim who was boarding with Mr Green as the message had entailed.

"I should like to hear all the monotonous details of how you came to be here, Lockie," Scrooge interrupted. "But since you are here, you are *now in the hunt*. We need clues desperately, and you may be our key to attaining them."

Lockie allowed, "I believe Abigail can escort Tim back on the next available ship. Therefore, as long as Abigail can inform my lovely wife at Tamperwind, I shall start immediately to work here."

"Fine," Scrooge said. "It's about time you got here." He marched off towards the library. He halted, gave an exasperating sigh, and called over his shoulder indignantly, "Well, make haste."

"Yes, sir. Coming." Lockie hurried after his employer.

In the library, Scrooge, Blevins, and Byrne informed Lockie of the details they had attained so far. Abigail took a seat near the gentlemen and listened without saying a word, which was not in her nature. She wished to help solve the mystery, but she had greater concerns for the mine and the aggravating lawsuit. *I must return to Tamperwind soon,* she thought.

Tim and his father made their way to the kitchen to talk. Mrs O'Malley had just taken from the oven some sweet raisin bread. Both Tim and his father agreed the slices were delicious.

In the library, after Scrooge and Blevins had relayed all the details to Lockie, Scrooge said, "This afternoon, we head to Sean's estate. Lockie, upon our arrival, I need you to do some of the scrounging you do so well."

STAVE FIFTY-FOUR

INSPECTOR SHACKLE LENDS A HAND

After the noon meal, Cratchit borrowed Byrne's cabriolet and took Tim and Abigail back to the inn. That afternoon, Cratchit listened to Mr Green's many exploits while Abigail secured passage for Tim, Mr Green, and herself on a ship sailing to Cornwall. Before Cratchit departed back to the manor, she told him, "I saw no point in waiting for a vessel bound for London. I will assist Mr Green and Tim in their return to Tamperwind. The daily coach will take them both to the rail station in Lazy Eye. Samuel will pay for tickets for the rest of the way into London. I shall inform Lucy of Lockie's plan and continue to help my brother with the mines. Bobbie has chosen to stay here a few days to visit some friends and is already seeking them. The ship sails on the evening tide."

The two friends bid farewell. Abigail grabbed her portmanteau and shillelagh, and she and Tim, with Mr Green riding in a barrow, departed for the dock. Cratchit mounted the carriage.

Just when Cratchit drove the carriage into the drive of the manor, and Thomas came forth from the stable, a cart barrelled down the road and turned into the manor. The driver reined in the running horse that pulled the cart and brought it to a shuddering stop. The driver was none other than

Shamus Shackle. He leapt from the cart, making no effort to secure the horse from galloping off.

"I say," he remarked, marching at full tilt towards Cratchit who was just dismounting from his carriage. "This is indeed fortunate to meet you here, Robert Cratchit." The men shook hands, and Cratchit introduced Thomas.

After a few cordial remarks, Thomas excused himself. He secured Shackle's horse to a hitching post then drove the Byrne carriage to the stable and unhitched the horse.

Shackle wasted no time. "Look here, Cratchit. I've been in pursuit of an underhanded fellow, an agitator, or as the newspapers call the sort now a 'rabble rouser.' He is touring Ireland after already stirring a pot of trouble in Manchester and its environs. He calls himself a *socialist*. He touts he's only expanding on the idea of Utopian socialism authored by the French heretic, Henri de Saint-Simon, but his real goal is anarchy." Shackle was becoming so flustered, spit was flying from his lips, and his face had turned scarlet.

"Slow down, Inspector." Cratchit placed a gentle hand on Shackle's wrist.

"Yes, yes. So, here's my dilemma. This insurgent has escaped me. I know he fled down this road, but I was unable to obtain adequate transportation to pursue him." He smacked his fist against his palm. "Now, I've lost him."

"It's getting late. I know our benefactor, Mr Byrne, will allow you a room and accommodations. You won't find your rabble rouser in the dark."

❦

Shackle joined the men for supper, and each one shared their findings. After the dessert, Byrne announced, "A courier came today with Sean's last will and testament. It is brief. I am his executor. He left to me his entire estate and house, plus his investment holdings. To Darragh Lynch, he left twenty pounds, and to his foreman, Doyle, he left one hundred pounds. He willed two hundred pounds to the Catholic church. I shall inquire if he has adequate funds in Tipperary Bank and then distribute them after the reading of the will. His final request is to allocate any remaining funds to a Mr Freddy McDevitt to do what he describes as 'continuing the hunt for Christ's treasure.'"

"Christ's treasure? Whatever could he mean?" Shackle remarked.

"McDevitt," Cratchit said simultaneously with Shackle.

Cratchit continued, "He was the public house owner who was murdered."

"'Looking for Christ's treasure' could mean anything," Blevins said. "What madness is that?"

"Unless," said Byrne, "he meant it to further the good will and charity of the church."

Blevins nodded. "Yes. That is most probably it."

At that moment, Bonnie Jean entered. "Excuse me, gentlemen." She courtseyed. "May I clear the table now? I feel rather unwell."

"Of course," said Byrne. "Go lie down, Bonnie Jean, and don't concern yourself with us for the remainder of the day." He rose. "Gentlemen, let us retire to my library. I have a telescope and can afford us the opportunity to look at the full moon."

While Bonnie Jean began removing the dishes, the men retired to the library that was festooned with tall windows on two sides. Out the western windows, the rising pale moon was evident. Blevins moved the telescope there, and each man took turns looking through it. Shackle showed the most interest and peered the longest at the pale orb.

"Is that the old castle there?" Lockie asked, pointing out the north window. "Up on the hill with all those torch lights?"

All the men rushed to the north window. They gazed at the fallen down edifice that was now highlighted by numerous torches. The shadows of many men could be seen passing in and out of the walls. One light glowed in the single tower window. The cadre of detectives and police and Byrne stood in awe for over a minute.

Byrne said, "There's not supposed to be anything happening there. Though the castle is not officially in the Byrne family, it sits astride Sean's and my estate."

"Whatever could be going on?" Scrooge inquired.

"Nothing good," Byrne said. "I shall get my musket and investigate." He headed for the fireplace, above which rested his long-barrelled firearm. He took it down and began filling the barrel with gunpowder from a powder horn.

"Wait!" Shackle said. "Blevins and I will go. We're the most trained in matters of large crowds, and we are officials of Her Majesty's police force. If they are just having an unauthorised party or are into some mischief, let us go put a stop to it. They will heed the voice of our authority. Stay here, gentlemen, and let the Metropolitan handle this affair. Come, Blevins." They strode towards the door into the hall, each one ensuring they had a Billie club. Blevins pulled out his pistol. Shackle stopped at the door and turned. "I mean it, friends. Stay safe here."

When the remaining men heard the officers close the door, they turned to the window. Byrne doused the lamps so they could see better. On the hill, there was now a bonfire spilling flames into the sky. A mass of beings cloaked in gloom, be they men or something else, circled round the fire in undulating patterns.

Scrooge was glad Blevins and Shackle had gone to investigate. He felt certain the beings on the hill roaming in and out of the castle and grounds were some form of ghouls. He wanted no part of it.

Cratchit said, "What will Blevins and Shackle do once they arrive? I cannot tell for sure but there must be upwards of forty men there."

"Men? Or phantoms?" Scrooge squeaked.

"Or leprechauns," Lockie added. "I've seen them. Perhaps it's just a harvest ritual."

Byrne put his hand on Lockie's shoulder. "I've seen a leprechaun too, though at a distance. But I doubt leprechauns would have a harvest festival. But they do like to dance. The one I saw was dancing a jig."

The men moved closer to the window, their noses almost touching the glass panes. They each could see the officers pacing stealthily up the slope. None of them spoke, though each one said silent prayers. The blaze grew large, casting fantastic shadows on the castle walls.

"Centuries ago," Byrne whispered, "there was a deadly battle for control of the castle. My parents retold the story of spirits of dead soldiers rising. I've never seen any. I hope this is not an abominable human sacrifice."

"Say," Cratchit noticed. "I see Blevins walking up the hill, but where is Shackle now?"

"Perhaps he's swinging around in a flanking movement," Byrne said, stepping on a chair to see better. He peered around the library. "Where's Holmes?"

Scrooge turned from the window. "Yes, where's Lockie?"

Each man looked out the window once more and soon saw Lockie's shadowy form striding quickly up the incline. Cratchit said, "Well, of course. There he goes."

"I'm not surprised," added Scrooge. "So long as he stays alive."

STAVE FIFTY-FIVE

THE BONFIRE AT THE CASTLE

Lockie crept like a cat pursuing its prey. He had not been asked to approach this ongoing matter of the castle and bonfire, but he assumed the beings on the hill were up to no good. In addition, based on what he knew of Christ's nails in the box at Tamperwind, and on the knowledge conveyed by Scrooge, Cratchit, and Byrne about Sean's focus on finding a treasure, he knew others also sought the treasure.

He could see there were no phantoms or leprechauns milling about the bonfire, but men. And he heard them chanting in unison, the language neither English nor Latin.

Drawing steadily closer to the castle, he reflected on what he had learned from the people along the Cornwall coast: Jesus Christ had come as a boy to Cornwall with his father's relative, Joseph of Arimathea. Joseph had accomplished the business of purchasing tin, and the Lord of Heaven had made friends with dozens of inhabitants of the isle. Now, he feared this inordinate band of men were playing host to great evil on the island across from Cornwall.

Lockie slipped carefully up the hill, ducking down into swales, checking no chanter was watching, and then racing to the next tree. The castle's walls and its single tower loomed to his left. A stand of trees ran to his right from the vale with a narrow stream. The long line of trees ran up the hill and down the other side into the dark. The bonfire began to give an aura of impending day, and the light and shadows slid as the men swayed and tramped around it. Lockie saw every man wore a hooded cloak. He dashed for cover behind the trees.

A sudden movement in the brush caught his attention. He turned, ready to fight. Then he heard Shackle's strained voice. "Holmes, come give me aid. I was attacked."

Lockie rushed to the Chief Inspector who lay on his back on the ground. His brow was covered with dried blood and a nasty cut, and his wrists and feet were bound tightly with rope. Lockie knelt beside him and whispered, "Quiet, sir. Are you seriously hurt?"

"I cannot tell. I was knocked out."

Lockie inspected the bump and the dried blood on the inspector's forehead.

"There must have been half a dozen of them." Shackle hammered his words. "I waylaid two of them, but they bounced my noggin. Now, I am unable to see clearly."

"'Tis a nasty blow, sir. Let me untie you."

Shackle took a deep breath. "No. I don't believe I could even stand. Everything before me is swimming. Instead, I don't know if Blevins knows I've been assaulted. I was attempting to flank the crowd when I was jumped. My officer is in peril. Here, take the pistol from my pocket and save Blevins if you can."

Lockie dug through the man's jacket pocket and retrieved the firearm. "I hate to leave you here, Inspector."

"Don't worry about me. Save Blevins. In my fight with the men, I saw several wore masks and long black robes. I fear something worse is occurring than I could ever imagine."

Lockie stood and sped at a dead run up the hill with both his pistol and the inspector's cocked and ready to fire. He arrived on the periphery of the bonfire and the milling throng. Cratchit's estimation had been right. He counted upwards of forty men, all in black robes with hoods, striding in solemn file in circles around the fire. The inner circle was moving clockwise, the outer one gliding like a snake counterclockwise.

Then he noticed the group of four men perched on a pile of rock rubble near the last vestiges of a castle wall. The three in front wore white robes with gold cinches around the waists. The one in back wore black and looked to be merely observing rather than participating. Rather than being hooded, each man wore an elaborate headdress, fashioned like the hood of a cobra. Lockie had seen enough illustrations in books during his education at the Ragged School to know the headdresses were equivalent to those worn by princes and priests of ancient Egypt.

He crept closer, looking for Blevins. He thought urgently, *Did they get him too?* He noticed a stand of muskets beside the castle wall. Next to the muskets stood a big, slouching man wearing a broad-brimmed hat covering his face.

Blevins was nowhere in sight.

Suddenly, the circling men stopped and looked at those standing on the rubble pile. The tallest man in priest garb shouted, "Jannes! Jambres!" The black-robed mob began a chorus, repeating those words. The priest held up an article which, to Lockie, looked like a piece of metal. *What is that thing?* The throng ceased chanting and prostrated themselves. While they had their faces to the ground, Lockie slipped around the outside edge of the prone horde for a closer look. The tall man still held up what Lockie considered to be some sort of talisman glinting in the firelight.

With stealthy steps, Lockie ventured within a few yards of the makeshift platform, his back pressed against a wall. He carefully examined the leaders standing with their arms upraised. Three were tall and elderly, but the fourth was somewhat shorter, and his facial features were those of a young lad.

The tall man exclaimed, "Behold! The head of the spear we have just received this hour. The blade that insured the *death of the One!*"

The mass of prone men glanced briefly then put their foreheads back on the ground.

The priestly garbed leader then shouted, "When the nails are ours, we shall have unlimited power!"

Lockie was baffled, but he knew he had to do something quickly. The ceremony boded a darkness he knew must be stopped. He immediately developed a plan to rush forwards and seize the spearhead, for it must be the one that had pierced Jesus's side after He died on the cross.

Lockie searched one last time for Blevins, then, brandishing both pistols, he had resolved to make his charge when, suddenly, his mind went dark.

STAVE FIFTY-SIX
LOCKIE IN HIS ELEMENT

Lockie awakened with a splitting headache. The tip of the rising sun shone dazzling just over the horizon, and the glare hurt his eyes. The first thing he realised was he was lying on his back on a pile of stones, some of which, with rough edges, rubbed his back horribly. Smoke from the dying bonfire drifted in wafts about him. He choked. Wiping his bleary eyes, he saw the face of Isiah Thrusher, the seaman, a few inches from his own nose.

The old seadog quibbled, "So, there ye be, ye measly piece o' meat, lyin' there with a gun in each hand, neither of which ye found a use for."

Lockie asked, "What?" He rose to sitting. "Thrusher, how is it I find you around me again?"

"I'm 'ere 'cause this be where me journey has led me. I be in search o' treasure, and, if me hunch be right, there must be some hidden 'ere in this forlorn, fallen-down castle."

"Treasure!" Lockie rubbed his throbbing temples then reached around to the back of his head and felt a lump. "Ouch. Wait! I just remembered. I've got to see about Inspector Shackle."

"Not to worry, laddie. Yer friends have already seen to his bindings, and he be free as a bird. Mr Byrne 'as sent Thomas for the doctor in Dublin to care for 'im. They were all out lookin' for ye ever since Officer Blevins came stumblin' into the manor just before the cock crowed. Misters Scrooge and Cratchit were especially worried about ye."

"Then I best return, lest they worry more."

"There be no need, laddie. They know yer here. I told 'em I'd sit wit ye till ye woke. I've sat through many the wake of some dead fellow. So, sittin' and waitin' be no issue for me."

"Did they all …?" Lockie turned to look at the smoldering bonfire, black and smoky, with a few bright orange embers glowing. "I was here last night. There was a bizarre ceremony with forty or fifty men in robes. They were chantin' and actin' like they were in the presence of a—"

"'Twas not in the presence o' any god, not a good one anyway. I wasn't 'ere for it, but I be aware o' the cult."

"So, it's an evil cult." Lockie picked up the pistols and closed down the hammers. He stuck the guns in his deep jacket pockets.

"Aye."

"I'm tired of this smoke. I'm heading to the house."

"Aye, ye best do that. Yer employers 'ave an important task awaitin' ye."

Lockie treaded down the hill. When Thrusher did not follow, he stopped. "Are you comin'?"

"Nay, I want to 'ave a look 'round."

Walking down the hill, Lockie struggled to recall all he had seen. His head throbbed. *Whoever hit me did a mean job of it.* He tried to recall the four priests and their appearance. *Who were they?* Only then did he realise the older boy on the rubble podium was none other than James Moriarty.

He never saw the lone man standing inside the doorway of the castle turret, barely a few yards behind the group of leaders … the one wearing a black cape.

He walked in through the kitchen door. Scrooge and Cratchit were drinking tea at the table while Byrne stood beside Mrs O'Malley near the larder. Shackle was seated at the end of the table as a doctor shone a lantern in his eyes. Shackle did not look well.

"You appear to have had a concussion," the doctor said. "Most likely, you'll be fine by tomorrow. Take these powders every four hours." He handed the man some small packets of a medicine. "This is an old recipe from the Indians of America. It is good for a headache." The doctor closed his bag and looked at Lockie. "Is this the other one you said would arrive soon?"

Byrne replied, "Yes, it is. Sit, Lockie. Let the doctor take a look at you. We would have stayed with you, but from what Blevins told us, there is much to consider. He's lying on the couch in the parlour, completely undone and highly nauseous. He's thrown up twice."

The doctor gave Lockie a once-over. Seeing the young detective's eyes contracted correctly when the light was shone in them, the doctor gave Lockie some medicine packets for the headache. "You have a tough skull, young man. You'll be fine."

Byrne paid the doctor and saw him to the door. Returning, he said, "Since we have most of you here, save Blevins who is asleep, I feel we should begin our discussion and decide on next steps."

"First of all," Lockie said. "Do all of you know who Isiah Thrusher is? He saved Bobbie Wheeler from being taken prisoner by a band of faeries, and he was at my side when I awoke this morning."

Byrne said, "I know him only because he had visited Sean a few months ago. I'm uncertain of his reason. Perhaps Sean was planning to purchase a sea vessel of his own, and the seaman had connections with a seller. I did discover Thrusher makes his living serving as a mate on ships, so his time on land is limited. The one time I spoke with him while he was involved with Sean, he espoused he was 'no land lubber.'"

"Our next move," said Scrooge, not caring he was interrupting, "is to speak again to Malachi Doyle. I don't believe he's told us everything we should know. Plus, I wish for Lockie to spend some time in your brother's library." He rapped his knuckle on the table. "I'm quite tired of getting nowhere in this case. We have needed Lockie."

Lockie gave a slight smile. "I'm at your service, Misters Scrooge and Cratchit." Lockie had come to care deeply for his employers whom he deemed his friends.

"I shall stay here and rest," Shackle said. "I still feel puny."

Malachi was coming in from the field when the men arrived in Byrne's landau. Upon entering the house, they smelled a mellifluous odour of a hearty stew. Malachi's girlfriend, Matilda, appeared from the kitchen, wearing an apron and holding a wooden spoon. In no time, she had invited them to dine with her and Malachi. As none of them had eaten anything since the night before, they readily joined in the feast. The stew was loaded with hearty chunks of beef, carrots, peas, and a tongue-delighting gravy. They even had potatoes.

"Those potatoes are from Mr Callahan's farm," Matilda said. "Untouched by any blight. We are so blessed."

After the meal, Scrooge again rapped his knuckle on the table. "Lockie, follow me into the library."

While the remainder of the men sat with Malachi and Matilda, Scrooge and Lockie ambled into the large library. Scrooge closed the door behind them. "Here is your task. Something in this room is a clue. Maybe there are many clues. I am fortunate I often have a sense that something weighs on a subject, just as I do now. But I don't have the acumen you naturally have to ferret out a salient point or item that can help us in this investigation."

Lockie was already looking about the shelves festooned with volumes and volumes of books—scientific journals and books on every aspect of biology, zoology, and astronomy. Large books detailed portions of history—from ancient times to the wars with Napoleon. Most plentiful were novels and books on the Bible, both Old and New Testaments, plus writings by the great theologians.

"Here is the conundrum," Scrooge said after clapping his hands to regain Lockie's attention. "We all know a drunk man would never leave his home or the town pub and venture out onto the moor unless he was in trouble. Perhaps Reginald's brother was being pursued. Sean had recently been looking for treasure, which is cause enough for someone to want him dead. Cratchit spoke with the gardener, Rian Simple, who explained that Sean never drank anything but milk. He only put on the appearance of drinking so as not to appear prudish. As the London newspapers claim, all Irishmen are drunkards."

"So, he was merely maintaining appearances."

"Precisely. Second, some man, who had hoped to gain entrance to the mayor's house, was disguised as an Irish pot and pan fixer."

"A tinker."

"Yes. When he was denied access, he stormed about the home, looking for what we now know was the small jewellry box found on Sean Byrne's body. A box we have yet to open. Later, in the evening of that same day, Mayor Kelly was murdered. The constables have done nothing to investigate the murder of an important man. Finally, Mr McDevitt, the pub owner, who may or may not figure into this mystery, was also murdered."

Lockie lifted an atlas book from the library table and thumbed through it. Distractedly, he said, "Three murders, and now, we have a large group of men—members of a cult, according to Thrusher—who are holding their ceremony at the very castle adjacent to Byrne's land."

"And we didn't tell you this, but the castle is where Sean spent most of his time looking for this so-called treasure. Now, search this library and find something to help us solve this case." Scrooge exited and closed the door behind him.

Lockie was alone and felt he was in his element. He had honed his observation skills by seeking out any bit of information in the many cases Scrooge had assigned him to find culpable evidence of a spouse's infidelity. He had never enjoyed finding cause to break up a marriage and was often happy to find there was no infidelity at all. Thus the marriage was strengthened.

He began combing through the books. Searching the bookshelves first, he found two books pulled out a tad. The first was a novel recently published in 1845: *The Count of Monte Cristo*. Inside, he found a most interesting letter, one with a broken wax seal on the envelope.

The second book, a large one, was on another shelf. Stuffed inside this tome on the subject of whaling was a partially completed monograph entitled, *Typee*, the pages loosely bound. The author was someone Lockie had not heard of, an American named Herman Melville. *For goodness' sake*, Lockie thought. *Who is this Melville fellow?* Included inside the stuffed book were correspondences from Melville to none other than Isiah Thrusher. The last item stuck between the pages was a New York magazine from the year 1839 entitled *The Knickerbocker*.* He opened the periodical and found an interesting article by a Jeremiah Reynolds about a hunt for a large white sperm whale called Mocha Dick.* He decided to keep it and read the article later.

His search went on for hours, taking down books, flipping through the pages, and considering every aspect. He turned last to the table. In one old book lying upside down, he found a three-column list. The first column bore odd letter markings. He surmised the second list to be translations of those unusual words into Latin. In a third column set across from the Latin, the words were in English. "Hmm," he said. "These scribbles and Latin phrases look much like what my dear wife was working on."

In a book on English law, he found two documents written in legalese. "Ah-ha!" he exclaimed. Finally, he opened the large world atlas once more. He thumbed through it, and, in between the last two pages, he found what he thought was most important.

Lockie emerged from the library when the sun was settling behind the Wicklow mountains, carrying all the evidence he had found tucked inside the novels, lawbook, and oversized world atlas.

"We've discovered some vital information from Malachi," said Scrooge. "What did you find, Lockie?"

"What we needed and more. I'll tell you when we return to the manor."

STAVE FIFTY-SEVEN
THE FALSE BOX, THE MISSING POLICEMAN

"I told Malachi of his inheritance in the will," Byrne said, seating himself in his favourite chair, happy to be home. Save for Blevins who was still weak from his ordeal and illness, all the men sat in a circle in the parlour. "He offered to move into town since the home and estate now belong to me. I told him he could stay but only if he promised to marry the lady he was courting and make an honest woman out of her. He agreed. Besides, I will need a good foreman to bring Sean's farm back to its former glory."

When Byrne paused to light his pipe, Cratchit opened the discussion of found clues. "The first thing we learned confirmed what the gardener, Simple, had stated: Sean did not drink. It was only a farce. Malachi later told us that when Sean went to the bars, he would slowly empty his beer or whiskey when no one was looking then act quite drunk by stumbling around and slurring his speech."

"Apparently," Byrne said, "Malachi and Simple were the only ones who knew his secret. I had no idea. He always seemed to imbibe heartily when we were together. Thus was the innocent deceit of my little brother." He smiled.

"I have a hypothesis," Cratchit said. "After being around enough milkmaids carrying milk in unclean cans, and spoiled milk left in cups by my own children, I can safely say the stench in the whiskey bottle found by Callahan when he discovered Sean is from poisoned milk."

Byrne gawped.

"Someone was putting poison in his milk," Cratchit repeated. "And I believe they poisoned him slowly so as not to arouse suspicions."

"What if you are correct in your hypothesis? How would you prove it?" Byrne said.

"Malachi said he was acting delirious and jigging," Cratchit responded, "which could be evidence he was slowly being poisoned. Just enough to make him ill so when he died, everyone would think he had always been ill or a drunkard."

"However," Scrooge said. "He was out on the moor, far from his home. I believe he was being chased by someone who wanted what he had in his possession: the box."

"What is this box you speak of?" Shackle, now sufficiently recovered, asked.

"We have been so busy looking for clues for the murders, I've completely forgotten about it," Scrooge said.

Byrne added, "That's right. Blevins was going to see if he could unlock it. Perhaps we can find some answers there." He called to Bonnie Jean, whom he knew was listening at the door. "Bonnie Jean, I know you're there. Come forth!"

The little, freckled maid with raw hands and wrists pushed open the parlour door and wobbled into the room. "Yes, sir," she said, swaying back and forth.

"She looks drunk," Shackle declared. "Fine attitude for help these days. Well, this is the land of the drinkers."

Byrne said, "Not so fast, Inspector. She's a teetotaler."

Shackle hmphed.

"She looks faint!" Cratchit called. He and Lockie rushed to her side and helped her sit on a spare plush chair.

"I'm sorry, sir," she murmured. "I'm not my usual self."

Byrne knelt beside her and closely examined her. He raised one of her closed eyelids then the other. "Her pupils are completely dilated.".

No sooner had he said that than she began shaking in a mild tremor, and her lips took on an odd smile. Byrne called for O'Malley who quickly brought smelling salts. Bonnie Jean revived somewhat but then gagged.

While O'Malley helped Bonnie Jean to her room, Grizelda arrived with several cloths and laboured to remove the vomit stain from the carpet.

Scrooge, ever fearful of death and disease, thought, *I hope whatever illness she has is not contagious.*

"I suppose she has whatever Blevins is suffering from. Some new malady," O'Malley said.

Byrne went upstairs to check on Blevins but found the room empty. He returned with a jewellry box, holding it up for the others to see. "This looks like the box, but Officer Blevins was nowhere in sight. Perhaps he went for a stroll."

"I find that odd," said Shackle. "An officer of the law should report to me of his whereabouts while on duty."

"He admitted he was feeling poorly," Byrne said. "He is probably seeking some fresh air. I'm sure he'll return soon." He lightly shook the box. "Nothing rattles. It feels empty."

"Let me see it," said Scrooge, rising.

Byrne handed him the box.

Scrooge was shocked. "This is not the box from the mayor's home. I expend too much of my time staying alert to details. This box, though similar, is a fake! Look, even the key lock is different. This one has abalone and tiny pearls on it but no sapphires."

All the men stood and observed the box.

"I recall it had blue sapphires along the edge," Cratchit said. "Where is the real box?"

"You know," said Shackle, his hand on his chin, "when I saw my officer in Dublin, he was just coming out of a fancy shop, carrying an item in a paper sack. I thought nothing of it at the time."

"Could he have purchased this substitute box, hoping to fool you?" Lockie, who had remained quiet all this time, took the box in hand. "Why, I can open this easily." He took out his pocketknife then paused, remembering how the simple knife had been offered as treasure to the faeries. He applied the blade tip to the key lock, and with a few twists, the lid popped open. He turned the box upside down. "Mr Scrooge was right. It's empty."

Grizelda finally rose from cleaning the rug. "I'll take my leave, sir," she said, bowing to Byrne. "I must prepare tomorrow's meals."

Scrooge plopped into his chair. "What about the mayor? He had the jewellry box for a time after the constable gave it to him. Based on how the mayor's wife spoke, she knew not of its even being in her home. The mayor had hidden it, conveying its location only to the maid, Sally."

Cratchit paced the floor. "What did the mayor know about this peculiar box? Did he know of its value, or was he only interested in the jewels that bedecked its lid?"

"That is a good question, but I have another," Lockie said. "Was the mayor formerly a sailing man?"

STAVE FIFTY-EIGHT

SAILORS ON *THE ACUSHNET* SHIP,
A SECOND TREASURE DESCRIBED

"Mayor Kelly often shared his sailing adventures," Byrne said. "He was a ship's captain at one time."

"Which vessel?" Lockie said.

"Let me think." Byrne put his hand to his chin. "It was the *Fair Wind*, and though it's old, it still sails to and from the Wicklow port."

Lockie sighed. "Did he ever mention any other ship?"

"Yes, he was on a whaler that sailed all the way into the South Pacific. It was, um … it was an odd name."

The room fell silent while Byrne thought. Finally, he snapped his fingers. "The *Acushnet*."

"Ah!" Lockie said with considerable joy. "Then we have a connection."

"What could that be?" Shackle inquired. "How does being a ship captain get one killed over a jewellry box, a small one at that? Someone's sentimental value?" He crossed his arms.

Lockie smiled. "I'll explain in a moment. Wasn't there another murder?"

"Yes," Byrne replied. "The publican."

"Whose pub is down by the docks where sailors often frequent." Lockie pointed at Byrne.

"Why, yes," Byrne said.

"And do the sailors and townspeople join in games of chance there?" Lockie asked. "And further, did your brother, Sean, ever go there of an occasion and participate in said games?"

"I know he did," Byrne said. "But he was always careful with his money. He knew how to walk away before losing more than a shilling or two."

Lockie pretended he was dealing invisible cards on an invisible table. "And I suppose Sean may have won some big pots and was well-acquainted with the pub owner."

"Right on both counts." Byrne stood. "I see a connection being made."

"Now," Lockie said, lifting the atlas book from Sean Byrne's library, "I shall attempt to put some of this together. First, what I saw last night in that crass ceremony was a group of priests of this nefarious cult that attacked me and Shackle and Blevins. One of the priests held what I believe to be the head of the spear that lanced the side of Jesus on the cross."

Each man's jaw fell open.

"I will tell you of an equally amazing and shocking fact." Lockie opened the atlas. "I feel I am correct because I found this letter stuffed away in one of Sean's books." He held an envelope with the royal wax seal of the Queen of England still evident but broken. He opened the envelope and removed the letter. "To summarize its contents, this letter shows how Queen Victoria encouraged Sean to pursue what she believes in all sincerity is the actual spearhead broken from its wooden staff."

"Let me see that!" Scrooge lifted the letter from Lockie and quickly scanned its contents. "I know this handwriting. I received such a letter from the queen when we put an end to the dog-men in London. This is her handwriting!"

Byrne was flabbergasted, his face showing wonderment. "My brother was working at the behest of Queen Victoria! He never said."

Scrooge pointed at the writing. "This letter demands he keep it secret for the sake of the realm, lest it fall into the wrong hands."

Each man became lost in his own thoughts.

Finally, Shackle rose and strode rapidly across the floor. He turned. "Our national security may be at stake. No wonder she called upon London's premier detectives." He exhaled deeply and sat, drumming his fingers nervously on the chair arms.

"Now," Lockie continued. "Here is the connection of Sean with the pub owner, McDevitt. Inside one novel, I found this partially completed manuscript by someone who I can only guess is an author, a fella named Herman Melville. In the pile of papers bound with twine, there is a recently published book entitled *Typee*. However, far more important than the book is this packet of numerous letters from a man demanding the return of a certain item. There are at least fifteen letters from this Mr Melville to Isiah Thrusher, whom I met in the strangest of circumstances two nights ago in Wicklow, and I believe you met him early this morning by the castle."

Byrne explained, "Yes, Thrusher offered to stay beside you until you awakened. I knew him from his earlier involvement with Sean. All of us encountered him when he was first mate on Thorn's ship and at the inn in Dublin. I consider him a good man. He seems convivial enough. The rest of us were busy putting out the fire at the castle lest it spread to the fields and sheep. In addition, we were tending to Blevins who was deeply nauseous and Inspector Shackle who was suffering severely from his head wound."

"I told them you were tough as nails," Scrooge said, "and a blow to the head would be of little consequence to your youth and vigour. So, each of us had no compunction to stay with you until you awakened. Just common sense."

"Er, thank you, I suppose, Mr Scrooge." Lockie cleared his throat. "Now, both Melville and Thrusher, in his youth, were on the whalin' ship, *Acushnet*, and became fast friends. At one point, the two jumped ship, along with another fella named Richard Tobias Greene. They spent several months in the Marquesas Islands."

While listening, Cratchit had performed a quick scanning of the opening pages of the manuscript, *Typee*. "Perhaps this tome is reflective of Melville's time in the islands." He set the stack of pages on a side table.

"I'd bet you're right," Lockie said. "Later, after bein' taken on as sailors on another passin' whalin' ship, Melville ultimately returned to Manhattan and Thrusher to Ireland and England. But the letters easily explain how Melville had given to Thrusher, for no particular reason, an old map, or rather, a poor reproduction of an original map that his father, Allan Melville, had somehow secured in his business dealin's in Europe. Melville had become quite adamant in his letters to Thrusher about wanting it back."

"But this sailor named Thrusher kept it," Scrooge finished.

"Right," Lockie said, "and I conjecture that every chance he's had, he's been lookin' for the treasure the map indicated was somewhere in the area of Wicklow and Kindlestown Castle."

"And he always carried the map with him, I'll wager," added Byrne.

Cratchit was almost shouting. "Reginald! In a card game at the Flying Corsair Pub when Thrusher thought he had an unbeatable set of cards in his hand, he bet the map and lost it to your brother. And McDevitt was aware of the entire betting episode and watched Thrusher turning over the map to Sean."

Each of the men were jubilant, giving backslaps and plenty of smiles to each other.

"But," Lockie said as the men calmed, "Thrusher also had no idea how to read the strange markings on the map, which were instructions to finding the treasure. For that, Sean, who was a well-educated man—"

"At Oxford," Byrne said.

"Yes, I saw his diploma and several awards on the wall." Lockie then lifted two items. One was a page with columns of words in three languages. The other was a map. "Here, gentlemen, in my left hand is the map which Sean won from Thrusher. In my right hand, I have his page where he translated Hebrew in the column on the left into Latin in the middle column and thence into English. He translated the Hebrew riddle on the map and solved it, which directed him to Kindlestown Castle where he found this: the other half of the map." He carefully lifted a sheepskin scroll with barely readable markings. "A scroll that, I believe with confidence, was left here by none other than Joseph of Arimathea. I can later explain how I know it was once the property of the very man at Christ's death in a moment. With this other half of the map and new knowledge, Sean found the treasure."

"And it had been hidden in the odd pile of rocks out on the moor," said Byrne, shaking his head in disbelief.

Lockie held up the paper map. "I believe some Irish folks coincidentally came upon the spearhead some centuries later, learned of its history, and placed it in the jewellry box before putting it back where they found it. Then someone recopied one half of the map, which was later recopied several times over the centuries, and it changed hands before it ended up in

Herman Melville's father's safekeeping, thence to Herman, and finally into Thrusher's hands."

"I read two lines from another document Sean had in his possession!" Byrne exclaimed. "It was written in Latin, which was often the language of Ireland for years."

"Of course ... the Romans." Lockie carefully laid a yellowed page so tattered, it was more holes than paper, on the table. "This document explained what was not entirely clear on the faded maps. It mentions an old legend of St Patrick tossing statues that turned into boulders. Once Sean had translated the Latin, he could solve the maps."

"The stones of Crom Cruaitch tossed by St Patrick." Byrne stood and fingered his lapel pin. "Erin, Go Bragh."

"What is this Crom ... whatever you said?" Shackle spit the question.

Byrne explained, "'Tis a stack of boulders of various sizes out on the Wicklow moor where Sean died. He was heading there to hide the treasure he had previously found."

"To hide a gift more precious than pearls," Cratchit said.

Byrne lowered his head and softly said, "And he gave up everything to find it. His land. His crops. His other goals in life. Perhaps even the love of a woman. Maybe he did love Lynch's sister. St Matthew's Gospel, chapter thirteen, verse forty-four. He found no greater use of all he had than to secure that treasure."

The silence in the room lasted for several minutes. Only the ticking of the clock and the chime of the hour could be heard. A low rumble of thunder sounded in the distance.

Finally, Cratchit stated what they all knew. "He found the head of the lance once plunged into the side of our Lord and broken loose. It must have fallen to the ground, and Joseph of Arimathea picked it up."

"And blood and water poured forth," Lockie said. "From another document in a box Pudge and Dimsight found in a secret room at Hopworth Mine, my wife was able to translate a message written by Joseph of Arimathea. The writings explained how Joseph's ship was being chased by pirates. It surely sailed to Wicklow where he disembarked with the spearhead. Though Christianity had not been introduced into Ireland, he must have found some locals who helped him hide the spearhead."

"Did he intend to return for it?" Scrooge asked.

"I don't know that." Lockie paced across the room and pointed east out a window. "I do know he hid the box of the nails used to hang Jesus on the cross in a cave within Hopworth Mine. It was just a cavern in his time. Lucy and Samuel are now in possession of those nails."

Scrooge suddenly remembered his accumulated notes. "Hold on! I have more important information." He rushed upstairs.

STAVE FIFTY-NINE

THE POLICEMAN RETURNS,
THE TREASURE RETURNED

Scrooge was plying his way along the dark hallway towards his room when he heard a moan coming from Blevins's room. He slowly entered, wary that the moan may have come from a ghost or other ghoul. Another moan issued from under the bed. Scrooge slunk closer and tentatively lifted the edge of the bedspread. Lying under the bed was Officer Blevins. "My, my," said Scrooge. "Whyever are you under there?"

Blevins's face was red from tears. In a trembling voice, he stated, "They're coming. Probably hundreds of them." He buried his head in his folded arms.

Scrooge got down on one knee and lifted the spread higher. Though the light from a single whale oil lamp was dim, Scrooge could see the bobbie held what looked like a spearhead in one hand. "What's that in your hand, Officer Blevins?"

Blevins raised his head. "It's the spearhead I wrestled from the hands of the foul cult priest."

"Then you must come straightaway downstairs and explain. Hiding here will do no good. I thought you a brave man."

"Indeed, at one time, I felt I was such a man." Blevins looked piercingly at Scrooge. "But before now, I had not faced this crass evil that was fully tangible at the castle last night."

"Fear not," Scrooge said. "We all have armaments. This is a strong house. Come forth." The old miser could barely believe his own words. He knew he had spent most of his life either cowering or blustering to cover his cowardice. Always apprehensive of shadows. Wary of any ruffian who had requested a loan, lest the tough man default, and unsure he would even want to try to collect on the loan. Mostly, he had been devastatingly fearful of not having enough money.

Blevins climbed out from under the bed, dusted off his uniform, and strode beside Scrooge down to the parlour. At the bottom of the stairs, despite his visage showing fear, Blevins announced, "Here I am. When you came looking for me, Mr Byrne, I was hidden under my bed. I apologise for my cowardice."

Shackle stood and hmphed. "Whatever would cause one of Her Majesty's Metropolitan police to hide?"

Blevins walked up to the inspector and handed him the spearhead. "This. It is an item the Jannes and Jambres cult desires to use for black magic."

Shackle opened his mouth to retort but clamped it shut. Then he said, "I have been a witness to great evil perpetrated against the entire empire. Tell us how you came to have this in your possession." He sat, clutching the steel weapon* of death.

"Yes," Cratchit said. "We are on your side. As detectives, we have seen horrifying evil transgress itself into the streets and alleys of London. Tell us why you are fearful."

Blevins clasped his hands together. "This may cause the loss of my position at the force. Regardless, I have no choice but to explain. Shortly before the four of us departed London, three men approached me quite benignly. Only one of them spoke, saying he knew I was going to Ireland to solve the murder of Sean Byrne. Also, he said the three of them represented a club. Can you believe it? He called it a *club*. They were interested in obtaining a box that had been mislaid. He described it in detail then told me if ever I came upon it, the club would pay me thirty pounds of silver." He held up a sack of coins and dropped it on a lamp table. "I have no desire for these ill-gotten funds."

Cratchit rose and patted him on his back. "Please continue. We are here for you."

"I was cautious and asked him about the box. Acting nonchalantly, he said its contents were only significant to the club, and a thief had pilfered it. So, I believed the box was not mislaid but purloined. Well, being an officer of the law, I felt it was incumbent upon me to return any stolen goods to the rightful owners. He did extend an unusual warning, claiming the Byrne family might attempt to stop me. I asked him why, and he merely stated it was due to an old rivalry."

Byrne said, "As far as I know, neither Sean nor I have any rivals."

"I was far too anxious to serve well Inspector Shackle and Her Majesty," Blevins said. "I honestly did not give the aspect much thought. I figured it was unlikely I would come upon the box. The odds seemed miniscule. So, there you have it."

"Why did you seek to obtain the reward?" Shackle blurted angrily. "That is against policy!"

"Yes, Inspector." Blevins raised his eyes to stare directly at his superior. "You see, I have a woman I love very much. She and I would like to get married. But on my salary, I can barely afford the flat in which I currently reside. I hoped to purchase a home for us so we could wed. Love overtook my sense of duty."

"I guess I can see that," Shackle said.

"When we were at the Mayor's house," Blevins said, "I knew not what the criminal wanted. I just wanted to solve the crimes. But when Mr Cratchit came forth with the jewellry box, I knew immediately from the description the man had given me that it was the one they wished to have returned. Since they told me the Byrne family might resist my returning what I believed was a filched item, I kept my moves secret. I had seen the tall man when we arrived in Dublin. He met with me secretly, though at that time I still had no idea what the box contained nor why he and his cohorts wished to obtain it."

"How did you open it?" Lockie asked. "I'm fairly skilled at picking locks."

"While attempting to pop the lock, I inadvertently destroyed the box. Inside, I found the spearhead wedged against the sides. Hence, it didn't rattle when shaken."

"That is why I saw you exiting the gift shop in Dublin," Shackle said. "You purchased a replacement box, hoping no one would notice the difference."

"Correct. I had travelled to Dublin first to send the letter detailing our progress to you, Inspector, via a packet to Manchester where I thought you were. I met the tall man there and gave him the spearhead, and he gave me the money. Then I purchased the similar jewellry box Mr Holmes now holds. And should I have to stand trial, I will admit as much. I knew not what was the intent of the bonfire. At first, I considered it was a lark for locals to celebrate Halloween. Such occurrences are not unusual in some rural areas in England. Walking up the hill, Inspector Shackle went off into the woods. I was not worried in the slightest at the moment, purely thinking the bonfire was some tomfoolery. In no time, I found I had erred."

"Last night, you appeared horribly ill when you returned," Byrne said.

"Yes," Blevins responded. "When I arrived beside the throng of men, I was welcomed as if my presence was anticipated. Then they insisted I sit down and watch what they called their 'celebration.' A young man brought me a small loaf of bread and insisted I eat it all since it was unleavened bread, like the Jews ate before escaping Egypt."

"Bread!" Scrooge exclaimed.

"Yes." Blevins rubbed his stomach then his chest. "Then he demanded I drink a foul, bitter mead. He was so persuasive, I gulped it down. Immediately, I was ill to my stomach and swooned, finding it difficult to breathe."

"You were poisoned," Byrne said. "Just as my brother was."

STAVE SIXTY

THE EVE OF ALL HALLOWS

"I was not poisoned badly enough to not listen and discover their plans for the weapon. The leader rambled on about their next steps, saying they knew the nails used to pierce Jesus's hands and feet were somewhere in Cornwall."

"Unfortunately," Lockie stated, "I know of what you speak. The nails of Christ have been found. They are in a box at Tamperwind Manor in Cornwall." He stood. "If this cult means to steal the nails, then I must return. My wife, the Jigginses, my friends, and the miner families are in grave danger."

Blevins took a deep breath. "When the cult followers heard the tall man announce the location of the nails, they cheered. I began to understand they meant to use them for considerable evil. They believe those nails, along with the spearhead, will let them gain inordinate power. I struggled to stand and gathered enough strength to grab the spearhead and run into the forest. After I wrested the spearhead from the leader, many of them with guns gave chase, firing at me. So, I headed in the opposite direction of the house. After several hours, I lost my pursuers but then began to feel dreadfully ill. It has passed now." He took Lockie's arm. "You may not get the chance to sail to your friends. The cult army will be coming here forthwith. I heard them say they plan to invoke some creature named Crom Dubh!"

"Crom Dubh. The 'Crooked One,'" Byrne said. "He took the place of Crom Cruaich. He was worshiped as a god of fertility. He required human sacrifice." His eyes widened. "And tonight is Halloween!"

The room fell silent. Scrooge remembered today was his birthday. He did not feel festive.

Shackle seemed unperturbed. "I've handled riotous mobs before. Let me ask you a question, Blevins. Did you say you were poisoned by bread and bitter-tasting mead?"

"You are correct, sir."

"Well, this afternoon, while you gentlemen were away, I started feeling better and took a stroll in the garden. Quite beautiful. However, now I recall several of those pretty flowers have poisonous qualities. Nightshade, oleander, and foxglove. I kept walking out towards the little work-shed, where I witnessed the cook and a tall, thin fellow standing quite close as though admiring each other a great deal. I was too far away to be sure, but the man may have stolen a kiss. My eyes aren't as strong as they used to be."

Byrne showed astonishment. "Mrs O'Malley?"

Shackle elaborated, "If that's her name. When I drew closer, I think the man looked a great deal like one I saw in a Dublin pub, though I know not his name. After I arrived, he barely gave a greeting and departed quickly out through a field of grain. The woman stayed there, running her hands over the stalks in a seductive manner, if you understand my meaning."

"I'm aghast," Byrne said. "Our Mrs O'Malley having an affair."

"That is not the real issue," Shackle said. " When I asked her what she was doing, she said she was making remedies. I merely listened but said nothing to her about the small crop of grain in which she was standing. Couldn't be more than a quartern of a half an acre."

"Wheat?" Byrne asked.

"No," Shackle replied. "A weed known as darnel.* Looks quite similar to wheat. Any farmer who is not careful can grow the weed along with the real wheat. It is *fake wheat* that makes what we who work the wheat farms call 'drunken bread,' or as the Greeks called it, the *plant of frenzy*. Growing up on a wheat farm north of London, one of my tasks as a child was to spread the wheat seeds on a table and carefully remove the darnel seeds. Our family grew only wholesome wheat."

"Darnel. That is the *tares* in the Bible parable," Byrne said.

"I've only recently begun reading the Bible," Scrooge said. "Please elaborate."

Cratchit answered, "'Tis about a man who sows a good wheat crop, but while he is asleep, an enemy sows the tares, or darnel, in his field with the good seeds. The owner learns from his servants that the good crop now has darnel growing with it. He tells his servants not to pull up the weeds, lest they accidentally destroy the good wheat."

"So …" Scrooge was struggling to grasp the meaning.

Cratchit smiled. "I believe Jesus was saying bad people are allowed to live alongside good people. They will be judged later at the harvest, at the end of their lives."

Scrooge gave a nod of understanding.

"My point is," continued Shackle, "that your poisoner is none other than your cook. She ground darnel into flour and put it into her bread and even the mead or milk."

Scrooge grasped his hands behind his back and strode rapidly about the room, all the while expounding, "This O'Malley woman has been slowly poisoning people she finds fault with. That much is evident. Since Sean Byrne was liked by everyone, she must have somehow learned from him what he was looking for. She wanted the map for herself or, more likely, for others willing to pay her for it. She told me she wanted to leave Byrne Manor." He stopped.

"And …?" asked Shackle.

Scrooge pivoted and paced faster. "She began poisoning Sean a little at a time, baking darnel into the bread and mixing some element of poisonous flowers into the milk in his whiskey bottles. Who would ever guess the bread and milk would be poisoned?"

"Exactly," Cratchit said.

Scrooge ceased his stride. "When she learned he had found the spearhead, someone vile convinced her to complete the task of killing him. The day Sean realised he had been poisoned, he tried to return the box where he found it. He must have used the last of his strength to fight against the poison."

"He was being pursued," Byrne said, "but when Mr Callahan approached, the assailant fled."

"That has to be it," Scrooge said.

Just then, Bonnie Jean stumbled into the parlour from the hallway to the servant quarters and leaned against the doorframe in exhaustion, panting as she spoke. "Ye all be correct. Grizelda 'as been poisonin' people and made me 'arvest the poisonous plants without any gloves, so me constant touching the plants makes the rash spread all over me 'ands. She kept tellin' me it was for her remedies which she sells at the Wicklow market, but with all that 'as been goin' on, I started askin' 'er questions. Now, she's poisoned me." She grabbed her head with both hands and collapsed.

Byrne and Lockie rushed to her side. Her breaths came in rapid bursts. Lockie felt her pulse. "It's racing."

"I'll have Thomas go for the doctor." Byrne hastened to the door. When he opened it, he beheld a mass of torches, the flames torn by the whipping wind, and more than a hundred hooded men. They were rapidly striding up the road and onto the lawn.

STAVE SIXTY-ONE
ATTACK OF THE CULT

"Quickly!" Byrne shouted, closing the door and locking it. "Take up your arms. Officer Blevins was right. A horde of robed men are headed this way." He rushed into his office to retrieve his gun from its rack. While Scrooge and Cratchit raced upstairs to retrieve their pistols from their rooms, Herbert O'Malley came into the parlour.

"Mister Byrne," he announced, "I'm setting about lighting the manor lamps. 'Tis quite dark."

Byrne came into the room, carrying two muskets and a shotgun. "Not now, O'Malley. Here, take this musket. You know how to use it."

"Yes, sir. Many's the time when a youth, I—"

"No childhood stories now, O'Malley. Check if it's loaded."

"Yes, sir." He began checking the gun. When Scrooge and Cratchit returned, both armed with pistols, O'Malley asked, "Has anyone seen my wife?"

Each man stared briefly at him.

"Herbert, if you of all people can't find her, she's gone. She was listening to us while she cleaned the floor. She knows we now know of her vile deeds." Byrne placed his hand on O'Malley's shoulder. "You may not ever see her again. For now, you must defend the manor and your own life." He pressed the musket against the man's chest.

"Oh, dear," O'Malley said, pointing at Bonnie Jean lying on the floor with Lockie attending to her. "What's happened to the maid?"

"Your wife poisoned her," Lockie said. "Grizelda is a criminal, a murderer."

O'Malley stumbled to a chair. "I long expected as much, but I couldn't admit it. I think she poisoned Darragh's daughter a year ago."

A loud knocking sounded at the front door. "Mister Byrne, it's me, Thomas, with Lorcan Duffy and Rian Simple. Let us in! A great mob of men are spreading out over the grounds. Many are armed with muskets."

Byrne unlocked the door and let his workers inside. Thomas bore a shotgun. Duffy looked forlorn, rolling his hands. Rian Simple limped to the couch and sat, holding a sharp trowel. No sooner had Byrne let them in than Darragh Lynch entered from the kitchen, holding a musket in each hand. Two pistols protruded from his belt.

The men froze. Cratchit swung his pistol at the man.

Lynch barked, "Thar gach ni eile, *fíoramaidí; corp díth céille!* In yer words, it means, 'Above all else, it would be the height of folly.' If ye mean to shoot me, man, I won't be much help."

Cratchit lowered his weapon, and Lynch tossed him a musket. "It's loaded," Lynch snarled. "And ye best post someone at the back door. The rogues are swingin' 'round to the back."

Shackle, two pistols drawn from his jacket pockets, headed into the kitchen.

Lynch pounded his fist against a wall. "And two of 'em are none other than the farmhands, Crimp and Lowe. I shoulda known."

"Crimp and Lowe?" Byrne exclaimed. "I thought they were good-natured farmhands."

"'Twas all an act," Lynch growled. "They 'tweren't no farmhands. Barely knew one end of a plough from the other. Oh, they worked hard, but 'twas only for show. I'm certain they was never travellin' to Dublin to visit no mother. They were part of the infernal conflagration at the castle last night. I watched 'em sneak away all secret-like and followed 'em. They put on white robes and joined in the wanton exhibition. St Patrick, preserve us."

A loud pounding came at the door. "Byrne!" came a deep bass voice like a lion's roar from within the crowd some thirty yards from the doorway. "There's no use in resisting."

"English accent, not Irish," Scrooge remarked, pulling back the hammer of his pistol and peeking out a front window.

"We only want the spearhead," came the voice like scraping metal. "We know the officer has it."

Byrne peeked out a window beside the door and ducked his head back and whispered, "There must be at least one hundred of them." Then he yelled loudly, so his voice passed through the door, "You'll not get any spearhead or otherwise, from us! Officer Blevins never returned last night."

"Oh, but he did return. Mrs O'Malley informed us. She's with us now. A hero for us all. Can you feel the darkness, Byrne? It is our domain. You and your friends cannot resist us all."

"We can try. Take some of you down with us."

"Good. More human sacrifices to Crom Dubh."

Byrne peered out again, talking to the others in the house now. "I can't see who's speaking. It's too dark, even with the torches."

Cratchit had taken a position on the stairs landing and looked past the heavy curtains. "It's a tall man in the front, wearing a white robe. It's ... it's Lowe, the supposed farmhand."

"I'll wager he has another job," Scrooge said. "One with great wealth gained by swindling people from their property ... like lawyers. Wait a minute!" He called, "Lockie, didn't you say the nails were found in Hopworth Mine?"

"Aye." Lockie had been able to urge Bonnie Jean to sit up and lean against the wall and was giving her some water.

"I'm seein' things," Bonnie Jean mumbled. "Strange beasts. Friendly but bizarre."

"You're having hallucinations. They'll pass." Lockie helped her drink more water.

"I say, Lockie!" Scrooge called. "Are not the law firm of Cragle, Schleege, and Pincher trying to gain ownership of the mines?"

"Aye." Lockie stood.

"And none of the Jiggins family, nor your wife, nor even our good friend and attorney, Abel Leggitt, has seen the two partners, Schleege or Pincher. Is that correct?"

"I know it to be so. Only Cragle has even been in court."

"Then I feel confident," Scrooge said, "the fake farmhands are none other than the two missing lawyers. They do the dirty toils in secret while Cragle works his filth at the Lincoln Inn Chancery Court."

Cratchit applauded. "Makes perfect sense, Ebenezer! Those two have been trying to obtain the spearhead, and Cragle has been squaring away at the Jigginses and Lucy in the court to somehow wrest the property from them in the hope of finding the nails."

"Except," Lockie said, rising. Bonnie Jean's eyes were beginning to focus, and her breathing had slowed. "Somehow, they've realised the nails have been recovered."

STAVE SIXTY-TWO

THE LAWYER, HIS GANG,
AND HIS BLACKMAIL THREAT

Angus Wheeler flung open the door to Tamperwind Manor. He called, "Lucy, Samuel, Cora, come quickly!"

Cora rushed from the kitchen, and Samuel and Lucy sped down the stairs. The three gathered around Angus. He heaved a sigh. "There's trouble brewin'. Some fool from London has brought a band of half a dozen men and has been threatenin' our workers. The women and children have all fled to their homes. Our workers are standin' firm, each one with a shovel or pick, just inside Tamperwind Cave, but these ne'er-do-wells have guns."

"For what purpose?" Samuel asked.

"Barnabas is talkin' to him, tryin' to get squared away with him. Stallin' for time." Angus wiped his brow. "He and I both left our pistols here in the house, thinkin' what use have we of carryin' them in the mines."

"Do you have any idea what they want?" Lucy asked.

"All I can tell is this fellow is requiring all the miners walk off the job immediately," replied Angus.

"Then I shall have a word with him," Samuel said.

"It will do no good. He's given us a deadline," Angus said.

Lucy went to the window and peered out. "I see the armed men. Seven of them. The one in the front is yelling, though I cannot decipher his words."

Both of Lucy's children began crying.

"I'll see to them, Lucy," Cora said. The clever, stout dwarf hastened upstairs.

"Thank you, Cora." Lucy turned back to the window. "Wait a minute, I recognise the arrogant posture. The man in charge is Cragle, the lawyer!"

Samuel stepped to the window. "Abaddon Cragle. Whatever would make him take such an outlandish action? We could report him. He'd lose the case against us and be disbarred. It makes no sense."

"I believe it does," Lucy said. "He means to bargain for the nails."

Dimsight and Pudge slammed open the door. Pudge spoke first, "Barnabas is right behind us. He's given up talkin' to the villain."

"And Pudge and I," Dimsight, the slim boy of eleven years who always wore shaded glasses, said, "we have pistols here at the house, though ancient they may be. I believe they might fire a ball."

"Barnabas is a crack shot with a musket," Angus added. "I've seen him bring down a deer at five hundred yards, though we were poachin' at the time."

"I hope it doesn't come to that," Samuel said. "Those who fight with guns can die by a gun. Maybe I can reason with him."

Barnabas came up the steps, and the group met him on the porch. He pointed. "Says his name is Cragle, and he rightfully owns the mine and intends to shut it down. He claims he will open it later and rehire each one of the miners at a higher wage. I don't trust a thing about him."

"He's persuasive to some of the miners," Dimsight said. "Mostly the new hires."

"Wayne, er, Dimsight, do you have a feel for how the men will react?" Samuel asked.

Dimsight put his skinny hand on his chin. "Hard to say. Not one has ventured to stand beside him."

"When you come demandin' with guns," Pudge said, wiggling his fat fingers, "folks is less likely to listen."

Barnabas shushed them and motioned for all to get close. "Somehow, the word got out to this fellow that Christ's nails were found. He dropped a *not too faint* hint. Told the miners he would share the wealth of the newly found treasure with all of them but never mentioned what the treasure was.

Then he said that you two, Samuel and Lucy, were keepin' the treasure all to yourselves."

"And yet, none of them have left the mine? Not one?" Samuel asked.

"Not one," Dimsight confirmed.

"That's a good sign we have developed loyalty with our crews," Samuel said. "Now what do we do?"

"One more thing," Barnabas again whispered. When the others drew close, he said, "This London lawyer, he called himself, set a deadline of one hour for them to walk away, or else he'll set fire to their homes."

"Whatever is Cragle thinking?" Samuel said. He looked out the window at the shoved-together, unpainted board houses sitting closer to the manor than the mine. Dozens of homes knit tight. A fire would spread quickly.

"He must be quite desperate," Lucy replied. "Barnabas, how were Cragle's men reacting? Were they tough-looking? Did they look like a trained militia?"

Barnabas grinned. "Not at all, ma'am. They looked pretty timid, 'cept they all have guns, o' course."

"No matter," Lucy said. "I have an idea." She paced to the stairs then stopped and turned. "Dimsight and Pudge, gather as much charcoal as you can and bring it upstairs. Once you've done that, bring me some horse droppings from the stable. I won't need much. Quickly now. Once I have the charcoal and droppings, I'll need only half an hour. Then I'll have a surprise for the dastard and his little militia."

STAVE SIXTY-THREE
THE BATTLE AT THE MANSION

"I'll go see if I can stall them," Samuel said.

"Yes," said Lucy. "Get them to come up to the house's fence and keep them there." She hurried upstairs as Pudge and Dimsight gathered old grain sacks and serving spoons from the kitchen, hurrying to scoop up charcoal pieces at each of the manor's hearths.

"Barnabas," Samuel said, "Angus says you're a marksman."

"That I am," said Barnabas.

"Good. Take my musket from above the fireplace. It's loaded. Take a position upstairs. If I signal you, shoot the crudest one but just wound him if you can."

"That will be simple." Barnabas headed inside.

Samuel and Angus grabbed a pistol each, and both stuck the guns in the backs of their belts, hidden under their jackets. They walked slowly down to the gate of the yard, stopped, lit their pipes, and tried to look unconcerned.

Samuel could see Cragle eyeing them, but the vile lawyer made no move towards the picket fence. He kept up his harangue at the miners. "I'm counting down, Tamperwind miners." He pointed at his watch. "My men have torches in this barrow." He pointed to the wheelbarrow with a half dozen unlit torches in it. "Don't miss this opportunity to leave and gain riches a short while later."

When two of the miners started to walk out from the cave opening, Angus, his short height being no hindrance, bellowed, "Don't you dare!"

The miners sped back to the rest of the miners and hid behind them.

"That's better!" Angus called with a smile. "The sound carries well from this hill."

Cragle decided to walk up to the fence and confront Samuel. He saw Pudge and Dimsight dash to the stable towards the rear of the manor. "So, Samuel!" he called. "Sending your boys to prepare your steeds so you can escape? I presume you'll be taking the great treasure to keep it from your miners."

Samuel took the pipe from his lips. "Not at all. Those two young men have duties. We're not the least bit worried about any plan you might have."

Cragle and his gang arrived on the opposite side of the fence. "Not concerned we'll burn the homes of your beloved miners to the ground? I'm sure they'll want to keep working for you and live like cavemen in your mine with no homes to go to." He guffawed, and the armed men behind him chortled. One aimed his musket at Samuel. Cragle pushed the man's barrel down. "Not now, you fool. I believe Mr Jiggins will see things our way. Light the torches."

Two of the men set down their guns and began lighting the torches.

"Just four with guns," Angus whispered to Samuel. He glanced back at an upstairs window and saw Barnabas aiming the musket. He also saw Dimsight and Pudge, laden with a scoop of manure, dash into the back of the manor. He spoke aloud to Cragle, "Surely, you are not so callous as to burn down these innocent people's homes."

"Look at it my way." Cragle swept his hand in a grand gesture. "This property is rightfully mine. I have a writ here from a judge, declaring my ownership." He briefly held up a document Samuel quickly deduced was a forgery. He knew no judge would make such a ruling without Abel Leggitt informing the Jigginses. Cragle continued, "We could belabour whose land it is in the court, and I could keep the trial going indefinitely. Costs me nothing, but you and your sister and cousin will soon run out of money. I'm trying to save you lost revenue and offer you a new way to keep your precious mines."

"But what you really want are the items we hold in our possession," Samuel said. "What you call a treasure."

"That would have to be part of the bargain, yes. You produce the items, as you call them, turn them over to me and my colleagues, and you get to keep your barely producing mines, I drop the suit, and everyone walks away unhurt."

The men lighting the torches handed one to each of the gunmen.

Angus nudged Samuel in the ribs. Samuel bent his ear to Angus who whispered, "Can't fire their guns if one hand holds a torch."

"Are you devising a last-minute plan, Samuel?" Cragle asked. "Or is your half-grown friend convincing you to submit?"

"Neither." Samuel put his pipe in his mouth, sucked in, and then blew the smoke towards Cragle's face.

Cragle waved the smoke away then looked at his watch. He turned to the mine and hollered, "Think of your families, men! Do you wish for your families to be burned alive? Ten more minutes!"

The miners, en masse, slowly moved a few feet from the entrance.

Samuel had an idea of what Lucy was planning but was not sure. "Give me time to confer, Mr Cragle. Come along, Angus. Let us speak with Lucy and the others."

"Ten minutes is all I'll grant you, Mr Jiggins. Be quick about it."

Samuel called over his shoulder, "Oh, we'll be right on time!" He and Angus made their way up the manor steps and walked inside. "Lucy!" Samuel called. "Are you ready?"

"Almost!" came her cry from upstairs.

"How much longer?" Samuel moved to the bottom of the stairs.

"Five minutes."

"We only have eight minutes left," Angus shouted.

"Let's go outside again," Samuel said. "If we have to shoot someone with our guns, at least we'll be closer."

Upstairs, while Dimsight and Pudge watched, Lucy poured a black powder she had concocted along with some green copper crystal into a tube of rolled heavy paper then stuck a fuse in it. She repeated her actions for a second tube. "I'm not sure why I keep fuses with me," Lucy confessed. "I guess it's because I'm married to a man who lives such a dangerous life." She handed a tube and matches to each boy. "Get in a good position beside the house. When Samuel gives the signal, light the fuse. You'll know what to do."

"What's that?" Pudge asked.

"Just don't hang on to it," Lucy replied with a smile.

"Oh," Pudge said. "I get it."

The boys slipped out the back door. One went left, the other right, and both stopped behind the hedges growing beside the front porch. They looked out and saw Samuel and Angus talking with Cragle who tapped his watch. "Time's up."

"Indeed, it is," Samuel said then yelled, "*Now!*"

A bullet pierced the shoulder of the most intimidating gunman, a perfect shot. The man slumped to the ground, dropping his gun and torch. Samuel and Angus ducked low and pulled their pistols. Dimsight and Pudge lit the short fuses, raced forwards, and hurled the paper bombs which exploded in the midst of the armed men. The gunmen dropped their weapons and fell to the earth. Only two gunmen fired randomly. Suddenly, a barrage of rockets, one after another, shot from an upstairs window, exploding in sparkles of green and gold over the fallen men. The gunmen, even the wounded one, jumped up and fled down the road away from Tamperwind.

Cragle called after them, "Come back, you cowards!" They did not stop.

The miners raced up the hill from the mine, and Cragle was quickly surrounded. He looked with dismay at the array of grime-faced and determined workers, each holding a menacing tool in their hands. He turned and saw Samuel's and Angus's pistols aimed at him.

"I'd have no sorrow for shootin' ya," Angus said.

Barnabas and Lucy strolled out to the group. "Good evening, Lawyer Cragle," Lucy said. "It seems you've lost your case. Angus and Barnabas are deputies in Lazy Eye. They will be arresting you on a variety of charges."

"That we will," Barnabas said. "I have some manacles in the house. I'll get them post haste." He turned to go.

"Nice shooting, Barnabas," Samuel called after him.

"Why, thank you," he replied over his shoulder as he trod towards the steps.

"Wherever did you get all those fireworks, Lucy?" Samuel asked.

"Oh, I don't know," she said. "Basic chemistry. I always find myself making explosive things. Oh, look, here comes Abigail with Tim. He's safe!"

Tim and Abigail walked up the hill past the mine from the dock in Tamperwind, both smiling ear to ear. When they arrived at the fence, great joy abounded in the group for several minutes. They hugged, smiled, and laughed. Barnabas came out with the manacles and secured them on Cragle's wrists.

"I shall want a lawyer immediately," Cragle growled.

The Jiggins siblings, Tim Cratchit, the Wheeler cousins, and Lucy guffawed.

Just then, Pudge ran up. "Come quick! Dimsight is down. I believe he's been hit with a bullet!"

When they arrived beside the prone, bleeding boy, Angus said, "One of those blackhearts must have fired and hit him accidentally."

Samuel knelt and felt the boy's pulse. "It's weak. Let's get him inside."

STAVE SIXTY-FOUR
THE OUTNUMBERED DEFENDERS TRAPPED

"They've got ladders!" Cratchit called. "Many are circling the manor house, going both directions. Most are twenty yards from the entrance. I've never seen so many hooded men."

A musket ball crashed through the window where Cratchit stood, barely missing him. Another smashed the window to pieces beside Byrne.

"Everyone, shoot!" Byrne called.

Lockie rushed to a side window, broke a pane of glass, and shot a robed man who was running towards the house. The man crumpled to the ground. While re-loading his gun, Lockie saw two men bash in a kitchen window and start climbing through it. Suddenly, both men fell dead. He saw both pistols in Shackle's hands poured out smoke. *Good for you, Inspector*, thought Lockie.

Musket fire was now pelting the walls and windows on all sides. Every man within the manor was firing back and re-loading. While Shackle was busy loading his pistol, Lockie saw two more men erect a ladder to the second floor, and one was climbing up. Seeing no cultist at the back door, Lockie jogged to it, opened it, and then raced around to the ladder. He clubbed the man holding the ladder in the head, causing him to collapse. Lockie pushed over the ladder along with its climber, and it slammed to the ground. When the climber tried to get up, Lockie kicked him in the temple. The man didn't rise. Lockie hastened back inside and locked the door just as Shackle, still at the window, nailed two more attackers with amazing accuracy.

Several attackers were now ramming the front door with a heavy tree limb, repeatedly pounding against it over and over. The wooden door cracked in the middle. Herbert O'Malley had overcome his measure of sorrow over his wife's treachery and was now loading the spare guns for Byrne and Blevins who were stationed at windows on either side of the door. They worked in tandem.

Lynch had sped upstairs, and Lockie could hear him firing and shouting, "That'll teach ye! Die, ye English vermin!"

Thomas had stationed himself in the library in order to see out the tall windows. He fired and loaded a single gun, dropping any man who ranged near.

Scrooge, who was not well-trained in the use of firearms, still managed to fire out a front window and then reload, though he could not say if he hit anything. Amidst the smoke and noise, despite his fear, Scrooge's thoughts oddly ran to a memory of a mundane newspaper article about some battle almost a decade ago in America. *It occurred in some city that began with San*, he thought. *A handful of men were holding out in a fort against a large Mexican army. Were they brave or merely trapped?* He took aim and fired out the window. He miraculously hit a foe in the leg, and he fell.

Scrooge's thinking would not let him rest. *What was the name of the fort? It started with A. I can't remember the name. I should remember the … Oh, what was it called?*

A loud crash sounded upstairs, and Lynch came running down. "They've breached the north wall!"

Cratchit left his post at the landing and followed Lynch downstairs. In a moment, the two were battling multiple assailants who were piling down the stairs, overwhelming them. The two defenders were swinging fists as fast as they could but were greatly outnumbered.

Just then, the door splintered. With another blow, it collapsed from the frame and fell into the room. Smoke poured into the already smoky parlour and hallway. Shackle and Lockie were backing their way from the kitchen. Shackle was swinging a heavy kitchen pot, knocking the invaders in the heads and arms while fending off their swinging of cudgels. Lockie was in a fierce fisticuff with two men but was forced into the parlour.

The army of hooded men began pouring through the front door. Blevins jumped onto four of them at once, driving them to the floor in a fantastic display. In the struggle, he kept beating the men with his Billie club. He had gotten the better of them when a robed man with a musket strode into the room and shot Blevins in the back. He slumped motionless.

Byrne swept up his shotgun, pulled back the trigger, and blew the hooded man and two others dead. He then began swinging his gun like a club. "I'll go down swinging!" he called.

Cratchit was fighting with all his might, using his pistol handle to bludgeon any assailant. O'Malley went down with a gunshot to his shoulder and another to his thigh. Scrooge ended up shoved against the wall behind Byrne and Cratchit who were finally knocked into submission by at least two dozen men. The manor owner and detective sat with their hands on their knees, guns far from them. Duffy, who had done nothing during the fight, cowered under a table.

Lynch lay on the floor, his face covered in blood. Scrooge could only guess he was dead. Shackle was on one knee near the couch, looking down and holding a hand to his bleeding head.

Finally, Lockie was knocked to the floor, and four men with bloodied faces stood over him, slapping their cudgels in their palms.

Scrooge looked about the room crowded with almost faceless men, their hoods pulled low, keeping their eyes in shadow. "Where's Thomas?" he asked aloud.

He did not need to wonder long. Two large assailants pushed Thomas, whose shirt was torn to shreds, ahead of them, shoving him to the floor at the feet of the gardener who had managed to plunge his trowel into an attacker before being knocked unconscious. He now lay limp on the couch. The attacker was on the floor, the trowel stuck in his chest.

"Thomas," Byrne said. "It looks like we'll have a little cleaning up to do come tomorrow."

Despite numerous wounds to his face and body, Thomas chuckled. He groaned and clutched his ribs.

The tall man in the white robe entered. Scrooge and all his companions recognised Barry Lowe, who spoke in a rough voice. "Ah, Reginald Byrne, keeper of the manor and land. I have reason to believe you stole it. At least, my law firm can drum up a reason and thus explain away why your house is in, shall we say, a state of disarray. Then I will tell the English constable you were attacked by a mob of Irishmen. The useless man will believe whatever we tell him, especially if I blame the Irish. The persona non grata. And I, merely a humble *English* farmhand, will be believed entirely." He sniggered with delight.

"So." Scrooge found a sentence coming forth from his mouth. "Which one are you? Schleege or Pincher?"

"Not that it matters, for you'll soon be dead," the white-robed man said. "My name is Malthus Pincher, and I'll have that spearhead now."

"Can't say I know where it is," Byrne said. "You said Blevins had the item, and you killed him. Go ahead, ask him."

Pincher kicked Blevins's side. "'Tis of no concern. One of you knows where it is. We'll simply start killing you one at a time until someone admits it. We'll begin with the young lady over there on the floor." He pointed at Bonnie Jean.

A broad, hooded man stuck a musket barrel against her head.

"I'll count," Pincher said.

"I don't know," the man with the musket said. "I've taken a liking to this lassie. Let me slice her throat like I did the mayor and pub keeper." He drew back his hood and revealed his face then slid a long knife from a scabbard.

"Simon Crimp," Cratchit said. "Actually Schleege."

"Festus Schleege, if you don't mind," Schleege said.

"Very well," Pincher said. "Let her be the first sacrifice to Crom Dubh."

"I think not!" a strong female voice called from just ten yards outside.

STAVE SIXTY-FIVE
CONFIDENCE AND FRIENDS BRING VICTORY

uddenly, the entire exterior of the manor lit up bright as daylight. Everyone inside turned to gaze out the front windows. Above the waiting crowd of hooded men floated thousands and thousands of faeries, each one holding a tiny bright lantern. Some were riding on insects, some rode on nightbirds. Others merely swam and dipped and floated in the ocean of air, their tiny wings fluttering.

In the midst of the Jannes and Jambres followers stood a strong, beautiful, dark-haired maiden with eyes flashing like lightning. The woman was none other than Abigail Jiggins, with her shillelagh in hand. The crowd of men stood back from her in a sort of semicircle. "I've already overpowered twenty men!" she hollered. "Shall we see how many more I can eliminate?" She tossed her shillelagh like a baton spinning high into the air. It landed back in her hands.

Just then, riding astride a huge owl, a leprechaun tribal king flew in. The owl landed, and the king dismounted and righted his golden crown. Immediately, Bobbie Wheeler advanced upon the king. They shook hands and grinned. Bobbie hollered to the house, "I've called in a favour. A really big one."

Pincher stood in the doorway. "What might that be, dwarf? And you, tiny shoemaker, go back to tacking nails into shoe soles. Ha! Isn't this marvelous? A woman, a dwarf, and a miniature shoemaker believe they can fight all these men with clubs and guns.

"Indeed," Abigail announced.

"Attack!" shouted the leprechaun king.

As swift as running deer, hundreds of green-clad leprechauns launched from the surrounding trees, each one with a cudgel or hammer or pick. In the span of two seconds, the wee men were attacking the cultists, jumping on their heads and pulling their hair, kicking the men in the legs with metal-toed shoes, and slamming picks, hammers, and cudgels into their ribs and stomachs.

Abigail held her staff in the middle with both hands and wheeled about through the crowd of men, knocking one in the head with one end, followed by clobbering another one's head with the other end. She waded into about thirty of them, dodging the swings of their cudgels. Though some tried to fire their muskets at her, she knocked the guns from their hands then rammed the end of the shillelagh into their throats. In three minutes, thirty villains lay on the ground, groaning and holding their beaten, broken bodies.

"Get them!" Pincher demanded. Every one of his followers in the house rushed outside to the conflagration only to be overwhelmed by the leprechauns and Abigail.

Not a single leprechaun was down, though one hopped about on one foot. "That big lug stepped on me arch," he complained. The members of the cult who were not unconscious slunk away as fast as they could limp or crawl. Only those who were knocked out or lying with a gunshot wound were evident on the manor lawn and drive.

Abigail scanned the pile of unconscious men around her and merely wiped her brow. "A little tougher than I thought it would be."

The tall, scar-faced Malthus Pincher and the round, balding Festus Schleege stood alone at the door.

"I'll take those guns," Shackle said, shoving pistols, one apiece, into the backs of the two villains. They dropped their weapons, not realising the firearms were empty. "Now, sit in those chairs." Both men, with dazed expressions flooding their faces, wobbled and tripped to the parlour chairs and sat. Shackle sat across from them, keeping the guns aimed at the wayward lawyers.

While Byrne and Thomas gathered the weapons and made sure the assailants on the floor were either dead or out cold, Duffy held cloths against O'Malley's wounds, stopping the blood. Bonnie Jean, though a little unsteady, rose and began checking on Rian Simple who was still unconscious on the couch. Lynch sat up, groaning and holding his head. Bonnie Jean brought him a couch cushion to hold to his wounds. Thomas and Byrne stood next to each other, both holding an aching side but smiling broadly.

Cratchit, Scrooge, and Lockie walked over the crushed door and out to Abigail and Bobbie.

Bobbie introduced the leprechaun king of tribe 12327. Each man shook his hand and offered extensive gratitude. "Now that I've helped ye," the king said, "don't ever be tryin' to find any o' our treasure. Nor be askin' any o' us for three wishes."

"I would introduce you to all my leprechaun pals," Bobbie said, "but they must go. And, Lockie, I only convinced the faerie queen to help provide light tonight on one condition."

"And what is that?" Lockie asked, smiling, for he figured what the request was.

"That you render unto her your pocketknife and a lock of your fine, golden hair." Bobbie crossed his arms. "Here she comes now."

Through an expanding gloom, the tiny, gold coach pulled by crickets wound its way up the drive before stopping. With the footman's help, the queen, no taller than ten inches and dressed in an elegant, red dress, stepped down and walked up to Lockie. Her expression was solemn and regal.

Lockie took a knee and bowed his head. "Your red dress is lovely, your majesty."

"One must wear red when one goes to war," she said in the tiniest voice. "I believe a bargain has been put forth. I would hate for ill happenings to occur were you to renege."

"Never, your majesty." Lockie reached into his pocket, drew out his pocketknife, opened it, and looked at it admiringly. "You know, this knife has been with me most of my life."

"Yes," she replied.

"And so has my hair." Lockie smiled, took hold of several blond locks with one hand, and sliced off the strands. He laid the hair and the open knife at the feet of the queen.

Her smile was brief, for her face returned to the solemn expression she had borne. She snapped her fingers, and a small wagon drove up, also pulled by crickets. This time, the crickets rubbed their legs together, creating a sort of triumphal chirping. The queen told the strong-looking band of elves who had stepped down from the wagon, "Be especially careful of the hair. It is of utmost importance."

The elves loaded the knife and hair into the wagon bed before climbing into it. The driver turned the wagon around, and it vanished in a twinkling. The faerie queen returned to her golden conveyance. Stepping onto the steps of the coach, she turned to Lockie and gave him a wink then entered. The driver cracked his gossamer whip, and the coach vanished, leaving only tiny sparkles of light glimmering for a second before disappearing.

Bobbie gave a wave to the band of leprechauns who were gliding noiselessly into the trees. "Very nice. Excellent end to my visit with my friends. I wish you could have spent more time with them, but leprechauns never stay visible long."

"Well," Scrooge announced, "it's rather nice to be visited by beings beyond our usual world who actually act in a considerate manner."

"Agreed," said Cratchit, looking out into the moonless night. A scum of darkness blocked any light coming from the stars or Wicklow. "What is that?"

Scrooge, Lockie, Abigail, and Bobbie turned to peer into what appeared to be a large inkblot blocking all light.

Lockie recognised the voice calling from the black landau carriage. It belonged to James Moriarty. "Once again, Sherlock Holmes, you have thwarted my plans. I was sure the Jannes and Jambres cult would prevail. No matter. However, know I will keep an eye on you and your family, especially Junior. I already have new plans for him and you, dear Lockie."

"I have plans for you, Moriarty!" Lockie called.

"I'm sure you have but I'm the one who's come closest to success. I feel my next plan will be magnificent in its malevolence."

"Not if I stop you first."

Cratchit said, "I wish we had a loaded gun."

"It's too dark," Abigail said, "and I can't even see him."

Moriarty gave a cackle, which rang among the trees, and the carriage pulled away quickly. "Oh, do be careful of the bat!" he called. The carriage soon slipped, unseeable, into the black night.

Just then, a bat with a three-foot wingspan swept inches over each of their heads. They all ducked then watched it fly away towards the lights of Wicklow.

"Oh, say, Ebenezer," Cratchit said. "I completely forgot. Today's October thirty-first. Happy birthday!" He patted his partner on the back.

Scrooge looked down and shoved his hands in his pockets. "And so I'm another year older and not one bit richer."

"Don't grumble, old friend," Cratchit admonished. "You are rich in friends. Look around you."

Scrooge scanned his grinning friends and gave a timid smile.

STAVE SIXTY-SIX

THE FEAST OF THANKS AND A MIRACLE SAVES A LIFE

The four friends returned to the house and passed by Malachi and Matilda who were removing a dead cultist's body out of the house. "We heard and saw the commotion," Malachi said. "We came as quickly as we could."

"Thank you," Scrooge said.

"Our pleasure," Matilda chirped. "On our way, we stopped at neighbouring farms. More help is coming. If fact, I hear some arriving now."

In a few minutes, ten local farmers arrived. The women set about helping those most critically wounded—O'Malley, Thomas, Lynch, and several of the hooded men.

Byrne came up to Shackle. "Officer Blevins is dead. He gave his life for us."

"It is a great shame. He was a brave man." Shackle's usual dour expression crumbled into a well of sorrow.

"Has anyone seen the spearhead?" Byrne called. "Surely, one of those criminals didn't take it."

"Ouch, ouch!" The gardener sat up, rubbing his head.

"I'm glad to see you've awakened, Rian," said Byrne.

"Me as well. Now I have a pain in my head along with my bent back. And … something is poking me in the arse." He reached underneath and lifted the spearhead. "Oh, yes. This looked like a fine trowel tool for my garden. I sat on it to keep it safe."

"That's what we were looking for," Byrne said. "But I must admit, using it as a garden tool would have been a better use for it than originally intended."

In late November, the Jiggins siblings held a feast at Tamperwind Manor to celebrate the bountiful load of tin ore and silver shipped away two days prior. All their friends and family were present, seated at the long dining table plus one more.

While most everyone was talking to each other and sharing the joy, Scrooge was intent on going over the figures from his new bookkeeper, his head bent over the list of numbers. Samuel tapped him on the shoulder and indicated for him to cease his work, which he reluctantly did. He put down his pencil and looked up.

Samuel then held high his glass of wine. "To a most successful mining operation."

Lucy and Lockie Holmes, each Cratchit family member, every one of the Wheeler family, Hiram Grumbles, Kitty Clutterbuck, Pudge, Dimsight, and Sergeant Eugene Hart who was sitting next to his betrothed, Snow, lifted their glasses and made a toast with those around them and then drank.

"And so much more to be grateful for," said Cratchit. He sat on one side of the table in the middle of his entire family, his wife on one side of him, Tim on the other. He had allowed Peter to sit at the head of the table. "I'm proud of you, son," Cratchit said. "You acted quickly, getting here to Tamperwind so Lockie and Abigail could sail to Wicklow in order to bring Tim safely home." He raised his glass to his oldest child.

Scrooge stood and raised his glass and bowed to his friend, Hiram Grumbles, sitting across from him. "Here's to Hiram, who kept our loan business afloat and even brought in more loans. To you, sir."

Each person toasted the gentle giant who blushed slightly.

Scrooge raised his glass once more. "Here's to my delightful housekeeper who helped make my previously dark abode into a home and keeps it so. To Kitty."

Everyone toasted her. She rose from her seat, crossed to Scrooge, and gave him a peck on the cheek. His many friends cheered. Scrooge blushed and plopped back into his chair. *I don't know what to do with so many friends.* He almost said aloud, "Humbug," but then he chose otherwise.

"I would like to toast as well," Sergeant Eugene Hart said while rising, "To the most elegant, charming, beautiful woman I know. Ginny Snow Wheeler, my soon-to-be bride." Snow grabbed his sleeve and pulled him close and kissed him.

The friends and families oohed and ahhed. The Wheelers each made toasts about the heroism of their family members in the previous month.

Cora and Abigail, the best cooks, appeared from the kitchen, bearing one sumptuous dish after another. Lucy tended to Mycroft and Sherlock Jr with motherly affection while Lockie looked on with fatherly pride.

After the meal, Samuel rose again. "First of all, we men will do the dishes. Second, a huge thanks to our wonderful cooks."

Scrooge snickered then remarked, "Abigail, is there anything you can't do? Cook a delicious meal? Almost single-handedly defeat a platoon of men?"

"Well," Abigail said, "after I took Tim to Tamperwind, I decided to take a tour of Ireland. It looked to me a fair isle. I went back to our dock at Tamperwind and obtained passage on the *Fair Wind* for its return voyage to Wicklow. That is one incredibly speedy vessel!"

"Fortunate for us you returned," Scrooge said.

Abigail smirked. "My only intent was to spend the night at the inn in Wicklow and join you the following morning, but then I saw two dozen men in robes disembarking another ship on the opposite side of the dock from the *Fair Wind*. I followed them through town and, on the way, ran into Bobbie Wheeler."

Bobbie dipped his head in acknowledgement.

"I spoke to him," Abigail said, "and he, too, knew something was amiss. It was getting dark while we followed the band of men out of town. Soon, they met with another eighty or so men. That's when I saw the man dressed like an Egyptian priest. One of the men hailed him as Pincher. I knew he was the lawyer, the beast. I wanted to go after them all and take them on right then, but Bobbie wisely dissuaded me. He told me to wait for him while he left to get help. I had no notion of the immense help he would bring."

"It was a gamble," Bobbie said, "but one that paid off. The tricky part was convincing the faerie queen Lockie would give up his knife and some of his hair."

"I still don't know what she wanted with my hair," Lockie said.

"Or your pocketknife," Lucy added, taking her husband's arm.

"Finally," Abigail continued, "Bobbie arrived with his green army and so many faeries flying everywhere, I am still in amazement. Thank you, Bobbie. I couldn't have done it without you."

"It is sometimes better," Bobbie said, "to have friends in low places than high-ranking government officials or judges."

Cratchit walked to the head of the table. "Most importantly, we all know the brave Officer Blevins was buried near his hometown in Ireland. Friends of his family held a beautiful wake. Chief Detective Shackle gave him a posthumous promotion to corporal. The London bobbies donated money to establish a soup kitchen for the Irish poor who are starving from the potato blight. I said I would visit the kitchen frequently to be sure it is functioning properly."

"And I gave him leave to do so," Scrooge said. "I never again want to see poor, starving people lying in a church cemetery simply to die on holy ground."

"Now," Cratchit said, "as far as the end of this affair. All of Byrne's staff have recovered from their wounds. Though a few of the hooded villains escaped, the cult criminals who were rounded up are either tried and imprisoned or awaiting trial. Most will be jailed for several years. Cragle, Schleege, and Pincher are awaiting trial for murder. They've somehow delayed their trial by way of their evil collusion with one of the judges. Abel Leggitt is trying to have him recused." He took a sip of the wine. "Nice vintage. Where was I?"

"Detailing the case," Lucy said. She held Sherlock Jr in her arms.

"Ah, yes. Schleege, under interrogation by Inspector Shackle, admitted that the reason the lawyers were in cahoots to purloin the mines was specifically to find the nails of Christ, which they knew were hidden there but had not discovered yet when they colluded with the Owsleys after they murdered Mr Tamperwind. He admitted there was a secret mastermind to their efforts but knew not who that person was."

"I think we all know who it was." Lockie was still angry Moriarty had escaped again.

Cratchit agreed. "At least Cragle can never take the Tamperwinds to court again, should he ever be released, due to Lockie finding the title to the mines free and clear in Sean's library."

"Who knows why he had it," Lockie added. "But the Tamperwind and Hopworth mines are in your family for as long as you like."

Everyone cheered.

Cratchit tapped a spoon on his glass and gained everyone's attention. "The O'Malley woman, Grizelda, has yet to be found. Schleege told the inspector she had been using darnel to taint the bread she gave Sean, hence his increasing illness and hallucinations. Then she poisoned the milk she gave him in empty whiskey bottles. Sensing the last draught was bringing about his demise, he was trying to hide the spearhead but died before he could. Inspector Shackle thinks Grizelda has fled the country.

"Now, here's some very good news. Reginald Byrne has taken over his brother's estate and hired Malachi as his foreman. Malachi married Matilda, and they seem happy. Come spring, Byrne plans to hire as many of the starving poor as he can to begin planting. And all the crops and sheep mutton will stay in Ireland."

All at the table applauded.

"Before I finish," Cratchit said, "I'll let Lucy explain what occurred with our dear friend, Wayne, or, as he prefers to be called, Dimsight."

The young bespectacled man rose, took a bow, and then sat.

"This is what happened when we defeated Cragle and his wanton bunch here at the manor," Lucy said. "As you know, a stray bullet hit Wayne in the chest near his heart. We carried him inside and laid him on the couch. We were deeply worried, for the nearest doctor was miles away. Cora knew some basic nursing, but she could only slow the bleeding. The bullet was deep inside his chest, as it had not exited. We considered trying to dig the ball out ourselves. All of us were praying. Suddenly, I had a fervent urge. Nay, 'twas more like I was coerced by a power stronger than any on Earth. I went upstairs and retrieved the box of Christ's nails. I took one out and placed the nail directly on his chest above the wound. We waited for what seemed like hours but probably was a mere minute."

"Then the miracle happened," announced Pudge who was seated beside Dimsight.

Lucy handed Junior to Lockie and stood. "Suddenly, we all heard a *clink*. Samuel picked up the nail, and the musket ball was attached to it like a magnet. No surgery was necessary. In a moment, the bleeding stopped, the entrance wound healed over, and then Dimsight sat up and looked at us in dismay." Tears rolled down her cheeks. "Our brilliant, unselfish young man, who once saved my husband's life, is alive and well."

Dimsight took off his dark glasses and exclaimed, "I asked, 'Why's everyone looking at me?'"

With tears of joy on their cheeks, the family and friends laughed. Pudge hugged his best mate.

"And now, we can feel abundantly safe," Cratchit said. "Inspector Shackle and Her Majesty's royal guard are taking the nails and spearhead to London for safe-keeping. All's well that ends well."

Scrooge muttered, "We'll see. I feel there's more to come."

A light snow drifted down, and the temperature was dropping, but inside of Tamperwind Manor was warmed by joy reigned.

Tim quietly said, "God bless us, everyone."

EPILOGUE

MORIARTY, HIS MOTHER, AND A NEW THREAT

On a curvy road in the middle of the Welsh countryside, a platoon of dragoons trotted their horses in front of a royal landau. Another dozen armed guards rode behind the carriage. Their final destination was Buckingham Palace. Inside the imperial conveyance, two relatives of the royal family sat opposite Inspector Shackle. On the seat beside Shackle was a newly sealed, square, wooden crate. Inside it was an elegant, gold-laden chest that contained the box holding the nails and spearhead. Shackle briefly opened the window shutter and then pulled his coat collar up, for he felt the wind of a frigid storm blowing in along their path. He watched the first flakes of snow fall.

A quarter of a mile back, a cross-looking sailor with one eye squinched rode a bandy-legged horse and kept apace of the carriage.

James Moriarty and his mother, Penelope, once again sailed on a corsair along the eastern coast of Italy. The ship would soon turn to starboard across the Adriatic to dock at the port of Dubrovnik, thence they would travel by train inland several hundred miles. They sat on the deck in heavy wooden chairs with blankets across their legs, and they were bundled in warm coats and woollen caps. A sharp November wind howled against the sails, and the masts creaked a thumping cello sound—sombre like a death knell or the drumbeat of a funeral march.

The dark-eyed man who was always wearing the broad-brimmed hat and who had driven the wagon for Moriarty and his mother to Wicklow climbed up from below deck. He bowed to mother and son. "The woman has finally fallen asleep," he said. "She drank some of her own tonic. Calls it a 'remedy.'" He returned below deck.

Moriarty cracked his knuckles. "Mother, is it necessary we take the tiresome hag Grizelda O'Malley with us?"

"She's adept at poisons, more so than you or I could ever learn, and she knows how to make the death appear natural. Poison a little at a time. 'Tis my kind of killing." Penelope smiled. "Additionally, she has more about the dark spirits in this world than either of us."

"Thank the stars she's below in the cabin. If she can't stand the cold, then why has she been living in Ireland?"

"She's not there anymore. She is with us. She has a new wardrobe and can finally attain some of the fashionable things in life. Think about it. She's no longer a servant. She's a partner."

Moriarty, growing irritated, changed the subject. "I think it's a shame our distinguished guest found no interest in our home country of England."

"I agree, son, but he has his own affairs and wishes to maintain his own castle." The pretty woman with eyes like pools of blackest ink stared out at the grey waves rising and falling.

Moriarty took a quick look through his telescope at craggy cliffs then said, "I hope he's comfortable in that crate below deck. It seems an odd way to live."

"Well, as you know, James, he's not really alive."

Author's Note

Dear Reader,

Thank you for reading *Treasure and Murder in Ireland*, a Scrooge and Cratchit: Detectives Mystery. I tried diligently to blend in elements of the writing tone, and even the actual sentences, from some of the works of Charles Dickens.

Let's all keep Dickens's legacy alive. Read his great books.

If you enjoyed this mystery, please write a review on Amazon, Barneandnoble.com, and Goodreads. Reviews are the lifeblood of authors.

And please check out the other two Scrooge and Cratchit: Detectives mysteries. Find them at my website www.curtlocklearauthor.com and all over online.

Thank you again and may God bless you abundantly.

APPENDIX 1

Passages from Dickens's Works Blended into the Novel and Other Unique Facts of the Era

- **Page 22:** Jarndyce vs Jarndyce—the legal case that hung over the protagonists' family in Dickens's novel *Bleak House*
- **Page 30:** "The best thing to maintain a porcelain white skin."—The fad for white women living in England and much of Europe was to have extremely white skin. Opium, too, was considered a natural way to relax the skin and make a woman feel refreshed.
- **Page 41:** "In trickery, evasion, procrastination, spoliation, botheration, under false pretenses of all sorts, there are influences which can never come to any good."—Passage from *Bleak House*
- **Page 44:** Tackleton's Toyshop—Tackleton was an objectively nasty man in Dickens's short story "Cricket on the Hearth."
- **Page 50:** "Fog would settle in the *stem and bowl* of the city's labourers' pipes."—Dickens
- **Page 51:** "Voice that demanded a great deal of room. A loud voice."—Dickens

- **Page 51:** "And his hat and walking stick in his hands, and his hands behind him, a composed and quiet listener."—Description of Inspector Bucket in *Bleak House*

- **Page 53:** Lord's Cricket Grounds—an actual location often used for the launching of the balloons.

- **Page 54:** Boot-blacking factory—Charles Dickens, as a boy, since his father was in Debtor's prison, worked in such a factory.

- **Page 57:** Abode of Love and Reverend Henry Prince—an actual locale of a religious cult run by the self-proclaimed Lamb of Heaven. The cult survived long into the twentieth century.

- **Page 57:** Spaxton—the actual town where the Abode of Love was located until the 1950s.

- **Page 65:** James Moriarty—character in Arthur Conan Doyle's writings about Sherlock Holmes. James Moriarty was Holmes's arch enemy and perhaps a math teacher, but he was also a master criminal. Sherlock Jr will grow up to be the great detective.

- **Page 74:** "Every piece of furniture had been shaken and dusted, the paintings wiped, the best tea service set forth, with an excellent provision made with dainty new breads, crusty twists, cool fresh butter, thin slices of ham and German sausage and delicate little rows of anchovies nestled in parsley."—Dickens's *Bleak House*

- **Page 86:** "Who was folding up his chin in his fat smile."—Dickens

- **Page 88:** Laissez Faire—the prevailing sentiment among many Englishmen of the era, assisting any human in hard times went against the best economic policies; therefore, if people died of want or illness, the government should do nothing to help.

- **Page 94:** Godfrey's Cordial—a sweet-tasting concoction of the day that contained laudanum to put fussy babies to sleep; often, tragically, the babies never woke up.

- **Page 101:** Dropping the menu to the floor—In an estate in Ireland, one woman so hated her Irish servants, this is how she communicated with them.

- **Page 102:** An actual manor house in Ireland where an English woman and man lived had a tunnel under the house so the owners would not have to see the Irish help very much.

- **Page 111:** Taxing a home based on windows—At the time, the law required homes to be taxed based on the number of windows and doors they had.

- **Page 132:** Irish 1798 rebellion—one of many Irish uprisings; Billie Byrne (not really a relative to the fictional character as stated in the story) was hanged.

- **Page 133:** General Cootes's army shoving every townsperson into a building and burning it down really did occur.

- **Page 227:** *The Knickerbocker*—an actual New York magazine

- **Page 227:** Mocha Dick—the name of a real white sperm whale that eluded whalers and damaged the launches and ships; the article inspired Melville's *Moby-Dick*.

- **Page 240:** Steel weapon—the Romans had advanced in the manufacture of primitive steel.

- **Page 244:** Darnel—an actual weed that often grows alongside natural wheat; a fungus that grows on it can cause anyone who ingests it to hallucinate and suffer several various disfunctions of the body; it was called *tares* in the Bible parable.

APPENDIX 2

English and Irish Old Terminology and Slang Words Explained

- **Arseways**—backwards
- **Bacca-pipes**—Whiskers curled in small, close ringlets.
- **Begrucchen**—complaining
- **Chartist Group**—a group of men who wanted to rewrite their Irish charter to allow more representation in Parliament
- **Costermongers**—hawkers of fruits and vegetables.
- **Dearg-Due**—the first Victorian-era vampire; a woman who rose from the grave, seeking ongoing revenge
- **Donkey years**—not having all day
- **Fluthered**—drunk
- **Hot Codlins**—an apple and cinnamon alcoholic drink
- **Jannes and Jambres**—the name of the sorcerers who opposed Moses in the Pharoah's court; their cult remained a long while in the Middle East
- **Knackered**—really tired
- **Lugger ship**—a medium-sized ship with lug sails, used primarily as a short voyage working ship

- **Mots**—unsavoury women

- **Night soil men**—the people, generally men, who would go down into the basement area sewers and dig out fecal matter from the houses and take it to dump in the Thames; this was a major, full-time employment.

- **Punters**—shoppers

- **Quarest**—unusual or odd

- **Scrivener**—the term used for a copyist individual who painstakingly copied legal documents

- **Smoking bishop**—a celebratory alcoholic fruit punch, named for the royal purple color, like a bishop's vestments

- **Spontaneous combustion**—Some scientists of the day had "proven" how people could actually explode spontaneously. Odd as it sounds, great numbers of people believed it because some scientists had "proven" it. Dickens truly believed it was possible, and it inspired the death of one of his characters in his novel, *Bleak House*.

AFTERWORD

WHY DO I WRITE? I set about my writing with three goals.

1. To tell a good story that people will long remember.
2. I write to keep history alive. Too many people today are trying to hide history. They tear down the statues, rename the streets and schools and army bases, doing it all in the name of their selfish concept of who they think are worthy to be remembered—when they really know nothing about history. After all, the Nazis and the Communists and ISIS have done the same. For sure, history has its warts, but hiding it only makes it impossible to learn from it. Thus people in the future suffer the same fate.
3. Most importantly, I write for the greater glory of God and that each person realizes how much God loves all of us and wants us to stay close to Him.

If you like this book, please take a mere three minutes to write a review on Amazon, barnesandnoble.com and/or Goodreads.

BRIEF SYNOPSIS OF THE OTHER *SCROOGE* AND *CRATCHIT: DETECTIVES* BOOKS

The first book, *Scrooge and Cratchit: Detectives, A Christmas Mystery* begins two years after Charles Dickens's *A Christmas Carol,* a few weeks before Christmas. Cratchit, who has taken on a second job on the wharfs and has now become lean and muscled, is partnered with Scrooge, though Cratchit is at 49 percent. Scrooge is striving to become a better man, but he still struggles with his old miserly and fearful habits. The pair have hired an office boy — Lockie, an accomplished pickpocket.

Suddenly, an old friend stumbles into their office begging for a loan to escape to France, for he's been accused of murder. They give him the loan, and he temporarily escapes. That night, however, the ghost of Jacob Marley (Scrooge's dead former partner) returns and coerces Scrooge to go to the dangerous tin mines of Cornwall on the west coast of England and solve the mystery to save the man.

Cratchit is visited by a friendlier ghost with the same motive, so the two set out for Cornwall where a dark-cloaked killer roams amid ominous, twisting tunnels and secret passages. Their newly hired office boy, Lockie, surreptitiously follows them and becomes vital to them solving the puzzling double murders. With multiple new characters, including three strong female characters (Lucy, Abigail, and Ginny), the detective trio must face incredible danger and more ghosts.

To give away one surprise in the mystery, Lockie's full name is Sherlock Holmes. He marries Lucy in the next book, and they become the parents of the famous detective—Sherlock Holmes—named after his father.

Who dies in this exciting tale? Will they actually solve the crimes? Who is the mastermind?

In *The Dark Malevolence*, the trio are faced with four mysteries: several murders, a stolen corpse, a kidnapping of Ginny, and a dark force that has followed the ghost of Jacob Marley into the world. Grown men begin acting like wild dogs. The plot twists and turns.

Lockie and Lucy get married. The strong female protagonists again play major parts. Scrooge, Cratchit, and Lockie must solve all the crimes or London will dissolve into Civil War. The clock is ticking.

THE GREAT HUNGER—
THE IRISH POTATO FAMINE

In 1845, a blight of all tubers (potatoes) began spreading across Europe. By 1846, evidence of its impact became widely known, and people who lived only on potatoes began to starve or suffer horrible disease from the malnutrition. By 1848, in France, Germany, and other nations, there were a number of revolts, but all of them petered out with no changes to the governments. The elites still ruled with an iron hand.

Though all other nations of Europe ultimately set about providing food for their starving people, the English government (and its rich elite) had such disdain for the Irish, bordering on hatred, they deliberately did little to help the Irish, almost all of whom subsisted on the potato. (By the way, the potato is nature's almost perfect food, supplying considerable nutrients and sufficient carbohydrates. If a potato farmer had a cow for milk, butter, and cheese, the potato was the only other food the Irish family needed to survive and even thrive.)

The Great Famine (*Irish Gaelic: An Gorta Mór*), also known as the Great Hunger, was the period of mass starvation and disease in Ireland from 1845 to 1852. The west and south of Ireland, where the Irish language was dominant, was the most severely affected. The period was known in Irish language as an *Drochshaol*, or the hard times. Over one million Irish died, and almost another 2.1 million emigrated to America, Canada, England, and to other European countries.

Most of the potato farmers lived on small parcels of land as tenants where a few acres of potatoes, unlike grains that required many acres to produce a quantity of food, could provide for a large family. These lands were owned by "absentee landlords" who had cruel overseers carry out their orders in taxing the poor farmers. Most of these wealthy, elitist English landlords had never even stepped foot in Ireland.

When the farmers could no longer pay their taxes, the landlords had their overseers and English police drive the tenants from their homes and burn down the homes. Hence, hundreds of thousands of Irish families roamed Ireland begging, then dying alongside the lanes. Many persons, knowing they were going to die (and caskets were unaffordable) crawled onto church lands so they could die on Sacred Soil.

Treasure and Murder in Ireland takes place in 1846 when the potato blight was spreading, and thousands flocked to the cities to find some sort of job and food. The Quakers tried to help, with kitchens serving free food. The English government set up "workhouses" that deliberately separated all the women from the men into different barracks and were really nothing more than disease-ridden prisons. Many protestant ministers set up faux soup kitchens and would only serve a starving person food if that person denied their faith.

Thank God that today, Christians of all faiths generally have much more respect for each other.

www.ingramcontent.com/pod-product-compliance
Lightning Source LLC
Chambersburg PA
CBHW020948260626
47169CB00006B/1877